Spirits of the Relentless

Mordena Dawn – Book 2

Morgan Biscup

Author's Note

WELCOME BACK, DEAR READER, to the spacefaring science fantasy universe of Vazdimet.

You hold in your hands the second installment of Mordena Dawn, exploring the formation of the Mordena mercenaries and the tumultuous pasts of its founders, most notably the formerly villainous necromancer, Shane Lawrence, and his quest for redemption.

I've realized, in the course of plotting out this series, that I have a love for charting the less-explored facets of life and human behavior. I love a good redemption arc, same as anyone, but it's the aftermath that fascinates me. How does one move forward when their entire history is constantly pulling them backwards? Each memory, each ingrained habit, each gut reaction, well-trained through the years to lead them where they *were*, not where they want to go?

I suppose it's my own history leaking through, as tends to happen when writing from the heart. I haven't conquered planets or shattered souls, but I've taken my own journey to fight myself free from the ingrained lessons of coping and survival – I'm still *on* that journey – and it's *hard*. I don't think I'll ever be done. It's a lifelong quest.

But it's worth taking, alongside all the discovery and self-discovery and all the emotions that entails. And I think that's why I love writing about Shane and his circle. His discoveries, as he works to untangle who he can trust and which of his regrets are his own doing versus someone else's, mirror our own journeys. His are more ruthless, perhaps, and certainly more fantastical, but that only makes them more appealing. A way to confront our own journeys, without feeling burdened by them. If Shane can do it, so can I.

And so can you. Here's to many more journeys together, in Vazdimet, and across our own mortal plane called reality. And as you make your way through your own life's journey, know that I am grateful to find my fictional stories featuring as a fraction of your own adventure. May they bring you as much enjoyment and comfort as they've brought me for mine.

To hope.

Even at our worst, may we always see our best.

1

2291.08.31 EVT

Shane Lawrence scowled at the oven timer's slow countdown to zero, fingernails digging into the edge of the worn countertop as he forced himself to remain upright. Sitting was perhaps the wiser option, given the extent of his unhealed wounds from his confrontation with the Sparnelli Admiral Kydell nearly two weeks ago, but he'd built his career on never admitting defeat and he had no intention of changing that now.

Or admitting he was slipping back into bad habits.

He could already hear the lecture from Feels about how he'd never heal on his own if he didn't allow himself to rest, soon followed by an offer of their magic to speed up the process. But the psychomorphic mage was back with the fleet, healing the minds of those crewing his accidentally adopted armada exactly as he'd ordered.

It was the only way Shane knew to keep Feels safe from his own possessive tendencies. Especially after he'd murdered them and imprisoned their soul in his mother's locket for two years. They'd asked for their freedom, and he'd finally granted it.

He wouldn't allow himself to hurt them again.

He already missed them. They'd been a constant presence, all that time. An angry presence, certainly, but he'd never faulted them for that. He'd barely had time to process their unexpected forgiveness before setting forth to battle against an entire combined Sparnell Confederation armada at the stubborn insistence of his adopted son, Jake, nearly dying at the hands of a magically-manipulated ally in the process. And here he was now, forcefully wrenched from his quiet life as a school janitor and thrust into the role of planetary hero.

Hero.

An undeserved epitaph. Despite Feels' insistence to the contrary, saving one planet meant little when measured against those he'd destroyed. One kind deed – performed at the insistence of his twelve-year-old son, no less! – did little to wash the decades of blood from his hands. He'd have to–

The timer interrupted his spiraling thoughts.

Releasing the counter, Shane attempted to reach for the oven door, biting down on the cry threatening to escape his lips at the bolt of agony racing down his side and squeezing at his chest from the movement. He forced his breath to steady and leaned into his Necromancy instead, jumping the breakfast casserole through the Afterlife and onto the counter before him.

The smell of leftover meats and vegetables filled the room. A reminder of happier days helping his mother in the kitchen of their humble farmstead, before the Space Defense Legion had come for his childhood and set him on the path of vengeful destruction.

Jake had saved him from that path. A Legion child, pleading for the life of his dying mother, his eyes already hinting at the growing sparks of the same hatred fueling Shane's rage. Only this time, that rage was directed at Shane, for perpetuating the same war crimes that had launched the necromancer's own military career. An echo of Shane's pain at the loss of his own parents, and the unquenchable thirst for vengeance that had followed.

He'd told himself he'd been fighting for justice.

Jake had proved him wrong.

Shaking the memory from his thoughts, Shane turned his attention instead to preparing his son's favorite fruit juice, to accompany his meal.

The past was the past. All he could control was what he did next, and whether or not he slid back into his old, dangerous patterns.

With a twist of the mortal plane, several fresh fruits appeared beside the juicer. A newer addition to the kitchen, the shiny device appeared out of place next to the other worn appliances and scuffed cabinets, but Shane had resolved to provide Jake with the comforts of his own childhood to the best of his abilities, and the juicer helped. Especially in his present state.

With a sigh, Shane reached through the Afterlife for a knife and then he went to work, gritting his teeth against the pain.

Showing weakness had been fatal in the Sparnell Confederation. He'd left that life behind when he'd deserted the Sparnell Armed Forces, instead taking responsibility for Jake's upbringing, with the blessings and insistence of his mother. But that was before his former fleet had attempted to conquer his new planet. Before they'd joined him in exile, surrendering to his leadership.

No. If he wanted to keep their respect, he couldn't afford to show weakness.

He *had* to keep their respect. He had nothing else to offer them.

"Breakfast!" he called, jumping Jake's juice and helping of casserole to the shabby kitchen table before beginning the laborious effort of filling his own plate.

Jeb Kane shuffled into the kitchen first, barefoot, tugging distractedly on his short, brown hair as he sniffed the air appreciatively. "We're going to gain weight, staying with you. Would've protested less about Raz and I taking your spare room if I'd known you could cook like *this*." He snorted. "Not that we've anywhere else to stay. Intact housing's at a premium these days."

Jeb had been Jake's bookish biology teacher, before the Sparnelli assault had flattened both the school and the apartment he'd shared with his sister. He'd proven his talent in Nature Magic during the boarding assault on Kydell's flagship, despite the frequent reminders he was a pacifist now.

Shane grunted, his attention still focused on his knife. "You could use it."

"The place to stay? Or the belly fat?" Jeb laughed, before frowning and reaching for the blade. "Let me get that. You shouldn't be doing all this, you're still hurt."

"I've got it," Shane snarled fiercely, eyes narrowing as Jeb took a step backward.

"No. *I've* got it."

The knife pulled itself from Shane's hand, completing its work with one smooth stroke before settling itself on the table.

Scowl drawing deeper, Shane turned to the doorway. "Razick..."

Razick Kane shook her head wearily, the unruly red curls cascading down her back bouncing at the movement. She offered a faint smile that didn't quite meet the dulled green of her eyes, and even the mass of freckles across her pale skin seemed to shout her exhaustion. "Lawrence. Stop. Please."

When he'd first met her, Razick had been a mostly quiet school lab technician, her free time spent experimenting with ways to replicate the Sparnell Armed Forces' protective uniform fabrics. He'd witnessed her talent as a highly-trained Sparnelli battle mage that same day, after she'd fallen prey to Kydell's Psychomorphation and turned those skills against him.

"I said I didn't need help."

"But you know I need to give it anyway." She glanced away, and Shane watched her pull her shoulders back before meeting his eyes again. "*I* did this to you. Least I can do is help you get better. Especially when you won't wear that powered body brace Jake and I made for you."

He *should* have been wearing it. Somehow, though, that felt like admitting defeat. Succumbing to his wounds.

Admitting he needed help healing after all.

"It wasn't your fault," he told her, not for the first time.

Razick kept her silence, the weary slump of her shoulders signaling her unwillingness to engage in their usual argument over who should shoulder most of the blame. Instead she used her telekinesis to tug out his chair and drop his overfull plate onto the tabletop where he usually sat. "Eat."

Shane's attempt to stare her down failed miserably as Jake chose that moment to stumble into the room. His hair was disheveled, as if he'd just climbed from bed, while his clothes bore the usual wrinkles of having been slept in. Again.

Jake slid into his seat with a quick glance at Shane, before silently lifting his fork to poke at his meal. He'd been silent and sullen since the Battle for Baden, and his own role in Shattering the soul of Kydell's personal TAG when Shane had been too weak to help.

It had been a feat worthy enough to earn Jake the respect of the rest of the fleet. TAGs served as the SAF's shock troopers, a living necromancer controlling a tactical assault group filled with the souls of dead mages, phasing behind enemy lines to cause as much damage as possible before dying, only to resurrect themselves to fight another day.

Kydell's TAG had been a Selkirk, trained by her Family since birth for the role. Shattering her had been the only way to prevent her eventual return, and Jake had risen to the challenge to save them all. The boy had been avoiding him most days since then, and while Shane had tried to give him the space he needed to work through his experiences on the *Inevitable*, his intuition said Jake now needed him to push the issue into a conversation.

But first, breakfast. They'd all be calmer on a full stomach.

"Eat, Raz." Shane motioned to the empty chair across from him, gratefully noting Jeb already happily digging into his own portion despite the tension in the room. "Arguing about who shoulders the bigger blame never gets us anywhere anyway."

When they'd first met, he'd been wallowing in it himself. Still should be, by all rights, but Feels' role in the battle had required them to strip his guilt, to use as a weapon against the fleet, and to protect him from Kydell's manipulation.

They'd replaced it with resolve instead. He'd no choice now but to undo what he could of his past transgressions. His own emotions would allow nothing less.

And part of that meant helping Razick heal.

She set her chin as if to argue, then sighed, nodding. With a wave of her hand, her own plate floated gently to the seat across from him, and she joined it. "You're right."

"Of course I'm right. I've more experience with guilt than you." His smirk faded. "Certainly have more to be guilty *about*. Many would say you'd be doing the universe a favor, killing me."

"Lawrence," Jeb warned, his fork frozen in midair.

Shane raised an eyebrow at the biologist. "I know who I was. I know what I did. *You* don't."

"You don't know what *I* did, either," Razick said quietly, staring at her meal. "I still see their faces. The nightmares..."

"Me, too." He caught her eyes as she looked up in surprise, and smiled sadly. Many regrets haunted his dreams. Faces, some nights. Other nights, entire *planets*.

"Does it ever get better?"

Jake's voice was small, a shadow of his usual self. Shane opened his mouth to answer, closing again as he realized the question wasn't directed at him, but rather Razick.

"I... don't know," she admitted, shaking her head at Jake before returning her attention to Shane. "Does it?"

"I'll let you know when I find out," he promised, but the words felt hollow.

The preteen looked away, brown hair shifting to cover his face as he began to slide from his seat at the table, but Shane grabbed his wrist. Time for that conversation he'd been putting off.

He kept his voice as soft as his grip was firm. "What's wrong, Jake? Talk to me."

2

Jake shook his head as his adoptive father motioned the Kanes for privacy, grabbing Razick's hand as she began to push away from the table.

"No, they can stay. Please." He felt the unspoken question as Razick's fingers tightened around his own and squeezed back reassuringly before meeting his father's eyes. "I like their company. It's... nice."

Not to mention, having them there meant he wouldn't be alone with his father for this conversation. He *knew* his father would never hurt him on purpose – anyone who'd ever seen the necromancer defend him would know *that* – but knowing didn't make him feel better about the impending conversation. Having Razick beside him *did*.

Jeb excused himself anyway, gathering his plate and used cutlery as he stood. "I'm done, anyway. I'll start the dishes."

Jake watched his father's frown deepen. "What's wrong, Jake? You know you can tell me anything."

"I know… It's just…" He swallowed. "Dad?"

"Yes, Jake?"

Jake hesitated, attempting to ignore the sudden dryness of his mouth, and the sadness held within his father's eyes. He'd hurt the necromancer often with his words over the last few years, wielding them as expertly as the Void knife he'd brought on the *Inevitable*, both finely honed weapons intended to cut as deeply and painfully as possible.

And now he was about to do it again.

Sighing, Jake averted his eyes to study his breakfast. One of his favorites, yet another of the many gifts from his father. His father did *everything* for him, without complaint. And once again, Jake was rejecting him.

But the necromancer had taught him to always tell the truth, and this truth needed to be said.

Jake met the concern on his father's face, forcing his breathing to match the calm rhythm of Razick's thumb against the back of his hand.

"I've been thinking. About what happened on the *Inevitable*. About that TAG, and how I…" He turned away, closing his eyes. "I don't want to learn Necromancy."

"Okay."

Jake looked up in surprise at the even tone in his father's voice. "You're not angry?"

"Why would I be angry?" His father reached out, grabbing Jake's free hand and squeezing, his face an unreadable mask.

Jake's words felt small. "Because that's *your* magic?"

"Jake." Another squeeze. "I don't want you to be me. I want you to be *better*. *One* of me is too many already." The necromancer released his hand, instead folding his fingers together on the table. "My job is to help you find your way, not make you follow mine. You're already a Shielding expert. Jeb's teaching you Telepathy. And your Rune Magic far outpaces anything I've ever seen." He shook his head. "You don't need my Necromancy. You've got enough to practice already."

"But you wanted to teach me how to protect myself!" Jake protested.

Why isn't he arguing with me?

"And I have." His father began counting off his accomplishments on his fingers. "You can Soul Call your mother. You've mastered the basics of sparring. You've Shielded a carrier *by yourself* in the middle of combat. You know how to break a Soulbind, so nobody can trap you against your will. You don't need anything else. Not from me." He frowned, eyes furrowing. "Is *that* why you've been avoiding me?"

Jake bowed his head, nodding through the sudden tears. "I thought you'd be mad."

His father sighed, balling each fist around a handful of his trousers. "If I'm angry at anyone, it's myself. I promised I'd protect you, and I didn't. And as a result of my failure, you ended up in a situation where you had to protect me, instead."

"I disobeyed your orders. You told me to stay with Alanis, but I left."

"And if you'd stayed, Kydell's TAG would have killed you, instead of the other way around. You forget, I *knew* Fleet Captain Selkirk. I've seen Larissa in action." His father tugged at his shoulder and Jake surrendered, letting go of Razick's hand to allow the necromancer to pull him and his chair closer. "I'm the one who brought you on that ship, Jake. I'm the one who put you in that situation, and I'm sorry."

Jake heard Razick stand, collecting her now-empty dishes before joining her brother in the cleanup as Jake buried his face in his father's chest, clutching tightly – then letting go at the necromancer's sudden intake of breath.

He's still hurt. Even though he tries to hide it.

His father was stroking his back now, soft and reassuring. "I'm not angry, Jake. I'm *proud*. You're working through feelings no twelve-year-old should have to work through. You're using them to figure out what you want to do with your life, and then doing what needs doing to make that happen." His father squeezed, and Jake could feel the necromancer's muscles tensing from the pain of the exertion. "I'm sorry my failings led you to this point... And I'm proud of you, for finding the good in it anyway."

Jake closed his eyes, relishing his relief at his father's understanding as he inhaled the smells of herbs and sausage permeating the necromancer's shirt, his father's hand still rubbing his back in firm and comforting strokes. He felt the dampness from his own tears soaking his father's chest and sat up, smiling nervously as he rubbed at his eyes.

"I'm proud to say you're my Dad."

"Void knows why. But thank you." His father sat back in his chair, tears glistening on his cheeks. Lifting his fork, he waved it at Jake. "If you think you'll want seconds, better grab them before Jeb finishes cleaning. He's efficient. Even though he does it all by hand."

"A little manual labor never hurt anyone," Jeb called from the sink, elbows deep in soapy water. He turned to wink at Jake. "But no need to overdo it."

Razick snorted from her perch on the counter, cleaned dishes held aloft with her Telekinesis as she air dried them with her Anemancy. "If you say so."

She neatly directed the plates to their spot in the cabinet before beginning the process again with the utensils.

Jeb snapped his wet dish towel in her direction. "Cheater!"

Jake couldn't help but laugh as Razick neatly caught the water droplets with her Hydromancy, instead directing them down the back of her brother's shirt. Jeb screeched, dropping the glass in his hand. Razick expertly arrested its fall with her Telekinesis just before it hit the floor, gently returning it to the sink.

"Careful," Jake's father growled. "We've got company coming later, and I'll need all the dishes. Don't have any spare place settings."

"Grilling?" Jake kicked his feet against the chair leg. His father had become a surprisingly good cook since his first tentative attempts after he'd adopted Jake, but nothing could beat his efforts on the rusty grill in their small backyard.

The necromancer nodded solemnly. "Been marinating since yesterday. Want to make a good impression. And Javon's been on deployment for over a year. She deserves something nicer than hydroponic vegetables and travel-packed proteins." He stood from the table, scratching the back of his neck. "Should probably get that started now – but I want to run through what we know about Janikk, first."

"Good idea." Jeb's voice was muffled by a mouthful of the breakfast casserole as he packed away the leftovers.

Razick nodded as she directed his father's now empty plate to the water filled sink. "Make sure we caught everything, before we brief the others."

"That was my thought." His father turned slowly, his steps stiff and almost hesitant as he made his way toward the stairs leading to the bedrooms. "Let me grab my notes."

Jake waited until his father was out of earshot before bolting from his chair. "Professor Jeb? Did you make the call yet? Let them know?"

"Doing that now."

"Good." Jake shifted his weight, watching as Jeb closed his eyes to focus his Telepathy, and turned to Razick. "Because if they don't do it right now, I don't think Dad will give us another chance."

SHANE PAUSED TO CATCH his breath before gathering his notes. He'd overtaxed himself preparing breakfast, and he'd be paying the price for the rest of the day.

But there was nothing he could do about it now. With Commodore Javon's visit mere hours away, he'd have to power through the pain again. Showing any weakness today might delay the trip to Janikk, and time was running out to find a more permanent home for the armada of defectors currently orbiting Baden. One more week and the Baden Defense Force would likely want more than their currently near-constant demand for updates. And that wasn't even accounting for the traumas they'd all face if Sparnell caught them first.

Although he didn't have to continue to overexert himself. His stubborn refusal to accept Razick's assistance was clearly bringing out the battle mage's worst emotions.

Not to mention, he needed to set a better example for his son. He'd caught Jake's recognition of his own pain. How could he expect Jake to accept his help in the future if he refused to accept anyone else's right now, when he clearly needed it?

He retrieved the body brace Jake and Razick had designed for him, tugging it free from where it had fallen between the bed and the wall, and pulled it on. It only took a moment to adjust the straps, tucking the harness snugly beneath his shirt, and he breathed a sigh of relief as the soothing hum of the exosuit's magic surged to life.

Buttoning his shirt over the brace, he quickly verified he'd gathered all his handwritten paperwork detailing his thoughts on their pending mission. After a pause, Shane also plucked the Sparnelli datapad holding the official reports of the mysterious Planet TR-75 from its perch on his scuffed nightstand before phasing into the Afterlife to emerge back in the kitchen.

Razick was right. There was no sense overtaxing himself physically if he didn't have to.

His houseguests had finished their efforts to clean the kitchen and now sat at the table, drinking water and sharing memories of their own childhood exploits. Jake sat between them, enthralled, his elbows propped on the table as he rested his chin in his hands, watching intently while Razick explained a particularly clever prank she'd played on her brother.

Shane wrinkled his nose and hoped they weren't giving Jake too many new ideas. The boy was creative enough on his own.

Razick nodded a silent acknowledgement of Shane's arrival, quickly wrapping up her story as he claimed the empty chair and organized his notes while the others burst into laughter. He waited patiently, only clearing his throat as the sound tapered toward silence.

They turned to him expectantly, and he pulled up the datapad, setting the screen to holographic projection mode. "TR-75. Let's start with what we know. Jeb?"

"Fleet Command authorized three different expeditions to Planet TR-75, set for different seasons, different locations on the planet and larger exploration teams with each attempt." The biologist keyed in the reports on the datapad, pulling up a sparsely mapped rendition of the planet with markers at three separate locations. "The first two? No survivors. But the third..." He rotated the globe to point to the expedition site. "The third attempt. They rescued my former coworker on his second day. The others were already dead by that point."

Shane consulted his notes, looking for anything they'd missed. "He claimed the planet itself killed everyone."

"He *was* known to embellish." Jeb tugged at his hair. "But from what I could gather, from him and the heavily redacted debriefings of the others, they were hunted relentlessly by the wildlife wherever they went. Those who survived *that* died to the vegetation."

"Do you remember his descriptions for any of the creatures on the planet?" Shane glared at his tablet. "How much do they correlate to the official reports? What are we likely to encounter?"

This was a train of thought they hadn't discussed before.

Jeb frowned. "Good question. From what I remember... The most prevalent were the red furred pack animals. He said they kept herding his team toward caves, trying to drive them inside. The closer to nightfall, the more desperately they hunted."

As Jeb continued to detail various plants and animals from the planet, Shane felt a familiar presence settle into the locket against his chest.

"You're early," he whispered, trusting Jeb's lecture to Razick's note taking. Instead he closed his eyes, reaching beneath his shirt to rub the necklace. He concentrated his thoughts on gratitude and affection, and received a burst of love from Feels in return.

I miss you, Grim. His empath sent thoughts of loneliness.

"I know," Shane murmured softly. "I miss you, too. I want to keep you all to myself and never let you go."

An enticing thought. Feels radiated amusement and mischief. *You should try it sometime.*

"Don't encourage me." Shane clutched the locket tighter. "You know I'll do it."

"So the creatures in his stories *do* mostly match the official report," Jeb concluded. "And they're *coordinated*. There's definitely an intelligence at work."

"Janikk?" Jake's eyes shone as he spoke. "Why did he say that's the planet's name?"

"Said he heard the wind speak." Jeb shrugged. "Wasn't any language he recognized, but it kept using the same word in every sentence: Janikk. He assumed it was meant as a name."

"So... Either we're traveling to a sentient planet who can coordinate with the wildlife," Shane summarized, "or we're chasing the frantic musings of a madman about a death planet."

"Pretty much." Jeb grinned. "Should be fun! And it's already chased off the SAF, so hopefully they'll be less inclined to hunt us down if we're able to settle there."

Shane had to admit, he'd been tempted to relocate the fleet for that feature alone, regardless of their success at winning over the planet. Sparnell *would* hunt them down – he'd personally dispatched Admiral Kydell's own retention teams often enough to recognize *that* inevitability – but Jeb's attempts at retrieving the full reports on TR-75 had met resistance in several roadblocks announcing the information as classified to Fleet Command.

He shook his head. The same secrecy that hid the admirals' shame at repeated defeat from an uninhabited planet would hide his fleet in turn. Few would risk the vengeance of Fleet Command for violating a classified system.

And those who would knew better than to do so at the first opportunity.

"Jake's staying behind this time, so it'll just be the three of us," he said, noting his companions had grown silent. "Although... Jeb, I'd like Hydroponics to come, too, if she's willing."

"Urla is happy to hear that." Jeb pointed to his watch, and Shane noted the presence of the *Inevitable*'s Hydroponics Afterlife Intelligence. "She made me promise to smuggle her in if she wasn't invited."

"Good. Given the apparent hostility of the plantlife, two agrokinesiologists will be better than one." Plus Urla had some additional skills Shane hoped to utilize, although it appeared she hadn't said much to Jeb on the matter. He turned his attention to Razick. "You ready to bodyguard? You're the only one of us equipped for offensive magic."

Razick nodded. "I'll raid the *Inevitable*'s armory before we land. What's left of it." She frowned at him. "Nobody'll order me to kill you this time, so I'm not holding back."

"Approved. Just, keep it non-lethal. Much as you can." He tapped the datapad. "Our mission is to gain the favor of the planet, not make her angrier. We'll fight back as little as possible." He held up a finger as Razick began to protest. "I'll admit, I don't know if that's possible. So yes, I'll feel safer if you're fully armed. If I'm wrong, we'll need you at your best if we plan to survive."

Razick quieted at his acknowledgement, settling back into her chair.

Shane closed his eyes as he rubbed his temples. "We're as prepared as we can be. We'll run it past Commodore Javon when she arrives, check in on the *Inevitable*'s repairs, and see if we missed anything. We're leaving for Janikk tomorrow, after I drop Jake of at Veris' house."

Jake frowned, but said nothing.

No. You're not going. Not without me. Not in this state. I forbid it. Feels' disapproval radiated from the locket.

"Feels…" Shane sighed. There was always so much work to do. "The fleet needs you. More than I do."

I disagree, Grim. And what about how much I need you? The empath paused, as if choosing their words. *You might want to go to your room.*

He raised an eyebrow. "You're sending me to my room? You're not my parent."

No. I'm your partner, and my vote in this relationship counts just as much as yours. There was no mistaking Feels' warning tone. *We need to talk about this. And I doubt you want to have this argument in front of our guests?*

Shane sighed, deflating. "Fine."

He turned to the others, each busy pretending to ignore his one-sided conversation. "We'll continue this later."

Without waiting for their reactions, he rose from his seat, phasing through the Afterlife to emerge in the small room he claimed as his. The mattress sagged at his weight as he sat, concentrating his thoughts on love and openness. "It's just us now. What's on your mind?"

Feels radiated frustration, mixed with fear. *After all these years, you're finally mine. I don't want to lose you now to your own stubbornness.*

"I'm a necromancer," Shane reminded them patiently. "Death means nothing to me."

And this body I made for you? Does that mean nothing, too?

Shane exhaled sharply. His current body was a masterwork of Feels' skills, back when they'd been a prominent fixture within the Baden underground. They'd managed to include all the alterations he'd requested in an effort to obscure his identity as Admiral Kydell's Commodore within the Sparnell Armed Forces, while still retaining enough of his own genetics that the process to bind his soul into its new home had operated like a resurrection.

Eying his reflection in the desilvering mirror above his faded dresser, he caught his own orange stare glaring back at him, his muscular frame clearly visible through his shirt. Shane had to admit in hindsight that the talented empath had maintained many of their own favorite features from his original physical appearance. He found himself wondering just how much love Feels had poured into the efforts of his body's creation...

And recognized with a start that if something happened to it, he didn't have the resources to obtain a replacement, and all their tender efforts would have been for nothing. Because of him.

"Shit, Feels, I didn't mean to–"

The empath interrupted, now projecting their own anger. *I may be dead, but I don't want you to join me just yet! You may as well murder me a second time.* Their anger shifted to frustration. *At least let me heal you before you go.*

"But the fleet–"

Can wait. *You're more important. Now and always.* Feels paused, and Shane felt the frustration dissipate into... mischief? *I can make it worth your while.*

He felt his breath catch as Feels' Psychomorpation sent a frisson of pleasure resonating along his Oath and throughout his body, the strength of the emotion amplified by the same spellworked vows eternally pledging his soul to the empath.

"You... don't fight fair," he gasped, clawing at the sheets to keep his balance.

I don't want *to fight at all. But you've made it clear it's either this, or I give you an order and hope Kydell's conditioning kicks in. Either way, I am healing you today.* The empath's voice was firm, the tone they reserved for him alone, most often to pull him out from emotional spirals. *So, what'll it be, Grim?*

Shane exhaled at the recognition of just how much he'd been worrying his empath, his breath still ragged from their spell. Feels needed this. Needed *him.*

He concentrated on his own memories of mischief, of the troubles he'd caused in the service during the early days of his conscription, and all the times Feels had rescued him from his own ill-advised ambitions. "Option two?"

He was rewarded with a snort. *You're incorrigible. You know that?*

"You offered." He shrugged, before turning his thoughts to apology. "I'm sorry I keep pushing you away, Feels. You matter to me. *We* matter." He hung his head, rubbing his feet against the threadbare carpet. "I get so wrapped up in everything that needs my attention, and in all my fears of becoming too possessive of you, that I forget you need me, too." He squeezed his eyes shut, finding his words. "I'll make it up to you. I'm all yours. Do what you want. Just... Tell me what you need from me."

Lay down. Hold still. And don't get up until I tell you. Feels' words were sharp, but the love beneath them was unmistakable.

Shane slowly unbuttoned his shirt, gently caressing the locket as he studied his own reflection. Kydell's claw strike against his cheek, the streaks of lightning etched clearly across his chest, the deeper burns and scarring where Razick's Electromancy had seared the locket into his ochre skin, and the soft powered brace she'd crafted with his son to allow him to maintain his mobility despite his injuries.

Feels was right. It had been two weeks since the duel against Kydell, and he was leaving tomorrow in an effort to tame a hostile planet. He needed to set aside his stubborn pride and let them take care of him. Let them *heal* him.

Taking a deep breath, he lay down on the bed, closing his eyes again as he sank into the mattress. He exhaled slowly to clear his mind and, for the first time he could remember, surrendered.

4

Razick frowned at the grill. It shouldn't have been *this* difficult. "Read me that section again?"

"About the temperature ranges? I really think we should wait for Lawrence…"

Jeb sounded unsure as he scratched his head, *Grilling for Pyromancers* sprawled open in his lap. He'd surrounded himself with the mismatched buckets containing every plant he'd managed to salvage from the *Inevitable*'s hydroponics bay.

"About searing the meat."

Razick closed her eyes and grabbed at the table beside the grill as she felt another large pull against her magic through the Apotheturgic link to the necromancer's healer. At her suggestion, they'd joined resources to provide Feels the Imperium required to complete Lawrence's healing, much as she'd done with her unit's medics throughout her career.

But this time was different. Given the waves of exhaustion periodically washing over her for the effort, she was grateful Jake had suggested including trusted members of Lawrence's orbiting fleet. She'd clearly injured him worse than he'd let on.

Probably hiding it from her. Trying to assuage her guilt.

"We don't know how long this'll take, and he wanted it ready in time for the Commodore's visit. He wouldn't need healing at all if it wasn't for me. The least I can do is get everything ready for him."

"I don't know about that." Jake sat cross-legged in the barren dirt that was Lawrence's back yard, eyes closed in meditation. A perfect model of stoic calm, despite his own contributions to his father's healing. "He's very particular about his grill."

"He's protective of *you*." Razick shrugged, flipping the lean roast over the hot flames. "Probably worried you'll burn yourself."

Jake cracked one eye to watch her. "That's what Shielding Magic is for."

Razick ignored him. "It's very crispy on the outside, Jeb. I *think* I did it right? How long am I supposed to cook this for?"

"Flip the steaks and grill for another three to five minutes for medium rare," Jeb read.

That can't be right...

Razick eyed the thick log of meat in front of her. "I don't think that's long enough. Why would he want to cook it so far in advance if it would be done that quickly?"

"That's a lean roast, not a steak," Jake corrected. "Dad always says you only sear the fatty cuts, but the lean cuts are the juiciest if you slow cook them just right. He always puts a little water in the grill to help."

"Jeb…" Razick sighed. "Have you been reading me the wrong recipe?"

"Maybe…?" Jeb reached into his pocket, retrieving a simple pair of reading glasses before turning to the back of the book.

"Ooh, yes. Thank you, Urla," he muttered to the *Inevitable*'s Hydroponics AI, his vision likely shared with her via his Telepathy. "Almost missed that."

Razick watched with sinking dread as he turned to a different page.

"Umm… Yeah. We're supposed to cook it at *half* that temperature. With a small pot of water."

"Great." Her shoulders fell.

First I kill him, then *I kill his carefully marinated roast. Nice going, Raz.*

But maybe a little water would do the trick.

"Jeb, fetch me some water while I lower this temperature. Let's double what the recipe says. Since I wasn't supposed to sear it."

"Mom says she doesn't think that'll fix it," Jake said softly. "We should really wait for Dad."

Razick ignored him, instead watching Jeb retreat into the house before turning back to the roast. She was debating if she should just cut it into steaks and cook it that way when another large magic drain hit. Sinking to her knees, she looked up in time to see Jeb stumble out the door, the water spilling from his glass.

Forcing herself to cast through the exhaustion, she caught the glass with her Telekinesis, using Hydromancy to direct the water into the grill before closing the lid. The device emitted an angry sizzle, its protests growing in volume and frequency.

It sounded like it was doing *something*, at least. And they hadn't broken any of Lawrence's cups in the process.

At that moment, Lawrence stepped out the back door to join them, offering his hand to Jeb and effortlessly hauling her brother back to his feet. The necromancer's shirt hung open, revealing a muscular chest completely devoid of scars and burns, his locket proudly displayed.

"Everything okay?" Jeb asked, when Razick didn't say anything.

The necromancer shrugged, shoving his hands in his pockets. "Not used to being married. Trying to get better at it."

"Don't look at *me*." Jeb laughed. "Razick's the one with the steady relationship."

Razick frowned at the reminder of her missing fiancée. She opened her mouth to speak, but held her tongue as Jeb cried out in surprise, suddenly cocooned in the *Inevitable*'s salvaged plants.

"I just meant this is all new to me, too, Urla!" he spluttered.

Lawrence smirked as he watched Jeb, before turning to Razick as if to say something. Whatever it was died on his lips, instead replaced by an uncharacteristic grin as his attention shifted to the grill. "Razick! I never knew you could grill!"

She smiled sheepishly, opening the lid for his inspection as he drew closer. A wall of steam and the stench of burnt charcoal assaulted them both.

"Oh." She could almost feel the disappointment in his voice. "You've... Huh."

She hung her head. "I'm sorry. I wanted to help."

"I think that's beyond even Necromancy, at this point," he observed, before straightening to rub the back of his neck. "Unless..."

A knife appeared in his hands, the burnt roast plating itself on the picnic table in the same moment. Lawrence sat in front of it and went to work, slowly sawing into the steamed and overcooked meat.

He bit his lip. "A bit too far gone for today, but I think we can bring it back as jerky for tomorrow. Jake!"

Jake rose from the dirt, dusting off his pants before joining his father.

"Cut it like this. With the grain, whenever you can." Lawrence demonstrated, leaning his weight on the knife to cut the charred yet somehow also rubbery meat before holding up the end result. "Pieces about this big. If it's too tough to cut through, move on and leave that part to me."

Jake nodded, accepting the offered knife and setting to work.

"I'm sorry, Lawrence." Razick hung her head. "I ruined everything today."

"Nonsense." He waved his hand as he rose from the bench. "You're going to learn to grill vegetarian today, while I sort out a protein for our carnivorous katanoji. Jeb! What plants are these? Can you get any fruits or vegetables from them?"

The backyard burst into full bloom as the salvaged plants flowered, then fruited.

"Perfect," Lawrence praised, clearly in his element. "Razick, halve the heat on the grill. We want to roast these, but they'll burn quick at that temperature. Jeb, we'll need some things from the kitchen. I'll make a list."

"I'll have to call the *Inevitable*, too. Get more hydroponics supplies." Her brother's brows furrowed as he ran a finger tenderly across a leaf. "We've put them through a lot, and they're still stressed about being outside."

Razick turned her attention to her assigned task, doing her best to tune out the self-doubt filling her mind.

Lawrence made it look so easy. He'd never once blamed her for her mistakes, instead calmly accepting them before taking charge and moving on with a contingency plan that somehow made best use of all his available resources. And whenever she'd pressed him for his thoughts, he'd never failed to express a confidence in her she wished she could share.

She listened attentively as he walked her through each step of prepping the grill, all the while helping her brother mix seasonings for their new meal *and* a new marinade to reconstitute the meat she'd ruined. In short order she was grilling under the watchful eye of the necromancer, the fruits and vegetables elevated above the flames with Telekinesis, her Pyromancy maintaining the ideal temperature. Lawrence had her heat up the remains of the breakfast casserole as well, shifting its form once more into some kind of meat and vegetable dip for use with a loaf of stale bread from the pantry.

"Nothing too fancy," he said quietly, and she found herself accurately anticipating his next directives until he seemed confident to leave her to her own devices at the grill.

"Thanks for showing me how to fix it." She set the latest tray of grilled fruits on the table, beginning to prep the final set of vegetables. "I'm glad you're feeling better."

"Who sent Feels after me, anyway?" He eyed her suspiciously as he chopped more herbs for the jerky marinade. "I know at least one of you helped. Fae may have higher Imperium reserves than the rest of us, but I know from personal experience that job would've required several days' worth, at least."

Razick silently raised her hand, and watched as Jeb and Jake paused their own efforts to do the same.

He attempted to glare at all of them, but gave up. "I was being stubborn. Thank you. I'd promise to never let it happen again, but... that would be quite presumptuous of me."

His features grew soft as he fondled his locket, and Razick was pleased to note no sign of pain in his movements now. "I know, I know. You already made your point... Would you like to join us? I... *Razick* grilled some of your favorites."

As Razick watched, reality twisted to reveal an iridescent fae perched in Lawrence's palm, their insectoid purple body displaying two pairs of pastel rainbow wings and a multicolored feathered tail splayed behind them like the train on a royal's dress. Their delicate white mane rippled in the faint afternoon breeze as they took flight, tilting their head to watch as Lawrence rose from his seat and twisted his shoulders to slip out of his shirt.

The necromancer stood awkwardly as his empath slowly circled before returning to land on his outstretched palm. "As promised. Can I put my shirt back on now?"

"Can't an artist admire their handiwork?"

Feels' voice didn't attempt to hide their amusement, and Razick stifled a snort. Despite her original misgivings at learning their specialties, she'd come to admire the psychomorphic fae.

"You could have asked while we were alone," Lawrence pouted.

"Where's the fun in that?" A kaleidoscope of color filled the air as they beat their wings in rhythm with their own laughter. "This is nice. And better than a hologram. Wouldn't mind a way to slip to the mortal plane whenever I want."

Shane rubbed his chin with his free hand. "Jake? Think that's something you could do?"

Jake paused his work with the knife. "I'd need to take your locket apart to see… But I *think* so." His words came faster after that, and Razick recognized his facial expressions from their afternoons puzzling over roadblocks together in the school lab. "If the holograms are stored in tyrellium crystal, I could set one for the necromantic phasing instead. You'd have to write out the spell for me so I can program it, since I don't know that one. When you get back, though. Wouldn't be able to finish before you leave, anyway." He grinned at Feels in triumph. "But then you could activate it from inside the locket, whenever you want."

Lawrence raised an eyebrow, his orange eyes fixed on Feels. "Is that acceptable? I'd like to put my shirt back on."

Razick caught movement out of the corner of her eye, turning in time to watch two katanoji and a fae materialize in the small backyard.

"*You're* looking much better."

Commodore Javon's voice was calm, but the wrinkles around her eyes betrayed her amusement. The tabby feline's tail danced behind her as she saluted, her orange fur blending into the standard tan and brown of her service uniform, the Sparnelli insignia now carefully removed. She nodded politely to Feels. "I see our magic was well spent."

Lawrence's scowl deepened at the revelation, but he merely shoved his arms back into his sleeves before deftly buttoning the front, his voice shifting into a growl. "Interesting timing as always, Alanis."

"Not my fault this time." The ice blue fae, Navigations AI from the *Inevitable*, crossed two pairs of arms as she landed on the table. "This is *exactly* when you told us to arrive. I hope it's a better party than your last one."

Lawrence nodded politely to the second katanoj, a stern mostly-black calico with mismatched eyes, one blue, one gold.

A noticeable scar ran across the feline's left eye, splitting the corresponding ear. "Jeb, Razick, meet Fleet Captain Haveid, the Commodore's XO on the *Relentless*."

Haveid saluted, pressing their right fist tightly against their left shoulder in response. "Thanks for having us, Sir."

"None of that here. Please." Lawrence waved his hand dismissively, although Razick thought she caught a hint of embarrassment from the necromancer. "We're all here. Jake, does Caroline...?"

Jake shook his head. "Mom says there's too many people."

Lawrence nodded, redirecting his attention to Jeb. "Would Urla like to join us?"

Razick watched her brother tilt his head as his eyes unfocused slightly, telltale signs of a telepathic conversation with the Hydroponics AI. After a moment, he nodded. "I've convinced her."

A red furred katanoj appeared next to the biologist, smiling shyly in his direction. He grinned back, grabbing her hand and sliding over in his seat to allow her space beside him.

Razick watched as Urla lay her head on Jeb's shoulder, her brother instinctively wrapping his arm around her to pull her closer, and wondered again what her own relationship with Nya had been like before Admiral Kydell had erased her memories.

I will find you, she promised again. *And I will* remember *you*.

But the fleet needed her first.

Lawrence motioned to the array of food across the table without looking at it, his attention held instead by a Sparnelli datapad. "Grab a bite while I set this up. Razick's been grilling all day."

No mention of how I ruined his original plan, Razick realized with gratitude as she filled her plate. She took a bite and briefly closed her eyes, sinking into her seat as a surprisingly array of flavors filled her mouth.

"TR-75," Lawrence began, and when Razick opened her eyes again he'd pulled up the globe Jeb had displayed earlier. "Also known as Janikk. And our destination tomorrow."

"Umm... Excuse me?"

All eyes at the table turned to watch the approach of the fair-skinned human stranger, his hard hat in hand. He shuffled closer, his almond eyes risking a glance in their direction before returning his attention to the bare dirt of the yard. "I'm really sorry for interrupting, but I honestly don't know where else I can turn. I'm told one of you is the Bastard of Baden?"

5

Razick and Haveid moved with precision to intercept, but Shane waved them away. "Stand down, I know him. He's my neighbor."

They halted, still watching the newcomer with vigilance, and Shane scowled. He commanded a fleet again; he'd need to get used to the traditional Sparnelli security details once more. At least until he trained them out of it.

The fact they hadn't yet assigned anyone to his house was either a major oversight on their part, or an acknowledgement of Shane's own confidence in Razick. He hoped for the latter.

But that was something to mull over later. Furrowing his brow, Shane turned to address the man. "Call me Shane. Please. Or Lawrence, if you want to be formal. What's wrong, Tom?"

Tom froze, blinking. "Sorry. Only talked to you once. Didn't expect you to remember me, much less my name!"

Shane noticed the man's furtive glances around the table, and motioned for him to sit. "Would you like to join us?" Whatever was bothering Tom, it must be important to him, if he was this nervous yet still willing to interrupt.

Tom shook his head. "No. I can see you're busy. I was just hoping... My house... The bombardment..." He motioned in the general direction of his house, his words coming in a rush now as he gripped his hat tighter. "Not that I hold you responsible or anything! Voids, without you, we wouldn't even have a *planet*! It's just that building materials are harder to come by right now, what with the demand and all, but I found a distributor who claimed to have the lumber in stock. They even agreed to sell it to me at half the current inflated rates, but I have to pick it up today or they'll sell it to someone else, but travel's a right mess right now and I was hoping maybe you knew someone who could help me? I already paid for everything, you see, and it wiped out my savings."

He pulled a tablet from his pocket, its screen displaying some sort of invoice, and thrust it in Shane's direction with trembling hands.

Rather than accepting the device, Shane reached for his magic, elevating his consciousness into the Afterlife and tracing back along Tom's approach. Unlike his own section of the Baden City suburbs, several streets away the whole block had been practically leveled, with little intact aside from a few personal bombardment shelters arranged in basements. Likely an SAF atmospheric missile knocked off course by Baden City's

Shielding defenses. Or perhaps one of Baden's, fallen to ground after losing track of its intended target.

He hadn't concerned himself with civilian casualties when he'd written the fleet's pocket Shielding engagement protocols.

The street was crawling with people of all ages in hats and heavy gloves, sorting through the remains for personal belongings and reusable materials. Several small sheds professionally constructed from clearly salvaged material dotted the streets, safely positioned away from any unstable structures.

"You've got the whole street working." Shane kept his voice soft, but it wasn't a question.

"And my crew." Tom scratched behind his ear. "Took a vote. Rebuilding my house first, then I can give everyone a safe spot to stay while we take our time with the rest. But we need that lumber."

"Razick? On me. We've got a shipment to move." Shane rose from his seat as Razick moved closer. "Jeb, it's your briefing. Start without us." He slid the datapad to the biologist. "Alanis, take over my spell for Feels and Urla. Keep them on the mortal plane."

He waited for her to nod, her wings shimmering with a light blue sparkle at the movement, before moving toward Tom in preparation for the jump.

"You're leaving me again." Feels hovered just in front of his face, all three pairs of arms crossed against their thorax. "I'm glad you're helping people. I know it helps you, too. Just...

Relationships also need time. I was looking forward to finally spending some with you. Preferably while not healing anyone."

"I know." Shane focused his thoughts on love for his empath and was rewarded with an overwhelming sense of affection in return. "Won't be gone long. Promise." He motioned to the array of grilled fruits and vegetables. "Besides. It's been years since you've eaten. Enjoy yourself."

"Don't get much meat on deployment," Haveid growled through a mouthful of casserole dip, their focus on Razick. "How'd you learn to cook like this?"

"Was all Lawrence's doing, really." She sat taller in her seat, even as she tried to brush off the compliment.

"I just gave her the recipe." Shane shook his head. "She did the rest."

"*My* family recipe. Just like my parents used to make it!" Feels said excitedly.

Shane growled as a new realization rose in his thoughts. "You don't cook... But I have your recipes. They don't share those with just anyone, do they? *You* told them how you felt about me. Before you told *me*?"

The multicolored fae showed no signs of apology. "They were so heartbroken when the holovids said you died."

"And you?"

Feels laughed. "I've seen the trouble you cause. Figured you'd find me again eventually. And I was right!" They tipped their head thoughtfully. "Should really let them know I'm okay, though. Last they probably heard, I was murdered. And I'd love if they got to finally meet you!"

Shane swallowed. "Not awkward at all."

"Oh hush. I forgave you. They will, too."

He felt a rush of calm settle into his thoughts, a psychomorphic gift from his gentle fae. Closing his eyes, he briefly savored the moment before opening them to turn to Razick. "Ready?"

She nodded and stepped closer. Wrapping an arm around her, he pulled her closer to conserve magic. She inhaled sharply but returned the favor, pressing herself against his side.

"What's the address?" He directed the question at Tom, grasping the architect's upper arm. Tom's eyes widened, but he merely offered the invoice once more. "Got it."

Narrowing his eyes, Shane pulled Razick and Tom into his awareness before phasing into the Afterlife. He bent reality around them, folding the distance between them and their destination before emerging from the jump at the lumberyard.

Razick surveyed their new surroundings as he released her, intuitively scanning for threats. Endless rows of heavy metal shelving stretched away in all directions, piled surprisingly high with a generous assortment of tools and building materials much valued across the still-recovering planet.

Tom blinked, frozen in place.

"Hyperjump. Sorry." Shane noted Razick tense as an angry-looking canid wearing coveralls bearing the lumberyard's logo ran down the aisle toward them, her dark brown fur standing on end. "Forget I should warn people. First time?"

"I'll... be okay." Tom had also spotted the distribution center worker and busied himself pulling up the sales agreement. "Certainly efficient. Thank you."

"This is private property! You're not supposed to be in here!"

"Apologies, ma'am. The network is a mess. This was the only available mode of transportation." Tom smiled amicably, turning his tablet to reveal his paperwork. "I'm here to pick up my order? XK7J9. For Tom."

She frowned, looking them up and down apprehensively before turning away and motioning for them to follow. "You'll want to talk to the Boss."

She led them through aisles of surprisingly well stocked building supplies, eventually motioning toward an office at the far end. Shane and his companions stepped inside to discover a large dracoling in an expensive-looking suit busy at work across multiple data screens, his thick green skin crisscrossed with patterns resembling scales. The man's ear fins fluttered faintly at their entrance, but otherwise he made no sign of hearing them enter.

The door closed behind them, and Shane found himself on high alert at the sound of the latch sliding into place.

Razick clearly heard it too, turning to him for guidance.

"We'll give it a minute. I'll Shield the civilian," he mumbled quietly, knowing she'd be using her Anemancy to augment her hearing and hoping the dracoling wasn't currently doing the same. He bolstered his own Shielding, this time including Tom in the spell, and felt the telltale spike of energy at the back of his neck as Razick followed his lead.

The lumberyard boss looked up from his work, scowling at their presence. It was easy to see why old folklore claimed the species a distant relative of the mythical dragons, although genetically they'd been proven to share a common ancestor with humans. "And who in Void's name are you?"

"I'm here to pick up my order." Tom seemed oblivious to the danger, turning his datapad toward the man to display the details of his purchase. "XK7J9? Name's Tom. We spoke this morning."

"Tom." The manager folded his fingers together above his desk, an awkward smile pasted on his face. "I remember. How'd you manage to get here?"

"Neighbor gave me a lift."

Shane noted Tom's voice shift toward suspicion, nodding faintly in approval. The architect hadn't mentioned who Shane was, or the spell that had brought them there, allowing them to keep the advantage of surprise. *Good.*

The lumberyard manager turned to Shane and Razick. "I'm sorry he dragged you into this. This business deal is between him, and me. If you'd be so kind as to leave, I won't be forced to involve either of you any further."

"That's a mighty fine offer." Shane calmly pulled up a chair and took a seat in front of the desk. "But I think we'll be staying."

"Your funeral." There was no kindness in his smile as he rose from his desk to tower above them. "And yes, I *do* mean that literally. The point of selling the same stock repeatedly, after all, relies on nobody being able to pick it up."

Allowing his eyebrow to rise at the audacity of the man's words, Shane leaned forward in his chair, folding his fingers together in his lap. "You've been taking orders, counting on non-delivery due to infrastructure and transportation issues, only to turn around and resell them somewhere else?"

He thought he'd seen his fair share of brazen arrogance in his career with the Sparnell Armed Forces, but even the most narcissistic admirals had known better than to admit their plans out loud. However many desperate Badenese the lumberyard had swindled since the Confederation's assault, Shane resolved today would be the end of it.

"That's about the shape of it," the conman manager agreed with a casual shrug and a confident sneer. He turned his attention back to Tom. "While I'd normally let you take your tiny order and chalk it up to a bad bet on my part, I just sealed a rather lucrative deal for my whole inventory. I'd apologize, but... Well, it's just business. You understand."

Tom paled, stepping backward. "But that's my life's savings! We need those suppliers!"

Shane calmly propped his feet on the manager's desk, ignoring the resultant glare. "Something tells me you don't recognize me." He turned to Razick. "He doesn't recognize us."

"No, Sir," she answered automatically, eyes locked on the lumberyard boss as she waited for direction.

"Think you have a chance against me?" The lumberyard manager rose from his seat, towering over them. "Three miserable humans. What are you going to do?"

"It's quite refreshing, really." Shane smiled cruelly, his expression hardening. "Most people freeze with terror, meeting the Bastard of Baden." His smirk grew at the man's panic, the expression still not meeting his eyes as the lumberyard boss struggled against Razick's Telekinesis. "Some even find themselves breathless."

The man's eyes widened as he gasped helplessly into the near-vacuum now surrounding him, his own genetic Anemancy unable to counter Razick's finely honed battle mage training. Shane held his gaze for several long seconds before motioning Razick to release her grip. She nodded once, sending the lumberyard boss tumbling back into his chair.

"I'm not a murderer," Shane told him conversationally, tilting his head. "Well, no. I am. But I'm *trying* to cut back. Been clean a whole two weeks!" He returned his feet to the floor, leaning forward menacingly instead. "You wouldn't want to cause a relapse, would you?"

The manager shook his head no, emphatically, still gasping for breath.

"Good. Good." Shane leaned back in the chair, propping his feet on the desk once more. "You keep that attitude, you'll do just fine. So, here's what's going to happen next..."

6

RAZICK POSITIONED HERSELF IN the corner next to Tom, allowing an easy vantage point of the cowering lumberyard boss, as well as the door. She winked at the architect, his knuckles white as he repeatedly attempted to turn the knob. "You're safe with us."

Tom studied her cautiously for a moment before releasing his grip. He turned to her, hand slipping from the door as he leaned his back against it. "Lawrence knew something was wrong, didn't he?"

Razick watched the lumberyard manager nod eagerly at each of Lawrence's demands, the necromancer maintaining his personable veneer. She shrugged. "Hard to tell. I can't figure out that brain of his. Always several steps ahead."

She'd come to rely on his planning intellect. By boarding the *Inevitable* and confronting her old team she'd given away her position, all but guaranteeing the Confederation would send someone to retrieve her.

But Lawrence made her feel safe, for the first time she could remember. Whatever happened, she remained confident they could face it together.

"He must have known. Why else would he bring you?"

Razick frowned. "What do you mean?"

"You know." Tom looked away, shoving his hands in his pockets. "You're his muscle, yeah?"

"No," she said, a little too quickly, and scowled. "Lawrence is a power unto himself. How do you think he ended up in command of an entire fleet of invading warships? Certainly wasn't from asking nicely."

She paused to watch Lawrence chatting conversationally with the terrified manager. The man kept his full attention on the necromancer, as if his life depended on it.

Realistically speaking, it probably did.

Turning back to Tom, she noted the architect seemed much more relaxed, his attention now focused on Lawrence.

"He just... I don't know how to describe it. People want to give him what he wants."

"Because they're afraid of what will happen if they don't?"

"Sometimes." Razick thought back to Lawrence's generous hospitality, opening his home and even his beloved kitchen to her and her brother while they decided what to do about the charred remains of their former apartment. "But not always. There's lots more than that. I mean, are *you* afraid of him?"

Tom frowned, scratching his chin. "A little? But probably not as much as I *should* be. He didn't have to help me, but here he is." He gave her a sidelong look. "Why do *you* follow him?"

"Well..."

Razick paused, shifting her weight. What should she even say? Friendship with his son? Gratitude for helping her destroy Admiral Kydell? Hope he'd help her find the fiancée she couldn't even remember? Guilt for killing him with her fear and secrets?

The necromancer didn't seem to hold a grudge, never once mentioning her failings aboard the *Inevitable* unless she brought it up.

Which only made it more difficult for her to forgive herself.

But Lawrence himself saved her from answering, rising suddenly from his seat to address her again. "Now that we've settled things in here, you want to get the door, or shall I?"

Hired muscle indeed.

"You get it." Razick motioned Tom to step away. "I can do it quickly *or* cleanly, but you can do both."

"Fair enough." She noted Lawrence's faint smile as he reached for the handle. His eyes lost focus briefly and then suddenly the entire knob and locking mechanism lay unencumbered on the desk as the door swung open.

He waved the lumberyard manager through the doorway. "Get. We'll follow you."

Tom moved to stand beside Razick, the pair watching their reluctant guide stumble slowly through the door, Lawrence following close behind. The architect looked up at her, eyes wide.

"So that's it, then? Just like that?"

"I doubt it. In my experience? Things are never this easy." She shrugged, motioning him through the door. "But you'll be fine. That's why you invited us."

Outside the office, they were greeted by four yard workers, including the canid woman who'd escorted them. A pair of matching katanoji wielded heavy looking construction tools, tails jerking with agitation, while the human and canid brandished heavy pipes.

Amateurs.

"Don't get many visitors?" Lawrence's shoulders remained relaxed from his position behind the manager, but Razick noted his spine straighten ever so slightly as he evaluated the potential danger.

"What are you *waiting* for?" the manager growled, breaking into a run. "Get them!"

"Get down," she hissed at Tom, stepping in front of him and hoping he obeyed.

The manager's henchman lunged toward Lawrence with their makeshift weapons, but Razick was ready with a quick Shielding burst that knocked them off balance and sent them tumbling to the floor.

"Protect Tom," she ordered Lawrence.

"I can help," he protested.

"By staying out of my way."

To her surprise, he offered no further arguments, a familiar sensation at the back of her neck informing her of his newly reinforced Shielding.

Further proof of his undeserved trust. But she'd no intention to argue, this time.

While their opponents were unlikely to hesitate before a killing blow, they'd never get the chance. Not when paired against a Sparnelli battle mage and... whatever Lawrence had been. Somehow she doubted he was merely a Void necromancer – the highly powerful mages tasked with transporting the Sparnell Armed Forces' capital ships through the vast Void of space – but he respected her privacy about her own traumas, and she'd vowed to grant him the same courtesy.

Many of those traumas stemmed from using deadly force on weaker opponents with no hope to withstand her. She wasn't about to add to them now and, despite his best attempts, she didn't quite trust Lawrence to temper his own offensive magic. If she wanted a clear conscience tonight, this fight had to be hers alone.

The two katanoji henchmen rolled to their feet with a feline grace, claws and teeth bared, their former weapons abandoned. They shifted their attention to Razick as their companions struggled to their feet, accelerating toward her at impossible speeds.

Telekinesis.

She countered with her own telekinetic spell, reinforcing the gravity beneath their feet and forcing them to pour more power into their own spells to compensate. A power of wills they'd surely win, one telekinetic against two, except they'd overlooked one simple possibility.

Razick released her spell.

No longer burdened by her telekinesis – but still supercharging their own – the pair unwittingly launched themselves toward the ceiling. Before they could react to save themselves, Razick cast her Electromancy, sending lightning chasing after the two flying felines for good measure.

Razick winced as the first katanoj, focused entirely on recovering from their errant Telekinesis, took the full force of her spell, slumping unconscious the same moment their feet hit the floor. The second had chosen to instead address her lightning, reflecting it off his Shielding only slam into one of the many reinforced metal shelves of the warehouse, knocking the wind from his lungs and sending him tumbling toward the ground.

She caught him with her own magic, gently settling him beside his twin.

"Watch out!"

She'd forgotten about their other assailants, an oversight quickly remedied as the canid woman landed a heavy blow against her Shielding, sending her reeling backward. Converting her loss of balance into momentum with a brief burst of Telekinesis, she pivoted to confront the human attempting to surprise her from the other direction to repeat the maneuver.

Her fist connected with his jaw, eliciting a sharp yelp of pain, but he'd managed to bring his heavy section of pipe inside of her defenses. It connected with her Shielding, and only an instinctive cast of Anemancy kept the blow from knocking the wind from her lungs.

"Razick," Lawrence said, tentatively. "You've nothing to prove. I can help."

She ignored him, instead pushing her assailants back with another Shielding burst. Buying a moment to think.

She was doing this all wrong. She didn't need help. She *shouldn't* need help.

But she was afraid. Afraid of making another mistake. Afraid of disappointing Lawrence. Afraid she already *had*. Afraid of losing herself to Kydell's conditioning, and the deadly nature of her training.

But Kydell didn't own her mind anymore. And she wasn't about to allow fear to take his place.

Forcing herself to exhale slowly, Razick locked her eyes on her opponents, and surrendered to her instincts.

And then she was in the thick of it, once more slipping into the familiar dance of combat. The universe slowed, her two assailants closing the distance, pipes held over their shoulders and ready to swing. She crouched, ducking beneath them and pivoting away.

Their weaponry collided, and they followed soon after, falling to the ground in a tangle of limbs and curses. Her Telekinesis kept them there long enough for her to crouch beside each, a careful spark of Electromancy sending them to join their allies in unconsciousness.

She rose to her feet, brushing her hands on her trousers as she grinned at Lawrence. "See? I had it covered."

"That you did," he agreed, his features softer than usual. "Are you okay? I saw you hesitate."

"I'm not hurt," she reassured him. At his raised eyebrow, she added, "Doubt."

He nodded, once, and opened his mouth to say something else, but Tom interrupted.

"Their manager got away."

"No, he didn't," Shane growled.

The harried lumberyard boss materialized in front of them, a large stack of bills in one hand, a small sack clutched tightly in the other. He blinked at the sudden change of scenery, eyes widening as he recognized them.

Lawrence smirked. "I'm sorry. Did we interrupt something?"

7

"You won't get away with this," the angry manager snarled, struggling against Razick's expertly applied Telekinesis.

Shane allowed himself a cruel smile. "I already did."

"I have friends. They'll come for you! You might control orbit for now, but *Nightbird* owns this planet!"

"And we'll grant them the same hospitality you've shown us," Shane said coldly, wrapping his fingers around the man's arm.

The glaring manager disappeared, jumped through the Afterlife into the brig of one of his orbiting ships. Shane watched through the Veil for a moment, well-trained crew quickly jumping to action to secure the cell and await further orders, before turning to Tom.

"See if you can find what you ordered. Give us a minute, and we'll come join you to send it home." He closed his eyes briefly, leaning into his Necromancy to search the warehouse for any other souls. "Looks like everyone else got the message. I don't think you'll see any more trouble."

Tom glanced briefly at Razick before scampering off, his datapad clutched to his chest.

Shane watched him go for a moment, ensuring he wasn't followed, before turning to Razick. "I know you swore you'd never use your skills to hurt anyone else. Thank you. For trusting me."

Razick shrugged, but there was a hesitation to the action. "Said I wouldn't *kill* anyone. I'll put the fear of the Void into bullying cheats any day." She watched him for a moment, her projected confidence slipping. "Thanks for caring enough to check how I felt about it. And for listening. When I told you to stand down."

"You said you had it handled." He tilted his head, watching her closely as she averted her eyes at his acknowledgement of trust, and made a note to talk to her later. He knew guilt when he saw it.

But now wasn't the time.

"Besides," he added instead. "Made it easier to track our cheating friend. Tried to empty out the safe before he left."

She nodded, biting her lip before meeting his eyes again. "Why'd you bring me, anyway? Did you know this would happen?"

"No." He probably *should* have, maybe. But the truth of it? "I asked you to come because I know I shouldn't do these sorts of things alone, and I enjoy your company." He rubbed the back of his neck, smiling sheepishly. "Plus... Was hoping to borrow your Telekinesis. Takes me less magic to jump things if they're close together. I know you used a lot already today, to help Feels heal me... But that invoice list was long."

Her nose wrinkled. "I *am* your muscle."

"You are my *friend*," he corrected her, frowning as he shoved his hands in his pockets. Despite his longstanding friendship with an empath, he'd never been good at words. Not the kind that bared his own emotions. But Razick needed to know. "I *hope* you feel the same way, at least. It's nice, having someone who understands things, without me having to explain it. I'm... not used to having friends. Not real ones. That I can trust. That trust *me*. It's... It's been a while."

Feels had been the only friend he'd had, and even then... Well, they'd spent decades separated due to his military career, and then he'd *murdered* them the first chance he got when they'd reconnected.

And now they were married. It was a lot to work through.

And that was before acknowledging his other chance at friendship. He'd sworn an Oath of loyalty, a promise to stand by his side, no matter what.

An Oath that ended on Loxira, when Shane had Shattered his would-be friend's soul to keep Jake safe. That face *still* haunted his dreams, and probably always would.

He shook his head, exhaling. No. He didn't have many friends. Didn't *deserve* any of them, if his past choices were any indication. But Razick mattered to him, and he was intent on getting this one right.

"You're not the only one with regrets," he told her, his guilt for the past swelling into resolve for the future, just as Feels had conditioned him. "Whatever you think you've done, I promise I've done worse."

"That's harder than you think," she told him, but her eyes reflected her newfound smile. "I'm the one with the special forces training, remember."

"Feels always said I was an overachiever," he said wryly, and she laughed. There was a shift in his necromantic awareness. "You'd better find Tom. He went... that way."

He watched Razick pull straighter as she followed his finger with her eyes, scanning their surroundings as her training kicked in. "Trouble?"

"Hopefully not," Shane reassured. "But I'd feel safer if he had backup. Just in case. Help him gather his supplies in larger groups, and I'll jump them once I've checked it out."

He shuddered slightly as her fingernails dug into his shoulder, her eyes lined with concern. "Be careful, okay?"

"Promise," he agreed.

She watched him suspiciously before turning to make her way in the direction he'd pointed, her steps purposeful.

He waited a moment longer before focusing his thoughts on loneliness and need, turning his attention to the sudden warmth in his chest as Feels settled into the locket. He let out a soft growl. "Missed you."

Then you shouldn't have asked me to stay behind, Grim. The words held a stern tenderness. *If you've already managed to break this body of yours after I spent all morning fixing it, I swear to everything you hold dear I will* never *let you leave the house again.*

Shane rubbed the locket affectionately, focusing his thoughts on love and reassurance even as he bit back a retort about the difficulties of containing interdimensional Hyperjumping necromancers. "I'd have healed eventually, you know."

A self-satisfied stubbornness emanated from the locket. *If you refused my healing today, we were grounding you from the mission.*

"You can't...."

But they could. They'd finally given in to his demands, and claimed Kydell's conditioning over his mind. They could order him to do anything, and as long as it didn't jeopardize Jake's safety, he'd do it.

You're mine, *Grim. When someone gives me a gift, I take* care *of it.* The empath now radiated a possessive frustration, but Shane could still feel a hint of amusement beneath the words. *Unlike* some *people.*

"Razick did all the fighting. I'm fine. Not a scratch."

I'll be the judge of that.

A healing warmth raced briefly through his veins.

"Perfectionist," he muttered.

No. Artist. The answer was smug, but there was a sadness to it, too. *What do you need, Grim? You never Call me these days unless you want something.*

The truth of their observation hit like a punch to the gut. Despite his best intentions, his efforts to ensure they kept their freedom, his desires to give them space...

He was still failing his empath.

"I *do* need your help," he admitted, shoulders sagging. "Tom's situated, but there's still a lot of building supplies here. Lots of people could benefit from these."

A wave of love filled his mind in return. *And you want to ensure they do. How can I help?*

Reaching out with his senses, Shane found the eavesdropping stranger's soul again. "I need your Insight, Feels. Just like old times."

At Feels' agreement, Shane folded the mortal plane, emerging directly in front of the young gray-furred katanoj doing her best to trail Razick. He grabbed her by the scruff, lifting her into the air before she could react.

"Please let me go! I mean you no harm!" She struggled against him, limbs flailing, to no avail.

"Then you have nothing to fear from me."

Shane carefully lowered his arm until the feline stood on the floor once more, his grip still firm as he studied his captive. She was a mere child compared to the others at the yard – perhaps nineteen, if he had to guess – although he'd had younger battle mage commanders in his military career. The young woman's whiskers twitched with fear, her claws digging into the back of the datapad she clutched to her chest.

Fear. Lots of it. This individual holds no threat.

"Please don't hurt me." The datapad moved upward to cover the lower half of the katanoj's face, fur still twisting against his palm as she tried to escape, watching Shane with wide brown-orange eyes.

Shane wrapped his leg around a bucket of some sort of fertilizer, sliding it behind himself for use as a seat. He kicked a second gently toward the young katanoj. "I won't. Promise." He motioned to the bucket. "I'll even let you go if you promise to sit and talk instead of running."

The young woman nodded emphatically.

Nervousness. Resignation. Curiosity. Seems to trust you, for now. Or recognizes they can't run.

At Feels' confirmation of his own gut feelings, Shane let go and settled onto his bucket. The girl grabbed the offered container, dragging it away as Shane watched quietly. Apparently mollified by the necromancer's lack of reaction, the yard worker finally sat and turned to Shane expectantly, claws still digging into the datapad now perched on his lap.

"You didn't attack us."

It wasn't a question, but the gray furred worker shook her head anyway. "I'm just the bookkeeper. Restocking, customer orders, finances, that sort of thing."

"And scamming people."

The katanoj recoiled. "I had *nothing* to do with that, I swear! I just want to *help* people!"

Your friend is insulted.

"You just said you kept the books," Shane pressed, cocking his head. He was careful to maintain an even tone. "And you're working for a mobster."

"He's my uncle." She sighed, pulling her knees toward her chest. "By marriage," she amended quickly, noting Shane's raised eyebrows. "Yard was my Mom's. S'posed to be mine, now, but I'm not good with people." She frowned, turning pleading eyes toward Shane. "When my uncle offered to take over that side of things, let me stick to the bookkeeping, I thought he wanted to help. Didn't realize he planned to fire all Mom's people, replace them with Nightbird's, and threaten to kill me if I did anything about it." She hung her head. "She'd be *so* disappointed in me."

Guilt. Shame. Despair. But also trust. A hint of hope. They could be yours, Grim, if you want them.

Shane weighed his options. This was the second mention of Nightbird that day, but he couldn't afford to pull on that string – the fleet needed him at Janikk tomorrow.

"What's your name, kid?"

"Gabbie." Her voice was a whisper.

Standing from the bucket, Shane stepped forward to place a hand on Gabbie's shoulder. She didn't even flinch, instead leaning into the touch as if it were the only warmth she'd felt in a while.

Mind made up, Shane knelt before her, using his other hand to direct the young woman's face to his own. "No. She'd be proud of you, for learning from your mistake and making something good out of it. People like your uncle live to prey on those they believe are weaker. But you know what to look for now, don't you? You learned his secret, so he can never hold power over you again."

She rubbed at her eyes, the short jerks of her tail betraying her thoughts. "You mean you believe me?"

Shane thought back to his own career, and the early days under Admiral Kydell. "Believe it or not, I've been manipulated by people I trusted, too. There's no shame in it. We learn, and we keep moving forward."

She leapt from the bucket, eyes shining with excitement. "You're right! I *can't* let him stop me! Oh, thank you! You gave me my *life* back today!"

You know how you always claim to be a monster? Feels' projected emotions shifted to love. *This is why I argue with you, every time.*

Closing his eyes, Shane fought back his discomfort at the unexpected hug and instead focused his thoughts on his son and the empath in his locket. Even monsters could do good, given the proper motivation. Even *he* could learn to do things for the right reasons.

He pushed against the embrace, standing up as Gabbie released her grip. "We're not done yet. I've got someone I think you should meet."

8

RAZICK FOCUSED ON HER breathing as she carefully lowered a sizable stack of plywood to the floor, already feeling the signs of Imperium strain. Not that she was in danger of hurting herself – at least, not yet – but she'd pulled heavily from her reserves today, between Shane's healing and the lumberyard. She needed to stop soon and rest if she intended to begin tomorrow's mission at full strength.

"Please tell me that's the last of it."

"And…" Tom's voice trailed off, still focused on his datapad. "Done! We've got everything on the list, and not a scrap more." He grinned, meeting Razick's gaze. "I don't know how I can ever thank you. I reached out in desperation. Never expected to actually get help."

"It's nice to help people for a change," Razick admitted, surveying the pile of supplies with a careful eye. "Build things. Instead of tearing them down."

Tom's eyes brightened. "In that case…" He shook his head as his voice trailed off. "No. No. You're busy enough as it is. I can't ask for more."

Razick rolled her eyes. "Let *me* be the one to say no. What's on your mind?"

He stared at her before nodding, once. "Fair enough. Someone with your skills would be quite useful in construction. If you're up for more work?"

"Need to be at full strength tomorrow," she admitted with a sigh. "Unless you've got someone I can borrow magic from, I'm no more use today."

"As a matter of fact…" Tom's brows furrowed. "I've a few minor mages looking for training, if you think you can help."

Lawrence appeared before she could answer, accompanied by a young female katanoj. "Tom. Razick. I'd like you to meet Gabbie, the rightful owner of this distribution center."

The woman blinked as she regained her bearings, smiling at them sadly. "Sorry my uncle tried to rip you off. Glad you didn't let him."

"Our new friend needs some help on the customer relations side of the business." Lawrence directed a pointed look at Tom. "Her uncle didn't work out so well."

Tom's brows furrowed. "You know… Always did want to get into the business. Much easier to guarantee my own supplies, and I've contacts already." He scratched his ear, turning to Gabbie. "If you'd like my help with that."

Gabbie turned to Lawrence, studying him, before turning to Tom with a toothy grin. "Yes, please! First plan is to figure out everyone else my uncle tried to scam, find a way to get them what they need. And go through Mom's old personnel files, see who I can hire back."

As the two began to discuss possible strategies, Razick lay a hand affectionately on Lawrence's arm. "You're quite the matchmaker today."

She felt him shiver slightly as he turned to meet her eyes. "Felt like the right thing to do." He shrugged, moving toward the stack of materials. "Easy to feel like it's my fault Baden took so much damage. That I couldn't stop Kydell sooner. Least I can do is help rebuild things."

Razick nodded, recognizing the same regret curled in her own stomach. "Speaking of... I want to help Tom and his crew today. My Telekinesis could really speed things up! And... I want to feel useful. For things other than violence and threats."

She'd spent decades mastering her magic. As much as she'd tried to branch into other things, it was what she knew *best*. And if she ever wanted to trust herself, she'd need to learn better ways to use it.

Lawrence nodded. "Just one question. How's your reserves?"

"Shot to hell!" she admitted. "But I'll be teaching today, which is easier. Full Apotheturgy. Give them a good feel for the basics, at least. We need more telekinetics in civilian jobs, and less in war. I *need* this." She snorted. "I'm no good at the planning anyway. I'll make sure I'm back to full strength tomorrow. If you're worried."

"You're better at planning than you realize," Lawrence told her, his voice uncharacteristically soft. "But enough talk. You've important construction work to do. And I need to jump this back."

Razick squeezed his shoulder. "Thanks for understanding."

"Of course." He offered a brief smile before stepping away. "Tom! Time to get you home. Is this everything?"

"One of twelve," Razick said, laughing as he blinked. "Don't worry. This one's one of the biggest."

"One of the..."

"You jump starships. This should be easy," she teased, motioning Tom toward the pile. "We'll jump with this one. Save you some effort."

"Right. Let's get you home then."

Lawrence's brows furrowed. She'd noticed they usually did when he pulled on the Void for his spells.

"You sure you're okay with me doing this?" Razick asked, motioning for Tom to lean against the pile of materials. "You know if you need me I'll–"

He held up a finger. "Go. I'm proud of you. This is a good thing."

And then the material plane was folding around her, shifting to reveal the scene at Tom's former house. Without blinking at their sudden arrival, Tom's crew swarmed the first stack of supplies, beginning the effort of sorting and arranging them based on type and need.

"I don't know how I can ever repay you for this." Tom adjusted his hardhat, surveying his crew. "But I will. You have my word on that. Maybe I can–" The architect froze before running off toward a pair of workers struggling with a portable powered saw. "For Void's sake! How many times do I have to go over this? You'll lose *fingers* handling it that way!"

Razick shook her head, grinning at the chaos. "Glad I'm not the only one nobody listens to." Seemed battle mages and construction workers had more in common than she'd realized.

Following Tom into the site, she accepted the hardhat offered by one of his crew, scanning the scene with excitement.

Time to make herself useful for once.

COMMODORE JAVON NODDED ALONG with Jeb's explanations of tomorrow's mission as she observed Fleet Captain Haveid studying the map intently. *Good.* She'd be staying behind with the majority of the fleet, but she wouldn't permit the Grand Navarch and his team to leave on their mission without doing her best to ensure their safety.

And part of that meant entrusting them to her second in command.

Her officers trusted her and her decisions, but this was the first test of the Grand Navarch's leadership, and his actions would either cement their acceptance or tear the fleet apart from within.

It didn't help that their entire future depended on his success. They'd all grown up hearing the stories of what happened to traitors. Chairman Starraze Louise, leader of the ill-fated Starraze Rebellion against the Fleet Admiral's leadership, had been Shattered for his crimes, his entire Family Dishonored and subsequently disbanded.

And *that* had been a mercy. In Fleet Admiral Valcore's place, Javon would have harbored concerns for a rescue mission. It wouldn't have worked – nobody left the tyrellium-lined maze of SAF Fleet Headquarters without Valcore's permission – but a second rebellion so soon after the first would have weakened her unyielding grip over the Confederation.

Nobody would risk their souls to rescue a fleet of deserters. If her people were caught, they'd face a prolonged existence in Headquarter's basement, yet more playthings for the sadistic spellcrafters even Fleet Command knew better than to unleash on the universe.

Shuddering at the thought, she turned her attention to Jake, watching the Kid carefully continue his work of slicing a rather burned-looking roast and placing the pieces in some sort of marinade. She'd grown worried when the Grand Navarch's psychomorphic mage, Feels, had suddenly requested Captain Yiven drop the spell holding them to the mortal planes, citing a request for their assistance, but the boy seemed unconcerned about the present safety or whereabouts of his father and so she forced her mind to calm.

"Why here?" Haveid pointed to their intended landing site, a frigid island near the southern pole. "Certainly that's not the best location for a long-term base."

The human biologist, Jeb, smiled at his companion, pushing his reading glasses higher up his nose. "Why don't you explain, Urla? Since this was your idea."

Urla beamed at his praise, her tail jerking uncomfortably as all eyes turned toward her. "Prior visits ended in disaster. From what we've found in the files, and what Jeb remembers from his coworker, the wildlife and plantlife itself was to blame." She pointed to the former Sharnelli expedition sites. "These locations were selected by the Confederation because they had the *highest* species varieties and populations. So I thought we'd try something different. Land somewhere with the lowest."

She zoomed in on the polar island, sliding her claw through the image. "Vegetation here is limited, and doesn't seem to grow large enough to pose a threat. The creatures are more predatory on average, but most are also smaller, and anything big shouldn't be able to take us by surprise."

Haveid's brows furrowed. "If that's the best place for a base, though... Many of our people would declare they'd rather continue to live on the ships."

Jeb stepped in when Urla hesitated. "Before we look into base locations, we first need to determine if we can even *use* the planet." He smiled encouragingly at the woman beside him. "Which means we need to survive long enough to find Janikk. Hopefully she's willing to talk."

"Jeb and my magic will be weaker at this site," Urla continued. "But Janikk's control over planetary life should be, too. Plus we'll have a battle mage and the Grand Navarch, who will remain unaffected." She bit her lip. "And since he's a Void necromancer, he can easily jump us anywhere else we want to go once we catch our bearings."

Javon scratched at the base of her whiskers. "Seems you've thought of everything."

The two biologists beamed at her compliment, with Jeb flashing a disarmingly proud smile at Urla.

"It's good to hear you say that," Jeb said evenly. "Wanted to run everything past you before departure. Needed some fresh eyes. To make sure we didn't miss anything."

"Mushrooms," Captain Yiven answered solemnly. "You forgot to grill mushrooms."

The table burst into laughter, and Javon almost missed the sudden return of Grand Navarch Lawrence himself.

"Glad you're enjoying yourselves."

She frowned, noting an edge of exhaustion to his voice that he was clearly attempting to hide. "You okay, Sir?"

"Will be," he reassured her, wearily sliding onto the bench across from her. "Ran into a little trouble. All fixed now."

Captain Yiven crossed two pairs of arms. "Can't you go anywhere without starting a fight?"

The necromancer frowned. "Apparently not. Old habits, and all that. But I didn't start this one." He paused briefly, tilting his head. "Okay, fine. But I *tried* to avoid starting this one." Another pause, this time ending in a faint smile. "Fair enough, Feels. Did you want to rejoin us?"

Javon watched as Yiven readied her spell, the fae also clearly aware of the Grand Navarch's depleted state but he waved her off, instead reaching between the buttons of his shirt to rub the locket. "No need, Alanis. Looks like I get them all to myself for now."

Jake slid the final pieces of meat into the marinade, standing to watch his father. "Where's Razick?"

"Helping Tom with the building." The necromancer eyed his son's handiwork. "Nice job. That looks ready." A growling from his stomach betrayed the present state of his appetite. "Grab me a plate while I fire up the grill again? Need to start these now if we're bringing them tomorrow."

Javon stood to join the Grand Navarch at the grill, readily accepting the tray he offered her and steadying it as he loaded it with the meat. "Your biologists have a solid plan for us."

He turned to watch the pair, Urla's head on Jeb's shoulder as he handfed her an assortment of protein-laden fruits with a gentle smile. "They're a good team." There was pride in his voice.

Javon shuffled her feet as the necromancer claimed the tray of meats and slid it into the grill.

"Few hours of that, and we'll have a nice travel snack for tomorrow," he announced, checking the heat and closing the lid. "You have a question?"

"I'd like to make a change. To the plan."

"Oh?"

She winced as he turned toward her, but his expression held only curiosity, not the condemnation to which she'd been accustomed when questioning Admiral Kydell's plans.

His stomach growled again, and he motioned her back to the table. "Mind explaining while I eat? It's... been a long day."

"Of course." She reclaimed her seat next to Haveid, noting the Grand Navarch purposely positioning himself across from her. "I know we agreed I'd stay behind with the fleet," she began.

He nodded, accepting his plate. "Only need one ship at Janikk. Don't want to risk offending her, showing up in full force." His eyes closed briefly as he took a bite, clearly savoring the flavors.

"I'm sending the *Relentless*."

He frowned, eyes snapping open. "Not the *Inevitable*. Repairs not going well?"

"In normal circumstances, we'd have scrapped her by now," Javon admitted quietly. "By all rights, we *still* should. She took a lot of damage. Entire sections of the ship are just... *gone*."

"We have a lot of salvage."

"We have a lot of ships that *need* salvage," Javon countered. "Only thing the *Inevitable* has going for her is the EMP. She's not a warship anymore, Sir. She's sentimental scrap."

The Grand Navarch shifted his gaze, and Javon braced for censure, but he merely sighed. "Alanis. If Janikk says yes, can we jump the *Inevitable*?"

Captain Yiven shrugged two pairs of arms, looking up from where she'd settled in the center of a plate of fruit. "Sure. You know how it works. I can jump her anywhere. It's keeping her in orbit that's the trouble. And it's not getting any easier."

He nodded, shoulders sagging. "We're *not* scrapping her. I'll figure something out. But you've made your point. No sense trying to fix her, we've limited resources as it is."

Javon exhaled in relief. "Thank you, Sir. For understanding."

"You're doing your job," he told her, waving his fork in her direction. "I can't argue with that. Anything else?"

"While the *Inevitable* was built to make a show of strength and power, the *Relentless* is about hiding them both behind an agile and nonthreatening exterior." Jerking her head toward her second in command, she continued. "Fleet Captain Haveid, on the other end, doesn't pretend to hide their experience. I trust them, and the rest of my crew, with my life. And now, with yours."

She paused, watching his reactions carefully, but he merely raised an eyebrow and continued to chew.

"Since we're keeping the *Inevitable*, I'd like to name her my flagship. For now."

His eyebrow rose even higher.

"She's vulnerable, and it shows," she explained. "We've caused a lot of damage to this planet, but the *Inevitable* took on the fleet and won us to your side. I think it sends an important message. A show of trust, assigning our command staff to our most vulnerable ship. And a reminder of the sacrifices we've made for Baden's freedom."

"Approved," the Grand Navarch said immediately. "What next?"

"Fleet Captain Haveid has been my right hand for most of my career," she pressed onward, "and has served as the head of my battle mages for more than half of that. But we've a shortage of officers I trust right now, and I need more. I'd like to name them flag officer of the *Relentless* and his supporting craft, and move their second into the top role for the mages. I don't know what processes you intended to implement for promotions, but–"

"Done. You know your people best. Write up your recommendations, and consider them all approved by me." He frowned. "And ask Alanis for her recommendations, too. Trust is important, but we don't want to show favoritism to your half of the fleet just because you know them better."

Javon sat taller on the bench, and felt Haveid do the same beside her. She'd been braced for an argument, not acceptance. This Grand Navarch was a far cry from the micromanaging admiral he'd defeated, and a lot more trusting of others. Or at least, trusting of her.

Which reminded her of another potential issue. "I'm concerned about the rest of the fleet. You'll be in good hands with the *Relentless*. For all his control issues, the admiral surprisingly left me a lot of leeway when selecting my own crew, so I've vetted them personally through the years. But despite the best efforts of your psychomorphic mage, I know we haven't caught all of Kydell's people yet."

Captain Yiven flitted back into the conversation, dragging a large slice of fruit behind her. "She's right. That medic of yours has been through the whole *Inevitable*, and we've already lost a third of the crew as either loyal to Kydell or too distrustful of another mage in their head. But I've got the feeling we've only eliminated the minor players."

"Admiral Kydell was a crafty son of a..." Haveid's voice faded as they spotted Jake, focused intently on the conversation. "Uh, traitor. His best people were, too. I guarantee we haven't caught all of them. And the ones we've missed? They'll be the most dangerous threats."

"No offense to your partner, but even after their efforts with the *Inevitable*, I only trust my AI." Yiven crossed her arms before looking up at Javon. "And the Commodore and her security detail, of course."

The Grand Navarch sighed, slumping as he pushed away his now empty plate. "Was worrying about that, too. Hoped I was overthinking things."

He exhaled, running his fingers through his straight, black hair. "We'll be cautious. They've been through enough. I don't want to traumatize everyone in the hope we catch some of Kydell's sleepers." He turned to Javon. "There's also something I wanted to talk over with you. It's a bit more... personal."

She felt her back stiffen.

"For *me*, not you," the Grand Navarch added hastily. "Your title. Commodore. It... brings up bad memories."

She eyed him cautiously. "What did you have in mind?"

"*Navarch* Javon has a nice ring to it, don't you think?" He leaned forward, orange eyes watching her intently. "Not as Grand as me, of course, but I think you've earned it."

Javon snorted at the offer of the second half of his own grandiose title. She was one of his, now. If she'd doubted it before, here was the proof.

"Navarch it is," she said, nodding acceptance. "Are you going to change everyone's?"

"Maybe." He shrugged, speaking with a level of candor that somehow continued to surprise her. "Given what the fleet has survived, it's good to change what we can. Add some distance from the SAF where possible. Rename some ships. Alter some ranks, if it won't cause confusion." He pursed his lips. "But there are more important things right now."

"Speaking of which..." Haveid leaned forward. "The planning for our expedition is important. So I've been struggling to understand why you'd leave your own briefing to help some civilian with a building project? Isn't that misplacing your priorities?"

Javon watched silently as the Grand Navarch met Haveid's eyes, her second in command crossing their arms to size him up, tail darting along the bench in short, quick motions. If Haveid had directed a challenge like that to Admiral Kydell, they'd have been shipped off to some dusty outpost to be literally forgotten, but the new leader of their fleets merely blinked slowly as he considered his words.

"We'll need a lot more than a planet if we want to succeed," the necromancer answered at last. "Funding will be difficult. Good will is a bit easier. We'll need both."

"And what will the good will of your neighbor give you?"

The Grand Navarch merely shifted in his seat, a calculatingly smug expression which Javon initially mistook as his answer. But then he turned and Javon saw the neighbor in question running toward them, only stopping to bend over and catch his breath upon arrival.

"Tom." The necromancer nodded his head, once, in greeting. "Everything alright? We didn't forget something, did we?"

"No, no." Tom shook his head, still panting. "Wanted to thank you again for transporting our building supplies, and making sure we could get them in the first place. That was... really something."

Javon caught the Grand Navarch's faint smile and wondered just how much trouble he'd caused. Not that she'd ever ask.

But Tom had finally caught his breath. "And Razick, she's phenomenal. Usually the framing takes a good week to finish, but we put it up in an afternoon." He offered his hand. "You ever need an architect, for anything at all, you let me know. Would love to set up a trade for more of your magic muscle."

"Of course." The Grand Navarch eyed Tom's hand before grasping it to shake on their deal, motioning to Javon. "If you or Gabbie need help moving deliveries from the warehouse, feel free to reach out. This is Navarch Javon, she can send you a Void necromancer or Portal mage to help. Won't be *cheap*, but I can promise fair market rates."

He turned to Captain Yiven. "Tom's was about a jump and a half. Have them bundle it first, to save Imperium."

Tom's face lit up. "That would *definitely* put us on the map if we could keep up deliveries while the infrastructure's still down. Think you could help us pull inventory *in*, too? Lots of manufacturers out there with no way of getting their products to distributors, either."

"If you can afford it, and we have enough people it doesn't impact our combat readiness. Captain Yiven Alanis can work the details."

Noting the Grand Navarch had directed that last statement to her, Javon ran a few quick calculations. Kydell's fleets had followed standard Confederation protocols, each capital ship carrying at least two Void necromancers to allow for emergency Hyperjumps in case they found themselves outgunned and chose to retreat. Coupled with their Portal mages, this left a sizeable force able to assist with the Grand Navarch's offer, even accounting for their reduced staffing from the purges of Kydell's loyalists.

As Tom excitedly pulled the fae away to talk logistics, Javon watched her former XO resume their confrontation with the Grand Navarch. It was a good thing the necromancer was patient. Haveid's thoughtful but endless questions would be nothing compared to the *Relentless'* Navigations AI.

Javon was almost disappointed she wouldn't be on board to witness *that* confrontation.

Almost.

"I can see the advantage in hiring out our services right now..." Haveid's tone was sharp, yet shied away from making accusations. "But I don't understand what you hope to gain from his good will."

The Grand Navarch shrugged. "Do you have an architect on staff?"

"Of course not." Haveid shook their head. "Why would we need one?"

"True," the necromancer agreed quietly. "You *could* live on the *Relentless* forever. Never have a home of your own. Nothing but metal beneath your feet for the rest of your life. Or maybe we try to design something on our own from scratch. Certainly we have a lot of intelligent people on staff, we could figure it out *eventually.*"

The Fleet Captain nodded their head with understanding. "I concede your point. I'm thinking too small. We're not just a fleet anymore."

Fact-finding mission complete, Tom returned to address the whole table. "Meant to tell you. Crew and I talked it over. We have this whole grill thing every evening, to feed the block. It's too much food, really, even for all of us. We'd love if you and your friends would join us today. Least we can do. Should be ready in a few."

"We'd be honored to accept. Thank you." Rising from the table, the Grand Navarch nodded his gratitude. "And if I could ask a favor...?"

"Anything." Tom spread his arms wide with the word, clearly still pleased with whatever had happened on their excursion to the lumberyard.

"She won't say anything to you about it, but Razick? Our telekinetic? Really wants to learn how to grill."

Javon let out a laugh. As the mention of his sister, Jeb's head shot up from his quiet conversation with Urla, blinking slowly as he acclimated himself to the discussion before extracting himself again, clearly amused by his thoughts of Razick's possible reactions to the Grand Navarch's suggestions, but more interested in his Hydroponics AI.

"Say no more. Dirk will happily talk both her ears off." He shoved his hands in his pockets. "Whenever you're ready, we'll be there."

As the architect turned on his heels to depart, the Grand Navarch fixed Haveid with an amused but pointed stare. Javon watched with pride as her second in command smiled sheepishly, conceding defeat. They'd always kept her on her toes, constantly challenging her decisions when time and level of urgency allowed, and she'd come to rely on their difference in perspective when refining her own ideas.

It was a relief to know the Grand Navarch didn't object to their unorthodox arguments against his authority, and she wondered if he'd already picked up on Haveid's own streak of unwavering loyalty for those who genuinely weighed their concerns when planning.

The Grand Navarch addressed the table, waving a spatula. "You should go now, if you want some meat to accompany all these vegetables. Being on deployment, I know it's been a while since you've had any."

Javon felt her mouth water at the thought. It had been *months* since she'd eaten something the fleet hadn't preserved, grown itself, or, Void forbid, reconstituted from those awful travel rations. This had certainly been the most *flavorful* hydroponics bay meal in that time... But nothing could compare to a nice, juicy steak.

The Grand Navarch waved his son toward the plates of fruit and vegetables. "Bring these with you. May as well be neighborly and share ours, too."

Jake's brows furrowed. "Aren't you coming, Dad?"

The Grand Navarch shook his head. "Someone has to watch this grill, and I can't do that from Tom's right now. Used too much magic already." He rubbed Jake's shoulder reassuringly. "You go, though. I don't mind being the only one to stay behind. And I still have to pack." He shot a glare at Jeb. "I'll probably need extra socks."

Javon rose from the table, reaching for Jake. "You can come with me," she said kindly. "I think your father wants some space by himself for a bit."

The Grand Navarch's veiled gratitude was all the confirmation she needed. Tomorrow was a big day, and everyone prepared differently. And after tomorrow...

She shook her head. Assuming everything worked out, it would be nice to have a home again.

Jake's hand slipped into hers as she set off across the gravel, the other guests falling in behind her at her silent command, leaving the Grand Navarch alone with his thoughts.

10

Usually his father was the first to rise, the nightmares of his past ensuring his sleep remained shallow and interrupted. This morning the necromancer was still sound asleep despite the light pouring in the window from where Jake had pulled back the faded curtain. A spiderweb of cracks across the pane cast shadows on the bed, patterns shifting in shape as his father's chest rose and fell in a calm, even rhythm.

Jake poked again, but his father didn't budge. He debated letting his father sleep, but the trip to Janikk was important, plus Razick's last disastrous attempt at making breakfast herself had ruined two pans and left the house smelling like sulfur for a week.

Closing his eyes, he sifted through his father's mantras for one that would apply. *If your plan isn't working, learn why and adapt.* There was only one possible explanation for the uncharacteristically restful night.

Locating the chain of his grandmother's locket, a constant presence around his father's neck, Jake gently tugged until his fingers brushed against the mechanical pendant itself. He wrapped it in his fist. "Good morning, Feels. Dad needs to wake up now."

Can't I keep him just a little longer? The empath's tone carried a silken smugness, with no hint of shame.

"Sure." Jake shrugged, even though Feels couldn't see him. "But you'll have to answer to *him.*"

Worth it.

"I heard Razick pulling out pots in the kitchen."

Feels sighed. *Put me back. I'll wake him.*

Tucking the locket back against his father's chest, Jake turned and made his way down the rickety staircase and into the kitchen.

Razick looked up sheepishly from the sink as she scrubbed something unrecognizably charred from one of the pans. "Please don't tell your father."

Jake offered a reassuring smile, opening the refrigerator to rummage its contents. "Where's Professor Jeb?"

"He and Hydroponics are doing some final prep on the *Relentless* to verify the equipment." She grunted, fighting against the last of the stubborn residue. "Told him I'd bring breakfast, but..." She glared at the pan. "It's not going so well."

Finding what he sought, Jake retrieved three small containers of leftovers from the prior day's picnics. "Here." He offered them to her, placing the stack in her upturned palm in exchange for the pan. "Warm it up when you're ready. There's one for each of you."

Hearing his father's footsteps on the stairs, Jake quickly slid the pan into the drying rack and returned his attention to the refrigerator, retrieving a juice-filled travel cup with his name carefully marked onto the side in his father's steady hand.

Every detail perfectly organized. Just like always.

Razick smiled in appreciation. "Where's your breakfast?"

"Jake is eating with Veris today." His father's voice carried a softer edge than usual, lined instead with a cheerful optimism Jake realized he hadn't heard before. He felt the necromancer's hand squeeze his shoulder. "Morning, son. Sleep well?"

Jake closed his eyes as he clutched his juice cup against his chest. He was dreading the trip to Veris', not to mention the separation from his father, but he'd promised he'd do his best to support it. Turning to look at his father, he forced a grin. "Not as well as *you*."

Shane scowled, releasing Jake to instead slip his fingers between the buttons of his shirt. "That's enough, you. *Both* of you." He turned to Razick. "I see you found breakfast. Where's Jeb?"

"He went ahead." Razick shrugged, the leftovers hugged carefully to her chest. "I'll have to catch a ride with you."

"I can ask the fleet." Jake beamed with pride as he caught the slight straightening of his father's spine. "I've been practicing."

"Would you?" Razick asked. "I'd like to check in with my brother. See if he needs anything before the jump."

Jake tightly closed his eyes as he concentrated his magic, reaching for the *Relentless* like Jeb had taught him. <Communications? Razick needs a Jump.>

<At your location?> came the professional reply. There was a pause at Jake's affirmative, followed by the appearance of a Portal to the *Relentless*'s hydroponics bay in the middle of the kitchen, the magic of the temporary linkage snapping and hissing in the relative silence. <Anything else I can do for you, Kid?>

Jake suppressed a frown at the nickname, earned as a sign of respect for his own role in Admiral Kydell's defeat. He was proud of what he'd done to help, but...

Another of his father's mantras came to mind: *Reputation matters. Make it a good one.*

His actions to Shatter Fleet Captain Selkirk, Admiral Kydell's much-feared TAG, had cemented his reputation among the Sparnelli defectors, green recruits and grizzled veterans alike. The pain of his choices still cut deep, and he wasn't certain if he *liked* the reputation he'd acquired, but even he had to admit it was nice to be treated like more than a helpless child.

His mother had always pushed him to be more, and his father had quickly grown to respect his talents, but they were his parents. They always saw the best in him.

This respect was different.

<That will be all.> He mimicked his father with the words, and *felt* the stiff professionalism of the *Relentless'* Communications AI solidify further in response before they severed the connection.

Razick graced him with a playful salute, making her way to the Portal. "Looks like my ride's here. See you when we get back?" She tousled Jake's hair before stepping through. It closed behind her, leaving a sudden uneasy quiet in the kitchen.

Catching motion from the corner of his eye, Jake turned to find his father watching him, his eyes glistening with tears. "Do you have your knife?"

Jake rolled his eyes. "Yes, Dad."

"Good. I asked Alanis to keep an eye on you–"

"I *know*." Crossing his arms, Jake glared at his father. "You've only told me a *million* times."

"–so keep it with you," his father continued, undeterred. "Let Alanis or Navarch Javon know if you need anything. Or if you plan to leave Veris' house for any reason. And–"

"I *know!*"

The necromancer sighed, running his hands through his hair. "I know. You know the drill." He sank to a crouch, his face earnest as he looked up at Jake. "You remember what I used to tell you? About people's opinions of me also affecting their thoughts about you?"

Jake nodded, forcing himself to listen. He knew where this was going, but he also knew his father needed to say it anyway.

"I'm a lot higher profile now... And I won't be here to protect you." The necromancer frowned at the floor, and Jake could feel the worry he'd been trying to hide. "You'll be safer if you stay behind this time. But I promised your mother I'd keep you safe, and this is the first time I won't be doing that personally." Rocking back on his heels, his father met his gaze again. "Forgive me for being a little too repetitive?"

Jake nodded, lunging forward to wrap his arms around his father's neck, twisting his fingers into the necromancer's hair as he squeezed. "I'm not a helpless kid anymore."

"No. That you are not." His father returned the hug, pressing his cheek against Jake's. "I trust you. Please stay safe, while I'm away."

"I will."

"I wanted to send some of Javon's security detail with you. Or Haveid's battle mages. Or Razick. Unfortunately they're all needed elsewhere. But the moment you feel threatened—"

"I'll Call Alanis," Jake promised. "I'll be fine."

He didn't *feel* fine. He'd be staying with *Veris*. But he'd promised to make the best of it, and wasn't about to break that promise now.

His father watched him for a moment longer before nodding and slowly rising to his feet. "Let's get you to your friend."

Jake wrinkled his nose at the assumption. Veris had been the school bully, terrorizing him for *years* before stabbing him with a knife. Jake had encouraged the fight that time, but he hadn't approved of *knives*, only fists! And even though Feels had healed him almost immediately, it had *hurt*.

But he dutifully tucked his head against his father's chest, breathing in the comforting safety of the deadly Void necromancer as the Afterlife wrapped around them both.

11

JEB FROWNED AT THE console, an errant leaf tickling his cheek as he furiously tapped buttons. He pushed the plant away in annoyance, a small expenditure of his magic ensuring it stayed put. "I don't remember things being this confusing. How do I–"

"Let me get that for you. I swear. Each upgrade takes us backward."

Urla's cheerful amusement at his frustration proved a surprisingly soothing balm. Usually the plants alone would suffice – much like the *Inevitable*, the *Relentless'* hydroponics bay was an expertly balanced arrangement of water-filled growing tanks and carefully selected plants, surrounded by well-stocked storage shelves of tools and fertilizers – but the importance of today's mission was weighing on his mind.

"Tell me about it." The gruff growl of the *Relentless'* Hydroponics AI joined their commiseration, echoing through the hydroponic bay's speakers. "And it's not like they ask *our* opinions, either. No. It's all 'Do this. Learn that.' And then they wonder why our efficiency drops right after."

"Volume, Tarvik," Urla admonished lightly, using her link with the *Relentless* to navigate Jeb to the menu he sought. When they'd arrived that morning, they'd discovered Lawrence had already prepped a crystal for her within the ship's main servers. "Jeb still has eardrums to worry about."

"Noted," the AI answered sheepishly. "Not used to having company. Especially *agreeable* company."

"The curse of a Sparnelli botanist," Jeb agreed sagely, checking the readings on the now compliant console. "We're not important until it's an emergency, and then somehow it's *our* fault that nobody listened."

"Exactly!"

Despite his grievances against the Sparnell Armed Forces for his conscription, Jeb rather missed the camaraderie of his fellow researchers, most often borne of their joint frustration at the SAF's blatant disregard of their insights and experiences. He'd been retired from that life for *years*, and even still it was reassuring to work through those memories with people who *got* it.

Raz had tried to be present for him, of course, but compared to her own psychomorphic traumas at the hands of Admiral Kydell, he'd always felt guilty leaning on her for comfort from his own, milder memories.

As if on cue a Portal appeared in the currently overcrowded jungle of the hydroponics bay, and one of the *Relentless'* mages stepped through with a nod. The Portal's destination shifted abruptly, revealing a glimpse of Lawrence's kitchen as Razick emerged, pushing plants aside as she made her way toward them. The Portal mage saluted quickly as the Portal shifted once more, returning to her prior post.

Razick held up a stack of three pre-packaged meals. "Someone order breakfast?"

Jeb kept his tone flat. "Depends. Who made it?"

The air left his lungs with an involuntary grunt as one of the containers hit his stomach with telekinetically-enhanced force. "Lawrence did, you jerk." But she was grinning.

This was the Razick he missed, buried as she'd become in memories of regrets and worse. She still carried the weight of her past abuses, both those she'd committed and those she'd survived, but ever since the canid admiral's demise aboard the *Inevitable* these glimpses of his mischievous big sister had been growing more frequent. It would take time... But he had *hope* now.

Heart still light at the thought, he lifted the lid to view the packaged contents, inhaling the familiar scent of Tom's barbecue from the night before. "Urla, Tarvik, is there somewhere I can heat this up?"

"Did you bring any to share?" Tarvik's voice betrayed interest, and Jeb thought he saw one of the bay's cameras shifting position to eye his meal. "Urla keeps singing its praises and I haven't had a good barbecue in... twelve years?"

"Mine." Jeb playfully wrapped his hands around the container, holding it to his chest. "Besides. You'd need to sweet talk Navigations if you want to be able to eat any."

"Oooof. Never mind. Definitely *not* worth it." Gone was the AI's formerly jovial tone. "Void necromancers are the *worst*. Act like they own the universe, but it's not even their own magic. Pompous Solar Skimmers, the whole lot."

"I used to think that..." Urla's voice faded thoughtfully. "But the Grand Navarch's been good to me."

"If it's all the same to you, I'll make that call myself," Tarvik growled. "The way you tell it, he was half dead for most of it. Makes it difficult to brag about your own superiority complex if you want anyone to believe you."

Razick's shoulders slumped, and Jeb's words came out harsher than intended.

"That's enough!"

Reminders were the last thing she needed.

Tarvik continued anyway. "Mustn't be as Grand as you say, if he needs a biologist to stand up for him."

"He doesn't." Jeb kept his sentences short and crisp in an effort to mask his own emotions. "Wasn't for his benefit."

He held out his breakfast toward his sister. Wasn't much of a distraction, but it was the best he could think up. "Think you could warm this up for me?"

"Not afraid I'll kill it instead?"

He winced at the bitterness in her voice but held his ground, making his concern with a lighthearted cheer. "Nope."

Gingerly accepting the proffered container on her flattened palm, Razick closed her eyes momentarily before handing it back. "Let me know if that's sufficient."

The steam and smells emanating from the container proved answer enough. "Perfection." Jeb eyed his sister with admiration. "And you say you can't cook."

"Different spell."

By the look on her face, Jeb realized this conversation, too, involved memories best left buried. He changed the subject again.

"Tarvik, give me a rundown of the *Relentless'* role at Janikk while I eat."

"Sure thing, Boss."

Jeb nodded into his barbecue while the AI continued, unsure if the new moniker was intended as a tease or a sign of resentment.

"The surveys we have of the planet are old, and the technology older. Bossman Kane says we need another survey before he'll risk His Royal Voidness on the planet's surface, so you'll have a few hours once we arrive before you head down, while we do all the work for you."

Tarvik was *definitely* annoyed.

Quickly swallowing the last of his meal, Jeb interrupted the surly AI. "Thank you, *Petty Officer* Tarvik. I'll take it from here."

He heard Tarvik grunt at the formal address, the reminder of a stunted career, but Jeb discovered to his surprise that he didn't care. Tarvik might be a biologist, but Razick was his sister. She came first, always. And he wasn't about to embarrass her by explaining the real reason for his stop on the Necromancy conversation.

"The *Relentless'* sensors are significantly more powerful, not to mention more precise, than anything used on the former expeditions. So we're checking our information is as accurate as I *think* it is."

Jeb pressed a button on the console, activating the holographic projector, and Urla erupted into a fit of giggles.

"Jeb..." Razick's own attempts at composure dissolved shortly after, and she doubled over.

"You're an ass, Tarvik," Urla scolded, still laughing.

"Not as big of an ass as your boyfriend right now," Tarvik answered smugly.

Only then did Jeb realize the surly AI had overridden his options with a view from one of the cameras, currently zoomed in on his own posterior.

"And to think I'm trusting my life to you lot," he scolded, nonetheless fighting to maintain his own composure. "Urla? Could you... help? Maybe?"

"You've had your fun, Tarvik." She broke into laughter again. "Although I must admit, it's a *beautiful* view."

Caught up in Urla and Razick's clear humor, Jeb allowed himself to laugh with the others. "That was a good one, Tarvik.

But Lawrence'll be here any moment, and I'd rather not have to try and explain... this? Please."

"Fine. Spoilsport." Seemingly content with the extent of his disruption, Tarvik set the holovid back to the proper display. He paused for a moment, then added, "Sorry."

Jeb watched his sister, her face red as she gasped for breath, eyes still dancing at the joke. "No harm done." Quite the opposite, in fact. "Moving on..."

He pointed to their intended island on the map. "We'll be starting here, give it a fully detailed scan with everything we've got so Urla and I can analyze it and verify we're still good for the landing. Tarvik will scan the rest of the planet while we're working that, just a preliminary check for starters. Then a more in-depth one, which probably won't start until we're on the surface."

Razick's demeanor shifted back into the careful battle mage who'd appeared on his doorstep several years ago, after her desertion from the SAF. "What do you need from me?"

"Not much, at the moment," Jeb admitted, tugging at his hair. "Can't do anything until we arrive. And then it'll be a bit to take the scans. Anything we discover, we'll run past you before we land. But you'll have several hours to yourself before we'll have anything useful to give you."

She nodded coolly. "Then I'll find the sparring room." Jeb's spirits waned as he watched the ghosts of her past return to haunting her eyes. "May as well spend the time practicing. Would rather not accidentally kill anyone this time."

Watching her walk away, regrets in her steps, Jeb realized with a start he'd fisted both hands so tightly his fingernails had left indentations in his palms. *Oh Raz...* Someday, he hoped she'd be able to let go of the traumas she'd survived.

He just wished he knew a better way to help.

12

LIEUTENANT RABERT ASIK WATCHED through the bathroom window as the strangers appeared from thin air on his front lawn, the younger clinging to his older companion, the elder sizing up the neighborhood with a practiced eye before ushering his younger charge to the door.

They're here.

His emotions bounced between some semblance of gratitude and dread at the thought of opening his home to the young man who'd saved him from his Sparnelli captors. He *knew* he should be grateful. By all rights he should open his arms wide and greet this Kid as a second son.

Veris certainly considered him Family, judging by the boy's latest habits of mentioning this Jake as often as possible, eagerly seeking ways to prove himself to the preteen who'd earned his devotion.

Rabert's wife, too, seemed enamored with the thought of their visitors. He suspected Fiara would extoll the virtues of *anyone* who'd managed to bring him home, but she also seemed to believe the strangers had helped their son with something, as well. It had been her idea to allow the boy to stay with them while his father was away on whatever constituted a business trip for a newly-fledged space pirate.

And yet Rabert found himself torn, as if his mind had been violently split into two halves, each fighting for dominance over his thoughts and actions. He'd been this way ever since he'd awakened in the hospital on Baden, surrounded by countless victims of the Sparnelli bombardment.

He'd remembered the endless questioning of his captors. Wondered if they'd finally succeeded in coaxing him to reveal critical defensive data. Questioning just how much of the damage to his planet could be traced back to something he'd said or thought in an unguarded moment.

And then the dreams had started.

They'd been vague at first, mere hints of memories as his mind tried to reconcile his return home with the horrors of Sparnell, but had grown in detail and intensity as his mind slowly unraveled itself and his time aboard the *Reckoning*. He wanted to know – to *understand* – everything that had happened to him and his wing, Lieutenant Fangela Starx, the unshakeable canid his son had grown up calling Aunt Fang.

Yet with each new memory he began to regret the knowing, longing instead for those brief, blissful moments when he'd first awakened to see Fiara and Veris hovering over him with tear-streaked gratitude as he struggled to remember how he'd ended up in the hospital in the first place.

Sometimes the knowing was unbearable as the not knowing. And sometimes...

Sometimes it was *worse*.

An excited commotion broke out in the entryway as the Bastard of Baden and his Kid entered to greet Rabert's Family as a welcome extension of their own. He heard them call his name... First Fiara. Then Veris. Then even Fang joined in.

"Coming," he growled, checking his reflection in the mirror. He attempted to twist his lips into a smile. Whether he was happy to meet them or not – the war in his mind had not yet decided – at least he could find a way to look pleased when he emerged.

Yet try as he might, he couldn't remember how, his best attempt merely twisting his green scale-like skin into a frightening grimace. His light violet eyes reflected back a stare emptier than the Void itself, the ice blue hair framing both finishing off the terrifyingly ghostlike visage.

"...don't know what we would have done..." "...not the same since his captivity..." "...been through a lot..." "...trouble sleeping..." "...these things take time..." "...never seen him like this..."

His natural-born Anemancy carried pieces of the conversation to his ear fins, his family sharing personal details about his present mental state as if these interloping visitors had any right to know. As if Rabert had no way of hearing anything they said on the other side of the wall.

But of course they'd expect him to pretend he hadn't heard them, their nervous whispers and terrified conjectures of whether or not he'd manage to "pull himself out of it" or if he would "drown in the bottle" or whatever new phrase was consuming people's thoughts about him this week.

He wished he'd never come back.

No. That was unfair.

Veris was genuinely happy at his return. Rabert's fifteen-year-old son eagerly stepping in to see to whatever he imagined his father might need. Even at Rabert's worst, Veris was already ready with a kind word and a cold drink. Sometimes Rabert caught the boy staring at him sorrowfully for minutes on end when he thought nobody was looking, as if he feared his father would disappear forever and stay gone this time.

Veris' happiness was worth whatever price Rabert had to pay. And yet...

Despite his best attempts to move forward, Rabert couldn't help but feel he was forgetting something important, some forgotten dangerous secret just outside his reach that threatened to destroy his son's newfound purpose in life.

He attempted yet again to probe his own mind, but the thought skittered away like a frightened animal. He'd have to rely on the nightmares, and hope they eventually brought the answers he sought.

The cries of his name grew ever more insistent until suddenly an angry banging intruded upon the solitude of his refuge, his wife talking through the door.

"You're being rude to our guests. After all they've done for you, the least you can do is say hello."

"In a minute!"

He should go out. He really should thank them both.

Instead he checked the lock on the door.

All secure. *Good.*

He barricaded it to be safe, pacing the tiled floor in stuttered, jerky motions.

"...so sorry..." "...not usually like this..." "...been through a lot..." "...don't know what's come over him..." "...going to be late..." "...apologies..."

The flurry of conversation took on a new intensity until Rabert heard the front door open and close again, the elder stranger finally departing. He directed a pointed orange stare to the window of Rabert's refuge for several uncomfortable moments, his terrifying frown sending Rabert's mind into another heated argument about whether or not he should hide himself deeper within the room.

And then, just as suddenly as he'd appeared, the man was gone. Rabert's yard stood blissfully empty once more, threat departed.

"I hope you're happy." His wife's disappointment drifted through the locked door, undiluted. "That man saved your life. We're lucky he's so understanding."

Rabert saw the door push inward slightly, her voice growing mournful.

"I don't know what to do, Rabert. You won't see any of the therapists work has sent, you barely talk to me outside your nightmares, and you spend days at a time locked up in the bathroom. Sometimes I wonder if most of you isn't still on that damn ship... What do you need from me? How can I help you?"

He stood there, tensed in the silence, until the door finally shifted back to its neutral position and her shadow disappeared from the crack beneath. He rechecked the lock as her footsteps retreated in the direction of the others.

Good. Perimeter secure.

He *knew* he couldn't interact with them. Any time he considered it, the threatening aura of danger filled his thoughts with its overwhelming insistence. Under no circumstances could he rejoin his family. He must defend the barricade.

But was he keeping the evil out? Or in?

He wished he knew.

13

Shane scowled. "I don't like it."

The empath at his chest projected their own feelings of encouragement. *Jake has the whole fleet looking out for him. Plus me.*

Concentrating on thoughts of gratitude, Shane gathered the powers of the Void around himself in preparation for the jump to the *Relentless*, even as he directed another glare to the bathroom window. "Doesn't mean I'm thrilled about leaving him with someone I've never met before."

Veris' father is absolutely terrified.

"He'll be in worse shape if his behavior causes any harm to come to Jake." The words were a growl.

He was a Sparnelli prisoner for months. You know *what they do to prisoners.* Another wave of reassurance washed over Shane. *He's lucky the terror is all he's dealing with.*

Gripping the locket tightly, Shane cast one last look at Veris' house. "That's what worries me."

I'll keep Jake safe while you're gone. Promise.

Focusing on thoughts of trust, the necromancer allowed the welcoming caress of the Void to wrap around him as he reached for the *Relentless*. The Shielding officer granted his request for passage, permitting him to emerge from the Afterlife into the middle of the command deck.

The bridge on the *Relentless* was significantly smaller than on the *Inevitable*, but just as functional, the endless array of screens and consoles cleverly arranged to make efficient use of the limited space. The ship's original layout would have included a small flag deck with supporting offices for the flag's aides, separated from the bridge by a reactive sheet of translucent smart glass, but renovations through the years to update technology had commandeered the deck space for the bridge, relegating any assigned flag officers to a cramped space in the corner boasting a trio of fold-out jump seats and collapsible smart screens.

The *Relentless* had been one of the last Ravager class destroyers ever manufactured, the most ambitious and expensive ship construction project ever undertaken by the Confederation. Designed with an eye to detail, the Ravager class engineers had accomplished the impossible, incorporating heavy firepower, high survivability, and the best speed and stealth of their day into a highly compact and reinforced design optimized for solo missions. The shipyard and its sponsoring

Family had gone bankrupt in the attempt, but not before producing twenty-five of the most prized destroyers in the SAF.

Less than half had survived to the present day, a feat in itself considering their commissioning predated Shane's own conscription at the tender age of sixteen. To his delight, Shane had inherited two: the SCS *Relentless*, which had been assigned to Admiral Kydell's personal defensive fleet, and the more familiar SCS *Subjugation*, one of a handful of mage-heavy screening ships he'd often ordered to scout ahead to soften future targets.

Not unlike today's mission, he supposed. Although hopefully this time the missiles and mages would prove unnecessary precautions.

He felt all eyes shift toward him, with Feels reporting an array of emotions ranging from curiosity to distrust.

"Grand Navarch on the bridge."

Shane's arrival dutifully announced by the officer of the deck, Fleet Captain Haveid rose from their observer's chair in the corner to offer a quick salute. "Do you wish to assume command, Sir?"

"She's *your* ship, Fleet Captain," Shane nodded, noting Haveid's faint smile at the reminder of their new role. "I'm just along for the ride."

"*He.*" A disgruntled voice emerged from the Navigations console, the younger mage behind the screen wincing as Shane with mouthed apologies for her superior's impending behavior.

You've upset someone, Feels cautioned from within the locket.

"My mistake, Navigations." Running a hand through his hair, Shane felt his shoulders slump slightly. Amidst the other preparations, he'd forgotten to review the *Relentless'* crew roster. "I'm more accustomed to the *Inevitable*."

"If you think I'll be a pushover like Commander Yiven–"

"*Captain* Yiven," he corrected firmly. Least he could do was ensure she was recognized with the promotion Feels had awarded her.

"–accepting some minor promotion in exchange for my loyalty, you have another thing coming. The Commodore trusts too easily."

Exhaling, Shane rubbed the back of his neck, noting the Afterlife Intelligence's reference to Javon by her former rank, as well. But this was nothing he couldn't handle.

"My apologies, Sir," Haveid said formally, watching him intently. "Navarch Javon *did* attempt to warn you."

Ignoring the grizzled fleet captain for the moment, Shane pulled his shoulders back and turned his attention to the Navigations console. Currently the fleet followed Shane because they followed Javon. If he wanted to earn their loyalty for himself, he'd need to win it here.

Which meant his next words were critical.

"Anything else you'd like to get off your chest, Navigations? I'm a firm believer in open communication. Let's hear your grievances, all out into the open."

"Since you're offering..." The voice grew in boldness, the rest of the bridge now listening to the exchange. "Don't think me ungrateful. You *did* free me and my Sub-Lieutenant from the Oath. But you can't buy my allegiance with a bribe. What have you done to earn it?"

Shane shrugged. "You'll have to decide that for yourself. I'm not Kydell. I won't choose answers for you."

"And I won't Hyperjump without a good answer. So we'll just sit here until I'm satisfied." The voice paused, briefly, before continuing. "And don't think for one moment my Sub-Lieutenant will do it for you behind my back."

The young mage at the Navigations console blushed as several members of the bridge crew turned toward her at the mention.

Shane graced her with a knowing look. A Navigations Auxiliary reported to their Navigations AI first, the ship captain second. This flew in the face of typical military command structure, likely contributing to Void necromancers' well-deserved reputations as conceited narcissists, but the alternative had led to an endemic of cosmic burnout and a critical shortage of trained Void mages when auxiliaries-in-training failed to properly gage their own limits.

"Wouldn't dream of it. I'll just do the jump myself."

"What?"

Feels dutifully reported the AI's surprise, a sentiment echoed by many across the crew.

"We'll find something else for you to do," Shane continued, wiping his fingernails nonchalantly on his shirt as he slowly paced the cramped deck. "Or you could leave if you'd rather.

Find a spot in the civilian sector. I hear they pay well. Great benefits." He shook his head, frowning, his words intended for the entire bridge. "Especially since I can't afford to give you anything except my gratitude. Plus my promise to do right by you. Whatever it takes to get there."

"You can't jump the *Relentless*!" But Navigations' protest rang hollow.

"Been a while since I jumped a ship," Shane agreed. He'd already won. All that remained was to provide the Navigations AI with a graceful way out to retain some semblance of his dignity, but not enough that this would happen again. "I was taught to always Hyperjump empty the first time, but we've got a full crew today. Hopefully I don't leave anyone behind. That would be... unfortunate."

"You crazy bastard..." Admiration replaced the AI's surly temperament. "I'll jump. I'll jump. You win."

The concession was followed moments later by the standard shipwide announcement. "Jump protocols engaged. Rig for hyperjump, twenty-three minutes."

"Impressive. Unless..." Shane raised a brow at the shorter countdown timer as the bridge crew moved to strap tightly into their seats. A half hour was considered the golden standard for Hyperjumping a standard fully crewed capital ship, and while the *Relentless* was on the smaller side of that scale, the missing minutes were significant. "You started prep the moment I jumped in." He growled with approval at the distinct lack of answer. "Well played, Nav."

Well done, Grim, Feels added from the locket. *You haven't lost your touch.*

As the usual pre-jump coordination chatter took over the bridge, a light touch on Shane's shoulder drew his attention back to Haveid. "Better buckle in, Sir." They pointed to an unclaimed jump chair against the wall, next to their own. "Make yourself at home."

"Thank you, Fleet Captain."

While a Void necromancer could learn to treat the ship as an extension of themself, the cargo and crew within remained a different matter. Standard protocol required strapping everyone and everything tightly to the ship itself to reduce the strain on their Void necromancer, and the chances of being left behind.

They grabbed his arm as he turned to move toward the offered seat. Shane shuddered at the unexpected contact, but turned back with what he hoped was a neutral face.

"We've transferred your codes from the *Inevitable* to the rest of the fleet. You have full access to the *Relentless*, and all her systems."

"Appreciate it." Shane nodded his thanks, politely freeing his arm to take a seat.

He was suddenly grateful he'd updated his name in the files. He needed to win over the loyalty of his old fleet to his new cause. That was better done with a clean slate, free from his former reputation.

Shane began the process of buckling himself in for the trip to Janikk. "Comms? Link me with Jeb, hydroponics bay."

<Aye, Sir.> The AI's tone was cool and professional.

<Jeb here.> The biologist, on the other hand, sounded strained.

<You set for jump?>

"Hyperjump protocols engaged. Fifteen minutes to jump."

<We've got everything we know to bring. Getting harnessed in right now.> Jeb remained distracted but calm. <We'll be ready when you are. But Lawrence?>

There was no mistaking the concern in the biologist's voice now. <Talk to me, Jeb.>

<Check in on Raz? I... I'm not the help she needs.>

<Soon as we arrive,> Shane promised. If Jeb was asking for help, it was important.

<Thanks, Lawrence. Jeb out.>

Only one more check to make. <Comms? Navarch Javon, *Inevitable*.>

<Aye.>

"Hyperjump protocols engaged. Ten minutes to jump."

<*Inevitable*.> The newly retitled Navarch carried a warmth in her voice as she answered.

<We'll be out of your fur soon. Ten minutes to jump.> Shane allowed a hint of smugness to transmit with the message.

She noticed, laughing with approval. <I'm impressed. Thought you and Navigations would need a longer chat.>

<We've reached an understanding. Any last minute updates for me?>

<Captain Yiven'll check in regularly with Jake. It's already on her schedule, along with a list of those I trust if she needs backup. Don't worry, he'll be fine.> Her reassurance helped, softening the edges of his nervousness at leaving his son behind with a stranger. <What are my orders, while you're away?>

"Hyperjump protocols engaged. Five minutes to jump."

<You don't get any,> he growled. <You'd have to follow them, and I won't be here to change them if I made a mistake. I trust you to figure things out on your own.>

<Highly irregular, Sir.> But she didn't protest.

<If you really want orders, you could always ask Alanis. She loves bossing people around, as long as she's not held accountable for the outcome.>

<I will take your suggestion under advisement, Sir.> Javon's laughter revealed she'd do no such thing. <*Inevitable* out.>

Calls complete, he turned his attention to the AI herself. <Thank you, Comms. That will be all.>

<You're welcome, Sir!> Her voice betrayed her own appreciation at the unexpected acknowledgement as she ended the link.

"Hyperjump protocols engaged. One minute to jump."

Formal business concluded, Shane swallowed before reaching a finger through the jump harness to rub lightly at the edge of his locket. "This is where we say goodbye, Feels."

I want to stay.

Shane felt a rising love at their pouting tone. "I know... I want you to stay, too." He tugged at the locket, pulling it free of the straps pinning it stiffly against his chest. "But right now? It's for the best. We'll pick this up again once I return. I promise."

Stay safe, Grim. Feels' sorrow radiated from the locket in unmistakable waves beneath Shane's fingers. *Come back to me. Preferably intact.*

"I'll do my best."

Closing his eyes, Shane felt the moment his partner slipped from the locket's bindings, the mental weight of the upcoming mission taking the empath's place upon his heart.

"Hyperjump protocols engaged. Jump in three, two, one..."

The familiar darkness of the Void wrapped around his soul, temporarily claiming the ship and his occupants as they slipped beyond the Veil, emerging at their destination. Shane delayed his own emergence to first glimpse the planet below, its surface unmarred by the scars of civilization, bearing instead the untamed wilderness which had claimed at least three Sparnelli expeditions and quite likely an assortment of others' attempts as well.

Janikk.

14

THE WORLD WAS ON fire.

Not that it was anything Razick couldn't handle. Quite the opposite, in fact. The *Relentless'* sparring room was well-equipped for the average officer, including a full set of nine functional sparring machines, each highly Shielded with their own unique complement of elemental or physical attacks.

But she was a finely tuned weapon, and she and her team had thoroughly dismantled thousands of this exact model when they'd first come out ten years ago. Even at the highest setting, with all nine active at once, she was having trouble devising ways to combat the boredom of their predictability. She'd barely broken a sweat, and the downright repetitiveness of their familiarity was doing nothing to silence the accusing memories haunting her thoughts.

Maybe higher stakes would help. They'd never get close enough to seriously harm her, but the threat of pain at the slightest mistake might be what she needed to force her mind into the exercise.

Decision made, she shrugged off her outer protective jacket before dancing her way to the center of the storm, catching flames and rerouting lightning as she wove through the dulled practice blades. Once assured she was fully surrounded, she dropped her Shielding.

Razick bit her lip, eyes shining, as she immediately found herself assaulted from all sides. *This* was more like it. The machines' simple programming meant they wouldn't react to her the way a person or Afterlife Intelligence would, but at this close range, that didn't matter.

She ducked under a fast-moving sparring sword, deftly catching a pair of Electromancy attacks as she did so. With a well-practiced grace she directed the lightning harmlessly through her arms, feeling its power temporarily augment her own as she spun to redirect it into another unit's sword, the sparks coursing through the sparring machine on their pathway to the grounding within the deck.

Her pride in the maneuver was promptly interrupted by a searing flame across the back of her wrist from an overlooked Pyromancy attack, her instincts kicking in to catch and redirect the flames before she suffered any serious harm.

She'd be feeling that one for a while.

Focus!

Surrendering herself fully to the dance, she redirected and dodged each attack with practiced ease, relying solely on her reaction times and Elemental Magic. Only the Hyperjump countdown slowed her exercise, as she donned an emergency breather and Shielding, lying flat on the floor to ease Navigation's efforts, the maelstrom of possible death and discomfort still raging above.

Upon the ship's return to the mortal plane, she immediately redoubled her efforts until she caught Lawrence's silhouette propped against the doorframe, silently watching as she dodged a particularly close blow from a spray of ice bolts, and determined she was done for the day.

Crouching to the floor, she kicked her feet to propel herself into a telekinetically-enhanced dodge roll toward the weapons rack on the far side of the room. A moment later she had a compact bow in hand, nine bolts loaded on the string, aimed at the ceiling. Mere seconds after, the deadly collection of machines whirred to a halt and pulled back to the edges of the room, an arrow firmly embedded in the top killswitch of each.

She turned to acknowledge her visitor, easing her breath back to neutral as she replaced the bow on the rack. "How long have you been standing there?"

"Distracting you seemed like a bad idea." His smirk dissolved into concern as he approached, his steps rife with grace and power. "You're just holding yourself back, all the time, aren't you?"

Ignoring his question, she instead motioned to the Special Forces uniform folded neatly on the corner bench, its Sparnell insignia carefully removed. "You should get dressed, Sir." She'd expected his visit, but that didn't mean she intended to allow that conversation. "While you're doing that, I'll warm your breakfast."

She watched his shoulders slump at her suggestion, but to his credit the necromancer dutifully donned the uniform as she cast a warming spell on the remaining food container, carefully aligned across her palm and splayed fingers. With a slight expenditure of Telekinesis, she sent the warmed leftovers floating toward Lawrence before finding her own seat and leaning her head against the wall, sweat running down her face.

"Thanks." He ate quickly in the silence, brows furrowed, setting the now-empty container beside him on the bench before turning back to her. "Was hoping to have our first sparring lesson today. But I don't want to tire you out before we even land."

Razick snorted as she counted the many lighting fixtures in the ceiling. "Didn't go so well the last time we fought. You should ask someone else."

"I made a great many enemies in the SAF," he said quietly. "Most tried to kill me. You're the first to succeed. Practicing with you seems the perfect way to learn not to die."

He *did* have a point. The sight of him waterlogged and dying on the hydroponics deck still haunted her dreams and, despite his apparent forgiveness of her deadly efficiency that day, she hadn't been able to shake the guilt. But perhaps this would help.

Grabbing a towel from the rack beside her, she dabbed at the moisture dripping down her neck. "If we're doing this, we're doing it for real."

She wiped the towel across her face, tossing it into the hamper at the far corner of the practice room, her Telekinesis ensuring perfect aim. With a twitch of her finger she drew water from the faucet beside it, her Hydromancy carrying it across the room to caress her face and neck. "I won't go easy on you, like I do Jeb."

"Wouldn't expect you to." He watched as she drank the water straight from the air. "Maybe we could start without magic first? Not used to fighting in this body. Need to fix that, first."

Razick snorted, returning her attention to the ceiling. "Nervous?"

"After what I've witnessed of your workout this morning? A little."

"Good."

And before he could answer she was upon him, lunging through the air in a well-practiced strike. His eyes widened briefly at the unexpected assault, but he recovered quickly, sliding to the side as he rose from the bench in one fluid motion. But she was faster, adjusting to meet his new trajectory and pin him against the wall with her forearm, her face mere inches from his as she met his startled orange stare with a fire of her own.

"I wasn't aware we were starting yet." Lawrence's voice betrayed none of the tensions Razick felt rippling against her.

"You can't plan for everything," she smirked. "So stay alert."

Spinning away as she released him, Razick caught him nod, mouthing something to himself.

And then she had his full attention, every muscle at the ready as he watched her move effortlessly across the floor, stalking her motions with the grace of a katanoj despite the bulky fabric of his protective uniform.

She lunged again but he was ready this time, her punch merely grazing his cheek as he blocked with one arm before landing a fist of his own with the other, the force weak as she used his own momentum from the block to shift her body the same direction as his swing.

He scowled his admiration, pressing his luck anyway. She met the renewed assault with a burst of magic, pushing him backward across the floor. He rolled quickly to his feet, but Razick noted a slight limp as he once again locked onto her movements.

"I thought we weren't using magic? You know I'm at a disadvantage to your Telekinesis."

"I never agreed to that," she teased, lightly darting away to maintain the distance between them. "And that was a Shielding spell, actually. Don't they teach you Void necromancers anything?"

"You forget, we're more valuable dead than alive." He gave a sad smile as he phased into the Afterlife to avoid her next barrage. "They tell you all the propaganda about the importance and value of the Hyperjump spell, but nobody tells you the career path ends trapped as an AI, a dead soul bound to a ship. Not until the Oaths are made and the escape routes sealed."

His words reminded her of her own intended fate, a soulbound prisoner of Kydell's personal TAG, one of many serving the emotionless Tactical Assault necromancer. She hadn't wanted to talk about it, but even listening to him relate his own struggles was a soothing balm to her tortured mind.

Not to mention the fact he fought back. His counterattack caught her lightly on the shoulder as she dodged away, shaking her thoughts loose from her worries. *This* is what she needed.

"Think you could teach me?"

"The Shielding?" She pretended to hesitate, but he didn't attempt to press the offensive. "If I teach you all my tricks, you won't need me anymore."

"I'll always need you, Raz."

Her breath caught at his honest tone, and the use of her nickname.

Seemingly oblivious to the full impact of his words, Lawrence took full advantage of her momentary distraction to land his first real blow of their engagement, a tight-fisted punch to the side of her jaw. Blinking at the sudden sharp – but manageable – pain, she retaliated on instinct, a sizable blast of Telekinesis and Shielding that once again sent him rolling across the floor.

He was slower to rise this time, his face a mask of triumph as he once again sank into a ready position that nonetheless failed to hide his efforts favoring the same leg as before.

She shouldn't...

But her emotions won out. Whether they were directed at him or herself she didn't know. It didn't matter. She lunged, faking a punch before twisting to sweep his good leg out from under him...

She found herself flat on her back instead as he revealed the deception, shifting his weight to his falsely favored leg and sending her to the ground in a motion so smooth she didn't even think to catch herself.

He looked down from above. "Never let them see your true weakness."

"Only the traps you want them to spring," Razick finished sheepishly, accepting his offered hand.

"What's on your mind? The Razick I know would've never fallen for that."

She leaned on his comforting strength as she gathered her thoughts, only turning away when she caught the lines across his face deepen. If anyone would understand, it was him.

"I don't like feeling helpless," she answered at last. "I need to be in control."

"You are the *least* helpless person I know," he offered earnestly. "And that includes me."

"I had an opportunity to take control for myself," she continued balling her fists, her back to him. "I could have told you the truth any time on the *Inevitable*. You could have helped. You *would* have helped."

She felt his gloved hand rest on her shoulder, firm and comforting, but she shook it away.

"I know the truth now," he answered softly instead. "You didn't know me then. I understand secrets. They want to be kept. There's a lot of fear, to overcome that desire."

"But you shared yours, and I still kept mine, and killed you with them. How can you trust me after that?"

She winced as her voice broke, but Lawrence merely reached for her again, this time grasping both shoulders with his hands. This time, she didn't pull away, instead leaning into the touch as if he could Shield her from the guilt she carried.

"Because you know me now." His fingers dug into her muscles, easing her tension with surprising expertise. "And, hopefully, you've learned I'll do anything in my power to help."

They stood in silence for several heartbeats, his thumbs boring into her back with excruciating bliss, before he continued. "You don't know half my secrets. And it's best it stays that way. The person I was died the day Shane was born."

Razick mulled on that for a while, rolling her shoulders to loosen his grasp before turning to face him.

"I've killed a lot of people who didn't deserve it." She bit her lip, averting her eyes from the understanding in his face. "I didn't want to... But Kydell had a lot of political rivals, and I was one of his favorite ways of dealing with them." She gave a bitter laugh. "At least, the ones whose minds he didn't want for himself! I was his reminder that death could find them, anytime, anywhere. Those who chose to return after the experience generally gave him a wide berth."

Instead of the pity she expected, Lawrence's face hardened. "That's because they knew who would visit next." It was his turn to look away. "Not all of Kydell's people were forced into things. I used to *revel* in it. Wasn't immune to his conditioning, of course, but I don't know anymore where I end and Kydell begins."

When he turned his face to hers, his pain was unmistakable. "I *do* know it's a lot further up the scale than I'd like to admit. I'm a cruel bastard, but believe me when I say that Grand Navarch Shane Lawrence is *nothing* like the monster I used to be."

Razick wanted to dismiss his claims as exaggerations for her benefit, but something in his voice stopped her. "How'd you deal with it all?" she asked instead.

"Would you believe I have my mother to thank for that?" The sorrow Lawrence carried in his unfocused gaze hinted at a lifetime of regretful memories. "I've never been able to reach her after her death, but we used to talk all the time before the attack. She..." He sighed, shoving his hands in his pockets. "She died to the war. Her and my father both."

Swallowing, he halted his pacing to meet Razick's gaze. "'You can't change the past, but you *can* change yourself.' She used to tell me that all the time, growing up. Was only two years ago when I finally realized what she meant." He closed his eyes, and when he opened them again she could see the slick sparkle of withheld tears. "And then Feels hardwired my guilt, so now I have to take her advice. Sometimes... Sometimes I wonder if she *knew* what I'd become after her death, and was trying to save me from it." He wiped his eyes on the sleeve of his borrowed uniform. "But of course that's not possible."

"With Divination, you never know..." Razick began, but Lawrence cut her off with a strangled laugh.

"We were *farmers*, Razick. And not very good ones. Didn't even get the planting window right half the time." He plucked a pair of practice swords from the rack, brandishing them with a playful flourish that revealed his own comfort in their use. "Shall we go again?

She made her own weapon selection, watching the orange flames behind his eyes rekindle with anticipation as she gripped a second pair with her Telekinesis, testing the balance of the dulled blades in her hands. He braced for impact, snarling as she lunged at him with all four.

This was *exactly* what they both needed.

15

"Thank you. That was delicious." Jake allowed Veris' mother to retrieve his empty plate, the flavors of pepper and spice and at least three different kinds of cheese still fresh in his mind.

She beamed back, her smile somehow brighter than the light catching in the crystalline accents woven through her thick black braids, even despite the worry lines cutting deep across the thick, scale-like skin of her face.

Her ear fins fluttered as she tilted her head at him. "Least I can do after all you've done, Sugar. Far as I'm concerned, you're family now. Anything you need, you just let your Aunt Fiara know."

The canid beside him leaned over, covering her snout with brown furred fingers as she addressed a conspiratorial stage whisper in Jake's direction. "And you'd best take her up on it, or there'll be Hell to pay."

She winked, dodging the dish towel Veris' mother flung her direction.

"You hush your mouth. What did I tell you about talking behind my back to our guest, Fangela?" Veris' mother glared in mock anger, fists on her hips, laughter in her eyes.

"That you can still hear me?" Veris' Aunt Fangela quipped, lips twisting upward to reveal her teeth.

Fiara snorted, shaking her head as she turned her attention to the counter, wiping it off with wide, firm strokes of her towel. "Where's that boy of mine gone off to? I swear. Some days he's as helpful as a screen door on a spaceship."

With the two women occupied in their search for Veris, Jake spared another glance around the kitchen. From the outside, the Asik's residence had looked about the same size as the home he shared with his father. From the inside, an efficient use of furniture coupled with the bright daylight reflecting off the cheerful pastel yellow walls made everything seem somehow both bigger and cozier.

He shifted his weight on the tall barstool, leaning his elbows on the counter to inhale the welcoming scent of the delicately spiced fruit tea Aunt Fiara slid his direction across the worn countertop. The exuberant hospitality of Veris' mother stood in stark contrast to Jake's father's quiet and unassuming love, his mother's fierce drive for perfection, and even the boisterous mischief of the Kane siblings during their prolonged stay. He wasn't quite certain what to make of it.

"Was hoping to offer you some fruit tarts," Aunt Fiara sighed, draping the ragged dish towel over her shoulder, "but now I'm wondering if Veris decided to keep them all to himself."

As if on cue, Jake's supposedly former bully appeared with an apologetic smile and a tray full of pastries bearing an assortment of shapes and fillings. Jake shrank backward from the older boy, his fingers wrapping around the Void knife in his pocket.

He still felt uncomfortable around Veris, always expecting the older boy to somehow find another knife to stab him with now that Feels wasn't there to heal him after – despite Veris' protests to the contrary.

He knew his father's trip to Janikk was important. The necromancer had an entire fleet looking to him for help now, and he'd always been one to fulfill his obligations. But he couldn't help but resent his father for leaving him behind with the boy who'd once tried to kill him. He'd have felt safer with the fleet. He actually *liked* Navarch Javon. She respected his need for quiet.

Aunt Fiara swooped in to retrieve the prize, clucking her tongue with a bemused smile at her son when she spotted a suspiciously empty section of the mouthwatering display. Moments later, Jake found himself faced with the entire tray.

The matronly dracoling winked proudly as she set a small dessert plate by his side. "Just dig right in, Sugar. Many as you want."

Jake shrank lower in his seat. "You didn't have to go to all this trouble for me, Ma'am."

"There's no Ma'am in this house, young man, just your Aunt Fiara," she said cheerfully, loading his plate when he made no motion to do it himself. "What took you so long, Veris?"

"Wanted to check if Dad needed anything." Veris bit his lip, shoulders slumped as he started blankly at the countertop. "He's still locked in the bathroom."

Jake felt another pang of loneliness for his own father, shoving a pastry – airy and sweet and deserving of more appreciation than he could currently muster – into his mouth in an attempt to distract himself. Maybe he and Veris *did* have something in common.

"That man..." For the first time since Jake had arrived, Aunt Fiara's face turned dark as she scowled down the hallway. "Rabert! Dessert!"

A clatter emerged from the bathroom. Veris' mother and Aunt Fang stiffened at the sound, their eyes fixed into the darkness at the end of the short hall. Moments later, Rabert appeared, wide-eyed and disheveled with his button-down shirt askew as he scratched at his check. If Jake didn't know any better, he'd have assumed the decorated fighter pilot had just awoken from a long nap.

But then Rabert noticed Jake, his face contorting into an angry scowl before he spun to stomp up the stairs.

Jake managed to down two more of the pastries before the air returned to the room.

"Hasn't been the same since you brought him back," Aunt Fiara admitted, brushing at her eyes.

"Should have been me," Aunt Fang said quietly, dropping her half-eaten pastry to her plate before pushing it away. "If I hadn't been unconscious the whole time…"

"None of that," Veris' mother said firmly. "Confederation did it, *not* you. You're just as much a victim as my Rabert."

Jake felt a tug at his sleeve, turning to find Veris watching him. "Is there anything *you* can do?"

He didn't want to help. Didn't even want to *be* here.

But he'd promised his father he'd be on his best behavior. And that meant *trying* his best.

"I don't know," he said honestly. "But I'll ask."

Looking away, he allowed the Void to lick at his consciousness, just as his father had taught him, and focused his attention on the forthright Navigations AI of the *Inevitable*. If anyone could help, Alanis would know. And if nobody could help? She'd tell him that, too.

The insectoid fae materialized into existence on the countertop, the early morning sun catching the fragile gossamer of her wings in a stunning display of shimmering purples and blues, her gray feathered mane fluttering as if in a breeze as she shook her head.

"What is it with you and sad parties?" she asked accusingly, her top two pairs of arms now planted firmly upon each side of her thorax. "If I didn't know any better, I'd think it was *your* fault everyone forgot to have fun."

"Aunt Fiara, Aunt Fang, Veris? This is Alanis. A friend of my father's." He plucked one of the pastries from his plate. "Would you like some dessert?"

She inspected the treat greedily, testing the flavors of the filling before devouring the peace offering with gusto.

"While you're lacking in proper celebration decorum, you Lawrences *do* understand the importance of good food." She eyed Jake's remaining pastries as he slid his plate her direction, fluttering her wings as she accepted the gift. "This tastes remarkably like a bribe. What do you want *this* time? Not my stunning looks or sunny disposition, I'm sure."

"I was hoping for advice," Jake admitted. "About Veris' dad. Rabert Asik? Kydell had him prisoner."

Alanis fluttered her wings again, her words almost reluctant. "I don't know everything that wolf had people do," she said quietly. "Your father *does*, but he'd actually tell you if you ask, and... I don't think you want to know."

"I just want my husband back." Aunt Fiara wrung her hands. "I'll do whatever it takes."

"He'll need a therapist. A good one."

Fiara's face fell. "He's refused everyone the Baden Defense Force sent. They stopped coming, after he tried to strangle the last one."

Alanis was quiet for a moment. "I'll talk to Navarch Javon. Maybe we have someone." She held up an arm in caution. "It's a long shot. Our fleet did this to him; I'll be surprised if he lets us help fix it."

"Is there anything else we can do?" Veris sounded close to tears.

"Well…" The fae groomed her antennae as she thought. "Admiral Kydell wasn't one to use curses and the like, but that doesn't mean his people don't. You could get some Cleaning Magic in here, to be safe."

"I could pick up some aural candles for the bathroom," Veris' mother said, brightening. "And burn herbs in the bedroom."

"The BDF would probably cover one of those fancy alchemical carbon-filtered room fans," Aunt Fang added excitedly. "I'll ask."

Jake offered her another pastry. "Thanks, Alanis."

"You sound like you want something else," she said accusingly, ignoring the offering.

"You'd have an easier time keeping me safe if I were closer," he told her firmly.

"No." She crossed her arms. "Your father decided you were staying here. I'm not going against him. Not on this."

"I don't think Veris' father likes me very much," Jake whined. "And I'd feel safer with the fleet. With *you*."

"He said you were staying with Veris," she repeated.

"Then he can come, too," Jake said stubbornly, sticking out his chin. At least then if the dracoling tried to stab him again, he'd already be near the healers.

Veris' voice carried more excitement than Jake had anticipated. "Can I? Mom? Please?"

"I don't know..." Aunt Fiara's brows furrowed. "Can you keep Veris safe?"

"Fine." Alanis sighed, throwing up her hands. "I don't want to argue with you. Yes. Yes. It's fine. It's not like I'm going against the Grand Navarch's wishes or anything. I'm sure it'll all be fine."

Aunt Fiara didn't look convinced, but seemingly relented at Veris' excitement.

"You boys stay safe, okay? Be back in time for supper!"

"Yes, Mom," Veris said dutifully, allowing his mother to plant a kiss on his cheek.

Jake wanted to protest, wanted to insist Alanis rescind Veris' invitation, but before he could open his mouth the mortal plane was already twisting around them, giving way to Void.

16

Jake watched Veris carefully as they emerged from the jump on the flag deck overhanging the bridge of the *Inevitable*. The older boy stared in wide-eyed wonder at the efficient bustle of activity down below.

The *Inevitable* appeared to be at full battle stations for some sort of fleet exercise, judging by the crowd below and Jake's father's descriptions of his own time in the SAF. Someone sat behind each of the consoles scattered about the deck, most staring intently at their screens, while a large holographic projection of Baden's orbitspace hung above everyone, even with the flag deck itself.

From what Alanis had told him, Admiral Kydell had preferred to run his operations from the bridge itself, micromanaging his flagship's crew alongside the rest of the fleet. Navarch Javon appeared to be of a different opinion, instead allowing her crew the appropriate authority to do their own jobs by absconding to the sparsely populated flag deck with her minimal support staff instead.

A trait she shared with his father.

"Good morning, Jake." Navarch Javon casually rose from her chair, crooking her finger to summon one of her officers into the seat instead. "Wasn't expecting another visit so soon. How can the fleet help you?"

"What's going on?" He hadn't expected this level of activity when he'd requested the jump from Alanis, and he suddenly felt guilty for bothering them.

Although Veris was too busy watching the bridge below to give Jake any further attention, so he supposed he didn't feel *too* guilty.

"Planetary authorities attempted to arrest someone for taking advantage of the aftermath of our invasion. Apparently the geniuses decided fleeing off planet would be their best bet. Baden's Defense Force is already stretched thin. Requested we help intercept." Her tail jerked behind her as she offered him a sorrowful smile. "Our fault, all of it. And we're stuck in their orbitspace, until the Grand Navarch finds us somewhere else to go. Least we can do is be good neighbors."

"Dad will fix that," Jake promised.

That's why he was stuck with *Veris*, after all. As much as he hated being left behind, he knew the importance of the mission to Janikk. He *liked* Javon. He wanted her, and everyone else, to find a new home to replace the one they'd left behind when they'd deserted in favor of his father's leadership.

Javon's whiskers twitched at the conviction in his voice. "I know. Your father's a terrifying bastard when he wants something. I'm glad we're on the same side, this time. He'll see it through." She jerked her head toward Veris with a faint smile. "But you didn't come here to talk about things you already knew. How can we help you?"

"I miss Dad," he admitted. "And..." He lowered his voice. "Veris *stabbed* me."

"You feel safer with the fleet," she said knowingly.

"Thought I'd see what we could do to help fix the hydroponics bay," he continued, scuffing his shoe against the deck. "Least I'll feel useful."

"Good luck. It's a mess." Javon bared her teeth in amusement, lowering her voice. "Fleet's not safe, either, Kid. Can't rush these things – my crew's been through enough already – but that means we haven't found all the Kydell loyalists yet. *And* you're the Grand Navarch's son. I know your Shields are solid, but you'll still need a security detail."

He shrugged in acceptance, before brightening. "I'd like that, actually."

Not that he'd actually expected Veris to try to hurt him again, but knowing he'd have trained battle mages nearby would likely quell the last of his unease.

She nodded her approval. "Good. And good luck. It's a mess. Comms?" Her eyes unfocused as the Communications Afterlife Intelligence provided her requested telepathic connection.

Veris wandered over, grinning widely, the intercept mission apparently complete. "Everything feels so much *bigger* up here. And that was *cool*. Can they do it again?"

"No." Jake sighed, rubbing the back of his neck as Veris waited for him to elaborate. "Baden *asked* them to do that," he added finally. "They can't just harass other ships for fun. That would be..."

"Bullying," Veris finished for him, frowning. "I get it. Look, I'm... I'm sorry, okay? I didn't mean..."

"You stabbed me on purpose." Jake narrowed his eyes. "For *fun*."

"I..." Veris looked away, whatever he'd planned to say dying in his throat. He kicked his toe against the deck, shoulders slouched, and Jake had to strain to hear him. "Yeah. Yeah, I did."

"Because you wanted to be *mean*."

Veris opened his mouth as if to speak, but closed it again before saying anything.

Jake felt a pang of guilt for pushing the issue. Perhaps Veris actually *was* sorry.

He shoved the feeling aside, instead directing his attention to Javon. "I'll need some of Razick's lab equipment, too." From his vantage point, the large pile of tools and materials his father had jumped to the bridge after the battle had been moved elsewhere.

Javon caught Jake's eye to acknowledge the request before shifting her attention back to the Telecomm.

Veris grabbed his arm in a vice grip, and Jake stiffened, prying the older boy's fingers loose as he watched three newcomers – two heavily muscled black-spotted canids, led by a brown-haired human with a dark tanned complexion betraying his frequent trips to the field – emerge from the door to the flag deck, holding themselves in a stance highly reminiscent of Razick's. Aside from the ceremonial sword strapped to their leader's belt the trio appeared unarmed, although Jake knew firsthand this did nothing to reduce the battle mages' lethality.

The one with the sword saluted Navarch Javon before turning his attention to Jake with kind copper eyes and deferential nod.

"Welcome back to the *Inevitable*, Kid. Sub-Officer Olixa Perry, at your service. We're your escort."

Jake waved away Veris' nervous protest. "It's fine. You get used to it."

Not that he'd had a security detail before, aside from his father. But he'd felt his nerves settle at their arrival, and that was all he'd really wanted.

"Glad you feel that way." The officer grinned. "Traded in a lot of favors for the privilege. Shall we be off?"

"You can trust them," Javon added, to Jake's sudden hesitation. "Olixa's team has served me for years. Haveid chose them personally to stay behind."

"Someone has to keep our Navarch safe," Olixa said, standing even taller. "And my team's the best."

"In that case, lead on," Jake ordered.

The others spun on their heels at a motion from Olixa, the Sub-Officer instead taking up a protective position behind Jake.

Jake felt a smug satisfaction watching Veris nervously eye their new escort, ear fins held flat against his head. When the older boy shrunk even further upon encountering Javon's own security at the flag deck's exit, then again once directed to step through the portal to the hallway outside the Hydroponics bay, Jake realized he needed to step in.

He reached a hand for Veris' shoulder, pulling it back quickly as Veris jumped.

"You're safe here," he said instead.

"I... I'm sorry. You know that, right?" Veris pleaded, eyes wide. "Not just for stabbing you. For all the times I picked on you. I..."

"I know." And for the first time, Jake actually meant it. Despite all his misgivings about spending time with his former bully, he didn't actually think Veris would hurt him. Not on purpose. Not again.

"And then you brought my Dad back, even after..."

Jake felt another pang of loneliness. He missed his father, but at least he knew he'd come back. Veris' father had disappeared completely.

"You're not the only person on this ship who tried to kill me," he said kindly, only to kick himself as Veris winced again. "That's not what I meant. Alanis tried to Shatter my soul."

"Alanis?" Veris asked in surprise. "But I thought she was your friend?"

"She is," Jake agreed. He'd forgiven her quickly, given the circumstances, and found himself wondering why he was still holding a grudge against Veris. Unlike Veris, Alanis had tried to end his existence completely.

Of course, she'd also only attempted it once. Veris had singled him out for *years*.

Veris let out a strangled attempt at a laugh, his eyes focused intently on Jake. "Do you make a habit of befriending people who try to kill you?"

Jake was saved from answering by a polite cough from their escort. "We're here."

The hydroponics bay was almost entirely empty, aside from the heavy-duty shelving firmly attached to the right-hand wall. Carefully organized stacks of metal occupied the lower shelves, while Razick's lab equipment claimed the higher spaces. Piping from the original layout sprouted from the floor at regular intervals, capped with faucets at varying heights, while a collection of lighting fixtures and sprinkles – some of them damaged or even missing altogether – hung in patterns along the ceiling.

A large reinforced window claimed the entire left side of the bay, the outer bulkhead the only barrier between the hydroponics bay and the Void. Through the window lay an unobstructed view of Baden itself, a sparkling ball of blue, green, brown, and white. A large portion of the Turncoat Armada – as they'd taken to calling themselves – was visible from here, the darkness of the fleet still twinkling faintly in the light from Baden's sun, a sharp contrast to the brighter colors of the commercial flights dotting Baden's orbitspace.

Jake allowed himself a sigh of relief as Veris broke away to stare at the view, his own footsteps drawn to the faint marks of red still visible on the floor.

The blood of the woman he'd Shattered. Stabbed, with his own knife.

He didn't know how long he'd been staring before he realized Veris was calling his name, waving a blue scaled hand in front of his face. "Jake! Jake! Hellooooo?"

"She was right here," Jake told him. "They cleaned it up. You can barely tell anymore. But she died. Right here."

"Who?"

"She just lay there... Staring. Trying to breathe. Her blood..." Jake turned, looking through Veris, the memory still fresh in his mind. "She was already dead. But she wouldn't stop *staring* at me."

"You can't save everyone," Veris said hesitantly.

"It was *my fault!*" Jake shouted, barely registering Veris' step backward. "*I* did it! I *killed* her with *your* knife, and *Shattered* her *soul*. She was Admiral Kydell's. He probably made her do it. Maybe she didn't have a choice, either."

He closed his eyes, forcing himself to remember his conversations with Razick. *The right thing to do isn't always a good thing to do.* But he wished with everything he had there'd been someone else to do it instead.

"She would have killed us all," he continued, hoping he managed to keep his voice level. "I *had* to do it. It was the *right* thing to do..." He turned to Veris, his voice cracking. "Right?"

He watched as Veris exhaled, his hands curling into fists and uncurling again for several moments before the older boy sighed. "I'm... not the best person to ask about stabbing people."

Jake stared at him, watching him shuffle his feet and shrink from his gaze. In that moment, he was struck by the ridiculousness of it all. If Veris hadn't stabbed him, he probably wouldn't have ended up with the knife in the first place. If Veris hadn't tried to kill him, he'd have never become a murderer. He'd have been another of her victims, right alongside his father and Razick and Professor Jeb and Baden and...

An unhinged attempt at laughter filled the room, and it took Jake a moment – plus Veris' mouth-open stare – to realize it was him.

"You're the *worst* person to ask about that," Jake agreed.

"Unless you want pointers," Veris quipped. "In which case, I can show you the pointy end."

They both burst into laughter then, and Jake realized that although Veris hadn't given him the answer he'd wanted, perhaps he'd provided the one he needed.

But Veris sobered suddenly. "I know I'm selfish. But if you hadn't killed her... She'd have stopped you from saving Dad." He stood taller, and Jake felt the conviction in his words. "So far as I'm concerned, you did the right thing."

"We saved the planet, Veris."

"Dad wasn't *on* the planet, *Jake*." But Veris was smiling, even despite the eye roll. "You changed my life that day."

Jake bit his lip, staring absently out the window before turning back to Veris with a nod. "Lots of people changed. Most for the better." His Dad's fleet would still be killing people for the Confederation, after all. "Me... I don't like how I changed. But I did help other people. Not just my Dad. Thank you, for reminding me."

"Dad hasn't been the same, either, since he came back." Veris shoved his hands in his pockets, staring through the window into the Void. "I keep worrying I did something to upset him, but... It's not me, right?"

Shaking his head, Jake put his hand on Veris' shoulder. "We like to pretend we're all grown up. But we're *kids*. Dad still has nightmares."

"Why would *he* have nightmares? He took on an entire fleet, and now it's *his*. What does *he* have to be afraid of?"

"Lots of things. Himself, mostly. Bad memories. Things he did for the Confederation." While the necromancer had never kept secrets from Jake, he knew there was still a lot they hadn't talked about. And probably wouldn't.

Some things, it was better not to know.

"...My Dad has nightmares, too. I wish I could help."

"I want to learn Alchemy. Find a way to help him sleep at night. He says not to worry, but he's my Dad! He worries about me, and I want to help him!"

"So... It's not my fault?"

"About your dad? *No.*"

Veris nodded, slowly sinking to the floor. "Thank you. I'm sorry. I'm..." He looked up, and there was pain in his eyes. "How do you focus? With all the stars in your head?"

Jake was instantly on alert. "Have you been offplanet before?"

Veris shook his head, his hands over his ear fins. "Please don't... You keep *shouting* at me..."

But Jake hadn't been shouting.

Reaching out with his Telepathy, Jake felt his thoughts connect with Veris. <Stop using your magic,> he ordered. <I'll get you home, then talk to Dad. When he gets back.>

He was likely on Janikk by now. And distractions could be deadly.

Veris' eyes widened, his ear fins fluttering with agitation. <What's wrong? Am I sick?>

<You're fine,> Jake reassured. <You just need training. I can help, but Dad's better at it.>

Veris blinked. <Better at what?>

Jake smiled patiently. <He's Cosmically Attuned. The mages who can borrow magic from the stars, to cast bigger spells. I can't, but then I don't have to worry about the Burnout that happens if you borrow too much, either.>

<Burnout? Cosmic Whatsit? What are you *talking* about?>

<Veris.> Jake sighed patiently, brushing errant strands of hair from his face as he sank to the deck across from the older boy. <You're a Void mage.>

17

SHANE HAD NEVER WORKED so hard for anything in his entire life. Razick's relentless pressure stretched his skills to their limit, her strategies always several steps ahead even as he maintained his own tactical mind at full engagement. He congratulated himself on the foresight of wearing the reinforced exosuit to support him during the mission, despite Feels' success in healing his prior wounds. But even the body brace's slight strength boost when countering the force behind her movements did little to mitigate the power of a highly trained battle mage.

He parried her next quick flurry of attacks a little too easily, recognizing too late she'd successfully driven him closer to the corner of the room. She was *good*.

She must have caught the flash of recognition in his eyes, as she grinned suddenly before pushing in for the kill.

Shane ran through his rapidly dwindling options. He still held both swords this time, his exercises with Razick driving home the fact he wasn't nearly as skillful at using this to his full advantage as his opponent. The stars of the Void called out to him, offering their powers to augment his own, but aside from strengthening his personal Shielding, this held little use against Razick. His most familiar offensive spell was Shatter, and he wasn't trying to *kill* her, just *survive* her.

Not that he was having much luck on that front either. Her next strike managed to disarm his left hand, catching the blade between her own telekinetically-wielded swords and twisting it free of his grip. The practice weapon clattered briefly across the floor before rising to join her own, leaving Shane's wrist stinging from the sudden impact as he brought his remaining sword to bear.

Razick lunged again, the battle mage likely augmenting her reflexes with her Telekinesis, judging by the impressive speed behind the attack. Shane attempted the Shielding trick she'd taught him in return, tapping into the Void to bolster its effects. The Shield burst caught her in the chest with its full force, sending her rolling backward across the room as Shane dodged to the side. Razick's telekinetically-gripped blades clattered to the ground where he'd been standing moments before, assisted by his quick parry as he passed, and her temporary distraction.

She grinned again as she leaped from the ground, and Shane felt his momentary elation falter at the determination in her eyes. And then she was upon him again, her face a mere breath from his as she twisted the remaining sword from his hand, his back pressed against the new corner.

He graciously nodded his defeat as she relinquished her grip, rubbing his wrists and waving off her offer to return his swords. "You win. Again. Think that's my limit for the day."

"Giving up?" she teased, replacing the blades within the rack. "I thought you Void mages were supposed to be all powerful."

"We can make our *spells* more powerful, but we're still limited by what we know." He shook his head, pulling off the uniform gloves to splash water on his face in the wall sink. "And your spells are much better suited to this exercise than mine. Besides." He grabbed a towel, wiping at the sweat still streaming down his neck. "The most important part of being a Void mage is knowing your limits. Live to fight another day."

"There's hope for you yet, Lawrence."

At a motion from Razick, the swords scattered across the floor zipped toward their home in the weapons rack.

"That's what Feels keeps telling me, too."

"Then it must be true," Razick said, her voice thoughtful. "You did well with that Shielding trick. I think there's a lot I could teach you, just applying your own magic."

"Why do I get the feeling you're *still* taking it easy on me?"

That had been the most challenging workout Shane had ever experienced, and yet while he sat gasping, Razick's breathing had quickly reverted back to calm and relaxed as soon as Shane had voiced his surrender.

"Because I am?" She shrugged with a laugh, a genuinely heartwarming sound, and Shane resolved to request more training with her, just to hear his friend happy again. "Don't want to discourage you. Not to mention, we don't know what Janikk has waiting for us, and I need to be able to keep you alive." She caught him with a sideways glance. "I'm not the only one holding back. You can *Hyperjump*. You could have phased through *any* of my pins, but you didn't."

"Felt that would defeat the purpose of the exercise." He tilted his head, mimicking her words. "Not to mention, we don't know what Janikk has waiting for us, and I need to be able to stay alive."

His attempt at humor was rewarded with a wet towel to the face, the cool against his skin a welcome distraction. He tugged at the sweltering uniform she'd insisted he retain for their practice. "Besides, I was at a disadvantage. How do you even *fight* in these things?"

His voice was muffled by the towel, but judging by her laugh, Razick understood anyway. "You have to turn it on first!"

Reluctantly removing the towel, he watched her shrug back into her own outer jacket before reaching into one of the many pockets to fiddle with something inside. Inspecting his own, Shane found a small control panel with various self-cooling options. He scowled as he selected one, her laughter growing in volume as a cooling breeze began circling within his shirt and trousers.

"When were you going to tell me?"

She merely snorted. "Turn it off before you jump us down. It'll be frigid on the surface, and these only have a cooling function." When he raised an eyebrow, she elaborated. "Self-heated uniforms show up on infrared. Have to manage that function ourselves."

They sat in silence for a while, the body brace barely enough to support his exhausted limbs. Leaning back against the bulkhead, he savored the lifesaving breeze of the repurposed SAF uniform until Razick interrupted the quiet with a polite cough. He opened his eyes to find her own stare focused on him, a nervous curiosity across her face.

"Lawrence? What was it like? When you discovered you're a Void mage?"

He hadn't thought about that for a long time. "Unlike many, I knew years before I was conscripted into the SAF. After my parents died they moved all the orphans to Sparnell, and kept a close eye on us to see who'd act different. One thing led to another, and I ended up one of the youngest recruits to ever take a Soul Oath." He balled his fists. "Kydell made certain I knew *exactly* how many favors he traded in to Claim me. Used to think that meant I owed him, which is exactly what he *wanted* me to think, but now I realize–"

"No," Razick interrupted. "I mean... What was it like when you first heard the stars?"

"Oh." This was a much happier topic. "I'm not sure I could ever really describe it. You look outside, into the darkness of the

Void, and it *looks* empty. But your mind says it's not, it's full of life and magic and mystery and all of it just... *calling* to you."

He still remembered the moment he'd set foot in that spacecraft, leaving behind the charred remains of everything and everyone he'd ever known, and how the welcoming call of the stars had carried him through his despair. Their song had been his only friend, until Feels.

"The more I learned Necromancy, the more I learned to open my mind to the higher dimensions of the Afterlife, the easier it became to trace the lines and current connecting us all within those stars. I... I don't know if that makes any sense?"

Razick watched him wistfully. "I wish I could feel that. Just once."

He'd never shared that part of his magic with anyone. Not even Feels. There was something deeply personal, intimate even, about sharing one's full unmitigated magic potential with another. Doubly so when that magic pulled from the very fabric of the universe itself.

But something in her voice, in the way she asked without asking, gave him pause. And with all the guilt she'd been carrying...

Maybe a glimpse of his true power would help. Maybe she'd realize that as much as she'd been trying to avoid hurting him, he'd have rather died several times over again than subject her to the destructive side of his own talents, and the dark inclinations he often felt lurking just beneath the surface of his thoughts.

"You can. Here." Shane grasped Razick's hands in his, offering an apotheturgic link to share his own experiences of magic with the battle mage. "Don't cast anything, though. The Cosmically Attuned automatically pull from the stars until we learn to control it, often with unexpected or unstable results, and I'm about to drop all my filters."

He swallowed hard at the absolute trust in her emerald green gaze as she obeyed, canceling her Shielding and squeezing his hands in hers.

"But maybe close your eyes."

One by one he dropped his own mental shields, first those holding the cosmic Void at bay, then those constructed to barricade the constant press of the Afterlife, allowing the full familiarity of both to wash through his mind. The caress of unbridled power.

"Don't fight it," he cautioned as he felt her tense. "We're surrounded by the magic of the universe. We can't change it. We can only experience it, adrift on the waves of an eternity we'll never truly understand."

She relaxed again, tentatively at first, her face a model of abject wonder and delight. "Now I see why you're so good at surrendering," she managed at last, her touch finally light within his palms.

"Can't fight the universe. Can only hope to survive it." He allowed himself a smile. "Just like sparring with you."

They drifted together in the dimensionless intensity of the stars, comfortable in their shared company. The waves of magical power rose and crashed around them in a harmonious symphony, an untamable chorus balancing the life and death of all of existence.

Jeb's telepathic sending recalling them to the hydroponics bay came much too soon.

18

Jeb looked up as his sister strode confidently into the room, followed by a surprisingly subdued Lawrence. Razick exhibited a smile and a lighter step than Jeb had seen in a long time, even despite her bulky backpack and the high-powered laser rifle gripped in her hands.

He nodded his thanks to Lawrence, exhaling in surprise as Razick thrust a uniform in his direction, already preset to show the same arctic camouflage she and Lawrence wore.

"Get dressed," she ordered, showing him how to set and manipulate the environmental controls within the suit, a courtesy Lawrence seemed to object to, given his sudden scowl. "Then we'll hear you out."

Not that he'd needed the instructions. He'd spent most of his conscription as a botanical surveyor, volunteering for any job requiring a battle mage escort in the hope the team would be Razick's. He recognized now how Admiral Kydell had likely kept them separated, despite Jeb's many formal requests to the contrary.

But there was no need to spoil her good mood.

"I see my backyard is barren again," the necromancer observed as Jeb donned the demanded uniform.

The bay was overcrowded, by people standards, although the hydroponics plants had been bred to grant more forgiveness on the matter, provided their needs were met. Aisles between the usual fixtures had been stuffed full of buckets bearing the *Inevitable*'s surviving plants formerly residing in Lawrence's backyard. He could have split them up across the remaining ships of the fleet, but he'd been a part of the destruction of their home environment, and he felt a sense of responsibility for their well-being as a result.

Besides, they were Urla's plants. The least he could do was see to their needs, since she didn't seem to have many of her own.

Jeb felt himself smile as he slid into the uniform jacket. "They're accustomed to an artificial environment, so they'll be happier here. And I wanted to keep an eye on them, after the way I overexerted them last night."

The necromancer's brows furrowed. "Can't you just use fertilizer for that?"

"Sure." Jeb shrugged, using the movement to tug the shoulders of the jacket into a better fit for his frame. "But too much at once stresses them, too, so I've had to spread it out."

Lawrence shook his head, shoving his hands in his pockets. "And now you know why there's nothing growing in my backyard."

"We'll make a botanist of you yet."

"We'll see. What've you got for us?"

"Tarvick? Sweetheart?" Jeb kept his words sickly sweet, smiling as he imagined the AI's discomfort. "Could you run the map? You're much better at it than I."

"All I said was that boss of yours needs to write some regulations against flirting in the workplace," Tarvick growled, nonetheless bringing up the map. "I didn't mean I felt left out of... whatever it is you and my coworker have going on."

"Jeb..." Lawrence cautioned, frowning. "*We* are the guests here."

"Well, what do you know?" Tarvick's voice betrayed his surprise. "There *is* a god."

"Most people just call me the Grand Navarch," Lawrence answered dryly. "What do you have for me?"

Jeb frowned. Lawrence was right, of course. "Sorry, Tarvick."

"Don't mention it, Buttercheeks," the AI growled back. "Ever."

Face flush, Jeb scrambled to regain his composure. "Uh, so..."

He was saved by Urla. "The *Reckoning*'s scanners show more wildlife on the arctic islands than in previous studies, but we expected that. Our scanners are better, so of course they'd see more. We haven't discovered anything of *concern*, so the island's still our best bet."

Razick tightened the grip on her pack, adjusting its weight on her shoulders. "Anything I need to worry about?"

"Tough to say," Jeb admitted. "Past expeditions never attempted to land in the arctic regions, so we don't have anything but scan data for them."

"Judging by the signatures, they appear fairly inactive," Urla added, and Jeb felt a swell of pride at the confidence in her words. "Could mean mostly plantlife, but given the location? My credits are on energy conservation. Add in the environmental profile, and I'd say we're not looking at many herbivores here. The main diets of these animals will be fish or each other. So expect good camouflage, and lots of hibernation and naps until they need to either hunt prey or escape predation."

Jeb watched his sister nod, biting her lip. "We can only react to what they do, until we learn enough to predict their movements."

"Pretty much," Urla agreed. "We already know Janikk wildlife is fierce. I'd expect that trend to continue wherever we land, and prepare for it."

"Here." Lawrence pressed the cold metal of an electropistol hilt into Jeb's hand, its twin already strapped to Lawrence's waist. "Kydell's. Purposely underpowered."

There was no need to mention why. The admiral's tendency to play with his targets before claiming their minds remained a recent memory for all of them.

"Should let you defend yourself without angering Janikk, if the need arises," Lawrence added, before lowering his voice. "I know you know how to use it."

"Been reading my personnel file?"

"I find it best to use all information available when planning a mission." Lawrence shrugged, while Razick winced, likely remembering how her own secrets had jeopardized their fight aboard the *Inevitable*. "Would you disagree?"

"Does this mean we get to read yours, too?" Jeb asked instead of answering.

Lawrence scowled. "No."

Jeb hid his disappointment. The necromancer had already revealed his prior role as one of Admiral Kydell's former Commodores, not to mention his part in the murderous Admiral Renkash's death to save the life of his son. What *else* did he think he needed to hide?

But Jeb had no right to press. Here he was, keeping his significant field mission experience a secret from his own sister, just because he didn't want to upset her. And Lawrence was keeping it, too, without judgment. Surely he was entitled to his own secrets.

Especially if they were anything like the secrets his sister still kept from him. Particularly the ones that still tormented her in the middle of the night.

"What we *really* want to show you," Tarvick interrupted gruffly, "is this." The globe shifted to reveal a network of multicolored lines, most of them green, spread across the planet. "I've never seen anything like it."

Lawrence's brows furrowed. "What am I looking at?"

"That's a Metamagic scan, showing the magic fields on Janikk herself." Urla's voice sounded slightly strained, and Jeb wondered if it was because of the information on the map, or his own silence.

The globe adjusted to display only the green-colored lines, a scattered collection of smooth vectors gathering at over a dozen poles across the planet. "As you know, Nature Magic relies on its surroundings. That's why us biologists are mostly useless in the Void outside the hydroponics bay, and also why medlab is on the other side of the wall. Whatever fields we've got here, we brought ourselves. Janikk's been left to her own devices for millennia, so *her* fields are... *really* strong. That's not unheard of on a planet of her type, but..."

A second globe appeared next to the first, a warmer planet by the looks of the readout. This one displayed a less cluttered network of green fields across its surface, with three poles situated within the densest sections of the tropics.

Jeb noted Lawrence lean in to study the new display, only to suddenly tense and turn away.

He knows this planet.

"This was Yarva at its height, before the Legion nuked the planet," Urla continued, unfazed. "Most people don't talk about it now, but Yarva was a highly effective farming planet with a unique approach to growing. Rather than clearing land for their animals and crops, they found ways to work in *harmony* with the native plants and animals, and used the increased strengths of their magic to improve their yield instead. As a result, they also became one of the few known planets with more than two poles in their Nature Magic fields."

The poles on both maps shifted into red dots. "On Janikk? I count *fifteen*."

"In other words, there's something unnatural about Janikk's Nature Magic." Lawrence had positioned himself to block out most of his view of Yarva and was studying the projected globe of Janikk again. "Where did the Confederation expeditions land, again?"

"Their last known locations were here, here, and... here." Jeb pointed at the globe, his fingers landing adjacent to three of the dots. "But also..." He hit a few buttons on the console, first turning off the projection of Yarva – earning a quick glance of gratitude from the necromancer – before splitting Janikk's projection in half to reveal her interior. "This is the first planet we've seen where the Nature Magic poles are entirely *underground*."

Lawrence frowned before turning to Jeb. "What does that mean, for us?"

"My magic and Urla's will be a lot stronger than we're used to, once we land." Jeb hesitated. "And the answers we need are probably at the poles."

"Where all the prior expeditions died," Razick added softly.

"Yeah."

"What did the Confederation scans look like?" Lawrence continued to study the projection, measuring the distances between each pole with his fingers.

"There aren't any," Tarvick growled. "I've found summaries of them, but the scans themselves? It's like someone removed them from the records. Navarch Javon couldn't even find anything for us."

"And I gave you everything I could access," the necromancer added, scowling. "Which means it's locked to Fleet Command."

Lawrence's comment hung in the uncomfortable silence until Razick stepped forward, waving a hand through the holographic display. "We need to stay clear of those poles until we know more about what we're getting into."

"Agreed. They're too evenly spaced. Someone clearly *built* them, and past records imply they're deadly." Lawrence rubbed the back of his neck, stepping away from the projection. "Stick to the original plan. Once we're planetside, I'll make contact with Janikk. See what we can learn."

"Any chance you could try from up here?" Jeb watched the necromancer closely.

"No," Razick answered instead, to Jeb's surprise. "Too hard to focus on a single target at this distance, especially if she stays on the planet. Too many voices in the Void."

"She's right," Lawrence agreed. "And the dead are nosy once they realize you can see them. Kydell's fleet is one of the few places I don't have to worry about blocking them out. He had a... tendency of binding them to work for him."

Jeb thought he caught a dark shadow pass over the necromancer's face, and wondered how many souls Lawrence had personally repurposed for the demanding admiral.

"Plus I don't know enough about Janikk to Call her specifically. I'll be reaching for anyone who can hear me, which means I need to get closer," the necromancer finished.

"Then it looks like we're heading down." Jeb grabbed his own pack from one of the shelves, carefully organized to include his own kit plus a few thoughtful additions from Urla's suggestions. He motioned to the shelf. "Packed one for you, too, Lawrence. Camping gear, since we're likely spending the night." He smiled apologetically. "Tried to keep it on the lighter end. I know you're not used to this."

Lawrence eyed the backpack before awkwardly slipping it on, reaching beneath his shirt to adjust something. The soft hum of his exosuit elicited a smile from Razick as she passed Jeb a knowing look from behind her helmet's built-in goggles. The necromancer knew he was the least experienced on this trip, and was doing what he could to take care of himself without slowing them down.

"Tarvick will stay with the *Relentless*, to keep scanning for the duration of our trip," Jeb continued, displaying his tablet and offering a spare tablet to Razick. "We'll be able to see any new changes here. I've set them all to manual updates, to conserve power. Lawrence, there's another in your pack." He ran through his mental checklist one last time. "Think that's everything. Janikk?"

"Janikk," Lawrence agreed, holding out his arms. "Let's jump."

19

THEY EMERGED FROM THE Afterlife along the northeast section of the island, atop a large glacier overlooking the eastern ice shelf. Red and orange from the dawning spring sun glinted in the dancing waves of the ocean below, casting their light in shimmers against the ice beneath the last faint slivers of Janikk's twin moons. Pristine snow, devoid of even a hint of animal tracks, covered every surface as far as Shane could see.

Not that tracks would remain visible for long.

He shivered in the frigid wind whipping across the glacier, before cursing and fumbling for the environmental controls of the uniform, half-frozen fingers pawing uselessly at his pocket. He'd forgotten to turn it off, the built-in Anemancy dutifully siphoning off his body heat to the environment.

"Can't take you anywhere." Razick shook her head, removing her glove to extend two bare fingers in his direction. "Let me through your Shielding."

He nodded, closing his eyes to concentrate on maintaining his personal Shield against everything but the battle mage. He felt the pressure of her hand in his pocket, deftly disabling the offending cooling, and shivered.

And then the warmth of her fingers tunneled beneath the stiff leather of his uniform collar before brushing lightly against his carotid artery, the sudden heat of her touch rushing to fill his veins as he opened his eyes at the invigorating sensation.

She pulled on her glove, retrieving her laser rifle from its resting place against her leg. "Let me know if you need it again."

"Where'd you learn to do that?" He rubbed the upturned collar of his protective leather epaulets, observing Jeb happily circling their landing site with a handheld scanner, seemingly oblivious to the cold.

"Basic."

She had her back to him, already scanning the vast expanse of nothingness for potential threats, her unruly red curls cascading down her back from beneath her helmet.

"Seems useful," he tried again.

She shrugged. "Once you master it." Her words were distracted as she rubbed at the side of her visor, her focus drawn by something in the distance. "It's a delicate spell. Get it wrong, and you boil from the inside out. Nasty way to go."

"Glad you mastered it, then." Shane winced at the thought of the earful he'd have received from Feels otherwise. "That sounds... unpleasant."

"They drilled us on the importance of keeping our focus, no matter what." Razick relaxed her shoulders, apparently appeased by whatever she'd seen through the enhanced vision of her visor. "Then one day when we were practicing blood warming, Instructor decided to demonstrate. Interrupted one of my squad as he was casting it..."

Her voice faded as she fixed Shane with an impassive green stare. "Something like that sticks with a person. Any time I started to lose my focus after that, all I could hear was his screams. And the *smell*..."

Shane swallowed. "You could have used it on me. On the *Inevitable*."

She shrugged again, turning to watch her brother dig through the snow, his own attention split between his scanner and whatever he'd just discovered within the ice. "You kept your Shielding up. By the time it failed, you were already dying. Kydell had no hold on me then, I'd already done what he wanted."

"Raz... I'm sorry. That's..."

"Life in the SAF?" She laughed bitterly. "I know. You. Jeb. The fleet. We've all been through it. No sense dwelling on it now. But I guess the Confederation is good at one thing."

"What's that?"

"They taught me to never give up until I achieve my goal. But now? *I* get to pick what that is."

Shane watched her pace their landing site with a purposeful stride, her focus astute and unwavering as she sought potential threats to their plans. He'd spent the years since his desertion lamenting his own pains and challenges under Kydell's thumb, but he'd begun to realize he'd been thoroughly pampered, compared to Razick.

He sighed, scuffing his boots against the powdered snow. Of *course* he was. Oathbound of Admiral Kydell? Void necromancer? And already an unhealthy dose of Sparnelli bloodlust.

He'd been well on his way to becoming the ideal SAF officer when he'd first been conscripted. Why wouldn't he be coddled in comparison?

"Speaking of losing focus…" Razick fixed him with a stare. "We're secure, for now. Don't you have a planet you're supposed to be contacting? Or did we just come here so Jeb can play in the snow?"

The biologist was hard at work digging again, a childlike glee spread across his face.

"He *does* look rather happy." Shane watched impassively as Jeb dusted a path between the two most recent holes, panning his scanner quickly between the pair as he excitedly mumbled to himself or, more likely, Urla. "But point taken."

"I was planning to walk the perimetler," she admitted, "but I can see for miles out here, so I'll stick close, instead."

"I'd appreciate the company," he said earnestly, settling into a cross-legged position in the snow. Shrugging off the backpack, he sat it beside him. "Been a long time since I sought out a spirit this powerful. Assuming our assumptions are correct."

"Anything I should watch for?"

Shane closed his eyes, relaxing his mental barriers against the Veil as he settled his mind for the Call. "Don't let me freeze to death?"

Razick's laughter echoed in his ears as he opened himself the Afterlife, the power of the higher dimensions rubbing against his thoughts and caressing his consciousness. The planetary files hadn't shared any insights into the spirit herself, so he concentrated his focus on the island instead, tracing his awareness along the snow dancing in the arctic winds, and the glacial walls of ice slowly carving their way across the frozen, barren wastes.

He felt a disapproval in his mind, pulling his attention closer to the ice. He allowed it to lead him, his thoughts subsequently lingering on Jeb's efforts to catalog the thriving variety of plantlife buried beneath the snow before driving even deeper to seek out a family of white furred creatures with thick, fluffy tails and long snouts of small, sharp teeth curled together for warmth, the occasional clawed paw twitching in their sleep within the ice-walled den.

His guide led onward, through the ice shelf itself and into the ocean below, pausing to watch a myriad of fish darting and weaving within the frigid waters in the eternal dance of prey and predator, both falling victim in turn to the sudden appearance of a large, quick shadow darting through the waves, the varied silvers of its skin camouflaging its true shape within the flickering light. They circled the island together, weaving through the plants and animals eking out a successful existence on the ocean floor before rising to observe a large predatory-looking colony of well-insulated hydrodynamic creatures basking in the rising light on the far side of the island, casually preening oiled color-shifting fur as they stirred in their slowly awakening slumbers.

So. Not barren, then.

He pulled away from the guided tour of the planet to inspect his host, earning another wall of disapproval as she darted away in turn, but even that brief glimpse revealed enough to drive the air from his lungs.

She felt *ancient*.

He'd never made contact with a soul carrying this level of power, not even in his early efforts practicing his Necromancy when he'd accepted and encouraged contact from any soul, learning all he could until Admiral Kydell had discovered and curtailed his side activities.

Shane shuddered involuntarily, and immediately felt the heat of Razick's warming spell fill him in response. He savored the feeling, allowing its warmth to chase away his regrets under Kydell. The way he'd trustingly mistaken the wolf's manipulations for kindness. The things he'd done to feel worthy of it.

That was *his* past. He needed to focus on hers.

"Janikk?" he whispered, softly, leaning into his brief but memorable glimpse of the planetary spirit.

She returned with a speed which revealed she'd never truly left, her own consciousness likely exploring his during his momentary distraction.

Communication with nonverbal spirits always presented its own challenges, but Shane had discovered emotions seemed to work within the Afterlife, a strange adaptation of his Necromancy he'd carefully honed with the help of his empathic partner. Filling his thoughts with friendship, understanding, and a hope of belonging, he projected those thoughts to his guide, his own personal emotions lingering on gratitude for Feels' patient efforts in developing this portion of his repertoire.

He felt a burst of love and relief from the fae in return, radiating along the tether of the Oath eternally binding his soul to theirs.

To Shane's surprise, Janikk seemed to catch both the feelings he'd intended for her, and his private exchange with Feels, despite the emotional Shielding they'd built into their bond. There was a brief drain on his magic as she plucked at the tether and then suddenly his mind was filled with a sense of the entire planet, every living creature upon it available in excruciating detail as if he'd reached out to hold them in his mind for a Hyperjump.

His instinctual training as a Void necromancer kicked in, his subconscious accepting the gift and reaching deeper to grab the details of the planet itself, even as his consciousness rebelled and attempted to extract itself from the mental overload and the drain upon his magic from the exertion.

She rescinded the gift immediately, its sudden absence interrupting Shane's misplaced reactions and allowing him to re-center himself.

A quick inventory of his reserves revealed the significant Imperium drain at the unexpected exercise. He'd have to be careful how he used his magic until he found an opportunity to rest and recharge. Although he *did* seem to have retained a surprising amount of detail from his unconventional geographic survey, including quite a number of underground cavern systems too deep for the *Relentless'* scanners.

Jeb was going to have a field day.

Turning his thoughts inward, he constructed several additional barriers to defend the remainder of his dwindling reserves before returning his attention to Janikk, his thoughts a mix of embarrassment and gratitude.

She seemed to understand, as his mind once again filled with the life of the planet, tentatively at first but faster and more exuberant as his prior distress failed to accompany the sensation. His thoughts wrapped around strange words and patterns as his awareness of the web of life upon Janikk's surface grew within his consciousness, consuming only the barest traces of his magic.

Before long he held the entire collection within his mind again, a vast and interconnected balance of life and death reminiscent of his own familiar connection with the cosmic Void, this one pulsing with vibrant footpads and soft flowers rather than the chaotic dance of the waves of eternity.

"Darrekknee," she whispered, her pride swelling across his thoughts in response to his overwhelming awe. "Darrekknee ivox Tenecknaab."

But he hadn't come for a zoological survey. It was time to ask Janikk her intentions, and whether or not his people would be permitted to count themselves among the planet's residents.

He attempted to word the question in emotions, and felt her pull back from his request, the network of life rescinded and replaced with her all too familiar disapproval. She tugged at his mind and he followed obediently, his awareness arriving at one of the many cave systems he'd discovered with his accidental survey. Reinforcing his thoughts with the limitless expanse of the Void in protection against his claustrophobia within the cramped space, he allowed her to pull them both into the waters filling the cavity within the earth, leading him deeper through the natural passageway.

They emerged within a large partially-flooded cavern, ancient stalactites dripping from the ceiling, the walls carved with intricate patterns and designs, the images half obscured by the uncaring ravages of time. The remains of a large petrified tree claimed the center of the room, once grown underground and now immortalized by the minerals of the cave water. An impressive vine wrapped around the columns and stalactites, to all appearances dead, and yet somehow Shane recognized the massive plant as merely dormant. Waiting.

"Nurekkee Tsekeht."

Janikk's unfamiliar, insistent words lay just out of reach, his thoughts tugging at his awareness as if he'd only just forgotten their meaning.

And then there was an insistent shaking of his shoulders, accompanied by the sound of faraway voices calling his name in distant, muted panic. The cavern and Janikk faded quickly from view, like a disappearing dream.

Opening his eyes, he watched the wave of worried relief pass across Razick's face, towering above him as Jeb desperately administered something from the first aid kid sprawled across his lap. The cold bite of the snow dug into his exposed neck as the late afternoon sun beamed through his shaded visor.

20

RAZICK EXHALED IN RELIEF as Lawrence struggled to sit, and realized she'd been holding her breath since he'd toppled backwards into the snow.

"How long have I been out?"

His voice was faint, a sharp contrast to the usual strength she'd come to expect from him, and he gave no protest as she pushed him back down, this time supported by a mound of tightly packed snow Jeb had quickly rolled into place.

"Hours," Jeb answered for her, repositioning himself to sit across from Lawrence as she fumbled through his pack for the nutritional soup powder. "And then five minutes ago you fell over and stopped breathing. Now that you're conscious again, I'll call the *Relentless*, get them to send someone to check on you."

"No." Lawrence shook his head. "I'll Call Feels, if it comes to that." He closed his eyes, settling deeper into the snow at his back. "I'm not hurt, just... exhausted. And cold. And..."

Razick lunged at his neck, her blood warming spell already at her fingertips as his Shielding faltered. "Oh no you don't. Stay with me."

Lawrence smiled weakly as she replaced his armored epaulets. She pulled the collar tight to help hold in the newly gifted heat before casting her own Shielding spell to replace his.

"You're a good friend, Raz," he muttered quietly, his breath calm and steady. "Always have my back."

"Except for the times I'm trying to kill you," she reminded him, scanning his face for any sign of distress.

The edge of his lips dipped upward slightly instead. The beginning of an uncharacteristic smile. "Even then. You push me. To be better."

"Shhhhh. Rest," she scolded, turning to Jeb. "Keep an eye on him. I'll make soup."

He was clearly delirious.

Catching Jeb's nod, she returned her attention to the necromancer's backpack, partially emptying its contents until she located a trio of lightweight camp bowls and several packets of fortified soup powder. Gathering a large helping of the snow around them with her Telekinesis, she mixed in the broth mix before heating the whole slurry with Pyromancy. She poured herself into the mundanity of the work in an effort to calm her racing thoughts, watching the soup bubble boil in midair before depositing it neatly into each bowl.

The largest portion she coaxed into Lawrence's hands, gently tilting to bowl to guide the life-giving liquid to his lips. "You're dehydrated. This will help."

He drank slowly, accepting her supervision without protest as he emptied the bowl.

Finally appeased, she shifted to sit cross-legged beside him, drawing her own bowl to her hands with a faint twist of her finger. "How do you feel?"

"Better." He cracked one eye, watching her drink as he rested against Jeb's manufactured snowbank. "Thank you."

The warm soup was a welcome distraction from the biting cold, the bland flavorings of the nutrient-packed powdered mix somehow a comfort despite the accompanying memories of past missions best forgotten. It was different, this time. Protecting Lawrence and Jeb. Knowing it was *her* choice. That she was helping to *build* something, rather than tearing down the accomplishments of others.

She placed her empty bowl in Jeb's waiting hand, and watched as her brother rinsed them thoroughly in the snow before wiping them out and packing them away.

She narrowed her eyes. Clearly, this wasn't Jeb's first mission.

Admiral Kydell wouldn't have risked assigning him to a hydroponics post in the fleet. Any chance encounter with her brother could have jeopardized Kydell's psychomorphic reconditioning, and the admiral wasn't the sort to take risks when he could easily eliminate them.

She'd hoped he'd been assigned to the labs instead. The letters she'd received after his conscription had implied as much. Urla's recognition of his lab work when they'd first set foot in her bay on the *Inevitable* had confirmed it, and she'd set the matter to rest.

Until Janikk.

She'd expected to be the only one with field experience, but observing her innocent baby brother approaching each moment and challenge on the planet with an expertly measured calm rivaling even the best surveying teams she'd escorted gave her pause. The way he'd packed Lawrence's bag. How he instinctively knew where her role ended and his began. The calm confidence in each of his interactions since they'd landed, a far cry from Lawrence's own determined inexperience.

But that meant he'd been reassigned to the survey teams. That meant he'd been one of the specialists sent across the Confederation's holdings, analyzing everything from potential sites for new colonies and military outposts, to recovery plans on recently conquered and often damaged planets, to customizing biological attack plans and forcing holdout civilizations into desperate surrender agreements to save what little population they could from whatever plague the SAF had unleashed.

From his continued sunny disposition, she hoped he'd avoided any involvement in the darkest uses of his Agrokinesis, and wondered what he'd seen in his own ten years of service to Kydell. How many of his missions had been the standard Confederation punishment for stepping out of line?

And how many had he *volunteered* for, in the futile hope of finding her?

She forced the thought aside. He was here – safe – with her now, and for the moment, that was all that mattered. She could protect him while they were on Janikk. And she could chew him out once they'd completed their mission, too, because he was *here*.

He'd adapted. Become a survivor. Just like she had.

And for the moment, Lawrence needed her more.

"You're developing bad habits," she scolded him. "Second mission in a row you've decided to take a nap while I do the heavy lifting."

"But you're so good at it," he said quietly, cracking one eye to watch her. "And breathing doesn't hurt this time, so I'm improving."

"Must have been some talk."

"She triggered my Hyperjump protocols." He scowled. "Almost tried to relocate the entire planet."

Razick's brows furrowed. "Why would she do that?" Nothing in the reports indicated an issue with the present orbit. According to Jeb, the planetary ecosystem had adapted perfectly.

"Don't think it was intentional. Void necromancers aren't exactly a staple in landing parties." Lawrence closed his eyes again, his breath shallowing. "Think she was trying to show me something. Seemed just as distressed as I was. Damn Confederation conditioning."

He sighed, cracking one eye at her. "I have an amateur geological survey in my head now, though, if Jeb can find a way to get it out."

"That sounds more like a puzzle for your son." Jeb scratched at the edge of his helmet, tugging on his hair. "I'll leave a message for *Relentless*, see if they have suggestions. And I can tug at the memory with Telekinesis." He held up his hand as Razick opened her mouth to protest. "After he gets some rest. I know. I know."

"Unfortunately, there are some things we *can't* wait for," Razick apologized, standing to resume her watch on the isolated island. "What does Janikk want? What did she say?"

"She says we shouldn't be here." He paused. "At least, that's what I gathered from what she showed me. I didn't understand the words."

"We already knew she didn't want us. Only one survivor from three prior expeditions – that we *know* about – makes that fairly obvious." She adjusted her visor, zooming in on a particularly bright flash of light, zooming out again as she confirmed the sighting as a particularly vigorous wave.

"No." Lawrence shook his head. "We shouldn't be *here*. On this *island*. We're in the wrong place. She wants us somewhere else."

Jeb was already pulling up the holographic globe. "Where?"

"According to the map in my head…" The necromancer pointed northeast. "Underwater cave system. That way." He grimaced. "That's the nearest pole, isn't it?"

"That's the nearest pole," Jeb confirmed.

Razick balled her fists. "I don't like this. If it's anything like the last missions, she's trying to kill us."

She wasn't about to walk her people into a trap she already knew was waiting for them.

"Didn't seem that way to me." Lawrence's conviction didn't carry the usual weight, his voice still weak from exertion. "Powerful? Yes. And *ancient*. Wouldn't be surprised if she predates the Enlightenment, and space travel. But when she triggered my Hyperjump protocols… She didn't feel malicious. She felt… apologetic. Worried. And she… She could have kept pushing, but she didn't. She gave me space to figure it out. To find a way to safely work through it, so she could…"

Lawrence's eyes closed as he drifted off.

Jeb reached to wake him but Razick grabbed his arm.

"Let him be. He'll be okay now. Just needs to sleep it off." She frowned into the setting sun, eying the frozen tundra to the west again. "We'll make our plans for the evening. Sort out tomorrow, tomorrow. I don't want to go where she's pointing, not until we have no choice, but I think it's clear we're not getting any more answers here."

"Doesn't want us here," Lawrence murmured in his sleep.

"Seems Janikk's been clear on that point, too," Jeb agreed, adjusting the weight of his backpack against his shoulders.

"But we'll save that worry for daylight," Razick finished, crouching beside Lawrence to check his pulse and gift him another warming spell against the encroaching cold. "It's getting dark. We need to make camp."

She stood again to retrieve Lawrence's pack, but Jeb grabbed her arm. "Raz, no!"

Lawrence bolted upright at the same moment, eyes wide as he grabbed at their legs. "*She doesn't want us here.*"

A rush of fur and sharp teeth emerged from the ice and snow between her and the errant backpack, accompanied by a multitude of growls rapidly growing in volume. An offensive burst of Shielding sent them scattering, but soon they were back, snarling and snapping at Razick's heels and draining her own Shielding.

She Shielded again, attempting to hold them off with her Telekinesis as she remembered Lawrence's insistence they avoid harming any of Janikk's inhabitants, but the creatures slipped and twisted easily from her grasp. "There's too many!"

And then the world twisted around them, the ground shifting away beneath their feet. Razick caught herself with her Telekinesis, but wasn't able to do the same for her companions. Lawrence exhaled sharply as he landed roughly on the ground, while Jeb let out a few choice expletives of his own as he stumbled indignantly to his hands and knees.

The ice and snow was replaced with a thick forest, the biting frozen wind now a chill but playful breeze against the leaves and vegetation. The beat of large wings sounded briefly from somewhere higher in the canopy.

"That's... all I have left." Lawrence's voice was a whisper as he collapsed against a tree trunk.

"What happened?" Razick asked, dialing up the night vision settings on her visor.

"She didn't want us there," the necromancer muttered, eyes closed.

"I think he's asleep again," Jeb observed, brushing himself off as he rose to his feet and tested his joints, but otherwise seemingly unconcerned by their recent brush with teeth and death.

She glared. "You stopped me. How did you know?"

"I didn't." Jeb caressed his wristwatch. "Urla warned me. She felt them coming." He frowned, turning his attention to Lawrence. "But how did *he* know?"

Scanning the trees, Razick spotted several potential sites for their overnight camp. "He dropped his Shielding. I cast my own, to keep him safe, but I don't know Necromancy. He must have dropped his mental filters, too."

"Which means Janikk warned him." Jeb voiced the same conclusion she'd already reached. "She's not trying to kill us. She's trying to *herd* us."

"Long as she lets us get some sleep before we do anything else." Narrowing her focus onto the most promising target – a healthy-looking tree with thick, sturdy branches – she climbed nimbly into the canopy, with assistance from her Telekinesis.

She directed her Anemancy to carry her words to Jeb. "We're in no shape for more travel tonight. Will be trickier without the tents, but your Agrokinesis should suffice."

"We've a bigger problem," Jeb admitted. "Lawrence had all the food."

She landed deftly beside him, arms on her hips. "You mean to tell me you put all the food in the same pack?"

Perhaps he'd less field experience than she'd assumed.

"Yeah," he said sheepishly, removing his helmet to scratch at his head.

"Good thing I didn't." She tossed him a nutrition bar from her jacket pocket, pointing to the tree she'd just vacated. "This one. You'll see my bag hanging on a branch. Get up there, see what you can do to make a sturdy perch while I get our sleepy friend."

By the time she arrived, Lawrence floating delicately beside her, Jeb had already used his magic to twist a tightly woven floor of vines between their tree and the next, the edges curving upward, reminiscent of a person-sized nest.

"I like what you've done with the place."

He shrugged sheepishly. "Urla's idea. She's got a talent for these things."

"Then give her my thanks instead," she told him, gently propping the still-sleeping Lawrence against the side. "I'll take first watch."

Jeb shook his head, settling into a small seat he'd apparently crafted within their hideout. "No, I've got it. I've a feeling he'll need you when he wakes up, and you'll need all the sleep you can get. Urla will help me stay awake."

Razick nodded, her own exhaustion catching up to her as she settled into the nest. She wasn't certain where Lawrence had brought them, but the chill in the air hinted at a cold night ahead. Pulling him close against her chest, she wrapped herself around him as she adjusted herself to a more comfortable position, refreshing her warming spell on them both in the process. He'd complain tomorrow, but without the camp gear, they'd need the warmth for the evening.

And she needed the company. Anything to fight off the memories of her past.

The stars shone above, a brilliant display against the otherwise unblemished darkness. She closed her eyes, focusing on the trusting warmth of the fearsome necromancer beside her, and attempted to shut out the reminders of her countless missions spent camped beneath the stars, a weapon of the Confederation's destructive will.

JEB POKED AT HIS uniform's controls, selecting one of the camouflage presets more adapted to their new environment. His knees still felt stiff from the unexpected fall at their arrival, but he'd retired from field work years ago to instead build a career as a Freehold biology teacher. As far as he was concerned, his joints were holding up better than he'd any right to expect.

<What'll he do when he wakes up?> Urla giggled across their telepathic link.

<I don't know,> Jeb admitted, watching his sister cuddle into Lawrence for the evening. <Should I feel guilty for wanting to find out?>

He carefully peeled the nutrition bar free from its protective wrapper, slipping the material into his pocket as he ate. Razick had chosen one of the tallest trees in their section of the forest, allowing for a mostly unimpeded view of Janikk's skyline, the night stars bright against the natural darkness. If he squinted he could also make out the merest waning sliver of each of Janikk's twin moons, visible tonight only with the help of the light-enhancing magic of his helmet visor.

Twin new moons tomorrow. Hopefully that meant the nightlife would be less likely to interrupt their sleep, but given the naturally untamed nature of the planet, he doubted they'd be so lucky.

<It's beautiful out tonight.> Urla's voice shone with wonder, the brightness of her tone rivaled only by the stars themselves, and Jeb felt a swell of love for the remarkable woman currently residing in his watch. <You'd think, having had access to a viewport in an actual spacecraft, I'd grow tired of watching the stars. But there's something magic about seeing them planetside, surrounded by so much life.>

<They sparkle, planetside. From the refraction of the atmosphere.> Jeb tensed as the shadow of a large, winged creature flitted past, blocking out a section of the stars. It continued on its path without turning their direction and he allowed himself to relax, although not before checking the pistol at his waist. Just in case.

<It's not just that...> The Afterlife Intelligence's voice grew thoughtful. <They're... warmer here? The Void is so cold. Sterile. The only life up there is what we bring with us. But down here... I could *live* down here.>

<Assuming Janikk lets us.> Jeb carefully wiped his fingers on his trousers as he chewed the last of the nutrient bar Razick had gifted him.

<Grand Navarch knows what he's doing.> There was a warmth to her voice, and for a moment Jeb felt a pang of jealousy. It was gone the next instant. <Between the two of you, I'm sure you'll sort it out. You always find your answer.>

<You're here, too,> Jeb reminded her.

<Yeah...>

He caught her hesitation and rubbed his watch in reassurance. <You've been a *huge* help so far. And good company. I'm grateful to have you with us. With *me*.>

They shifted into a comfortable silence, allowing Jeb to turn his attention to the local plantlife.

Wherever they were, Lawrence had picked a beautiful spot, particularly for an enthusiastic biologist such as himself. While the interlacing colonies of vegetation thriving beneath the ice on the island had been an impressive find for future ecological study, the biodiversity of the forest around them now would sustain countless papers just to *catalog*.

He pulled his jacket tighter to ward against the cold before grabbing his tablet, bringing up their current information on Janikk with the intention of adding these observations to their files.

<I was just going to suggest that!> The warmth in Urla's voice proved an equally effective defense against the frigid night air. <We don't know how long the Grand Navarch needs to sleep. We need to pinpoint our location, with what we know so far.>

Jeb felt his cheeks flush. <I... honestly hadn't considered that. It's a good idea. What've you got so far?>

<Hyperjumping is practically instantaneous, and night fell quickly after our arrival, so we're most likely not far from the island where we started. Certainly the same hemisphere. Given the positioning of the moons, the fact the sun sets in the west, and the tilt of the planetary axis, I'd say he jumped us northeast. Which tracks with Janikk's insistence we travel that direction.>

Jeb stroked the vines of the living nest he and Urla had constructed together. <Research says our spells should feel stronger if we're near a pole. But I didn't feel that when we were casting.>

<No, I don't think he jumped us that far. But I wouldn't be surprised if we're on a straight line in that direction.> She laughed lightly. <He was *tired*. What happens if a Void necromancer falls asleep during a jump? Maybe we just found out.>

Jeb shook his head with a chuckle. <You can ask when he wakes up, if you want. Personally, I'd like to keep living.>

She grew silent at that, and Jeb kicked himself mentally. *She's an AI, numbskull. You can't go making jokes about dying.*

<Urla, I'm sorry, I didn't mean–>

<Jeb. I know. I forgive you.> The sorrow in her voice stood in stark contrast to her happiness mere moments before. <You didn't mean it that way. Can we talk about something else? Please?>

He frowned. <Anything you want.>

<What were you doing with your tablet, before I interrupted?>

<I was just going to start cataloging the different plants.> He tugged at his hair, shaking his head. <Your idea was more practical.>

Her laughter at his admission broke the awkward tension, and Jeb relaxed.

<Let's catalog, then. I'll help.>

The next several hours passed quickly as they compared notes about the immediate environment. They marveled together at the towering trees they hung between, observing how they stretched high above the rest of the forest and wondering at why the remainder of the local tree species hadn't adapted to attempt to match their height. The many vines entwined into their nest provided an engaging study as they compared the differences between them, most notably the methods used by each to claim the tree limbs for their own support structure. Jeb's admission of gratitude at Razick's selection of the lower branches directly above the forest canopy, rather than expecting him to climb the tree's full impressive height, elicited another round of laughter from the Hydroponics AI within his watch.

The pair of flirting biologists had just turned their attention to the moss and lichen varieties growing upon the bark of their temporary home when a series of muffled curses erupted from the far side of the nest. Jeb turned to witness a rather disgruntled Lawrence attempting to disentangle himself from within the overprotective embrace of a soundly sleeping battle mage.

Urla snickered. <Now we find out.>

"Sleep well?" Jeb asked innocently.

Shane paused his efforts long enough to direct a glare in Jeb's direction, before calming and closing his eyes.

<I think the vines are starting to wilt,> Urla observed with a giggle.

Jeb couldn't hold back any longer, bursting into laughter.

And then suddenly Lawrence's shadow was towering before him, blocking out the stars. He swallowed, hard. "Um... Hi?"

"Glad to see you're enjoying yourself." The necromancer's orange eyes flickered with menace as he scowled from above.

"Sorry." Jeb brushed at his face. "It's just... watching you like that..." He blinked in realization. "Wait. Did you just use the Hyperjump spell to–"

"She's got a strong grip!" Lawrence protested. "And I wasn't sure what she'd do if I woke her up. Training tends to hardwire your reactions. Mine almost relocated the planet, and *she's* a *battle mage*. Already killed me once, and I promised Feels I'd come back intact."

<He has a point.>

At Jeb's apology, Lawrence settled next to the biologist, leaning his back against the side webbing. "Where are we?"

"Was hoping you'd know," Jeb admitted, watching Lawrence wince. "Urla very cleverly predicted you jumped us northeast, but we don't seem to be near the pole Janikk wanted us to visit, so..."

"I... don't remember what I was trying to do," Lawrence said at last, tilting his head back to stare at the night sky. "But that sounds right. And Janikk seems to agree with your assessment."

"She's here?" Jeb straightened in his seat.

Lawrence rubbed his temples, his eyes staring blankly across the treeline. "It's hard to explain. She's everywhere. But also not? Never made contact with anyone quite like her." He turned to catch Jeb's eyes with his own. "You were right, in a way. Janikk *is* the planet... But also separate." He shook his head. "I don't know. Doesn't make sense to me either."

"Right now, I just want to know if she'll let us survive the night." Jeb dialed up the sensitivity of the visor, but aside from an assortment of small, rapidly moving shadows he *hoped* were as distant as the visor suggested, there was no sign of an encroaching threat.

Yet.

"Remember. Aside from my coworker, none of the expeditions survived the first night. And we don't have the SAF's resources to resurrect anyone."

"I think we're okay for now," Lawrence said slowly, massaging the back of his neck. "She's not happy we're here instead of where she wanted us to go. But she seems to understand I was trying to get us there. We have a reprieve. For now."

<How long?> Urla asked, her tone thoughtful. <She was impatiently insistent until we jumped here. Seems rather strange she'd just... *stop.*>

Jeb opened his mouth to relay the question, but Lawrence was already answering, as if the same thought had already occurred to him. "Can't make any guarantees if we're not there by tomorrow night, though. I think we have until then. Whatever she wants us for, it happens in the evening."

"How are you feeling?" Jeb settled back into his perch, frowning. "You gave us quite a scare when you toppled backward like that."

"Spent a lot of magic, all at once, with no prep. Wears out a person. I'm fine." The necromancer leaned forward. "Not full strength. But close enough. Even ran the medical diagnostic spell Feels taught me. Came up clean. Just exhaustion."

<Urla? Mind if I drop the Telepathy for a bit?> Jeb bit his lip. He hated asking time away from her, but he'd been meaning to have a private conversation with Lawrence and now seemed the perfect time. <Just a few minutes?>

<Take your time. I've been hoping to catch up with Tarvick anyway. I'll hop to the *Relentless*. Link me if you need me.>

Jeb thought he caught a hint of relief in her voice but forced himself to brush it aside. Instead he caressed his watch in gratitude before dropping the connection, turning to Lawrence with an embarrassed smile. "There's... something I've been meaning to ask you. It's... personal."

The necromancer eyed him warily. "Personal for me or personal for you?"

"Both, really... It's about relationships."

"I see." There was a pause as Lawrence considered. "Fine. Ask away. But if you start asking pointed questions about my personal relationship–"

"Like whether making love is better on the mortal plane or in the Afterlife?" Jeb teased.

"–I'll send you past the Veil to find out personally," the necromancer finished with a snarl.

"Razick would kill you."

Shane fixed him with an impassive stare. "Wouldn't be the first time I recovered from that."

Jeb blinked. He couldn't argue that. "No. No. Nothing like that. It's just..." Running his fingers through his hair, Jeb shifted to stare at his own feet. "I want to give her everything she needs from me. Wondered if you had any suggestions."

The seconds ticked past until Lawrence finally spoke, his words slow and measured. "Relationships are give and take. Ideally you give more than you take, but both are important. Everyone needs to feel needed. Wanted, even."

He paused, returning his attention to the delicate panorama of the night sky. "And then there's time. Time is the more important thing to give, and to take. You want to give your time, and take their time. This is difficult for me, because I want to hoard all Feels' time to myself, so instead I overcompensate by giving them too little of my own time. I'm... working on it." He turned back to Jeb. "I suspect you have the opposite problem."

"I want to take her time, too!" Jeb protested. "I want to spend every waking moment with her until–"

"That's what I mean," Lawrence interrupted. "It's important to have space, too. You're a biologist. You know this."

Jeb exhaled at the realization he might be overwhelming Urla. "All good points," he muttered, shaking his head. "You don't mince words. I'll keep them in mind. Thank you."

"Of course." Standing again, Lawrence turned to Jeb with a pointed look. "Invite her back. I've got my magic again. I can pull her to the mortal plane, if she likes."

"You just said to give her some space!"

Lawrence held his gaze, blinking slowly. "*You*, not me. *You* are going to bed in a moment." His quick glare silenced the protests already forming on Jeb's lips. "She and I have some things to talk about."

22

SHANE WATCHED JEB CLOSE his eyes to cast his spell, the biologist's relationship questions still echoing in his thoughts.

No time like the present to make good on a promise.

Opening his mind to the Void, he focused his thoughts on the fae medic who so thoroughly possessed his soul, bolstering his mental defenses against the insistent planet-bound Janikk in the process.

"Feels... are you busy?"

<<Little bit.>> The empath's words were distracted but warm. <<What do you need, Grim? Is this an emergency?>>

"No." Shane tried to keep the disappointment from his voice, even knowing Feels would discover it anyway, courtesy of their perpetual Insight spell into his soul. "My turn for watch soon. Was wondering if you wanted to spend it together."

<<Oh. *Oh.*>> A deep love filled Shane's mind, projected along the Oath tether. <<Let me finish up here first. Untangling

the last of Alanis' psychomorphic conditioning, and you know what she's like. If I stop now, *neither* of us will hear the end of it.>>

"You're making good progress." Shane knew his pride would be unmistakable.

<<I've had plenty of time on my hands,>> Feels pouted instead. <<Making the best of it.>>

"I'm sorry. I'm trying." Shane frowned, focusing his attention on all the apology he could muster. "Who's next? Javon?"

<<She asked to go last. She's as stubborn as you are.>> Feels gave a bitter laugh. <<Fleet Captain Haveid.>>

"You'll be closer to me, then." Shane discovered that despite the inconsequential meaning of distance when traveling the Afterlife, he liked this thought.

<<Not if you keep talking my ear off I won't!>> Feels snapped, but there was warmth in their voice. <<Let me finish, before Alanis grows impatient with the both of us.>>

Shane massaged his temples at the memory of the last time he'd crossed the opinionated Navigations AI. "Agreed. I'll be here. Always."

The empath sent a flash of gratitude wrapped in longing as Shane ended the Call to find Jeb watching him expectantly, Urla's soul clearly present within his watch. A mere thought later, a katanoj with blue-green fur stood before them, her camouflaged uniform matching the green eyes shyly watching Jeb from behind the visor of her helmet.

The biologist scratched his head. "I could have sworn you were red this morning?"

She laughed. "I'm dead, Jeb. I can be whoever I want to be."

"Only the mortal plane relies on genetics." Shane shrugged at Jeb's questioning glance, leaning back against the woven vines behind him. "Afterlife is about your essence. Your soul. How you see yourself. It can change, over time."

"So... What would *you* look like, then?" Jeb bit his lip, brows furrowed. "Like this? Like you used to be? Or something else entirely?"

"*This* is who I am now. Won't say I don't have anything left of the old me. I *know* I do..." Shane felt his expression darken as he turned away, digging his nails into his palms as he forced himself to remain calm. To deny his former self, and all the accompanying violence that lurked just below the surface in his darker moments. "But I *like* being Shane. Would take a lot to pull me away from him."

Not as much as he wanted. But he was *trying*.

"Like what?"

Jake.

Ever since Loxira, everything Shane did came back to Jake. His desertion, his defense of Baden, his presence on Janikk, all revolved around Jake, and the better future Shane intended to leave behind for his adopted son.

But the fewer who knew that, the better. Jake had already learned the power behind that fact, and used it with impunity to manipulate Shane into situations and decisions he'd attempted to avoid. Feels recognized it, although they'd never use their power over him to harm him.

No one else could know. Not even the Kanes.

Instead, Shane fixed Jeb with a stare. "If I die and come back as anyone other than me? *Run*. And don't look back. Assuming you're not who I'm after, you might even survive." He shook his head, narrowing his eyes at the awkward smiles of his companions. "No, that's not a joke. I carried enough guilt on my shoulders to paralyze *both* of Kydell's fleets, remember? *Run*."

He could never afford to forget the monster he was. Someday, perhaps, he'd be able to undo the worst of his past.

Unlikely. But possible.

He'd spend the rest of his existence trying.

It was Jeb who broke the silence. "I shouldn't have pressed. I'm sorry." He frowned. "I know you wanted me to hit the sack... But would it be possible to eat something first? All my food was in the pack we left behind."

The necromancer reached into one of the countless pockets of his uniform jacket and pulled out one of the carefully wrapped packages of homemade jerky. "Will this do?"

Urla's eyes lit up at the treat. "May I?"

"Sure. Why not?" Shane shrugged. Food was a more comfortable topic. "Worst case, I'll jump more provisions down from the ship. Or ask Janikk what's safe to eat."

He paused to bolster his mental filters against the Afterlife again. The planetary spirit had become particularly insistent since he'd pulled out the jerky, but now wasn't the time.

They munched in silence, Urla mumbling in enjoyment, Jeb nodding his agreement. It was a little tough. A little bland. A little too salty. But not too bad, considering.

Shane decided he'd have to teach Razick the recipe.

Jeb grimaced. "Any water to go with it? Didn't bring that, either."

"Fruit would work, too," Urla offered as Shane shook his head, his own throat dry from the jerky. "If Janikk has a suggestion?"

"That one." Shane pointed to the branch directly above their heads and felt the pressure of Janikk's frustration dissolve into an almost nervous anticipation. He scowled. "She's been insisting I try it."

<<Zegae ivojox yukkan. Munokkee. Yukkanee.>>

Urla traced a light claw across the branch, her Agrokinesis rewarded with a sudden burst of intricate pastel flowers in a variety of purples, pinks, and blues. They erupted in an aromatic cascade of delicate white sparks, followed by a cloud of pollen. A round sphere of blue and green grew from the branch where each flower had been, ripening to a rich, gold-flecked purple.

She plucked one, holding it out to Jeb, the magic of the moment still dancing in her eyes.

Jeb eyed the fruit, suddenly wary. "Maybe Lawrence should take the first bite? Janikk likes you. And you said she wanted *you* to eat it."

"I see how it is," Shane growled, readily accepting the fruit. The cool, smooth skin gave slightly beneath his fingers, releasing a smell reminiscent of his childhood and the fresh, clean damp after a sudden spring shower.

Janikk leaned against his consciousness from behind the Veil, watching intently, her attention mirrored by both of his companions.

He took a bite.

All thoughts fled from his mind at the explosion of juice and flavor once his teeth punctuated the strange fruit, his eyes closing as he leaned his head back to savor the fleshy sweetness against his tongue. He faintly registered Janikk's smugness as she faded from his thoughts, seemingly content now to leave him to his own devices as he devoured the heavenly orb in his hand, sucking the last of the juices from the pit and his fingers before reaching for another.

"Should eat a second," he offered, his thoughts filled with a sudden affection for the planet and its inhabitants. "Just to be certain."

Visibly relaxing at Shane's pronouncement, the biologist plucked several more to pass around.

"I've never eaten anything like this." Wiping at the juice dribbling down his chin, Jeb grinned up at Urla. "Wonder what we should call it?"

"Tsijturikk." The word felt foreign yet familiar on Shane's tongue.

Jeb blinked. "You just making up words now?"

"That's what it's called."

"Janikk tell you that?" Urla's feline eyes reflected back concern in the darkness.

Shane bit his lip, searching his thoughts. "No. I just *know*."

Where *had* that name come from? He felt the presence of the plants around them, an echo of the experience Janikk had shared the day before on the island, but she herself was nowhere to be found.

The biologists nervously inspected the remains of their own fruits before dropping them, half eaten, to the forest floor below. "Perhaps this wasn't such a good idea," Jeb sighed, his words filled with regret.

"Jeb, go to bed," Shane ordered. He took another bite, finishing off his second helping at a slow and purposeful pace, savoring every last drop as Urla and Jeb shifted cautiously within their camp.

"Not sure that's a good idea, Lawrence," Jeb began, tugging at his hair before catching himself and attempting to rub his juice-stained hands clean against his uniform trousers instead. "Someone needs to keep an eye on you."

"I have Urla." Shane looked up at the apprehensive katanoj. "And Feels agreed to stop by later. They'll give me a full checkup, whether I want it or not."

Jeb appeared unconvinced. "If you murder me in my sleep because of some homicidal planet, I'll come back and haunt you."

Shane shrugged. "Wouldn't be the first. Wouldn't be the last. You'll be fine. Go." He smirked. "If you're worried, Razick can keep you safe. She likes to cuddle."

Jeb snorted. "If you let her get away with it, she's only going to do it again."

"Sleep. *Now.*"

That wasn't something he wanted to think about right now.

As the biology teacher reluctantly made his way to the other side of their elevated camp, Shane turned his attention to Urla. "Thank you for agreeing to talk with me."

She slid to the floor, watching Shane as he claimed Jeb's former perch. "You're the boss."

"I don't have to be. That's your choice."

Leaning against the woven side of the makeshift next, Urla studied him intently. "You've been good to us so far, Sir. And to me. Navarch Javon trusts you, and so does Jeb. If this is who you really are now, and who you intend to remain, then I'm content to follow you."

She threw up her hands as she laughed. "Not like I have anywhere else to go! Turncoat Armada's the closest thing I have to Family. But I don't want to talk about that. Is there something I can help you with?"

Shane noted her phrasing, and wondered how much she'd recognized of his past self, but shook his head. "As a matter of fact..." He waved his arm to indicate the forest around them. "I wanted to ask your opinion on what we'll face tomorrow."

"You've been reading my file, too." Urla's face broke into a grin, then faltered. "I didn't want to say anything to Jeb, but... I think we're in for some trouble, come morning."

23

"Tell me what you think."

The Grand Navarch's interest in her opinion sent a shiver of excitement down Urla's spine. *This* was what respect felt like. She hadn't felt that since... Since the last time she'd spoken with him, in his prior incarnation, if he truly was who she believed him to be.

Not that Jeb didn't respect her, of course. But he was *Jeb*. Her sweet, thoughtful, over-attentive Jeb, who always put her first before everything even when she protested otherwise, because that's who he was. He didn't know how to *be* anyone else, and she adored him for it.

But the Grand Navarch had an entire *fleet* of options, countless experts at his fingertips, and here he was asking for *her* thoughts. She swelled with pride, and knew Jeb would do the same when she told him about it later.

If she decided to tell him. He'd be hurt that she hadn't voiced her concerns to him first, but she hadn't wanted to worry him about something he couldn't solve anyway.

"You may want to put your helmet on. If you can extract it." She waved a claw toward the discarded headgear, now firmly wrapped in Razick's grip. Urla spared a longing glance at Jeb, curled up with his back to his sister, before turning back to the necromancer. "Most of the signs are rather subtle. Tough to see in the dark."

The Grand Navarch raised an eyebrow at his helmet's current predicament before turning to Urla, orange eyes flickering in the dim light of the stars. "Unnecessary. Courtesy of Feels, I have the eyes of a cat."

"Must be nice, having someone who looks out for you like that." She smiled wistfully into the night, her tail curling slowly behind her. "With the skills to put that much work into a new body, even. Give you a whole new life."

"Your genetics are in your file," he said levelly, sending hope beating in her chest where her heart once resided. "We don't have the resources to *do* anything with it yet, but that's my next priority. Everyone deserves a chance at the existence of their choosing." He caught her eyes in his. "Something to think about."

She'd have held her breath, if she still had any. The Sparnell Armed Forces made their own decisions on the career paths of those within its influence, and Admiral Kydell had taken that authority to the extreme. Becoming an Afterlife Intelligence hadn't been on her career plan, but the fleet had encountered a shortage and she'd been the least influential candidate who'd met all the requirements.

The offer to live – and die – on her own terms definitely held an appeal.

And she *knew* he meant it. She hadn't meant to eavesdrop on his conversation with his healer, but the name "Grim" had revived old memories. If he was the *same* Grim…

Not even Kydell's favorites had been able to change the wolf's mind. But, Nature bless him, Grim had *tried*.

"Thank you, Sir." Her ears twitched at the promise of a second chance at living. "Then let's succeed at our current mission. Our camp tonight? From what I've seen, we shouldn't be alone here."

Urla traced one claw along the bark of the nearest tree, pointing out a series of deep scratches into its trunk and branches. "See how the ages of the marks vary? This set here is deep, but old. The tree has slowly been healing over it. But then right on top are fresher marks, maybe as recent as yesterday. And then here…" She traced the frayed edges of several smaller branches. "I'm guessing either a predatory bird, or a rather large rodent, sharpened its beak or teeth here. Given the haphazard arrangement of claw marks surrounding it, my credits are on the bird."

"They're all over," the Grand Navarch observed, tapping his finger against similar marks higher up. "Whatever made these, there's either a lot of them, or they're very active."

"Or both," Urla agreed, pointing over the side of their constructed nest. "Before Jeb climbed up, I noted a lot of droppings on the ground, particularly around the taller trees. There's more on the leaves of the canopy below us. And..." She jerked her head upward, toward a dense shadow in the trees above them. "I don't think we're the only ones with a nest."

"We're not alone."

"That's just it, though. We *are*. All signs say we should have company, but we don't." She watched him expectantly. "Janikk's doing?"

His expression darkened. "I don't know. She left when we ate the fruit. I've never been this nervous about *not* being pestered by a spirit."

"Sir..." She exhaled slowly as she gathered her words, catching his eyes with her own as she flexed her fingers. "I'm worried about you – about *all* of us – after eating that fruit. You had a lot more than the rest of us. Are you sure you're okay?"

"No," he said, honestly. "Physically, I'm fine. I checked. But..." He looked away. "I feel... *different*. In my mind. It's not... I'm still *me*. It's just..." He ran his fingers lightly along a branch. "Since I learned Necromancy, I've always had to ward myself against the Void. People and places from beyond the Veil tend to slip into my awareness if I don't. But now... I have to build new, stronger walls. To keep the *trees* out."

Urla took a quick inventory of her own perceptions, briefly relaxing her control on her Agrokinesis and Zokinesis to gage her own abilities. All the calculations warned of stronger effects planetside, particularly on a planet like Janikk, so...

They both jumped as the branch above suddenly flowered and fruited a second time.

"Sorry," she said sheepishly. "Misjudged. My Nature Magic is even stronger than Jeb and I predicted. And what you're describing... Are you sure *you* don't know Agrokinesis?"

The Grand Navarch shook his head, scowling. "If I relax my filters, all I can say is there's a lot of trees, and they're content. Also that nest you found belongs to something called a... gromdornis? Gromdornox? I don't know what they are, but it feels important that they're not home right now."

"I don't know of *any* kind of Nature Magic that just... names things." Urla frowned, whiskers twitching as she watched Jeb's chest rise and fall in his sleep. "I don't know what's going on, but it definitely sounds Nature Magic related. I could ask Tarvick. Or Jeb, once he wakes up."

"Speaking of..." The Grand Navarch's tone took on a sharper edge. "When are you going to tell him?"

"That's not your concern." She crossed her arms over her chest, scowling. "Nor is it your business."

"He'll find out eventually," the necromancer warned, his voice soft. "He'd rather learn it from you."

"But you'll tell him if I don't?" she spat.

"No." The Grand Navarch looked down, shaking his head, before returning his gaze to her face. "That's your business. Not mine. But he deserves all the facts, if you want this to work."

"I..." Her shoulders slumped. "I don't know what I want."

The necromancer's voice was kinder than the truth in his words. "I think you do. I think you're afraid of what that might mean."

"He's such a sweet guy. I don't want to hurt him. I want him to be happy."

The Grand Navarch raised an eyebrow. "He'd want you to be happy. Don't assume the two are mutually exclusive."

"I don't know if I remember how." She attempted to bite back the bitter laugh rising in her throat. "When'd you turn into my therapist?"

"When I took responsibility for your well-being." There was no sign of hurt or recrimination in his voice. "I know you're happy. And worried. I want you to know I'm here for you, whatever you decide."

She knew she should be appreciative but instead she lashed out, her frustrations dripping from every word. "You dare tell me how I feel?"

"I'm married to an empath. I've picked up a few things." The necromancer snorted. "It's *your* Afterlife. I won't presume to tell you what to do. I'm not Kydell. Your choices are yours." He offered her a sad smile, his eyes gleaming in the darkness. "You have my word, I won't mention it again unless you bring it up, or I need your expertise. Just, promise me you'll think about it."

"I'm sorry, Sir." She bowed her head in apology. "I know you're trying to help. Relationships are *hard*."

His face took on a faraway look, one hand clutching at his chest as if reaching for something within his jacket. "No arguments from me."

He shifted his weight, biting his lip, an uncharacteristically boyish smile teasing at his lips. "Are you ready to return to the Afterlife? Don't tell the others, but... I asked Feels on a date tonight, and they've just arrived."

She nodded, once. "Enjoy your evening. Both of you."

As the mortal plane faded into a memory, Urla found herself wondering if, several decades from now, she and Jeb would have a chance at that same giddy excitement when spending time together.

The Grand Navarch was right. She needed to tell Jeb.

But when?

24

SHANE FELT A WEIGHT lift from his shoulders as the familiar presence of his beloved settled into the locket against his chest, the warmth of their magic exploring his body as they checked for injury.

"I've been keeping my promises," he purred, eyes closed as he savored the moment. "I even wore the brace."

Mostly, the fae conceded, a faint burning sensation against Shane's neck betraying their healing efforts.

He growled in amusement. "Perfectionist."

Artist. A caress of Feels' love filled Shane's mind, lingering as it entwined with his own emotions and devotion toward the fae. *I didn't expect your Call.*

"I *did* promise I'd try." Shane opened his eyes briefly to survey his surroundings for potential threats before settling back into his seat, content at the night's stillness. "I don't break promises."

Thank you. The accompanying wave of gratitude and affection said more than words ever could. *What were you doing while waiting for me, anyway?*

"Eating fruit."

No, I mean... The empath sent a cascade of reassurance. *I felt your pleasure. Over the Insight spell.*

Shane felt his cheeks flush. "It was really good fruit."

Grim... Feels' words were gentle, their touch against his mind a delicate massage of love and compassion. *I know there are things I can't–*

"I'm *yours*. No one else's!" Shane snarled, undoing the zipper of his protective outer jacket to clutch tightly at the locket nestled against his skin beneath the undershirt.

You could, though. If you wanted. Mischief filled Feels' words. *I put a lot of work into this body of yours. I like to know my art is admired. And your emotions? Intoxicating. I love to bask in your enjoyment.*

Shane arched his back as the psychomorphic mage clamped down on his emotions, shifting and locking his thoughts into a wildly passionate love that left him gasping, his mind imprisoned within their own tightly coiled possessiveness.

Just remember. You belong to me.

"I *am* yours," Shane repeated with a possessive growl of his own, his breath jagged at Feels' unexpected assertiveness. "And you're *mine*. And I. Don't. Share."

The moment ended all too soon, Feels releasing his emotions with a sluggish reluctance. Sensing Shane's disappointment, the empath cast another spell, gently curling their own love around the necromancer's mind, entwining the feeling with Shane's resultant gratitude.

So... Fruit, huh?

"There's still some left. I may let you try it, if you can figure out what it did to my mind."

What am I looking for?

"I don't know," Shane admitted. "But since I've eaten it, I've felt emotions from trees and announced strange names for things I've never seen before." He released the locket, allowing it to settle against his chest as he zipped his jacket once more. "You'll need Kydell's conditioning, to keep me compliant. Just in case. Use the fear."

Shane felt the nervousness bloom in his chest, growing quickly into an abject terror before settling into a low-grade fear which curled beneath every thought. He fought against it, striving to appease the emotion with justifications and bravado, but Feels held firm.

"That'll work," he said, finally, swallowing. "Whenever you're ready."

Keep your watch, Feels ordered in reply. *Let me handle this. Don't interfere.*

"Yes, Sir." Shane muttered his conditioned acknowledgement, surrendering to the sensations within his mind as the psychomorphic mage cycled his emotions and skimmed his related recent memories with their diagnostic spellwork. At their direction, he repeatedly relived pieces of the team's first day on the planet, Feels cataloging each under an array of emotional filters.

His fear lingered in his mind, insistent tendrils wrapping themselves throughout every portion of the retelling, Feels' orders ensuring he remained powerless to stop them.

The familiar pressure of a telepathic request pushed against his thoughts and he answered immediately, Feels' manufactured fear mixing with his apprehension at the interruption. He gripped the sides of the makeshift nest. <Comms? Go.>

<I've a secure link request from Baden for you, Sir,> the Communications AI apologized. <Navarch Javon said you'd want to know right away.>

<Put it through.>

An array of possibilities paraded through his mind. Was Jake okay? Had the fleet worn out their welcome? Was the Confederation attacking again?

But instead of a report from Javon, he was greeted by Jake's former headmaster, the woman's voice betraying an uncharacteristic uncertainty. <Mister Lawrence? I know you have a lot of responsibilities right now. Is this a bad time?>

<No, no. Now works.>

Jake came first. Before the fleet. Before Feels. Before the fate of the war-forsaken universe.

Whatever Janikk's fruit had done, Shane sighed with relief at the confirmation it hadn't changed his priorities.

Headmaster Corbin paused, as if to weigh her words, before continuing. <I wanted to talk about Jake's schooling. Perhaps we can come to an agreement?>

<Jake broke the rules,> Shane acknowledged cautiously. <As did I, by encouraging him. I won't hold you responsible for the repercussions of our choices.>

The day of the Confederation's attack on Baden, Jake had been offered a chance to join the school's advanced classes, only to be expelled an hour later after engaging in a fistfight with his former bully, Veris. Jake had *won* the fight, of course – even after an unexpected knife wound from the larger boy – but a fight was a fight.

That *did* leave the question of his son's continued education, although with a fleet full of well-trained professionals deserted from the Sparnell Armed Forces now reporting directly to him, Shane assumed he could figure out *something* to keep Jake busy.

The presumed loss of his janitorial position, on the other hand, would cause a larger problem. Deserters and traitors weren't known to draw salaries, after all, and Jake had made it clear he wished to remain on Baden. Shane had always done his best with what he had, but he needed that job to keep the house.

He still wasn't sure how he'd see to the needs of the fleet and its people, or the massive repairs they required after their battle against Baden's defenders – his team included. He felt the fear of failure twisting in his gut, his breath shallowing as it sped up to match his racing thoughts. He juggled so many responsibilities now, he'd never catch up. He'd never–

No. One crisis at a time.

He pushed at the panic, settling deeper into his seat as Feels smoothed the rough edges away, forcing his emotions back to a stable, albeit still fearful, baseline.

The headmaster still hadn't answered, and Shane was preparing to end the telepathic connection when she finally spoke again. <That's... we need to talk about those repercussions. I find myself in... an uncomfortable predicament.>

Shane held his silence, his thoughts focused on keeping Feels' manufactured fear at bay as he waited her out.

<You're not making this easy on me, are you?> Headmaster Corbin sighed. <Very well. In light of recent events, the Office has determined we can no longer afford to retain your services as our janitor.>

Shane bowed his head in resignation. While Veris had quite clearly informed them Jake had been included in his own expulsion, there'd been no official communication on the subject of his employment before he and Jake had Hyperjumped with the Kanes to the fleet battle in orbit. In the aftermath of that battle, not to mention the destruction of the school, he'd assume the headmaster had more important matters to attend to than providing those formal notifications.

It appeared that oversight was about to be corrected.

<I appreciate the opportunities you've provided, for my son and for me,> he told her honestly. Jake had expected him to fight against the expulsion, and Shane had intended to do just that,

but now faced with the final choice he discovered he couldn't. <I've already said I don't regret our actions, and so I cannot argue your holding us accountable.>

<What are you *talking* about?> Her words came faster now, and Shane had to focus to understand them. <You're a planetary *hero*. Can you imagine what the rest of the planet thinks of our school, employing you as a *janitor?*>

<Thankfully, the rest of the planet doesn't know,> Shane said quietly, wincing. It was bad enough they considered him some sort of planetary champion. The last thing he needed was for them to figure out where he *worked*.

<Your face is all over the holovids,> Headmaster Corbin said curtly. <Along with the Kanes, and your *son*. In full school uniform. Didn't take long for someone to figure it out. We're already buried under requests for enrollment. The Office is talking about raising tuition. Using the reconstruction as a chance to expand.>

Shane scowled. <I see. So now what?>

<I've been tasked to offer you the position of head of security,> she answered solemnly. <And a 20% raise.>

I didn't find anything, Feels reported, as the fear retreated from Shane's thoughts, the fae's affection rising to soothe any unease left in its wake. *But you didn't fight me, either. And now that I have an emotional reconstruction of your memories, I can more easily dig into specific moments.*

<Let me think,> he told the headmaster, massaging his temples. He'd had a reputation as demanding when he was a

Commodore. He could certainly negotiate something to Jake's advantage now.

But Feels needed an answer, too.

The fear may have covered something, the fae continued, when he didn't answer. *I want to run it again.*

"Do it," Shane ordered, gripping the sides of his perch.

The psychomorphic fae set to work once more, this time slowly adjusting and repeating each iteration to hone in on every subtle shift in Shane's emotions throughout the prior day. He closed his eyes, gaging the new rhythm in the manufactured shifts to his emotions, before returning his attention to Headmaster Corbin.

<I don't want any new responsibilities,> he told her. <Have too many already. Janitor suits me just fine. But Jake loves your school. Only reason I engaged with the fleet in the first place. >

<We never got around to the expulsion paperwork,> Headmaster Corbin admitted. <Far as I'm concerned, it never happened.>

Shane nodded quietly, fighting off a particularly strong wave of smugness as he chose his next words. <I'll take the raise.>

<Not if you're staying janitor.> The headmaster sighed. <That raise was the standard salary for chief of security. But... I *can* waive all of Jake's costs, in addition to continuing your current salary, for as long as he's a student with us.> She laughed nervously. <Different budget. One where I've got more leeway.>

Shane rubbed his chin. This was information he could work with. <Counter offer. Waive everything for Jake *and* Veris–>

<*Veris* brought a knife to school,> she interrupted coldly. <He stabbed your *son*. Surely you don't–>

<Was his expulsion paperwork completed?>

<No,> she managed, after a moment. <No, we... we hadn't gotten that far.>

<If you're giving us a second chance, he gets one, too.>

<You must understand, Mr. Lawrence,> Headmaster Corbin said crisply. <I cannot allow Veris Asik's actions to go unpunished.>

<Then give him to me,> Shane said firmly. Veris had chosen to lash out, leaning on violence to cover his insecurity. Given his own choices in similar circumstances, he couldn't fault the boy, even despite the attempts to harm Jake. <He can help with janitorial. After school.>

<You'll have to take full responsibility for him and his actions,> she cautioned. <Especially if he pulled another stunt like that.>

<He won't,> Shane promised, the growl deep in his throat carrying clearly across the connection. <I stay janitor, and take personal responsibility for Veris Asik. You reinstate Jake and Veris, tuition free. Jake gets his advanced classes. Jeb and Razick Kane get a raise. And if you're still looking for help with security, I can put together a few names.>

<You drive a hard bargain, Janitor Shane.> She sighed. <I can guarantee Jake's classes now, and you've given me enough

to make a good argument on the rest. Give me some time to convince the Office, and hopefully I'll have the paperwork by the time we're allowing staff back on site. I'm working out of the bunker office, in the vault.>

<Let me know when they decide. Anything ready for me now?>

<Just the approvals for Jake's classes,> she answered immediately. <I have them here on my desk, ready for your signa...>

Her voice trailed off as the paperwork appeared in his hand, alongside a pen plucked from her desk, both called to his reach with a casual use of his Necromancy to bend the distance between them. Propping the papers in his lap, he signed with a flourish, Hyperjumping them back to her desk seconds later.

<Anything else?>

<No...> She coughed lightly. <Suppose I'll have to get used to that.>

<Good. Just let me know. Lawrence out.>

He severed the telepathic connection, exhaling. He hadn't realized how heavily Jake's schooling had been weighing on him. Now he'd have good news for his son upon their return, regardless of Janikk's answer.

A wave of exhaustion washed over him, then, in echo of his earlier conversations with the impatient spirit on their initial landing. Shane settled himself deeper into his seat, propping himself up against the edge of their elevated camp to focus on Feels' efforts unraveling whatever the fruit had done to his mind.

This time Feels was taking their time, adjusting and repeating each iteration to hone in on every subtle shift in Shane's emotions throughout the prior day, amplifying them to sift through the associated memories. He allowed them to work unimpeded, interrupting only once to bolster their magic reserves with an apotheturgic link before returning his attention to his role as watchman.

The night remained quiet as the hours passed, his travel companions sleeping peacefully at the far side of the camp.

An unexpectedly strong wave of euphoria hit his thoughts, and Shane clutched desperately at his chest, inhaling sharply.

Caught you.

25

Shane stiffened at Feels' announcement, his thoughts immediately shifting to concern. "So it *did* alter our minds, then."

Not exactly. A wave of reassurance flowed along the tether binding him to his empath. *More subtle than that. Less harmful, too. Here.*

He felt Feels' magic against his emotions, amplifying them to impressive proportions as he relived the moment he bit into the fruit. The curious frustration at Janikk's insistence. The nervous desire as he held it in his hand. The anticipation as he brought it to his lips. And then...

Not sorry for this bit.

Feels' projections of glee were quickly buried in overwhelming pleasures at the mere memory of the explosive flavors within his mouth, and Shane found himself momentarily fighting for breath.

What we want is next. Feel closely now.

A subtle sense of belonging rose behind the more obvious emotions within the memory, as if he felt the planet had accepted him as one of its own. He closed his eyes, reaching inward toward his present mental state, and discovered it still purring contentedly within his thoughts, quiet but unmistakable.

Feel that? Now feel this.

His memories skipped ahead, this time to the moment Jeb and Urla bit into the strange fruit. Here he felt an increased awareness of their presence, as if somehow they'd become more real than they'd been mere seconds before.

It's so faint, I almost missed it. But it's there.

Shane exhaled. "Janikk showed me a web of life on the planet. Accidentally triggered by Hyperjump training." Relaxing his barriers against the trees, he pressed his hand against the nearest trunk and felt its existence rise to meet him. "I'm part of it, now. So are they."

That was my guess, too.

"But then where did all these words come from? The others don't have them."

Janikk shared her experience of the planet with you, Feels said thoughtfully, their curiosity entwining with his own. *Maybe those are* her *words, for everything in it. Maybe she tied herself to you somehow, and now that you're linked to her planet...*

"Some of her memories are bleeding through."

Does she have a name for you, then? His empath teased.

"Klaael." The term popped into his mind at Feels' question. "I don't know what it means."

I like "Grim" better.

"You would," Shane said quietly, resisting the urge to wrap his fist around the locket. "*You* gave it to me. And I don't have to *share* that one. Jeb and Urla are also Klaael."

And Razick?

Shane searched his thoughts, but came up empty. "Not sure."

Grim... Feels paused. *Not that I mind spending the entire evening wrapping myself in every flavor of your emotions, but we really need to work on your definition of "I just want to spend time with you."*

He gave into his urge to clutch the locket, then, channeling his Necromancy to draw his beloved fae to the mortal plane, their delicate pastel wings shimmering with a kaleidoscope of iridescence despite the starlit darkness.

"Even when I plan a quiet evening, I end up demanding everything from you," Shane observed, holding out his hand as the fae settled into his palm. "I'm sorry. I *wanted* to just sit and enjoy your company, and let myself get distracted."

He motioned to the clear night sky, the gentle breeze quietly ruffling the treetops surrounding them as a faint blush of pink peeked cautiously over the far horizon. "It's peaceful here. For now, at least. Reminds me of that night on Baden. By the lake."

His already-overtaxed emotions swelled at the memory of that evening, when they'd finally confessed their love for each other. By the affection and pleasure vibrating along the Oath tether, Feels appreciated the reminder.

"It *is* beautiful," they murmured, spotting the laden branch above them, "but I want to try some of this fruit you enjoy so much."

"Is it safe?"

"Is *anything* ever safe?" Feels laughed lightly. "I'm married to one of the deadliest men in the universe, with a list of war crimes to rival the length of the Hydell Order's Natural Order Manifesto and a stubbornness I swear could overpower a black hole. You've bound your soul and emotions to a psychomorphic fae, and selected the only person to prove herself capable of *killing* you as your most trusted travel companion. I think a mildly clingy planet ranks rather low on *our* scale."

Shane felt his guilt and subsequent resolve surge at the reminder of his past, but brushed it aside, reaching upward instead to pluck a tsijturikk – it still unnerved him how these unfamiliar words kept popping into his head – and offer it to the fae.

Feels accepted the gift eagerly, and Shane felt the now recognizable boost to his awareness as they bit in and allowed Janikk's web to claim them as one of her own.

"Well?"

The fae looked up from their meal, eyes wide, mouth full. "Grim, I *need* this planet, do *not* mess this up for me!"

"Told you." He didn't even attempt to mask the smugness in his words.

"What are you *doing*?"

Razick was upon them in an instant, telekinetically tossing the half-eaten fruit to the forest floor. "We have no idea if these are even *safe*. Didn't they teach you *anything* about planetary survival missions?"

"Looks like date night's over," Shane sighed, releasing Feels back to the Afterlife.

Good luck. They both knew he'd need it. *I'll be on the* Relentless. *Unless you* want *me to stay*? Hope radiated from the locket.

"I'll see you when I get home," Shane promised, smiling wistfully at Feels' farewell caress against his mind before they slipped from the locket. Straightening his shoulders, he turned to confront the glowering battle mage. "It's okay. I had Feels do a full check on me before they–"

"*You* ate it, *too*?" She turned away from him, setting her jaw as she growled. "Of all the foolish, impulsive..."

Shane suddenly found himself pinned to the side of the camp, Razick's diminutive form somehow towering above him, in all her fury.

"*Who else?*"

Shane swallowed, but kept his tone even. "Everyone but you. Jeb and Urla had some, too."

"Everyone but..." She held his gaze, scowling, before visibly crumbling to slouch on the vine-woven floor of their makeshift camp. She cupped her head in her hands, her voice pained. "I *knew* I shouldn't have gone to sleep. You... Jeb... We know *nothing* about this planet. This could compromise our entire mission."

"Which would be my fault. *Not* yours," Shane reminded her. "I'm leading this mission. It was my call to make."

The dawning light caught in the single tear running down her cheek, her face now cast in the same red as her hair as she looked up at him. "I *feel* like I failed you. You brought me here to protect you."

"From *Janikk*. Not from myself."

It was an important distinction. He'd carried enough guilt for his choices, before Feels' impromptu emotional surgery. Razick deserved better than to carry it for him.

She studied him thoughtfully. "I can't leave you unsupervised, can I?"

"That's what Feels tells me. All the time," Shane said solemnly.

That earned him the faint beginnings of a smile. "You actually mean it, don't you?" When he didn't answer, she stood, moving to stand beside him as she looked out over the trees. "All my life, I've been taught to shoulder the blame of others' mistakes. It didn't matter how much control I had over the situation. It couldn't be their fault, so it had to be mine. And if you're told something often enough... You start to believe it."

The fierce defiance in her shoulders and proud angle to her chin stood in stark contrast to the sadness in her words.

Or perhaps they were simply opposing sides to the same coin. A life spent shouldering the faults of others, learning to become strong enough to carry the burdens which had never been hers in the first place. Allowing people like him to ignore the responsibilities of their own damn choices.

"They were wrong," he said softly, continuing quickly before she could argue. "I never wanted a military career, you know. Always planned to just... Serve my time. Settle back with my parents. Be a bad farmer, but a *happy* one, just like them. And then one day the Legion came. And my dreams, and my parents, died in an agony of fury and fire. And everything changed."

"I'm sorry," she began, but he wasn't done.

"Anger was all I had left, after that. Ambitious revenge. I'd unleash on them the nightmares they'd given me. Repay the deaths a billion times over. I poured everything I had into that plan. Sharpened my teeth against those anti-resurrection fanatics of the Hydell Order, until the day I earned enough prestige for Fleet Command to approve my request to unleash my fury against the Space Defense Legion."

"Loxira."

"Loxira," he agreed. "And you know what I learned? Get called a war hero long enough, and you start to believe it. But there's no such thing, is there? Just a lot of hurt people, trying to drown their pain by perpetuating the very things that caused it in the first place. I wasn't solving the problem that killed my parents. I was making more people like the ones that killed them. More people like me."

"*Heroes* exist," Razick said fiercely, turning to face him. "*Wars* don't deserve them, but the universe does. What you did for Baden–"

"Doesn't even *begin* to heal the wounds I've inflicted," he finished, waving her off. "Not the point I'm trying to make. The universe we know is built on lies, Razick. Some, we believe. Others, we pretend to believe, because the truth feels unbearable." He exhaled, staring at the horizon. "I think I always knew this, on some level. I made a point not to lie to others, after all. But it wasn't until Jake that I realized I'd never stopped lying to myself."

Her brows furrowed, a sudden realization dawning across her face. "He's not yours, is he?"

"He's my son," Shane said defensively, before catching himself. He felt his protective conditioning swelling within his thoughts, his Necromancy just on the tips of his fingers. "You can't breathe a word to anyone. Not even Jeb."

He'd never forgive himself if he hurt her, not even to protect Jake. He'd already murdered enough friends.

A familiar face rose to the surface of his memories, and he clenched his fists, anxiously awaiting Razick's response.

"Not even Jeb," she promised, and his magic subsided, his conditioning appeased at her words. "Does Jake know?"

"No secrets," he told her. "Not from Jake. Not from Feels. And now you know that one, too."

"I'll keep it safe," she repeated. "You have my word. Thank you. For trusting me."

It felt *good* to have a friend. Someone who understood the pain without trying to fix it, or carry it for him. He briefly wondered if someday he could share more of his past, of the cruel secret of his former identity, but Kydell's conditioning reared in his mind once more, pressing unbearably against his thoughts as it planned its reaction.

No. Nobody could know. Jake's safety depended on it.

"You're the most trustworthy person I know, Raz. No one else I'd rather have at my side." He watched her stand taller at his familiar use of her nickname, and followed it up with a smile of his own. It felt *good* to have something to smile *about*. "But preferably at a distance. I'd better not wake up in your arms again."

She blinked at the sudden change in topic, before grinning. "It was *cold!*"

"Then use your damn blood warming spell. I'm *not* your body pillow."

He attempted to scowl again, although judging by her expression, he hadn't quite succeeded.

"I did," she told him brightly. "But you don't want me to cast it in my sleep. We'd end up like your jerky."

That was an image he hadn't needed. Memories of his past crimes trailed through his thoughts again.

And hers, judging by the sudden shadow in her eyes.

"You were a victim of Kydell, from the very beginning, Raz. I wasn't. Unlike you, not all of my past mistakes fell on that Void-cursed wolf's shoulders. A lot of them were entirely mine." He closed his eyes, inhaling slowly. "But that's the past. I've spent too long, wrapping myself in guilt for my mistakes. It's the future that needs my attention. As my mother always told me, 'You can't change the past, but you can change yourself.' Every day is an opportunity to do better. To *be* better. Every moment is a new chance to get closer to the person I want to be. The example I want to set for Jake."

He shook his head, standing as he caught her eyes with his own. "If you copy *anything* about me, pick that. It's the *one* thing I'm proud of." He snorted. "Well, that and Jake, but that kid's got a mind of his own. Sometimes, I wonder just how much he actually needs me, and how much of it is an act for my benefit."

"He's a great kid. He'll change the universe someday," Razick agreed, narrowing her eyes as she looked up at him, her next words accompanied by a playful but pointed poke to his chest. "Just like his father."

He still disagreed on that last point, but decided to accept the compliment as she'd intended, rather than arguing. His protective conditioning settled happily within his chest, at the reminder of Razick's promise to keep his secret.

"He looks so much like you," she marveled, biting her lip. "I really thought you were related."

"Technically, we are." He chuckled, settling back onto the small bench Jeb had built into the nest. "But he doesn't have half of my genetics. I have half of his."

Recognition dawned in her eyes. "Feels."

"Feels," Shane agreed. "They used to run the Phoenix Assembly, before I mucked it up for them. After we find the fleet a home, I want to try and get it back. Hoping you'll help with that, too."

"Relations are difficult enough with Baden," Razick observed. "How would they feel about you taking control of Baden City's criminal underground?"

"I'm hoping they don't find out," he admitted, rubbing the back of his neck. "Failing that, I'm hoping they'll recognize a return of Feels' priorities as an improvement over the violence it's devolved into now. Sure, they faked paperwork, but the promise of a fresh start and a new face kept a steady stream of highly skilled Sparnelli refugees flocking to the planet. They've never *admitted* to it, and likely never will, but the Assembly used to have a measurably positive impact on the planetary economy. And we'd be bringing that back, too."

Razick crossed her arms, leaning against the edge of their camp. "I'm not used to honesty. Or having choices. I won't use my training to hurt anyone, I've too many memories I can't outrun, but this is a good cause. I'll help. I'll *enjoy* helping."

He opened his mouth to thank her, but she held up her hand.

"You've entrusted me with enough of your secrets," she said firmly. "And your trust. Anything more and I'll feel like I owe you." She wrinkled her nose. "Already too late for that, if I'm honest."

"Then pay me back," he told her, as a new thought occurred to him. "Tell me a secret of your own. Something Jeb doesn't even know. Something you've been wanting to get off your chest, but never trusted anyone to talk about."

She narrowed her eyes. "You've spent too much time around that empath of yours. I know what you're trying to do."

There was no sense in denying it. "Yes."

It was the right answer, judging by the way her smile still reached her eyes, even despite the heaviness to her gaze. "Alright. Fair enough. Jeb was too young to understand this at the time, and now that he's older, I've never had the heart to start the conversation..." She squared her shoulders, and he felt the telltale buzz at the back of his neck as she bolstered her Shielding, as if to protect herself from the pain. "You want to play therapist? Then I need to tell you about my father."

26

Razick settled to sit cross-legged at Lawrence's feet, tugging at her hair and nervously pulling it over her shoulder until it pooled in her lap. "This is harder to talk about than I thought. Guess that's what happens when you bottle something up for too long."

"Take your time." Lawrence's eyes reflected starlight and patience.

"You know how ruthless the service can be," she began hesitantly. "People like Jeb, they're the lucky ones. Discarded as useless from the beginning, they suffer through the stigma of weakness for their kind hearts and thoughtful ways, but they don't have to *see* the true cruelty of the Confederation. They don't experience the same violent indoctrinations as the SAF molds us into heartless tools to satisfy the Empress' bloodlust."

At least, she *hoped* he'd escaped with his innocence intact. Memories of some of her escort missions, protecting the most brilliant and twisted scientific minds of the Confederation as they unleashed unspeakable biological crimes upon innocent civilian populations, flooded her thoughts.

She pushed them down.

"And they don't have to learn to pick up the shattered pieces of their lives after they get out. Not like us."

Lawrence watched her quietly, his face betraying the violence of his own memories, as his silent attention encouraged her to continue.

"Father was a battle mage. A damn good one. Probably why I was selected for the training as soon as my conscription came due, when I stop to think about it. He had a box full of medals tucked into the back of his closet, all the way on the top shelf. Used to play with them when I was younger. When he wasn't looking. There was always hell to pay if he ever caught me, but that only added to my determination, back then."

She laughed, a hollow sound against the calm morning. "I was naïve. Didn't realize what they all meant, back then. But each accolade takes a piece of the soul away, doesn't it? We become less of us, and more of what they want, with every acknowledgement of a successful mission. And knowing that now..." She looked away, wiping her watering eyes against her sleeve. "There were enough ribbons collecting dust in that horrid box, it's a wonder there was anything left of him to come home."

"Raz, you don't have to–"

"Yes. I do." Shielding her eyes against the sun, she gazed out at the clouds above them. "It feels good to finally talk about it with someone. Mama had enough trouble on her hands trying to hold everything together. And Jeb... Sweet, thoughtful Jeb always sees the best in people. Last thing I want is to damage his relationship with Father. I'm happy for him. He has a good life. I'll do whatever it takes to defend that for him."

"You need to care for yourself, too."

"That's why I'm telling you," she said, as the realization dawned. "I mean, I know you asked. But you'd let me say no. And you said you'd listen." She turned back to face him. "Jeb doesn't need to know, but maybe you do. Maybe I *need* you to."

He nodded, once. "I'll listen to whatever you want to tell me."

"There's good credits to be made off those trying to transition back to civilian life. I had Jeb to help me through the worst of it, and Kydell to blame for most of it. Father had Mama, but with all the memories in that box... I don't think she was enough."

Razick began to bat against the tears threatening to spill down her cheeks, but stopped herself. She'd have many more before she finished explaining. She could trust him with her emotions.

"She dragged Father to all the specialists. They tried all sorts of fancy therapies, and he tried all sorts of medications. And after a while, he just retreated into whatever temporary numbness he could find at the bottom of an alchemy bottle."

Biting her lip, Razick turned to watch her sleeping brother. "Jeb doesn't remember any of this. Not really. He can tell you how our parents used to fight a lot, and Father spent a lot of time away from home, but Mama always told him they were business trips. That Father had to leave for work a lot and she wanted him to spend more time with us. Truth was, those were the times she couldn't take it anymore, and kicked him out."

Razick sighed, searching Shane's face and finding compassion staring back at her, his attention still focused wholly on her words.

"She could never keep her distance for long, though. They'd grown up together. Married young, during training, with the foolish dream they'd be assigned together on deployment. And through it all, she kept hoping the man she'd fallen in love with would find his way back to her."

"Did he?" By his tone, the necromancer already suspected the answer.

Razick shook her head. "No. But he *did* eventually pull himself out of the medication. Started living again, instead of slowly dying, and the two of them found a way to build a new happiness. Away from the memories of the old."

She shrugged. "Course, by then I'd gotten used to covering for him. Protecting Jeb from the truth, and everything else I could think of. Helping Mama pick up the slack. She used to tell me I reminded her of Father, back before he lost himself. Father must have felt the same. We never had a good relationship, even after he got clean. I don't know if he resented me for it, or was just trying to protect himself from relapsing when my conscription came due. Maybe both! But it only got worse as I got older, and then when Mama died... Far as I'm concerned, Jeb's the only family I have left, now. But the two of them still write sometimes."

Turning, she offered Lawrence a half-hearted smile. "He gave Jeb all the love he'd never show me. Mama's death hit us all hard. Jeb got him through it. Without a relapse. Probably saved Father's life." She exhaled, staring at her hands. "Jeb used to try and get the two of us to make up. Said it would help both of us if we just... moved on from whatever there is between us. But there's too much hurt there. Fathers are supposed to *protect* their children. Prepare them for the future. But I had to learn how to survive the SAF on my own. Starting with the traumas he'd already inflicted on me!"

"Jeb isn't the only one you have left. As far as Jake and I are concerned, you're family, too."

The dam burst then, her tears flowing freely as she leaned against his leg. She felt him shudder at the touch, but before she could pull away he settled a hand on her shoulder and squeezed.

"I'd like that," she managed at last, leaning into his touch to sandwich his hand between her cheek and shoulder.

Lawrence's grip tightened, and Razick turned to apologize for upsetting him, only to find him scanning the horizon. She felt the telltale static of power at the back of her neck as he bolstered his Shielding and quickly followed his lead, casting a second Shield on Jeb.

"Wake your brother," the necromancer ordered. "*Hurry.* Janikk's restless again. Think she's decided we've wasted enough time."

Catching movement from above, Razick scrambled to don her helmet, adjusting the settings on her visor for a closer look. A thick-beaked raptor with comically bright plumage and surprisingly sharp teeth stared back at her, wings expertly tucked into a high speed dive, the hint of several more like it following its slipstream.

Shit.

27

"Juslemmesleep." Jeb rubbed his eyes groggily at the insistent, pounding prodding in his ribs. He poked the offending party, only to find the stiff fabric give beneath his fist, the contents of the backpack below him shifting to accommodate.

He opened his eyes to chaos.

"Just run, Raz! I'll hold them off!" Lawrence's voice sounded in the distance, insistent but strained.

"Like hell you will," Razick growled.

Jeb winced at each bounce of her footfalls, the equipment from her pack digging into his chest with every step.

"Just once, Lawrence, I'd like a mission where you don't die on me."

"Last time I was dying *next* to you," Lawrence panted, his voice quieter but closer. "So there's that. I need a break."

"Put me down." Jeb squirmed, immediately finding himself unceremoniously dumped butt-first on the ground between his companions.

At a motion from Lawrence, several large draconic birds twice again the necromancer's height tumbled backward in a protest of teeth and feathers. The largest recovered quickly, its long-necked leathery head lunging toward the party, only to be caught in Razick's telekinetic grip.

"Don't know how you slept through all this," Lawrence growled. "Let your girlfriend know you're okay, would you? Can't jump while she's pestering me. Too many distractions already."

Urla. She must have been worried sick.

He made the connection, her frustrated demands filling his mind before he could answer. <Jeb! Jeb! Grand Navarch won't tell me anything. What happened? What's wrong? Are you hurt?>

<I'm here, Sweetheart. I'm okay,> he soothed, surveying his surroundings as he widened his Telepathy to link her experiences into his. A quick glance revealed five of the oversized birds, squawking and circling above the large, brightly lit field where his companions had chosen to make a stand. <Looks like Janikk woke up.>

Jeb covered his ears as a shrill, modulating droning noise filled the air. He scanned their surroundings for the source, his eyes settling on Lawrence himself.

"Distractions. You mean the bugs?" Razick muttered loudly, a quick Shield of fire emerging between them and the giant birds of prey. "Thought they taught you Void necromancers to concentrate through anything."

Lawrence shuddered, dropping his pack to the ground. His outer jacket followed soon after. "No insects in spacecraft. Least, I've never *heard* them."

Razick snorted. "I've worked with a few."

With a twist of her fingers, the closest charging bird froze mid-dive, sending up a cloud of feathers and squawks as it attempted to escape its invisible prison.

It was *huge*, with a beak large enough to crush a canid's skull with ease. Its struggles revealed an impressive musculature within the bare skin of its head and neck, while its long, feathered tail lashed in protest at its current predicament.

The others shifted their trajectory, angling in on their trapped companion.

"We used to bring bugs with us, though," Jeb said brightly. "Was before my time, but there's a whole history class about it for biologists. Hydroponics is actually the most *expensive* way to generate a Nature Magic field in the Void. They're just also guaranteed not to contaminate the food supply."

<Not the time, Jeb,> Urla suggested. <Think everyone's busy. Gromdornox. The giant death birds. Probably live in that tree we slept in last night.>

<Why'd they wait until morning to attack? We were there all night, no problems.>

"Did they teach you how to decontaminate people during that lesson of yours?" Lawrence growled, clawing at his undershirt.

"Pyromancy," Razick suggested cheerfully, sending the captured bird reeling back into its companions. "Burn them right off you."

The impressive birds tumbled toward the ground, but righted themselves quickly before organizing themselves much like Jeb had seen in the old fighter pilot war propaganda movies he'd grown up watching in school.

<They weren't home. Grand Navarch thinks Janikk gave us the night off, to rest. But this place she's driving us toward... He said she wants us there by nightfall.> Urla's voice took on an edge of admiration as the circling predators dove at them, breaking off at the last moment before taking to the skies again. <They're really quite beautiful. Look at their pack tactics. We don't often see this kind of behavior from birds. Especially birds of *this* size.>

<Are you *seriously* admiring those things? Now? When they're trying to kill us?> Jeb surveyed their surroundings for a plant to recruit to their defense, but the forest from last night was nowhere to be seen, and the grassland currently surrounding them offered no viable options he could think up.

<No better time to study hunting strategies.> Urla was unapologetic. <A show like this... Distraction? Maybe? But from what?>

Lawrence's voice was pained, although whether this was in response to his sister's offer or a direct result of his attempts to evict the insects that had settled inside his uniform, Jeb couldn't tell. "I don't want to beat her up and take her stuff. I'd rather earn Janikk's favor. If she wanted to kill us she'd have done so already. She's certainly capable."

As Jeb watched, his sister pushed her hands forward at the carnivorous birds, palms out, fingers spread, muscles straining. Her stance for giant Shielding spells. He remembered several times when she'd been startled enough to cast it on him in public, after her escape from the Confederation.

Unlike those incidents, this time the Shielding caught fire, fueled by her earlier spellwork. The birds took to the air, circling and tilting their heads as if studying the new challenge.

"You didn't have many friends growing up, did you?" Razick asked, the sarcasm thick in every word. "This is *not* how normal people say hello!"

"I survived worse at the orphanage," Lawrence grunted. "Even the bugs. *These* ones don't seem to bite. Did you want me to get us out of here or not?"

Razick readied her laser rifle as the birds swooped in at them again, the first several impacting with her Shielding at full force. They spun away with dazed expressions but otherwise seemingly unhurt, the flames sparking harmlessly across their feathers.

Jeb grabbed his own pistol as Razick aimed for the last bird in line and began to pull the trigger, the creature careening directly toward Lawrence at an impressive speed.

The shrill noise filled the air again, sending Jeb's shot wide at the unexpected noise. Razick's own aim struck true, the highly concentrated laser striking close enough to the bird to send it veering off course in a cloud of brightly colored feathers.

"Oh, come *on!*" Lawrence shouted, beating at his trousers and stomping his feet. "Janikk! I'm *trying* to do what you want us to do, but *you won't let me*. You've got the gromdornox trying to kill us, we're stuck in the open because of the tekkirkk crawling inside my clothes and *screaming* at me every time I figure out how to ignore them, you already sent those yinit menaces who ate all our food... I'll do what you want, just *let me do it*!"

One of the birds settled into the long grass, propping itself on its wingtips as it reared to its full height, squawking indignantly at Lawrence but keeping its distance.

The necromancer walked toward it instead, nostrils flaring. "Darrekknee. Tsekeht. Yukkanee. I don't know what any of this means but you keep saying it to me and I'm *listening*. I'm *trying* to work with you."

"Lawrence!" Razick screamed, and suddenly the necromancer was struggling in a telekinetic hold, several inches in the air.

"I need to do this, Raz. If it eats me, *then* you can say 'I told you so.'"

"It's my job to protect you."

"And this is my choice, Razick. Not yours. Let me go."

<He knows what he's doing,> Urla said across the link. <Tell her.>

"Let him go," Jeb said quietly, resting his palm on Razick's arm. "He knows what he's doing."

"I don't like it," she told him, but relented.

Lawrence closed the rest of the distance to the large, single bird towering above him, his hands held in front of him, palms outward. "Please. Let me do it my way. I promise I'll do it."

The bird tilted its head at him, as if in thought, before lowering its neck to meet his eyes, its beak mere inches from the necromancer's head. It huffed slightly and hopped back, once, before letting out an ear splitting shriek directly in his face.

He raised an eyebrow. "And the tekkirkk?"

A winged cloud emerged from every possible opening into his uniform, temporarily encircling him with a massive swarm of insects.

"Thank the Void."

Jeb exhaled sharply as Lawrence appeared before him, shoving a pack at his chest. The biologist silently donned the backpack as the necromancer slipped back into his shirt and jacket.

"You could have died," Razick hissed.

"But I didn't," Lawrence told her, grabbing her arm. "Good work. We ready?"

The world twisted around them before either of them could answer.

28

Razick scanned the horizon as they emerged from the jump.

All clear. For now. Lawrence had dropped them in a semi-circular clearing full of oversized ferns, a craggy cliff face at their back. Beyond the clearing, at a healthy distance for her riot rifle, stretched a densely wooded area, its inhabitants strangely quiet to her Anemancy.

Despite his sheer disregard for his own safety, he at least understood the importance of defensible ground. Of all the locations they'd landed so far, this appeared the most easily protected, although the foreboding maw of a natural cave gaping from the cliff face left a knot of anxiety twisting in her stomach. There was no doubt in her mind this was the location Janikk had been driving them toward.

Or that the necromancer would insist on doing just that.

Lawrence slowly sank to the ground. "I don't suppose either of you have a first aid kit?" His hand was clamped tightly over his shoulder, and Razick caught the faint sheen of blood between his fingers.

She scowled, preparing to offer her commentary on his foolish confrontation of the giant bird, but it was Jeb who answered the request, expertly retrieving the first aid kid from his pack.

"Your partner busy?" her brother asked, offering Lawrence an all-too-familiar alchemical tablet to dull the pain as he prepped to clean the wound.

Razick raised an eyebrow. If she'd retained any doubts about her brother's experience in the field, he was certainly doing all he could to dispel them.

"I sent reassurances so they wouldn't come. It's just a scratch." The necromancer had the good sense to smile apologetically in her direction. "But as Razick pointed out earlier, we don't know anything about this planet. For all I know, they're poisonous, too. Would rather find out now than later."

"Would serve you right," Razick snorted, strangely appeased at his acknowledgement of her warnings about the risks, her attention now split between her companions and their surroundings.

"Was going to say Feels'll put me on house arrest once they realize I'm hurt," he told her, "but now I suspect you'll beat them to it. I'd rather be done here, first. I'll be the perfect patient, after. You have my word."

"You don't sound worried," Jeb observed, his voice distracted as he inspected the wound.

Lawrence's breathing relaxed as Jeb applied a Curative poultice. "There are worse things. Could use a vacation. Although... One of you will have to get the groceries for a while."

Propping her back against the cliff behind them, Razick crossed her arms, continuing to scan the space ahead of them. "Why am I not surprised you're the only one who got hurt?"

"Didn't you notice? I'm the only one they were aiming for." Lawrence flexed his arm to test Jeb's bandaging skills. "I think she likes me."

Jeb snorted. "I don't think I can trust your relationship advice anymore."

"I'm not letting you carry anything important anymore," Razick added with a glare. "Where's your helmet? If you really want us to go in that cave next, you're going to need a visor."

Lawrence laughed bitterly, dusting off his trousers as he rose to his feet. "Never realized how much I always had others looking out for me." He rolled his shoulder, nodding appreciatively at Jeb. "Not that they'd have dared let me know. And I can't blame them for that."

"We *did* have to leave in a hurry," Razick conceded. "And you brought the pack this time."

"And since nobody's trying to kill us for the moment..." Lawrence added absently.

The missing helmet materialized in his hands.

Jeb blinked as the necromancer adjusted the helmet on his head. "You can just... What about our camping gear? And the food?"

Razick suspected none of their supplies had survived the furred animals that had swarmed their original camp, but had to admit it wouldn't hurt to try.

"Probably shouldn't leave our trash lying around," Lawrence agreed, closing his eyes and leaning against the cliff beside her. The tattered and twisted remains of the pack and its contents appeared at his feet, one piece at a time. "Don't think we can use any of it now, after what the yinits did. But at least Janikk can't get angry at us for littering." He attempted to rub the back of his neck, awkwardly lowering his hand again as he merely bumped against his leather epaulets instead. "Or maybe I should jump it to the ship?"

"Yinits?" Razick furrowed her brows. He'd been leaking strange vocabulary into his sentences since his first encounter with Janikk, and it was only growing more concerning.

"Small white furry creatures. Sharp teeth, big groups. They came after us on the island." Lawrence shrugged, turning to enter the cave. "Apparently I know the name of things now. Ever since I ate the tsijturikk. Are we ready to go? Janikk says the Tsekeht is this way."

"Oh no you don't," Razick ordered, gently wrapping Lawrence in her Telekinesis before raising him into the air. "Your mind is compromised. I don't intend to blindly wander into the dark hole in the wall, hunting for the next thing to try and eat us."

"Janikk says we need to find the klaaeturikk before nightfall," Lawrence protested. "I'd rather not learn firsthand what happened to the other away teams."

"You're only proving my point." She crossed her arms. "Do you even know what those words mean?"

"No." He shook his head, pointing to the cave. "But there's an easy way to find out."

"Which is exactly why we're not doing that yet. Jeb?"

"You saw what happened back with the birds, Raz," Jeb told her uncertainly. "As soon as he told her we were going, they backed off."

"I gave my word," Lawrence added, still floating obediently within her Telekinetic grip. "That means something to me."

"You promised you'd do it *your* way. Does your way involve ignoring my advice?"

"Of course not." Lawrence scowled, then softened. "Is that how you feel?"

"Right now? Yes. You brought me to keep you safe, then keep overriding me whenever I try to do just that." She held up a hand when he started to protest. "I *know* the nature of our mission demands you take some risks. That doesn't mean you should take *all* of them. I've been working with you. All I'm asking is that you work with me, too. Let me do what you brought me for."

He sighed, nodding. "I concede your point. But you'd better hurry. She's getting impatient at our delays again. We'll have some new friends soon. *Very* soon."

Razick felt a weight lift off her shoulders. "Thank you. Jeb? You don't have any strange names in your head, do you? Or a sudden compulsion to go running into that cave unprepared?"

Jeb tugged his hair, brows furrowing. "No? At least, not yet."

"It'll have to do." She squared her shoulders, carefully lowering Lawrence to the ground as she turned to face the unknown in the surrounding woods. "We don't know what we're getting into, which means I need to scout our surroundings for unwelcome surprises first. Keep an eye on Lawrence while I'm gone. If he does anything out of character, grab him with your Agrokinesis or something, and recall me with your Telepathy." She turned to face them, crossing her arms across her chest. "And stay out of the cave until I return. I'll take point. Understood?"

"Yes, sir," Lawrence told her solemnly.

Jeb merely nodded.

"Good. And when we get back from this mission? I am making *both* of you sit through every single away mission training holo *ever* made."

With that promise in the air between them, Razick spun on her heels and set forward into the unknown, her thoughts gnawing on the problem of protecting her charges in the dark caverns beneath Janikk.

29

SHANE REACHED OUT WITH his senses, his Necromancy somehow mingling with the web of life on the planet – at least, he assumed that's what was happening – to yield a surprisingly accurate radar of the large pack of lanky quadrupeds currently stalking his position. Fylox, apparently, if the strange list of disjointed vocabulary in his head was any indication. Jeb and Urla were there, too, their souls readily visible to their Necromancy even as their presence within Janikk's network lent its own inputs.

There'd be no hiding from Janikk now.

Opening himself further to the Void, he reached for another audience with the planet's restless spirit, but aside from her familiar disapproval of their continued delaying tactics and the ever-growing pull in the back of his mind to enter the cave she granted him no further guidance.

"Jeb, please tell me you feel them, too." Shane turned to the biologist. Razick was no longer visible, but he could feel her soul wandering straight toward the fylox pack.

Jeb shook his head. "Not unless you mean the plants. But Urla says she feels a pack of animals stalking this way."

If Urla felt them, too, then it wasn't just his mind playing tricks.

Shane's decades as a necromancer meant he'd grown accustomed to building mental walls against the Afterlife, filters to ensure he knew where his mind ended and the Void began, even as he had come to allow the Void constant access to his consciousness. But whatever Janikk and her fruit had done used different channels, leaving Shane scrambling to sort through his thoughts to identify which were his, which belonged to his new network of information, and whether any of it was manufactured completely by his overtaxed mind.

Of course, the fact Urla confirmed this new threat as real opened up its own list of concerns.

"We need to warn your sister. She's walking right into them."

"On it." Jeb's eyes unfocused as he concentrated on his Telepathy.

The necromancer allowed the Void and Janikk's network equal space in his mind, tracking Razick's positioning in relation to the stalking predators as they adapted to her presence. A nagging sense of danger brushed repeatedly against his thoughts as the fylox drew closer to their target.

Jeb's frustration broke the silence. "She won't turn around."

As his emotions of caution spiked, Shane reached out with his Necromancy, but stopped himself.

No. He'd promised to let her do her job. He couldn't stop her now. She needed to know he trusted her.

Instead he focused on the group of fylox sneaking up behind her, wrapping his magic around one and dropping it in front of her with its brethren before moving to the next. It took a great deal of Imperium – and concentration – to jump moving targets. But she'd been right. He couldn't undermine her again.

"Link me in," he ordered instead. "She needs to feel what I feel."

<They're trying to surround me,> she told him moments later. <Where do they keep coming from?>

<I've got your back,> he promised, relocating another fylox back into her field of vision. <But Janikk doesn't like what you're doing.>

<No surprise there. It's set to stun, but no matter how many I knock unconscious, more keep coming.>

<I'm worried about your riot rifle,> Urla added softly. <It's calibrated for people. Not... whatever these things are.>

<Janikk hasn't hurt us yet,> Shane added, purposely ignoring the throbbing in his shoulder. <I'd prefer to return the favor.>

He could feel her sign over Jeb's Telepathy. <Fine. This isn't working, anyway. Bring me back.>

Shane wrapped her in his magic, elevating Razick to the Afterlife before dropping her in front of them, facing away. She pulled the trigger on the laser rifle in the same instant, its barrel now split to direct a widening beam of energy into the empty forest before them with a loud buzz of magical power.

Cursing, she shifted her position to watch him, even as she scanned the trees. She'd lowered her rifle, but kept her finger on the trigger, its barrel still splayed in riot control settings. "I don't like being out in the open like this. Where are they?"

<Not far.> It was Urla who answered. <They're gathering at the tree line, watching us.>

Shane nodded in agreement, setting his own weapon to scattershot to blanket the general direction of his aim with small, distributed stun beams. His new senses revealed at least twenty fylox observing them patiently from the shadows, with more in the distance. At those numbers, accuracy was *not* the most important thing.

"We don't have to be in the open," he suggested. "There's a perfectly good cave, right there."

"I'm not comfortable with that yet," Razick admitted.

Shane nodded, then tensed, raising his weapon as he felt the nagging sense of danger return to push against his mind.

And then the creatures were upon them, a dangerous bundle of red fur with black and cream accents barreling toward them on thin, agile legs, their shoulders even with Shane's chest. Reptilian mouths of sharp teeth snapped in anticipation as they ran, twin tails beating the air with powerful strokes, their focus now entirely on Shane.

He fired at the animals to the right, striking several and sending them tumbling to the ground, heads shaking and limbs twitching, but still very much conscious.

He doubted that would slow them for long. A quick glance to his left revealed Jeb's similar results.

Beside him, Razick's beam of energy exploded with a high powered whine, catching the vanguard of the middle wave. The front three froze as if in surprise before collapsing silently, their companions behind pausing briefly to shake off the weakened effects before distancing further from each other and resuming the assault, their focus now on Razick's weapon.

She cursed, tossing the closest several backwards with her telepathy as she aimed to fire again. "*People* don't figure out the angle limitations on this thing."

"I told you, Janikk's *ancient*," he grunted, pulling from the planet's network to focus his awareness on the four partially-stunned fylox before him. He hyperjumped them several miles away, his pistol working overtime as the remainder somehow adapted to anticipate the random patterns of his shots.

He shook his head in an effort to clear the mental strain. Hyperjumping moving targets was always tricky. He needed to conserve magic for whatever they'd be facing in the cave.

"I don't think we can hold them off much longer." The strain in Jeb's voice made Shane wince, the fylox near the biologist quickly ripping through the agrokinetically-enhanced foliage holding them back.

"Behind me!" Razick ordered, readying yet another beam of energy from her rifle as the fylox drew into physical range.

And suddenly several pairs of jaws were on the rifle itself, metal and energy alike shrieking beneath the incredible clamping power of their reptilian snouts. Shane phased Razick to the Afterlife on instinct as several sets of teeth lunged for the battle mage herself, his magic driving them back with a Shield Burst before returning her to the mortal plane.

She resumed her stance, retaliating with a will of fire, her Pyromancy trapping the small away team against the cliff face as the fylox paced frantically along the side of the new barrier with a chorus of frustrated yips.

"I'm not going to burn them," she promised, scowling. "Even though they tried to eat me."

"I know." He studied the fylox through the flames, several of the creatures pausing their digging efforts to study him in return. "I don't think this will hold them for long."

<They're tunneling underneath,> Urla reported. <Fascinating creatures.>

A round of Electromancy bolts sent the creatures scattering, returning just as quickly once Razick's spell ended. "I don't think I can deter them, either. You'll have to jump us out of here, Lawrence. Again."

Shane shook his head, pointing once more to the cave. "We're here to confront Janikk. She says we do that here, or not at all. We've clearly used up her goodwill, and I refuse to leave empty handed. Too many people are relying on us."

Razick sighed, shoulders slumping. "I can't believe I'm saying this... Fine. Into the cave. I'll take the rear, defend our retreat. At least those things can only fit through two at a time."

"No." Shane poured his full authority into the word, noting as his companions reflexively snapped to attention. "You take the lead, Raz. I'll go last."

"Sir," Razick protested, eliciting a faint smile from Shane at her sudden slip into the formal address. "I'm the one with the offensive magic. I'm the one best equipped to–"

"Sweep for threats ahead of us," Shane finished for her, holding up his hand. "Janikk wants us in that cave. Wants *me*. As long as we're heading in the right direction, we'll be fine."

Skeptical green eyes met his before Razick nodded, biting her lip. "I'll drop the barrier once Jeb and I are inside. You'd better be right about this."

The sudden hint of approval within the back of his mind as Razick stepped through the entryway of the cave confirmed his suspicions. Especially once the fylox halted their posturing, instead sitting to watch with alarmingly intelligent eyes.

The planet would remain on their side, so long as they did what she wanted.

Shane scowled. He and Janikk were too much alike. They'd need some ground rules.

Razick's wall of fire spluttered and died, leaving nothing between them and the fylox within the clearing, aside from a burnt line of grass and scattered piles of soil. The creatures stood again, slowly gathering to converge on Shane, the closest several greeting him with a low growl in their throats but seemingly content to halt their main offensive.

The necromancer summoned his memories of his old self, growling ominously in return as he backed toward the cave. The fylox yelped, leaping backward to widen the distance between them, waiting silently with twin tails tucked between their legs, ears flattened.

Good to know they recognize the bigger predator. He smirked to himself, turning to join the Kane siblings in the darkness.

Janikk's approval shifted into triumph as a heavy rock door slid closed behind him, cutting off their escape. The force of the closure reverberated within the narrow passageways of the cave, severing Shane's constant connection to the infinite possibilities of the Afterlife.

He clawed at the unyielding stone, barely registering the shouts of his companions as he tore at the walls and the confines of his jacket. His rapidly shallow breath gasped within the tightening grip of his claustrophobia as he struggled against the sudden absence of the Void from his mind.

30

Feels found their mind wandering, once more returning to the prior evening and their date with Grim. The thrill of his immediate and willing surrender to their assertiveness. The hours spent wrapping themself in every nuance of his emotions. His apologetic overtures about the envisioned romantic evening under the stars.

And of course their mutual appreciation for that phenomenal fruit.

Grim's stubbornness had always been a point of contention in their relationship, but they'd always found ways to work through the conflicts, and after last night, Feels had no qualms about their future with the dangerous necromancer who'd stolen their heart so long ago.

He really was theirs. Even now, it hardly seemed real.

They resisted the urge to inundate him with their presently overwhelming adoration and affection, Grim's own emotions over their Insight revealing an analytical frustration of varying intensities. They'd promised not to distract him while working. The least they could do was stand by that promise.

They Shielded their emotions instead, temporarily burying them to unwrap with him later, upon the completion of his mission on Janikk. Feels could already imagine their subsequent celebration, the taste of Grim's self-satisfaction mixing with his typical earnest ferocities of emotion, hopefully complemented by further samplings of Janikk's delectable vegetarian offerings.

"You ready?" Fleet Captain Haveid's gentle prodding brought them back to the present. "I'll be honest, I'm surprised it's my turn already. I'm far from the most impacted by his mind magic. The admiral spent as little time on me as he thought he could get away with. I was never a favorite."

"Navarch Javon requested you specifically." Feels directed their hologram to tilt its head. "And since you've been so generous in helping power my efforts, plus you're currently commanding the destroyer escorting the Grand Navarch..."

"Fair enough." The *Relentless'* flag officer threw up their hands in surrender with a canine-tipped smile. "I defer to your judgment. And Javon's".

"How'd you climb so high in the ranks without Kydell's approval, anyway?" Feels had been wondering the answer to this question, and now seemed as good a time as any to ask.

"He *approved* the promotions. He just wasn't *happy* about them. But even Admiral Kydell knew sometimes diplomacy is the best avenue of attack." Haveid's tail twitched in elegant curls of amusement as they bared their teeth. "Was Javon's doing, though. He needed her loyalty to tie her to himself, but it also tied her to us. He needed her, which meant he couldn't deny her requests for her people without risking his own hold."

The katanoj snorted. "Only got worse for him, after he lost Admiral Renkash and the landing party at Loxira. *Especially* Renkash's second-in-command, Void preserve his soul." They tapped their claws on the desk, mismatched eyes staring blankly through the wall. "Commodore Lawson Zane. Wish *I* could've met that one. From the stories I heard? Standing his own against Renkash *and* Kydell? Man's a legend. If he walked through that door right now, my battle mages would drop everything to line up and shake his hand. Every last one."

Feels debated adding their own opinions to the fleet captain's assessment, but decided to hold their silence and allow Haveid to finish. Grim had buried his past. Feels wasn't about to disrespect him by digging it up again.

The fleet captain shifted their attention back to Feels, eyes sparkling in the dim light of their office. "Javon's a legend, too, though she'll never admit it. Never dealt with Renkash, but no doubt in my mind, she'd have given him hell. Course, I'd have had to defend her afterward. That cat was a menace." Their ears twitched as they shrugged. "With Lawson gone, Kydell needed someone else to cement his fleets together. Someone they'd follow without question, regardless of whether or not they'd received his Psychomorphation. And Javon's the best he had left. Add in her stubbornness and... Whatever she wanted? She usually got it. *Including* my promotions."

Feels groomed their antennae through the katanoj's retrospection, the fae's own promotions through the ranks one of the many concessions Kydell had made to satisfy Grim through the years. Javon had certainly given Grim a few earfuls – *and* procured another promotion for Haveid – and it hadn't even been a month yet.

More affection bubbled to their attention at the memories, but Grim's current smug satisfaction was lined with a worry Feels knew better than to interrupt. They tucked their own emotions away for later, returning their attention to Haveid.

But before they could reply, a sudden unfamiliar sensation stopped Feels cold: silence.

No. Not silence, not exactly, but a distinct lack of...

Grim!

Their Insight spell, vivid with emotions mere seconds before, now lay still and empty as if his intoxicatingly enjoying feelings had suddenly dissipated to leave nothing in their wake. As if their beloved Grim had abruptly disappeared in his entirety.

"Fleet Captain! Sir!"

Feels barely registered the new voice demanding Haveid's immediate attention, or the rushed report that immediately followed. Grim had finally been theirs. He *couldn't* be gone.

"...and I can't reach them! It's like they've disappeared!"

The newcomer's words finally broke through Feels' panicked haze. "Tell me everything. From the beginning."

"I'm sorry, sir." The new voice filled with concern and apology. "I didn't realize you had a visitor."

"It's okay, Tarvick." Haveid nodded their approval at the Hydroponics AI's hesitation. "This is the Grand Navarch's psychomorphic mage. You can tell them anything."

"I don't know how much you understand about how Nature Magic fields work, or why Janikk is unique from any other planet I've seen..." Tarvick's voice faded.

"Summarize." Feels hadn't realized just how much they'd come to take their emotional connection to Grim for granted, but its absence now made even concentration difficult. "Where's the Grand Navarch?"

"I don't know!" Tarvick lamented. "I was just monitoring the scans like he'd asked when suddenly one of the poles disappeared. I counted three times, there's only fourteen now. Tried to push an update to their tablets, asked Comms to contact them, had Nav Call..." The rising anxiety in Tarvick's thoughts only served to elevate Feels' own fears. "It's like they *vanished*. Even tried the trackers in the tablets. Can only find one... And it's alarmingly close to our missing pole. Something they did must have triggered its disappearance, and theirs."

Feels didn't wait to hear more, slipping from their bindings within the *Relentless* to trace the Oath back to Grim. The necromancer had explained it would remain intact so long as Feels retained their possession of his soul, only breaking if he was Shattered. The tether's continued existence now quelled the worst of Feels' panic, but did nothing to answer their question.

Where *was* he? What had *happened*?

A sudden, unexpected barrier blocked the rest of their journey, their sense of the Oath tether's location ending just as abruptly. It hadn't broken – a close inspection of their own soul revealed a gossamer thin proof of that – but somewhere between them and their Grim was an invisible wall none of their magic could cross.

Remembering Grim's emotions as they ate the fruit to join him in the planet's living network, Feels attempted a different tactic, reaching for their own sense of belonging to Janikk in an effort to find their necromancer among the many lives within. They reached out with all their thoughts and memories, brushing against anything and everything even remotely familiar...

There.

The feeling was faint but unmistakable, the rising panic of their beloved, cut off from the limitless expanse of the Void that usually held his claustrophobia at bay.

I've got you. Feels broke the Shielding on their emotions from earlier, reaching deep into their own understanding of the Afterlife at the same time, and sent all of it into Janikk's network. An infinite Void of possibilities, wrapped in their unyielding love and devotion, injected directly into Janikk with all of Feels' desperate desires for their necromancer's safety.

Hope you're okay, Grim. I'll do whatever you ask of me, but I can't reach you. Whatever you need to do next, you're on your own. But never *alone.*

31

RAZICK CURSED AS THE cave system shuddered around them, the entryway closing behind them. She heard someone – Urla, perhaps – cry out across Jeb's Telepathy, but she was already in motion, spinning on her heels and sprinting back toward the entrance to...

She wasn't sure what. Maybe she could find a way to pry it open again?

The riot rifle could have burnt through rock at its highest setting, at least for a few minutes, but she'd lost that to the frightfully intelligent furred reptiles outside. Her Pyromancy wasn't quite so concentrated. She could melt their way out maybe, but that would likely take days and she hadn't packed enough water or provisions to sustain three people for that long. Telekinesis may have worked, if she'd been close enough to realize what had happened.

"I *told* him I should go last," she muttered to herself.

Once again, she was out of her element and scrambling for a solution.

All she'd ever wanted was to know someone was proud of her. Jeb was, of course, but he was *Jeb*. Her newfound knowledge of his own experiences in the SAF had only furthered her assessment that her brother always saw the best in people, even when they were at their worst. She envied his optimism, but couldn't share it. Not after what she'd seen. Not after what she'd *done*.

Nor could she share his opinions of her competence, his steady encouragement contributing little to soothe the wounds in her own confidence.

Lawrence, on the other hand... He was talented, powerful, and he *understood*. He was everything she'd always wanted to be, wanted to be *recognized* as being. If she could earn his approval, truly show him just how useful *she* could be, perhaps he'd quell the self-doubt she'd learned from an early age.

Not that he'd be much use at the moment, judging by the sight that greeted her as she turned the corner. Lawrence clung tightly to the wall behind him in wide-eyed terror, as if attempting to claw his way through, a far cry from the limitless necromancer she'd come to know, who readily bent the universe to his whim.

Janikk. There was no other explanation.

"That damned fruit," she cursed, unleashing the full fury of her magic to wrap him in an Antimagic field. "I'll get this planet out of your head."

She silently thanked her instructors for the strictness of her training, repeating each stance and spell until they'd become second nature. She didn't *need* hand motions, they'd drilled those out of her, but she used them now anyway in an attempt to hide how much her hands were shaking.

<No, no!> Urla shouted again across the telepathic link. <Razick, stop! That's not what he needs!>

"This... Antimagic field... isn't the favor... you think it is," Shane managed between tight breaths, his knuckles white against the cold stone walls. "Please, Raz... I just need..."

<Stop, so I can talk to him,> Urla commanded. <Jeb, the link.>

Razick dropped her spell, forcing herself to turn away. Once again, she'd done the wrong thing. Once again, someone else was better suited to resolve the situation.

She cast a Shielding spell on him anyway. Just because she didn't know how to help didn't mean she should stop *trying*.

<Sir. I'm here. Focus on my voice,> Urla commanded across the link. <I'll get you through this.>

Razick squeezed past her brother, reclaiming her point position and scanning for potential threats from within the passageway. "Making myself useful," she explained to his questioning glance. "Last thing we need's an ambush."

<Good,> Urla praised, and Razick's heart ached. <Now concentrate on this.>

The cave ahead of them was dark but silent, her Anemancy detecting little other than Lawrence's quick breathing behind her. She adjusted the settings on her goggles, pulling in a grayscale representation of their descent into the darkness.

<It's not as infinite as the Void, Sir, but Janikk has a lot to offer, just the same,> Urla continued. <It's like tapping into the special channels at Headquarters. Limited, but enough to soothe the worst of the claustrophobia.>

Razick hissed through her teeth. *That* would have been nice to know earlier. He'd told Urla he was claustrophobic, but not her?

Maybe they weren't as close as she'd believed. Maybe she'd only imagined she'd earned his trust.

It didn't matter. She had a duty to fulfill, and she'd do it. Maybe she'd lost her edge since she'd deserted from the SAF, grown complacent in her quest for a quiet civilian life, but she wasn't *that* rusty. Fleet Captain Haveid's battle mages would make good practice partners. Or maybe she'd hunt down Vernell, see if he'd survived his unexpected trip to the Void during the Battle for Baden.

She had options. She could fix this.

<Sir.> Urla's voice had adopted an awkward edge. <I appreciate your gratitude, but...>

"Feels," Lawrence sighed. "Feels came for me, too."

Razick spun at his voice, appraising him intently. He'd moved to sit on the floor of the cave, his back pressed to the wall, his eyes closed. The very opposite of the power he typically embodied.

Urla crouched before him, ears folded back, her tail jerking behind her as she stared intently at his face. Her fur shone a sickly green in the enhanced vision of Razick's visor, as if projecting her own concerns for the necromancer's well-being.

Lawrence looked up at the katanoj then, his face carrying a soft pride. "Thank you. That was a good idea. It's not the Void, but I can work with a planet in my mind."

Razick scowled, unable to stop her frustration from redirecting itself to him. "You mean to tell me you've been pushing us to go exploring in an unfamiliar cave, and never thought to tell me you were claustrophobic?"

He poked the cave floor awkwardly with the heel of his boot. "Wasn't expecting to get boxed in."

"It's a *cave*," Razick growled, throwing her hands in the air. "That's what caves *do*."

"Claustrophobia is rather common among necromancers," Urla interjected. "The stronger the necromancer, the more severe the claustrophobia. Usually. That's why SAF Headquarters has that specialized tyrellium wiring, for channeling magic through the walls. They say it's for easier communication, but it's actually so their necromancers can still function despite the tyrellium shielding."

"A side effect of the job, I'm afraid," Lawrence said with a sigh. "When you're accustomed to carrying the limitless expanse of the universe in the back of your mind, anything less feels confining. We try not to advertise it, of course. Particularly us Void necromancers. We're an arrogant bunch. It's... not good for the image."

"So when I used Antimagic on you, back on Baden..."

Razick could have kicked herself. Why hadn't she known that? With all her other training, shouldn't someone have told her?

"I'm sorry."

Lawrence grimaced, rubbing the back of his neck. "Mine is particularly debilitating. For me, Necromancy was the cure long before it became the cause, so I've come to rely on it more than most. But I'll manage now. Urla's quite clever. She's given me a good strategy."

At least one of them had been helpful.

Lawrence turned back to the dead biologist, frowning. "I'm afraid I'll have to break a promise, though. I'm sorry. I said I wouldn't mention it again, but I need your expertise. Take a look at the door."

"You think it's enchanted."

The necromancer nodded. "For starters. It takes a lot to cut me off from the Void. I want to know what we're getting into."

Urla moved toward the unexpected door, ignoring Jeb's half-hearted request for explanation of Lawrence's words. The inner surface shimmered as she passed her hand along its frame. "I think you're right." Her fingers caressed various points along the door as she studied it, shaking her head. "But this enchantment isn't meant for us. It's not cutting off the outside. It's amplifying everything *inside*."

"Why would they do that?" Jeb tugged at his hair beneath his helmet. "Disrupt magic only to cast spells to make it stronger?"

"This wasn't built with all magic in mind, though. Given the varieties of life we've seen on the planet... I'd hypothesize those who originally lived here built their society around Nature Magic specifically." Urla gestured to the wall, and the various mosses growing within the cave briefly illuminated the path with a delicate green iridescence. "Nature Magic is still at full strength here, and then some. They wanted to amplify whatever was cast in this cave, without spreading those effects to the rest of Janikk."

"Not sure it worked," Jeb said quietly. "At least, not when the door's open. This was one of the planetary Nature Magic poles. I don't think that's a coincidence."

Razick wrinkled her nose as she watched. "So then what's cutting off Lawrence's magic? If yours is fine, and mine feels okay..."

"Probably the same thing that's carrying the enchantment through the entire cave." Lawrence closed his eyes, reaching a hand to the wall until his fingers slipped through the structure up to his knuckles. Sliding his hands along the stone, fingers still immersed, he finally withdrew to wipe his palms against his trousers. "Tyrellium shielding. Same as Headquarters. This *looks* like a natural cave system, but the whole wall is lined with it. It's conducting the enchantments of the Runework, but magic can't pass through it."

"It's surprisingly elaborate." There was awe in Urla's voice. "Quite the find! I've never seen anything like it. No one has, to my knowledge. And just imagine how old it must be..."

"You're not a biologist, are you?" Jeb asked, with an edge of something Razick couldn't quite place.

But Lawrence was already talking again. "Necromancy pulls its strength from the limitless powers of the Void and the Afterlife, so in here I'm limited to whatever corresponds with this exact cave system. I can still cast, thanks to the amplifications carved into the door, but I can't jump us anywhere. We'll have to travel the old fashioned way."

He focused on Razick then, and she felt herself stand taller at the intensity of his attention. "The only way out is through, so I'm *hoping* Janikk's done sending her friends. But if I'm wrong, I can't help down here. I'm relying on you."

"You can count on me, Sir," she told him, determined to finally prove herself.

"I know," he said quietly, although his frown suggested perhaps she didn't sound as confident as she'd intended. "Let's see what surprises she's planned for us."

32

Fleet Captain Haveid frowned at the remains of the expedition pack scattered across the clearing, its contents thoroughly shredded and mangled beyond repair. A quick adjustment of their borrowed visor brought their field of vision into focus despite the rapidly fading light, augmenting Haveid's own enhanced night vision to reveal dimensions on the small bite marks and deep gouges in the metal of the camping equipment. "Whose pack was this?"

"It's camping gear." Petty Officer Tarvick Nalonni stood from where he'd been crouching to measure bite marks across a shockingly mangled riot rifle. The human Artificial Intelligence had chosen to manifest in an unmarked variant of the SAF working uniform, the khaki and brown a flattering compliment to the rich brown of the human's skin. He scratched at his short, wavy hair, biting his lip as he met Haveid's eyes. "Kane Jeb gave that to the Grand Navarch to carry. Was also his tablet I found."

Haveid's heart sank. Actual trouble then.

Grunting, they squared their shoulders and surveyed their rescue team. All experts in the field, hand-picked for their role. They'd get the mission back on track.

Besides, the missing team had already survived the full attention of Admiral Kydell. A murderous planet should be easy to stall until Haveid's arrival, in comparison.

They turned to the *Relentless'* auxiliary Void necromancer, Sub-Lieutenant Xalis Cassandra, a surprisingly young fair-skinned human with flowing blonde curls and color-changing eyes which currently shone a brilliant, deep violet. "What do you see?"

"No one." She frowned, her voice and attention far away as she scanned the Afterlife for clues. "As far as I can sense, it's just us here."

"Perimeter secure." Commander Kane Tammi nodded to Haveid as she jogged over to make her report. "Caught signs of a large pack of quadrupeds circling not far into the trees, but my team drove them off easily enough. We're keeping watch in case they come back, but it's quiet out there otherwise."

A slim-built canid with blonde fur and hazel eyes, the commander's quick mind and driven personality had quickly caught Haveid's attention soon after Kydell's Claim on her future career. According to her files she was a distant cousin-by-marriage of the Grand Navarch's accompanying Kanes, a relationship she'd traded on to claim leadership of the present away team.

"Think it's the same creatures that demolished the backpack?" Haveid held up one of the gnawed poles for inspection.

"No. Trust me, you wouldn't think so, either, if you'd seen the teeth on those things. These bites are too small in comparison." The commander motioned toward the riot rifle Tarvick had been inspecting earlier, unleashing a feral smile that revealed her teeth. "They're definitely responsible for disarming my cousin, though."

"I don't think the local wildlife was involved in their disappearance," the Grand Navarch's psychomorphic mage added, landing lightly on Haveid's forearm. "He was feeling triumphant before he disappeared, not hurt or afraid." They motioned to a specific section of the cliff face behind them. "I believe your necromancer would have better luck checking underground. And I'd like to return to the Afterlife, to try and contact Janikk directly."

Haveid nodded their approval at the Void necromancer's questioning glance. "Get them whatever they need."

The fae's relative position within the command hierarchy was uncertain, their relationship with the Grand Navarch holding a level of power which likely outranked the fleet captain's, but the psychomorphic mage seemed content to serve in a largely advisory role and permit Haveid to direct their people as they saw fit. A notable improvement from the SAF. Similar circumstances within the Confederation's military typically devolved into shouting matches, political sabotage, or violence, the outcome determining the future career paths of both victor and victim.

"Commander, which way did your team drive those creatures you found earlier?"

She pointed, shaking her head. "I'd tell you not to wander off, to let my team handle it, but I know that look."

"I've spent more time in the field than you, pup." Haveid's eyes sparkled in the starlight.

"I'll tell my lieutenant to keep an eye on you, but stay out of your way unless you tell her otherwise." The commander offered a casual salute, tapping the tip of her fingers against the brim of her helmet. "Enjoy your hunt, sir."

Haveid removed their own helmet and closed their eyes, nose tilted upward to take in the cool scents of the evening, unfamiliar and yet comforting all the same. They didn't regret their agreement with Navarch Javon, watching her back and defending her position against more threats than she'd ever realize as she rose through the ranks, but their days as a battle mage in the field had always remained a fond memory. It felt *good* to be back planetside for a change.

The faint breeze wafting from the direction the commander had pointed carried none of the expected scents of an animal on the run. And no true predator would remain downwind of their prey for long.

Decision made, Haveid set off in the opposite direction. They slipped from their boots to silently traverse the ground in bare feet, the cool earth a welcome sensation beneath their footpads after months spent on the unyielding metal of the *Relentless'* decks.

Time to run.

They made great time through the trees, easily slipping into their old stealth training to cover the distance with minimal sound, the soft yips and barks of their quarry faintly audible in the distance. They *had* circled around. Clever beasts. Finding a particularly sturdy tree, Haveid extended their claws, nimbly climbing to spread their weight across one of the lower branches. They settled to wait, whiskers splayed, tail tense with anticipation.

The red furred creatures emerged into Haveid's field of view moments later, their footfalls light and delicate on long slender legs, a sharp contrast to the razored teeth within their thickly scaled snouts. *Commander wasn't kidding.* Haveid counted over two dozen as the pack passed beneath their perch, the faint rustling of the underbrush to either side hinting at more.

Too many. If the creatures reached the clearing, the rescue team would be easily overrun, and Haveid couldn't allow that. No, they'd have to distract the creatures. Buy their team enough time to find and rescue the others.

They dropped from their perch to land lightly behind the predatory creatures, breaking off a portion of a dying tree with a loud *Snap!* The pack froze at the sound, quickly spinning to confront the newly-emerged threat with open-mouthed growls as the former battle mage wielded the branch as a long-handled club.

In a moment, Haveid was surrounded, the creatures maintaining a healthy distance from the branch but leaving no opportunity for the fleet captain to slip through their ranks. The ferocity in the predators' stance reminded Haveid of their own healthy bloodlust, a Family trait well known within the Confederation.

A Haveid rarely ran from a fight. And when they did, it was a bad omen for whoever they ran from.

Grinning at the challenge, the katanoj dropped their makeshift weapon to once again hoist themself into the branches of the tree with well-honed muscles and a strategic telekinetic push.

I love this planet.

The pack closed quickly, encircling both Haveid's position and the tree trunk with a calculated hunger, twin tails beating in triumph. Haveid was ready, launching themself into the next tree with a graceful running leap augmented by their Telekinesis, their claws finding quick purchase against the rough bark by instinct alone. The pack eagerly followed beneath as Haveid leaped from tree to tree, their agile dance of well-honed magic and feral muscle leading the predators further from the rescue party's efforts in the clearing. The katanoj snarled their pleasure at the ferocity of the chase, several of the furred creatures beneath launching themselves upward off the backs of their comrades to snap at Haveid's heels, often missing by mere inches as the fleet captain propelled themself forward to the next perch.

The chase ended too soon, Haveid's weight sending a particularly precarious branch swinging downward with a loud crack. Before they could react, one of their pursuers managed to catch the fleet captain's ankle in an unrelenting snap of stubborn teeth and broken bone as they both tumbled to the ground.

Haveid felt their ankle shatter at the twin impacts, their Telekinesis unable to pry open the locked jaw of the successful predator as the creature's packmates circled closer with triumphant barks and cautious steps.

Squaring their shoulders in preparation for the end, Haveid prepped a spell to prolong the predators' efforts.

This wasn't a bad way to go. They'd always worried their death would come at the claws of Admiral Kydell or his TAG, the white wolf finally determining the fleet captain's loyalty to Javon rather than himself was a barrier to his control over the fearless woman Haveid had begun to consider as precious as a daughter.

But there were no twisted politics out here. Just the honest relationship of predator and prey.

Ignoring the throbbing in their leg as the creature's jaw clamped down harder, Haveid instead gripped the broken branch with their Telekinesis and prepared to pull it toward themself. Just because they'd accepted their end didn't mean they'd make it easier on the creatures. Instead, they bared their teeth in their own predatory smile, whiskers splayed in warning.

The pack erupted in a flurry of fierce snarls, spinning once more to engage a new threat as a trio of arrows sailed forth from the treetops to impale three of the furred predators, including the one gripping Haveid's leg.

Lieutenant Tashford. Haveid had forgotten he'd been following.

"You could have just called for backup from the *Relentless*, sir, instead of taking them all on by yourself," the green-skinned dracoling chided with a shake of his ear fins.

"Now where's the fun in that?" Haveid laughed, carefully prying their ankle free from the now-whimpering creature.

Tashford was right, of course. They *should* have.

It had been so long since they'd been on a hunt, though; they hadn't wanted to share.

"I'll draw them off, sir," Tashford promised. "You get the help you need."

His words were accompanied by another spray of arrows, this set easily sidestepped by the creatures as they tore off after their new prey, their snarls fiercer now as if this hunt was personal, leaving the fleet captain alone with the injured.

Haveid shook their head. Grand Navarch wouldn't be happy if the planet refused his request because they'd hurt some of her pets.

The closest of the trio snarled as Haveid carefully removed the arrow from its chest, Haveid's own blood still in its teeth, but quickly collapsed into whimpers from the pain of the exertion.

"It's alright," Haveid soothed, running their fingertips over stiff fur now knotted with blood. "I got you."

The beast stilled at the warmth from Haveid's fingers, a simple healing spell they'd used often in the field, its strength now boosted by the planet's unnaturally powerful Nature Magic fields. It wouldn't heal everything, but it would keep the creature breathing.

As Haveid removed their fingers, the creature rolled to its feet, tentatively testing its footing before trotting to its injured companions and sitting, tilting its head expectantly.

"Of course, little one." Haveid gently poked their ankle, casting a quick spell to staunch the bleeding as they cataloged the jumble of snapped and misaligned bone. The rest of the injury was beyond their capabilities, but it wasn't life threatening. They could get proper medical treatment later.

For now, a walking aid would suffice.

Haveid's eyes caught on a promising stick, but before they could retrieve it with their magic the healed creature had followed their gaze to bite it first, dragging the thick branch to drop it beside Haveid. The fleet captain scratched the beast behind its ears in thanks, eliciting a friendly thump from its dual tails and a firm but gentle tug toward the creature's injured companions.

"I know. I know." Haveid pushed themself upright, balancing their weight on their good foot and the stick, stabilizing their steps with their magic. "Let's see what I can do for your friends."

The second creature had been pinned to the ground, the barbed arrow passing through to embed itself deep within the dirt. Haveid broke the shaft, carefully lifting the bundle of whimpering fur free before gently probing the wound. Verifying the shaft had passed through cleanly, Haveid cast their healing spell, mending the flesh to allow faster recovery.

Their third patient was younger, the arrow pinning it to a tree by its neck, its frenzied efforts to free itself serving only to sap its strength and increase blood loss. Haveid carefully leaned against its flank, pressing the beast firmly to the tree as they gripped its head and neck with their Telekinesis before gently directing their magic to press against the surrounding skin, closing the nicked blood vessels to staunch the flow.

It had missed the main artery, at least.

A quick snap of the arrow shaft granted the creature's freedom, and Haveid turned their attention to carefully removing the panicked animal in agonizingly slow motions, finger pressed against the arrow's entry point to mend each newly released portion of the wound as they moved. An eternity later it, too, was free, yipping weakly at its rescuer in cautious excitement.

Haveid patted the creature's fur, gently digging their claws into the awkward hard to reach spots behind its thickly furred ears, and was rewarded with a friendly scaled headbutt and demands for more.

"Thanks for the chase, little one," they growled, obliging. "Hopefully next time we won't be so rudely interrupted."

Haveid's first patient howled, a low-pitched wave of sound and emotion which carried through the evening with a chilling beauty. The other two joined in soon after with an overwhelming exuberance.

The fleet captain stared into the canopy of trees, leaning against the trunk behind them to enjoy the unexpected song, only to find themself nudged from all directions with a persistent urgency. They looked down in time to watch a large, dead rodent cascade into their lap, one of the furred pack creatures sitting expectantly between their legs, head cocked and waiting. A quick survey of their surroundings showed their former patients eagerly devouring a second rodent, while many of the others contented themselves with an assortment of large fruit.

The pressure at Haveid's sides continued, several of the predators impatiently demanding their attention, as the hunter in their lap nudged the rodent with its snout.

Haveid accepted the gift, gripping it in their clawed hands – much to the excitement of their new friends – and took a bite. The intoxicating taste of fresh flesh and warm, salty blood flooded their senses, and Haveid closed their eyes to savor the carnal flavors between their teeth and dripping down their throat.

This, they had missed the most.

The pack erupted in gleeful yips and howls, and this time Haveid joined in the song.

Feels reached for their necromancer again, the complete absence of his emotions growing into an unsoothable ache scratching against their consciousness.

Where are you, Grim? What could possibly separate us?

"What do you need from me, sir?" Sub-Lieutenant Xalis, the *Relentless'* auxiliary Void necromancer, eyed the cliff face before them expectantly as she awaited orders.

"He'd prefer this remain private knowledge..." Feels began hesitantly. But they needed to find him. "The Grand Navarch and I took the Oath. Can you use that to trace him?"

Her violet eyes flashed understanding as she readied the spell with a nod, phasing into the Afterlife to appear moments later against the cliff before them. Brows furrowing, she tried again, this time keeping her physical form on the mortal plane as her consciousness traced the gossamer thin tether of necromantic magic tying Grim's soul to Feels', her fingers dipping slightly into the natural-looking rock before them.

"It's not real," she breathed in wonder. "I mean, it's a real cliff. But right *here*... I think this used to be a cave."

"Used to be?" Feels tilted their head. "How can a cave just... disappear?" A sudden fear gripped their thoughts. "It didn't collapse, did it? Are they trapped?"

Xalis shook her head. "Trapped? Maybe. But not from a cave-in." She traced her fingers along the stones, her fingertips phasing once more into the rock. "There's a barrier here, blocking even magic. There's a whole section underneath I can't see into."

Feels landed on her arm to poke at the stone. "And he's in there?"

"Your Oath leads there." The necromancer shrugged helplessly. "So probably? But unless we find a way in ourselves, we can't know for certain."

"I need to talk to Janikk." Feels gripped the stone with their arms, fluttering their wings in frustration. "Drop the spell. Return me to the Afterlife. Soul Call me if you learn anything new, and I'll do the same."

The mortal plane twisted and faded as Xalis nodded, and Feels found themself once more in the higher planes beyond the Veil. Concentrating their thoughts on the network of life they'd begun to sense on the planet, Feels reached out with a rising sense of urgency.

Their mysterious host arrived in a burst of life and curiosity, her form and intentions clouded.

Shifting their thoughts into gratitude, then their concern for Grim, Feels addressed her tentatively. "Janikk?"

"Turikkael ij Tergerael." The fae caught a hint of a bow, respect in her voice as she plucked lightly at the Oath tether. "Nikkeer."

"Do you know where they are?" Sensing her confusion, the empath cast to share their emotions. Their love for Grim. The loneliness left by his absence.

Janikk nodded understanding, her own emotions now detached. "Klaaelox dirkkatae aja Tsekeht."

That didn't help. They tried again, this time their emotions centered on a fearful uncertainty. "Are they okay? I don't understand."

"Tsekeht esaukkee yukkan."

The words were heavy with importance, and suddenly the network of life bloomed in Feels' awareness, as if the planet itself was reaching out to them. Calling to them to experience a greater joy of belonging.

The sensation faded as quickly as it had arrived, leaving Feels to grapple with the emptiness left in its wake.

They turned to her, longing and wonder in their mind. "What was that?"

"Yukkan."

The word felt like a confirmation, although of what, Feels was uncertain. They reached out with more questions, the unknowns in their thoughts only compounded by their interactions, even as Janikk herself faded from their senses.

They still had no idea what she wanted. But there had been something in her *emotions*...

They recentered their thoughts, this time on Haveid's Void necromancer, and were rewarded with a response. <<Sir? Did you get what you needed?>>

"I don't know," they admitted, "but I'm ready to return. You can pull me to the mortal plane again."

Xalis obliged, twisting the Veil until the fae's gossamer wings once more fluttered in the light breeze as a flurry of contented howls echoed in the distance, the stars clearly visible in the night sky.

"Will that be all, sir?"

Feels nodded their gratitude. "Thank you. If there's something else you need to-"

"Actually..." Xalis' anxiety spiked as she looked away, shifting her weight on her heels and twisting her hands in front of her.

Pausing their own thoughts, the fae watched patiently as Xalis fought her inner struggle. She met their eyes briefly before squeezing her own shut, her words spilling out in a soft flurry of sound.

"What's he really like? The Grand Navarch? Everyone says he must be immensely powerful, to have defeated Admiral Kydell with such a small team. And the way Fleet Captain Haveid talks about him, many of us have been wondering if he used to be Sparnelli. But then why haven't we heard of him before?"

Xalis cracked one eye, embarrassment joining her concern. "I hope it's okay I'm asking this? I trust Navarch Javon. I know she wouldn't have sided with him if she didn't think he'd be good to us. I just want to... understand? I want to know what to expect. And what's expected of *me*."

Sighing, she directed a sorrowful smile at the empath. "With Admiral Kydell, at least I knew his plans for my future. And now that he's gone... I'm *glad* he's gone, but I feel... lost." A small spark of gratitude shone through her thoughts. "And you've been kind to me. And the Grand Navarch clearly trusts you if he'd swear his soul to you like that... So I'm hoping maybe you can help?"

Her burning questions now out in the open, Xalis blinked anxiously in the sudden silence, shifting her weight frequently as she waited for Feels' answer with a mix of trepidation and relief.

Her questions were reasonable. Xalis and the others had been through a lot. They needed to know they'd be safe now.

And Grim would approve.

"The Grand Navarch and I were both Sparnelli, once. Both in service to Admiral Kydell. I served my ten years and got out. The Grand Navarch, though... As with anyone who finds themselves in Kydell's Collection, the Grand Navarch has... regrets. He deserted, when the opportunity arose. Shane Lawrence is a new name, for a new life. He'd prefer the universe forget who he was, although he himself swears to never forget. So he can do better – be better – than he was."

"So he understands…" She bit her lip, her next words thoughtful, and Feels couldn't help but gleefully inhale the hope held in her mind. "And the fleet? What is he planning to do with us?"

"Right now?" Feels fluttered their wings in reassurance. "He's taken responsibility for your well-being. This mission is exactly what he said it was: a search for a safe place of your own, free from the Confederation and anyone else who'd try to harm or take advantage of you. And after that?" They opened their arms, tilting their head. "I suspect it's up to you."

"On the bridge this morning. When he promised he'd do right by us…"

"He's very careful with the words he gives. He doesn't lie, and he'd move the stars themselves to keep a promise. He meant every word, same as always."

Holding out her hand, Xalis smiled as Feels landed gently on her offered fingers. "Thank you. For answering." She turned from them to survey the rest of the rescue team, deep in their investigative efforts. "I'm not used to receiving straight answers, outside the *Relentless*. It's… nice. Being treated like a person, I mean. Someone caring how I feel, beyond simply the impact it has on my efficiency."

Feels began to remind her they were an empath, that feelings were an important part of how they experienced the world, when a commotion broke out on the outskirts of their camp.

34

Feels watched as their battle mage escort converged on a spot not far from where the fleet captain had entered the woods. The team's tensions wound tightly into a cautious agitation among the well-practiced troops, before exploding into an amused excitement.

Moments later, Haveid limped into the clearing, their ankle bound in a simple splint, their shoulder supported by a stern-faced Lieutenant Tashford. Despite the clearly painful injury, the cat's spirits were high, the triumph in their thoughts resonating in the night air.

Feels spotted the team's field medic, a young brown-speckled canid with an overfull kit, preparing to address the fleet captain's ankle. With a quick nod of thanks to Xalis, the fae flitted over to join him and offer their services.

Something tugged at the back of their mind. The fleet captain felt... *different*.

"Who caught who?" Commander Kane slapped Haveid on the back with a grin before turning with a growl to her lieutenant. "I thought you were supposed to keep them *out* of trouble?"

"Nobody can keep a Haveid out of trouble when they go looking for it," Tashford quipped back, feet planted firmly on the ground to offer additional stability as Haveid slid to the grass. "My job is merely to get them out of it again, in as few new pieces as possible."

"He did a beautiful job of it, too," Haveid admitted, wincing slightly as the medic poked at their mangled ankle with a practiced claw. "How'd you know it was safe to come back for me?"

"Those creatures of yours gave up the chase as soon as your injured friends started howling." He shook his head, hands on his hips. "Doubled back to make sure you were okay. Didn't expect to interrupt a whole damned dinner party."

And suddenly Feels recognized the sensation scratching at the back of their mind. "You ate the fruit."

"Not exactly..." Haveid's fierce smile revealed traces of blood within their teeth. "But something like that."

"There's something you should know," Feels began, pausing. "Hydroponics probably needs to hear this, too."

The fleet captain looked up expectantly as Tashford motioned for Tarvick's attention. "Food's not poisoned, is it? Last thing we need's to colonize a planet where we can't *eat* anything."

"No, nothing like that," Feels reassured, landing on Haveid's good leg after verifying the expertise of the other medic's efforts. They turned to watch Tarvick join the group, his grizzled face lined with worry. "Good. Maybe you know how this works? Janikk has some sort of network. The Grand Navarch and I ate some fruit last night, and it pulled us into it. And now Fleet Captain Haveid... So it seems if you eat *anything*, you become a part of Janikk, too."

Tarvick scratched his beard, directing a puzzled look at the fae. "Janikk has extremely strong Nature Magic. Are you sure that's not what you're picking up? You're a healer, you feel it, right? It's so much stronger here than elsewhere. You sure that's not what you're picking up?"

Shaking their head, Feels took flight to meet Tarvick's eyes. "Grand Navarch and I went through it in great detail last night. This is something different. Besides. If you ever saw his attempts at gardening, you'd *know* the Grand Navarch doesn't have the aptitude. But his draw to the planet is even stronger than mine."

They turned back to Haveid. "I also knew you'd eaten something. I felt a new closeness to you, more than just from our Psychomorphation sessions. Almost like we're family now."

"That would... explain some things." Haveid turned to the commander, a glint in their eyes. "Tell your team to stand down. I made some new friends."

Commander Kane raised her arm in the air, elbow bent, before suddenly tightening her hand into a fist. She waited a moment before giving a quick nod to Haveid, propping her own rifle against her leg in the process.

The fleet captain raised their chin, unleashing a short trio of yips into the night air. Their cry was greeted by an excited series of short barks in return, and Feels watched in delight as a pair of exuberant creatures rushed to greet Haveid. Their coarse fur was a dark scarlet on slender, black-tipped legs, the cream tips of their twin tails vibrating with excitement. The animals carefully sniffed the night air, casting a curious eye to the rescue team before sitting on either side of Haveid in a protective stance, their soft growls directed at Lieutenant Tashford.

"They don't like you very much," the fleet captain observed, baring their teeth.

He shrugged, maintaining a respectful distance. "I shot their friends. I wouldn't like me, either."

"You're always such a good sport," Haveid laughed, accepting the offered hand of their medic. Their new guardians tensed at the movement but made no efforts to stop it as the fleet captain rose before stepping forward tentatively, then more confidently as their ankle held. "Much better, thank you."

They returned the medic's salute before turning to Feels. "But what of the original landing party, and Janikk? Were you able to locate either?"

"The Grand Navarch is inside a magically-shielded cave beneath the cliff." Feels motioned to the rock face before them, Sub-Lieutenant Xalis still carefully probing for the hidden doorway. "We're assuming the others are with him."

"And Janikk?" The fleet captain scratched absent-mindedly behind the ears of their new companions, much to the creatures' delight.

"She had a lot to say," Feels reported, "And I understood very little of it, although a few words stood out. 'Klaael,' which refers to the landing party, according to what the Grand Navarch told me last night. And 'Yukkan,' which I *think* has something to do with the network you and I are now part of."

"Hmm…" Haveid scratched their own chin with their claws, the creatures now jumping against the fleet captain's legs with indignant yips until Haveid resumed scratching them instead. "Anything else?"

"Janikk felt pleased to see me. And worried about the landing party. I don't think she's trying to hurt us, I think she's genuinely happy we're here, and wants to help." They paused, tilting their head as they watched Haveid's new friends roll happily in the ferns of the clearing. "There was one other word that stood out. I've no idea what it means, but she said it a lot. 'Tsekeht.'"

The creatures froze in their play, ears alert, at the word. Leaping to their feet they darted south, turning excitedly to howl at Haveid to follow.

"*You* don't know what it means," Haveid observed, "but *they* do." They squared their shoulders, turning to address Commander Kane. "I'll take Lieutenant Tashford and two others, see what they're so excited about. Have Sub-Lieutenant

Xalis with Petty Officer Tarvick jump to us when they're caught up here."

"I'll join you as well," Feels added, receiving Haveid's relieved nod of approval in return.

Hold on, Grim. We're coming.

35

Jeb had taken the lead without asking, dropping his sister and Lawrence from his Telepathy before they could stop him and darting ahead into the winding passages of the unnaturally natural cave.

Urla had protested, of course, before finally admitting herself perfectly capable of scanning for signs of an ambush across whatever secret magic training she'd been hiding from him. Somehow he didn't *mind* that argument – for all his frustration at her secrets, she was still Urla, and that *meant* something – but the thought of an audience as he pressed for information twisted further knots in the emotions settled deep within his chest.

No, he didn't want company for this. Just answers.

<Jeb... Please talk to me,> she protested, not for the first time.

He wasn't angry. Or even surprised. They'd known each other less than a month. In that time, they'd been focused on the mission to Janikk and the needs of the fleet. Getting to know each other had been a pleasant way to pass the time while working. Her life before the *Inevitable* and her role as its Hydroponics AI simply hadn't come up.

Or... Maybe he *was* angry. Just not at *her*.

<When were you going to tell me?> he asked, finally.

<I'm sorry,> she said immediately. <I... after Janikk. I think. Probably. Maybe?>

Jeb allowed himself to pick up the pace, putting even more distance between himself and the others as if that would somehow lessen the distance he currently felt between himself and Urla. <You let me talk on and on about myself. I never even asked about you.>

<And I love that about you. I don't *like* talking about my past. You didn't force me to relive it.> Her voice carried a heaviness he hadn't heard from her before. <Until now, I suppose.>

<Where'd you learn all that?>

He already felt guilty for asking. She hadn't *wanted* him to ask. But the question had formed as she'd talked Lawrence through his debilitating claustrophobia, and now he had to know.

<I loved learning about your Family,> she told him instead. <I'd *known* about the Kanes before. Never got to talk to one, thought. Aside from pointing out plant types for alchemical field curatives, or helping brainstorm what they could ferment in a smuggled still, or something. Work stuff.> She sighed,

longingly. <From what I'd *heard*, though, I was envious. Not many well-regarded Families put their members' needs before the Family prestige. I'd always wondered what that would be like.>

Jeb frowned. When he'd flunked out of battle mage training, his Instructors had seemed surprised he hadn't been Disowned. That had always confused him. His parents had always supported him, as had his sister. They had enough battle mages in the Family, he'd been told. It was good he was charting his own path, and building a career he enjoyed, instead of being forced into what had been handed to him.

That same excitement for plants had carried him through the full ten years of his conscription. The countless missions he'd volunteered to support. The decade apart from Razick. Her sudden appearance on his doorstep on Baden after he'd left and she'd deserted.

<That's what Family *is*. We look out for each other.>

<Not everyone feels that way,> Urla said quietly. <You're one of the lucky ones.>

He hadn't *felt* lucky.

At least, not at first. As he'd pushed himself to learn more, and then to seek opportunities to reconnect with his sister, he'd come to realize just how privileged he'd been to escape the usual pressures of military service, instead devoting his attention to his research and his plants.

Even when he'd branched out into field work, he'd always had the opportunity to review each mission's objectives. He'd always enjoyed the missions like this one, cataloging new planets for potential colonization and alchemical reagents. He'd had his pick, too, courtesy of the lesser prestige attached.

Jeb shuddered. He'd witnessed fights erupt over some of the other ones, particularly those seeking "biological solutions to biological problems," as he'd seen them advertised. Back when he'd first been assigned to the labs he'd wondered what the hype had been about. After he'd been approved for field work, he'd looked into it, and...

Simply put, he'd decided then and there he preferred encouraging and cataloging life, rather than gathering prestige.

A horrible thought occurred to him.

<How many field missions have you gone on, Urla?>

<None,> she told him sadly, and suddenly he could breathe again. <That's why I agreed to the Agrokinesis in the first place. Figured I could apply for trips to the field. Apply my other skills, while I was there. But Admiral Kydell had other ideas.>

<Like what?>

<Like serving as a damn Hydroponics AI!> Urla spat.

<No, I didn't mean...>

Jeb's foot slipped on a collection of loose stones, his thoughts distracted by the present conversation and his own inability to properly voice his question. He reached for the wall to steady himself, instead pulling away a patch of lichen before landing roughly on his behind.

He dug his heels into the packed dirt lining the bottom of the cave to avoid sliding further down the sloped passageway, studying his unexpected sample, a rather bushy fruticose lichen with countless colorful hairlike tendrils branching out from the base where it had once clung to the wall. <I wonder how this grows down here.>

<It's not dormant,> Urla observed immediately, her voice slipping back into the cheerful tone that accompanied all her scientific observations. <It's quite vibrant, and didn't crumble when you grabbed it. Looks like it's growing quite happily. Or was, until you pulled it off the wall.>

<Wasn't on purpose,> Jeb grumbled, nonetheless happy at her apparent forgiveness. Or at least gratitude for the change in topic.

<I don't know of any species that can grow in the dark,> she continued thoughtfully. <But there's been too many twists and turns for the outside light to reach it. And since we already know this cave's sealed off from the outside world, we're not likely to encounter an opening up ahead, either.>

<Maybe it doesn't need light?>

<Even carnivorous plants need photosynthesis.>

<But lichen's the only fungus that does,> Jeb reminded her. <Maybe Janikk's doesn't.>

<Not much energy to be extracted from a cave wall,> Urla said slowly. <Unless...>

Jeb waited. Talking biology with Urla was easy. So easy, he hadn't realized how successfully she'd avoided most conversation about herself. He had full intentions to fix that omission, now that he'd realized, but for now the biology would clearly have to do.

<This would be easier if I were alive,> she grumbled. <Jeb. Hold it near your watch.>

<And then what?>

<Just... I'll tell you when to move.>

With a shrug, Jeb did as he was told, pressing the accidental lichen sample against his watch. <I feel rather silly.>

<How do you think I feel? Trying to catch magic without any hands. I can't even see what I'm doing. You keep looking away.>

He bit back a quip about watch faces and hands, instead forcing himself to focus in on the lichen, counting the seconds as they ticked past into minutes on his wristwatch.

<Magic!>

The cry made him jump, dropping the sample in the process.

<It consumes *magic*,> she repeated, reverently. <I think it was even casting Anemancy. I wonder if that's how it gets its other nutrients, by pulling them in with air?>

<From what you and Lawrence said earlier, there's plenty of magic down here to pull from,> Jeb observed, caught up in Urla's excitement. <And it's not a natural cave. Which means whoever built it would probably want some form of air circulation, yes? In fact...> He smelled the air. <This doesn't *smell* like a cave. It smells fresh. Like there's a filtration system, but better. It's not stale, like in spacecraft.>

<Selkirk Shatter me,> Urla swore. <You're right! I'd bet credits whoever built this *also* built the lichen. Think about

it. We like to think we're lightyears ahead of our predecessors, technologically, but if you actually *look* in the records for signs of Agrokinesis and Zokinesis, they're right there. They predate the Enlightenment, and space travel. They *had* to, or we'd have never survived the Void in the first place, without Curative Magic. And Biomicrokinesis like they'd have used on lichen is even *easier*, the only challenge is figuring out how to see what you're doing since everything's so small. Which is why all the spells are made to affect creatures as a *group*, rather than *individually*...>

<This isn't a cave.>

<Oh, no, it's a cave,> Urla said confidently. <But it has a *purpose*. Whoever lived here built it with intention. And whatever those were, Janikk wants us to experience it, too.>

Jeb felt the knot twist in his gut as he forced himself to stand. <We should probably tell the others.>

<Jeb...>

<Lawrence needs to know. Maybe Razick was right. Maybe this *is* a trap.>

<I don't think so. If Janikk wanted to kill us, she had plenty of opportunities.>

He couldn't argue that statement. Except... <What do sentient planets eat?>

<Jeb!> Urla's laughter, at least, was genuine. <If she needed to eat people, she'd have starved a long time ago. No, I think it's for *us*, not *her*. The Grand Navarch told her we want to live here. Maybe she's trying to show us what that means.>

<Or maybe there's a recipe she's been dying to try.> He loved her laugh. He wanted to listen to it, all the time.

<Then I guess I'm safe. I'm already dead.>

<Soul food.>

<Possible. Janikk's dead, too.>

<You're not seriously considering that, are you?>

Urla laughed again. <It's doubtful. But possible. I like considering the possibilities. Was the reason I studied the things I did.>

And *here*, finally, was the opportunity he'd been waiting for. Returning his attention to the path forward, he carefully picked his way down the sloped passageway. <What *did* you study?>

She didn't hesitate this time, still caught up in the excitement of her discovery. <History, mostly. Anthropology, especially. Biology, too, and the Nature kinesis classes. Civilization is fascinating. Especially when you think about the impacts of plants and animals on how civilizations form, and then that civilization's impact on the plants and animals in turn.>

<And Metamagic,> he guessed. <You'd need to be able to feel magic, to figure out the lichen was eating it.>

<And Metamagic,> she agreed, more subdued. <I meant what I said earlier. About how I don't want to talk about it right now.>

<I know. I'm sorry,> Jeb apologized. <I won't bring it up again. But Urla?>

<Yes?>

<You're absolutely fascinating. I want to know everything about you that you'll let me learn.>

<Someday,> she promised. <Just... not today? Please?>

<Not today,> he agreed, eying the passageway before them. <What would you like to talk about instead, while we wait for the others? Want to hypothesize about the lichen some more?>

A deep pool of calm mineral-laden water sparkled mockingly in the enhanced vision of his visor, completely submerging the path in front of them as far as he could see into its murky depths.

<We're not getting past that without Razick,> Urla agreed. <The cave's in remarkably good shape for its age, except here. Do you think this leaked in afterward? Or was it built this way?>

<The tyrellium shielding is intact.>

<Could have trickled in from smaller cracks. Or the entrance itself. This planet has so many mysteries I can't wait to unravel.>

Jeb poked the floor of the cave with his boot. <Ground's too porous for something that slow. Unless its builders sealed it up somehow.>

<Probably did, even if it's intentional. Whatever we're traveling to, it's strong enough to generate its own Nature Magic pole. Would water muffle that effect?> The passion in Urla's voice ignited a similar emotion in Jeb's chest. <I have a *theory*...>

36

Shane kept a steady pace along the cave-like passageway Janikk's former inhabitants had carved, deep beneath the surface, Razick maintaining a comfortable position behind and slightly to his left, much as his own escort had done, a lifetime ago. He'd considered saying something, directing her to walk beside or in front of him instead, just to avoid the memories, but had decided against it. Either she'd have done it without complaint, or she'd have requested his reasoning, both of which would have led his thoughts further down the path he'd been trying to avoid.

She'd initially attempted to follow her brother but he'd held her back. Shane's requirements for Urla's Metamagic had clearly sparked the conversation she'd been attempting to avoid with Jeb, and the two needed some time alone to sort through the resultant emotions.

If uncomfortable reminders of his past sins were the price required for their own closure, he was happy to pay it.

"Are you sure he's okay?" Razick asked into the silence, not for the first time.

"I still feel them ahead of us," he confirmed patiently, pausing to glance back at her. "I can share my magic again, if that would help?"

"No." Her voice was quiet, almost ashamed. "No. It's fine. I'm sure he's fine," she said, more forcefully.

Turning to study her, he frowned as she took an involuntary step backward under the attention. "I worry about Jake all the time, too, you know. There's nothing wrong with worrying about the people you care about. Especially the ones you feel responsible for."

"He's a grown man," Razick protested. "He's survived without me."

"No." Shane shook his head. "He's survived when you weren't with him. But he's never been without you. And he never will be."

Razick's brows furrowed, and he sighed.

"Raz... You've spent your entire life looking out for him. Building up his confidence. Protecting him, first from the truth about your father, then from the shame of not following in his footsteps. Yes, he's fine now. He can look out for himself. But you're ignoring everything you did to help make that true. Everything he learned from *you*."

Deciding to grant her the courtesy of privacy as she worked through the truth in his words, he turned to continue deeper into the cave. "I think my parents tried to do that, and look how I turned out." He snorted, bitterly. "But you. You succeeded. Which means maybe I can, too. With Jake."

"You really mean that, don't you?" Razick marveled, quickly resuming her position behind him. "Growing up, I just had Father taking offense to everything I did, and Mama trying to pretend we were happy. And I was stuck in the middle, trying to show I was strong enough to navigate it all. But for Jeb... I wanted Jeb to have someone he could rely on. The sort of person I'd always wished I had."

"So you became that person."

"At least one of us could have a happy childhood," she agreed. "I already knew it wouldn't be me. No need to take him down with me."

"He wasn't your responsibility," Shane reminded.

"No. He was my *brother*."

There was defiance in her voice, and Shane allowed himself a smile. "Which is why he'll always need you."

"I... thank you."

They walked in silence for several minutes, Shane's footsteps heavy with the ghosts of his past mistakes, Razick's lighter behind him. Her presence was a comfort, a stability of sorts he hadn't experienced often since the death of his parents – and had thoroughly destroyed each time he had.

He was deep in his own regrets when Razick spoke next.

"All I ever wanted was his approval."

Shane froze, past and present suddenly merging in one unbearable moment.

"I did so much for him," she continued. "But it was never enough. No matter how much I tried."

Exhaling, Shane struggled loose from his memories to focus on her with his full attention. He swallowed, his mouth unbearably dry. "Those who fail to acknowledge your efforts," he managed at last, "aren't worth your energy."

"He was my father. His approval meant *everything* to me."

Stepping toward her, he grabbed Razick's shoulders. "You deserved more than he gave you. More than he was *capable* of giving you. He was hurting, and so he hurt you. It wasn't right. It wasn't fair. And it wasn't your fault."

"I want to believe you." Her voice cracked as she looked up into his eyes. "But then why didn't Mama even acknowledge how I felt? She taught me that if I was strong enough, he couldn't hurt me anymore. And I tried. I tried to be strong, for Mama. But it never stopped hurting."

"Raz..." What could he ever say to that?

She straightened, shaking free of his grip. "Not now, Jeb needs us."

Refocusing on the mission, Shane set off down the tunnel, checking for their souls through his Necromancy. "They're not moving. Did Janikk bind them in something?"

"Jeb needs *me*," she clarified, with a faint laugh. "The path's flooded. Let's go."

It was a short but treacherous walk to catch up with the others, including a steep section where Shane likely would have lost his footing, if not accompanied by a telekinetic battle mage.

Not that Razick would ever admit to it. But he'd been around enough battle mages through the decades. He knew the signs.

"Janikk is *fascinating*," Jeb informed them upon their arrival. "I don't know who built this cave, but they thought of everything."

"Except drainage," Razick observed.

"Urla has some thoughts on that, actually." Jeb turned to Shane, holding out his arm with the watch. "If you could...?"

The cheerful katanoj appeared a moment later, her fur literally glowing a muted yellow. "There's runes buried in the wall," she announced without preamble, tapping one claw on the rock beside her. "They're damaged, so I didn't notice them at first. And I'd suggest against charging them this trip. They might do something... unexpected."

Pressing his palm against the cool stone, Shane drew on his Necromancy to see around the wall. "We can try and map them later. Might be a good project for Jake, until school's open."

Razick coughed politely. "Until then, you might want to stand in the middle. There's a lot of water here, and I've limited spots to put it."

There was no need to tell him twice. Shane stepped smartly to the middle of the passage, reinforcing his Shielding as a precaution against the water. He'd survived their last adventure with wet socks, but he'd resolved before they'd even left Baden he'd avoid a repeat this time.

The water before them churned, then bubbled, then split, the liquid wrapping itself against the walls and ceiling to clear the path.

Razick grinned, showing no sign of the tremendous draw of power Shane knew the spell required as she motioned toward her handiwork. "After you, Sir."

37

THE PASSAGEWAY TURNED UPWARD again, and Razick found herself steadying her companions with her telekinesis as they made their way across the slick rocks along the bottom of the cave.

She'd always enjoyed these sections of her missions, with the accompanying usage of her magic to help instead of harm. And working with Lawrence... For the first time in her recollection, she had no concerns she'd be expected to act against her own morality.

Attention drifting from her task, she lost track of the telekinetic assistance she'd been providing her companions. Lawrence's foot slipped, sending him sliding backward down the path. She reacted quickly to regain control, but not before allowing her hold to loosen on the water lining the cave, sending a large wall of water careening down the path.

"I *did* shower before we left yesterday," Jeb protested, grinning. "I don't smell *that* bad, do I?"

"I'm sorry, Sir," Razick apologized, wringing her hands as Lawrence scowled at his now-soaked socks.

"Nothing to apologize for," the necromancer reassured her, taking a step forward and wincing at the accompanying squelch from his boot. "You're doing great."

"I lost control, Sir. It won't happen again."

He shook his head, rising to full height. "Stop. You're getting stuck in your own head again. I meant what I said."

He was right. She'd been shifting back into her old patterns.

"And don't call me sir," he continued, wrinkling his nose. "I'm Shane. *You* of all people have earned that."

She inhaled sharply. Within the Confederation, Family prestige was everything, as was the Family name. Aside from the Disowned – those who had lost their rights to their Family name, and hadn't joined or created a new one – everyone used their Family name. To use someone's personal name without permission was a sign of disrespect, and a show of power over both the individual and their Family. *With* permission, on the other hand, was a mark of the highest levels of trust.

An honor Lawrence – *Shane* – had just bestowed upon her.

She opened her mouth to speak her gratitude at the gift she didn't quite feel she deserved, the words dissolving as the necromancer halted suddenly, his attention fixated further down the tunnel. Razick twisted away at the last moment, scowling as she shifted her attention to confront whatever new threat had arrived. She froze beside him instead.

Any further attempt at conversation dissolved at the sight of their destination, the water along the floor of the massive chamber doing little to detract from the sheer grandeur of the space. Detailed carvings covered every surface of the walls, the damages of time doing little to obscure the skill and care of the ancient artisans or the importance of the site, and Razick found herself enthralled.

Dominating the center of the room stood a large tree, once alive but now clearly petrified by the continual dripping of the mineral-infused waters seeping through the ceiling of the cave and pooling below. A large vine wound its way around the preserved tree and every other uneven surface within the space, pulsing with a living strength.

"It's alive," Urla breathed, breaking the awed silence as she reverently approached the vine-entwined tree. "And *ancient*."

"Klaaetael," Lawrence breathed.

At the sound of Lawrence's voice, the vine flowered in an awe-inspiring cascade of delicate pink, the large lacy petals gently drifting to the ground throughout the cave with an accompaniment of shimmering pollen. The klaaetael continued its display, large clusters of smaller, deep-red flowers forming along the base of the vine before merging into four shimmering red fruits, easily within reach.

One for each of them.

"Janikk says we need to eat the fruit," the necromancer continued, approaching the tree. "I'll go first, make sure it's–"

"No," Razick ordered, then softened. This *was* Lawrence's mission. "I'd advise against it, Sir."

"Shane," he corrected gently. "Please."

"Shane," she repeated, awkwardly. "I'm supposed to keep you safe. I'll go first."

He reached for her, then, wrapping his fingers tenderly around her wrists. "Janikk showed me this room, the first time we spoke. She wants *me*. If it's a trap, we'll find out once *I* spring it. If you go first, that just means she'd spring it on both of us."

His logic was sound, but it didn't sit right with her. "Jeb, Urla, did either of you...?" She motioned toward the tree.

"No," Urla answered for both of them, ears folding back as she shook her head. "It *felt* like it came from Janikk."

"My Agrokinesis isn't that precise," Jeb added, tugging at his hair. "I could make it flower, but exactly one fruit for each of us?"

"She wants *all* of us," Razick concluded, with a pointed look at Lawrence.

The necromancer shrugged, stone-faced.

"This chamber is *fascinating*," Urla continued, tail curling happily behind her as she stepped deeper into the cavern. The water puddles scattered across the floor sparkled in reflection of her faint luminescence. "Do you think Janikk will permit me to study it later?"

"We can ask." Lawrence plucked one of the fruits from the vine, holding it up with a purposeful look at Razick. "You're the strongest of all of us, Raz. Whatever this does, I need you clear-headed in case you need to stop me."

"Or save you."

"Or save me," he conceded, waiting.

She exhaled. He was asking this time. But she knew the only answer he'd accept. She pressed against the visor over her temples, nodding. "Okay."

He waited a moment before sinking his teeth into the deep red skin and emerging with a large mouthful of stringy white flesh, his nose wrinkling at the taste. Blinking, he popped the rest in his mouth, eyes watering as he chewed and swallowed, grimacing as he attempted to scrape the taste off his tongue with his teeth.

Razick kept her focus on Lawrence. Calling him 'Shane' still didn't feel right. "Jeb?"

"On it," her brother confirmed, stepping forward with the field medic kit.

Lawrence kept still as Jeb worked, the biologist eventually stepping away with a quick look between them. "He's fine."

"I don't feel any different," Lawrence observed, his eyes scanning around the room. "Except..." He pointed. "Is that a portal?"

Razick craned her neck in the direction he pointed, studying the worn etchings in the wall. "I don't see anything."

"Me neither," Urla observed, reaching for a fruit of her own. "But if I eat one of these..." She popped the fruit in her mouth, squeezing her eyes shut as she chewed. "That's *bitter*. But there's the portal. Now I see it, too."

Razick growled. She didn't like the thought of what came next, but couldn't think of any way to stop it, either. "You're going through the portal next, aren't you?"

"Seems like it," Lawrence agreed. "I'll go first."

"Not by yourself," Razick ordered. "Jeb? Telepathy. Now. In case we get separated."

Marching to the tree as Jeb cast his magic, Razick popped the entire fruit into her mouth at once, the condensed sensation of bitter regrets filling her mind even as she did her best to swallow it quickly with as little chewing as possible. The taste lingered, tainting her thoughts with an aura of overwhelming sorrows, and she found herself grateful it was a dry fruit, with very little juice to swallow.

<I feel you,> Lawrence said softly across their shared Telepathy. <You're part of Janikk now.>

Sure enough, she felt the life within the room light up within her consciousness, including not only her three companions but also an intense sensation of ancient vine.

<I'm going to test the portal now,> Lawrence continued, calmly walking toward the shimmering magic doorway. He reached through hesitantly, holding his hand within for several minutes before withdrawing it again and wiggling his fingers.

<I can't sense anything on the other side, not even with Necromancy, but I appear to be all in one piece.>

Squaring his shoulders, he turned to Razick with an intense stare. <Here I go.>

He stepped through the portal, and immediately dropped from the link.

Chaos erupted around her as Jeb shouted and Urla disappeared from view. A small part of her thoughts acknowledged that Lawrence's spell holding her to the mortal plane would have failed with his disappearance, but she didn't have time to dwell on her thoughts.

"Stay here," she ordered, already sprinting toward the portal, diving through before Janikk could close it.

38

Shane blinked in the sudden darkness, willing his eyes to adjust. He'd no idea what he'd be facing. Janikk had only provided a mix of hope and trepidation when he'd attempted to ask.

He reached out with his Necromancy, his breath freezing in his chest as he realized the Void no longer responded to his requests. He checked and double checked his reserves, once more running his consciousness through the familiar tendrils of existence beyond the Veil, verifying its presence within the back of his mind and noting a return to its full power rather than the limited resources he'd had available in the cave.

Everything seemed correct... And yet.

Attempting his search again, Shane reached out to catalog the souls around him, and once more came up empty.

There's nothing wrong with my magic. But then... how can the Afterlife *be broken?*

He dropped his filters, opening himself fully to the Void, the overwhelming silence of its continued absence contributing its own uncomfortable impersonation of sensory deprivation. Feeling the sharp claws of claustrophobia wrapping around his chest he reached instead to Janikk's network of life… and once more came up empty.

Something was *definitely* wrong.

Having exhausted all other options, he shouted as loud as he could manage around the growing panic. "Hello!"

A light shimmered ahead, a flicker of flame illuminating unruly red curls. His heart flooded with relief as he rushed forward, his damp socks squelching with each step on the uneven ground.

"Raz!"

She turned to greet him, her face an illuminated darkness of pain and shadows. "Lawrence."

Something in her voice gave him pause, the hair on the back of his neck standing on end as her Pyromancy flickered in warning across her face. "Raz. Please. I told you to call me Shane."

He'd finally felt comfortable admitting to himself that she was a friend. That he was *allowed* to have friends. If she was in pain, she needed to know he would help.

"Poor Lawrence," she said quietly, frown deepening. "Always on the run. You tell yourself you're running to a brighter future, but you're only running from the pain of your past." The flames danced across her fingertips, tracing a path from one hand to the other and back again. "But it's that pain that makes us who we are, isn't it? The fires that forge our destiny. Who would you be, without your pain, I wonder?"

The handful of fire paused, growing hotter and brighter in her palm until the flames burnt blue before finally shifting to a blinding white. And then, just as suddenly, she closed her fist and returned his universe to darkness. "Would you be anything at all?"

"I'd be a farmer, like my father," he answered honestly. He let out a short bark of a laugh. "A bad one, probably. But I'd have brought more life into the world, instead of destruction, and that alone would've been an improvement."

He wasn't sure why she was asking him these questions *now*, in the middle of their mission to Janikk, but she'd been highly protective of him the entire trip. If she felt comfortable enough to question him, he'd answer. He had little to hide from her.

With a snap of her fingers, the faintest flicker of flame returned. She left it to float in midair as she circled him, slowly, hands clasped behind her. "And who are you now?"

"A father," he answered, without hesitation.

Everything had changed on Loxira. And Jake had been the center of it all. The *reason*, for all of it.

Jake had saved him from himself.

"But who are you, really?" she pressed, tilting her head to study him as she stopped, green eyes boring into his with an intensity few dared direct at him. "Who, exactly, *are* you?"

"I can't tell you who I *was*." The shame – and spilled blood – ran too deep, their friendship too new. It was one thing to understand the depths to which he'd sunk. It was another thing entirely to give her the name he'd used. "But I've never tried to hide *what* I was. What I *still am*. I Shattered my own people, just to keep Jake safe. You helped me take on my own fleet!" He shook his head. "You don't know my *name*, but you know *me*."

"You're a war criminal," she told him flatly. "On the run from your past, hoping desperately to find something, some way, to undo your past regrets."

She'd resumed her pacing again, the flames of her Pyromancy casting eerie shadows on the nothingness surrounding them.

"Yes," he admitted, honestly. "I don't ever expect to succeed. But perhaps by trying, by doing my best to unlearn who I became, I can empower someone else to succeed where I've failed."

"Jake." He could hear the sneer in her voice then. "That's a lot to lay on the shoulders of a twelve-year-old."

"I was sixteen when I started," Shane said quietly.

"When you were conscripted," Razick corrected.

Razick had fought against her expected role in the Sparnell Armed Forces, though. He had embraced his with a hunger for purpose, belonging, and revenge.

"When I *started*," he repeated, more forcefully. "Jake saved me. And he can save the universe, if I give him what he needs."

Not that those lessons would involve Necromancy; Jake had already made his thoughts on that subject clear. But he didn't *need* Necromancy. He needed–

"If you *groom* him," Razick spat. "As Admiral Kydell groomed you. Because you'll never outrun your past, will you? No matter where you go, no matter what you do, you'll always find the old, familiar patterns waiting for you to inflict them on the universe. On your *son*." She turned to face him, her face unreadable. "You can shed your skin, but not your training. Can't outrun *yourself*, after all."

"So why try?" A familiar pair of golden eyes emerged from the darkness behind Razick, the white furred wolf baring his fangs as he lay claim to the battle mage, his hands resting firmly on her shoulders. "You were mine once. You can be mine again."

"Raz! Behind you!"

Shane bolstered his Shielding, expecting her to do the same, but she merely smiled.

Admiral Kydell slipped past her to address him, slowly closing the distance between them. "Surrender your mind to me, and together we can finish what we started. You believed in it once. I can help you believe in it again. Take away your pain, just as before."

"That was before I knew the truth," Shane snarled back, baring his own teeth as he shifted to circle Kydell. "I don't know how you escaped, but I will *not* let you hurt Razick. I should have Shattered you when I had the chance. I *won't* make that mistake again."

"Why would I hurt her?" The wolf oozed confidence. "She's already mine. And I have *you* to thank for it."

Shane's blood ran cold. He didn't know how Kydell had escaped, or even how the psychomorphic admiral had *found* them again, but clearly his attempts to befriend Razick had done little but endanger her.

That was the danger of it, wasn't it? He'd hurt everyone he ever cared about. He'd murdered Feels, led Razick back to Kydell's control, disappointed his parents, Shattered–

"Let it go, Lawrence," Razick encouraged, her conjured flames now larger as she gently spun them in her palms. "All your pain, your regret, your fear... He can take them *all* away. All you need to do is surrender."

No.

Resolve burned in his veins, and he clenched his fists at his sides. He'd *seen* what happened when he followed Kydell. When he allowed the admiral to manipulate his emotions until he forgot who he was.

No.

The admiral's conditioning wrapped itself around his thoughts, its power redirected to Jake. He had to protect his son. Whatever it took – his life, his soul, his very existence – he couldn't allow himself to fall to Kydell's magic. Everything he did was for Jake's protection.

No.

A new determination flared to life. Razick was his friend. He wouldn't – *couldn't!* – allow her to come to harm, simply for her misfortune of falling into his orbit. If he intended to turn his life around, his first step needed to be protecting those he loved.

"Oh, I'll let it go alright," he sneered, every muscle tensing as he reinforced his Shielding. "I'll give him *everything* I've got."

And with that he let loose, a barrage of carefully spun magic assaulting the psychomorphic admiral in an effort to fracture his defenses and Shatter his soul.

"So that's how it is?" The admiral merely smiled, shrugging off the concentrated arcane barrage. "Very well."

He lunged at Shane, claws and teeth bared, quickly closing the distance as Razick watched with an amused disinterest. Ducking the admiral's fanged jaws, Shane nonetheless felt claws connect despite his Shielding, the large slash against his check echoing his wound from their duel on the *Inevitable*.

Feels would give him an earful when he returned, but he couldn't afford to dwell on that now. The necromancer smiled savagely, his flesh ripping further at his movements, the pain a dull, familiar throb.

Time to finish Kydell, once and for all.

ADMIRAL KYDELL TWISTED AWAY as Shane pounced, but the necromancer was ready, his fingernails scraping harmlessly against the thick fur at the wolf's throat as he countered his former sparring partner's familiar evasion. He felt Kydell's claws rake across his arm, peeling back layers of skin despite the thick reinforced fabric of the uniform jacket Razick had provided for him a lifetime ago.

Shane lamented his lack of claws. *Only one of us is fully armed.*

Preparing another offensive spell to weaken Kydell's Shielding, Shane leaped forward again. The admiral attempted to add space between them, but Shane released a Shield burst behind him at the same instant, propelling Kydell closer instead. Snarling in triumph, Shane felt his claws deftly slice through Kydell's neck fur to draw blood.

The wolf howled in rage, lunging at Shane in a blind fury, but the necromancer twisted to the side at the last moment. Taking advantage of the admiral's bared neck, Shane bit down hard, his fangs sinking through Kydell's flesh as the metallic saltiness of blood filled his mouth and nostrils with a sweet satisfaction.

Wait.

Letting go in surprise, Shane spit out his opponent's blood as he backed away, staring at his fingers and running his tongue across his teeth.

Claws? Fangs? He exhaled sharply. *Of course!*

He'd thought about them and they'd appeared, exactly as he'd imagined them, with the carnal instincts to match.

This isn't real.

He'd heard about Dreamwalking, back during training. The ability to interact with another's dreams through Divination, often touted as an effective aid in the practice of more advanced spellwork.

Shane had never done it himself, of course. Death during a Dreamwalk merely woke up the spell's target. No one wanted to risk testing whether or not a Soul Shatter worked the same way.

Not that he could blame them for the caution.

But his current experiences matched the descriptions he'd heard, with its presently empty Afterlife and its prompt adaptations to his thoughts. This wasn't the real Admiral Kydell.

Or the real Razick.

"There's no need for us to fight," Shane said instead, holding his hands at chest level, palms facing the admiral. "You're the past. I won't fall for your tricks again. I'm not the same *person* I was then."

"It doesn't matter what you do. Who you think you've become," the dream-Kydell sneered. "My legacy will follow you wherever you go. You were Sparnelli, and one of our best." Golden eyes glittered, reflecting Razick's flames. "How long will you blame us for your own choices? What would your companions think if they realized how many of my accomplishments were because of *your* decisions."

"I've told everyone who needs to know who I was." Shane shook his head, turning to Razick. "The past is the past. I've buried that guilt, and the man who carried it." He met the admiral's eyes once more with a snarl. "He holds no power over me, and neither do *you*."

With those words, the wolf dissolved back into nothingness, the throbbing in Shane's cheek subsiding as the wound, too, disappeared.

Shane exhaled, allowing his shoulders to slump. *This is a test. On facing my demons.*

He turned to Razick, the battle mage watching him with a calculating interest as he approached.

"Razick." He shook his head, forcing himself to meet her eyes. "Raz. I..."

Why were the words so hard to say?

"I don't know if I'll ever feel comfortable telling you who I was," he tried again. "But I'll never hide who I *am*. Not from you. It's been a long time since I've trusted myself to make a friend. I seem to destroy everything I touch. But you're important to me. And so I'm going to try." He let out a short laugh. "Hell, Raz. If anyone'll hold me accountable for screwing something up, it's you."

"So what am I then?"

Shane froze as Razick dissolved, replaced instead by the figure of his beloved fae, their disapproval radiating openly along his Oath.

Of course. We still have unfinished business, too.

He exhaled, squaring his shoulders. He'd spent a large part of their mission puzzling over ways to fulfill his promise to the empath without leaning on them further. Their appearance in this trial was to be expected.

"Hello, dear friend." He smiled softly, holding out his hand as the fae gracefully landed on his palm, their wings revealing a particularly gorgeous display of shimmering color within the otherwise bare void of the Dreamwalk. "I always demand so much of you, and you never fail to meet those demands, while asking so little of me in return. But all of me is yours. I hope you know that."

"And why is that, Grim?" Feels tilted their head, watching him carefully. "Why are you always so eager to throw yourself at my mercy? You keep granting me these powers over you. Demanding I accept them. Begging that I use them?" They crossed their arms. "Why is it so important to you that I be able to override your own free will and bend you to mine instead? You just escaped Kydell. Why am I any different?"

"Because I trust you. More than I trust anyone else. More than I trust *myself*." Shane closed his eyes, inhaling. "You're a construct from my memories, you know what I've done, more than anyone. What I've done to–" He stopped himself, clenching his free hand into a fist at his side as he gathered the strength to continue. "What I'm capable of doing to *anyone* my subconscious identifies as a threat to my goals. Even *you*. And I know you'll stop me from taking advantage of anyone else." He opened his eyes, shoulders slumping as he brushed at the threatening tears. "More than anyone, I trust you to help me find a way to be better than I am."

"And what if I take advantage of that trust?" Feels' words carried an uncharacteristic danger. "What if I take these powers you've given me and actually use them? Use *you*?"

Laughing, Shane shook his head. "That's not who you are."

"What if I've just been biding my time? Waiting for you to trust me implicitly?" Tilting their head, Feels projected a wave of intense longing, overriding Shane's analytical calm with an overwhelming desperation that left him gasping, his thoughts suddenly and completely fixated on the fae. "Waiting until I own you so completely you can't find the line between yourself and my desires?"

"Then we'd have been married twenty-five years ago, and you'd already rule the universe." Shane's words carried an echo of his own longing, eyes half closed as he savored the fading remnants of the empath's Psychomorphation spell. "Admiral Kydell always wanted my absolute obedience, but I could never give him everything he wanted because a part of me always belonged to you. You could have always had it, but never wanted it, because that's not who you are." He fixed the fae with a soft smile, tentatively caressing them with his finger. "I'm already yours. I *want* to be yours. I throw myself completely at your mercy and you still won't take me."

"Then why do you keep pushing me away?"

"What?" Shane blinked in surprise.

"If you're not afraid of me, and you're not afraid of Kydell, who are you afraid of, Grim?" Twisting their head to fluff their feathered mane, the empath fluttered their wings, impatience resonating down the Oath tether. "Who is the nightmare that keeps you up at night? And why does it upset you so much, that I won't take possession of your every decision?" Unblinking purple eyes met Shane's perplexed orange. "Who are you *really* running from?"

As Shane watched, Feels disappeared into the dark nothingness of the Dreamwalk, leaving him alone to scour his memories.

They're wrong. He shook his head, scowling. *There's no one left for me to fear.*

A familiar shadow stalked across the edge of his vision, a bitter darkness of feral muscle and unashamed cruelty, voice swelling with a savage confidence. "Hello, Grim. I think it's time we talk."

Swallowing, Shane turned to meet the new threat, his blood frozen in his veins.

Renkash.

40

Razick blinked in the bright lighting of her parents' living room, brows furrowed. Everything was just the way she remembered it, but entirely wrong, all at the same time.

How had she gotten here? She tried to remember, biting her lip as the thoughts slipped away.

"There you are, Raz! Who's my big helper?"

"Mama!" Razick grinned, running to the kitchen and her mother's outstretched arms, burying her face in Mama's neck.

"There's my good girl," her mother crooned, running gentle calloused fingers through Razick's hair. "Your brother's napping. Can you help me with something before he wakes up?"

"I want to help!"

Mama was always happy when she was helping. Sometimes the sadness even left her eyes.

Although... She hadn't come here to help Mama. She'd been rushing to help someone else. Who was it?

"We need to set the table. Can you do that while I get dinner ready?" Mama pointed to the stack of plates and silverware carefully piled on the tabletop.

"Oh yes, Mama!" Razick grinned as she grabbed the plates, counting as she placed them around the table. "One... Two... Three..." She paused, confused. "There's four plates. Is someone visiting us for dinner?"

Was this who she'd been trying to help?

"You could say that," Mama laughed, the *chop, chop, chop* of her big cutting knife beating a regular rhythm as she began the dinner preparations. "Your father's coming home today."

Razick dropped the third plate on the table with a loud *thunk!* "Please don't let him visit, Mama. He's always so angry. I..." She exhaled slowly, choosing his words carefully at Mama's deepening frown. "I'm afraid of him, when he's angry."

"Raz..." Mama carefully wiped the knife on her apron before placing it on the counter, turning to kneel in front of Razick. "He's your father. He's trying. Why don't you give him another chance?"

"How many chances do I have to give him?" Razick pouted, crossing her arms. "All he does is yell and remind me I'm not good enough. I don't like when he visits."

Mama knelt beside her, gently tucking stray curls of hair behind Razick's ear. "He's not visiting, Sweetheart. He's moving back home. Your Papa promised to be good this time, so let's be good for him, alright? He's been through a lot. It's not his fault. Can you be good for me?"

Razick sighed, looking away. "Yes, Mama."

She always made mistakes. Father didn't like mistakes. This time she'd finally get it right, so Father wouldn't have to leave again. So Mama wouldn't be sad around her eyes anymore. She *had* to be perfect. For Mama.

No.

She shook her head, slipping free from her mother's arms. Something was wrong. This wasn't her anymore.

She'd been trying to do something. Help someone. Mama wasn't...

"You're getting so big!" Father crowed.

Razick stood taller, turning proudly toward him at the compliment, only to suppress her disappointment at the realization he'd directed it at Jeb. Father's brown eyes shone as he bounced her baby brother in his lap, grinning at his nonsensical babbling.

She must have finished setting the table without realizing. Mama had already piled the serving dishes high with all of Father's favorites.

She allowed herself to hope for a moment that this time would be better. This time she'd be good enough. Just the way Mama wanted.

"How's dinner, Sweetheart?"

Razick turned to tell Mama she wasn't really hungry, but her mother's attention was also focused on Father, a large smile pasted across her face. One of the fake ones grown-ups used when they asked a question but were afraid of the answer.

"Passable," Father growled, scowling as he tucked an errant strand of brown hair behind his ears. "Was hoping you'd have learned to cook while I was away. But no such luck."

He turned back to Jeb, grinning at the cascade of giggles as he tickled her brother's belly, his words softer but no less abrasive. "She won't learn for me. No, she won't learn for me. But maybe she'll learn for you? Wouldn't that be nice?"

Razick watched Mama begin to deflate and grabbed her hand, looking up with one of those large smiles grown-ups seemed to like when they were upset. "*I* like your cooking, Mama. Do you need any help?"

If she was helping in the kitchen, maybe Father would continue to ignore her. It would be better than the yelling.

"Thank you, Sweetheart." Mama squeezed back, and Razick smiled wider as her mother stood taller, dabbing the tears from her eyes with her apron. "You're the best helper I could ask for. Go get dessert. It's cooling on the counter."

Slipping into the kitchen, Razick leaned against the counter to catch her breath and her bearings.

This didn't feel right. She'd grown past this, hadn't she? Everything felt familiar, but *wrong*, as if filtered through the memory of a dream. But she'd come here for *something*. What had she–

"The pie, Sweetheart?"

The pie. How had she forgotten? She'd let everyone down.

She spotted the fruit pie, Mama's intricate patterns woven into the lovingly glazed top crust, and quickly slid it from the countertop with both hands.

Another of Father's favorites. She wondered how long he'd be home this time, and whether or not Mama would ever have an opportunity to make any of *her* favorites again.

It didn't matter. If Mama was happy, that would be enough. But why did her happiness need Father's?

She turned her attention to stare at her father, the faint green veins on his face and neck betraying his continued reliance on the alchemical concoctions he valued more than his own family.

Her attention distracted, she caught her foot on a chair, pitching forward as she lost her grip on the pie.

"You clumsy, useless little–"

Mama rushed forward, wringing her hands. "Sweetheart. Darling. It's not her fault. I shouldn't have asked her to carry it in."

Razick bowed her head, staring at the floor as Mama pressed her apron against the mess of pie dripping from Father, attempting to appease his anger and Jeb's sudden tears.

She'd made a mistake. Again. She *was* a mistake.

Balling her fists, she squeezed her eyes shut in an effort to push down the welling tears. He'd leave Mama again now, and Mama would be sad and it would be all her fault.

"Raz? Go fetch some towels from the kitchen." Her mother's voice strained against the attempted cheeriness. "There's my good girl."

Razick rose quietly from the floor, rubbing her still-stinging cheek from where it had scraped against the unexpected chair, her fingers now tipped with traces of blood. Turning to her mother for comfort, she witnessed Mama's focus on dabbing pie off Father's shirt with her apron, her baby brother a sticky, wailing, pie-covered mess as Mama bounced him on her hip.

Her father glared back at her. But no, that wasn't her father, it was Admiral Kydell, murder blazing in his yellow eyes, thick white fur perfectly framing his face as he growled at her. "It doesn't matter how far you run. You'll always be mine."

She fled to the kitchen, heart beating staccato as it attempted to escape her chest. Clutching at her mother's towels, she willed her breath to slow, drawing on her training to settle her mind and center her magic.

This wasn't real. Whatever was happening, it wasn't real.

She laughed bitterly, twisting her fingers through the memory of her mother's tea towel, the cheerful floral pattern a sharp contrast to her jagged emotions. Her father had been so afraid of her following in his footsteps, he'd primed her for worse, carving large pieces from her own self-confidence and stability. Enough to allow the damned admiral to anchor himself in her pain, bending her tortured thoughts into his service.

But he was the past. She'd defeated him, hadn't she?

Brows furrowing, she wet the towel in the sink and pressed it to her face, allowing the cool dampness to quench the fire of her emotions as she wracked her brain for answers.

Lawrence.

She'd been looking for Shane Lawrence. They were on Janikk, locked in a cave, and he'd disappeared through the portal, and she'd promised to protect him.

Janikk *wanted* him. That much had been clear, and now that she had him, Razick couldn't allow her to keep him.

She'd failed him before, and he'd found a way to survive anyway. But that had always been against a physical threat. He couldn't afford for her to fail him now.

Squaring her shoulders, she bolstered her Shielding and set it on fire, turning to face the phantom of Kydell once more. Whatever mind games Janikk intended for her, she had to overcome. She'd had *time* to work through her emotions of her father. And Lawrence had helped her confront Kydell. She had what she needed to succeed. But Lawrence?

Whatever past Lawrence was facing now? Selkirk Shatter her soul if she left her friend to face those nightmares alone.

41

JEB SURVEYED THE CAVERN through his light-enhancing visor, scuffing his boots along the waterlogged dirt and stones covering the tyrellium-lined rock beneath them. <They've been gone a while.>

<We need to go after them,> Urla repeated, no longer attempting to hide her frustration. <This is why we came to Janikk. I want to finish it.>

<Razick said to stay here,> Jeb reiterated, shoving his hands deeper in his pockets.

<That was an hour ago.>

<She knows what she's doing.>

<Do you even *hear* yourself?> Urla let out a laugh that was anything but happy. <Has she ever been to Janikk before? This planet is unlike anything else I've ever *seen*. How would *she* know the right thing for you to do?>

"Because she's my *sister*!"

The force of the admission surprised him, and he tugged his hair, trying to work through his emotions.

<She's always looked out for me,> he continued finally, softer. <Whenever I didn't know what to do, she did. And then her letters stopped coming and I thought I'd lost her and I had to figure out how to survive my conscription on my own.>

<She found you again,> Urla reminded, softly.

<But it wasn't *her*.> Jeb sank to the floor, leaning his back against the wall as he cupped his face in his hands. <She was all silent and angry and needed me to protect her. And I did my best, but I'm not her. And then the Confederation came and I thought I was going to lose her again, this time for good, but instead I'm finally starting to recognize bits and pieces of who she used to be and *I don't want to lose her again*.>

The cavern was silent for several moments, Jeb's sobbing the only sound, before Urla reached out again. <She'll never be the same as she was.>

<Don't you think I *know* that?>

<I only meant–>

He cut her off. <I know what you meant. And I know you're right. And I know I have to find a way to come to terms with that. But also, she's finally back, *really* back. Sometimes I catch her smiling when she forgets she's not alone, and it's easy to forget everything we've been through. And I can't...>

His voice trailed off. He couldn't finish that sentence. He couldn't admit his fears to himself, let alone out loud.

But Urla wasn't going to let him off that easily. <You can't what?>

<I can't protect her.> He ground his teeth, planting his fists against the rock on either side of himself. <If she's in trouble in there, I can't keep her safe. I'll only get in the way. Like I did on the *Inevitable*.>

<You were great on the *Inevitable*.>

<I was a liability,> Jeb said honestly. <I'm a botanist, not a battle mage. I thought on Janikk maybe I'd be able to help at least, but now she's off to save Lawrence and I'm here doing all I can to stay out of her way.>

<She'd have given in to Kydell if you hadn't stopped her,> Urla said softly. <I watched you hit him over the head with that wrench.>

<She'd have figured it out,> Jeb protested.

But he'd seen the way his sister had genuinely considered the admiral's words. Seriously weighed information about Nya against her own future freedom.

He'd done what he'd had to do. That was all. But if he hadn't...

He shuddered. <I did help.>

<You did,> Urla agreed. <We each have our strengths. You don't have to be a battle mage to be able to help. And right now, I think they need our help.>

He smiled, lightly caressing his watch. <Have I told you how much I appreciate you?>

<Not today.> The smile in her voice was contagious. <But you're welcome to compliment me as often as you like.>

Rising to his feet, Jeb began his slog through mud and water, back to the vined tree at the center of the cavern. <I appreciate you. And not just because of your intelligence. You have a way of seeing the universe. Of finding the truth in a situation. And I'm all the better for spending time with you.>

<If I wasn't dead, I'd be blushing right now,> she protested.

<Good. You *said* I could compliment you.> He laughed, reaching to pluck the last fruit from the tree. <You're the kindest person I know, and I'm grateful to have you in my life.>

<In that case, I have to warn you. That fruit is *gross*. I've never tasted anything so bitter in my entire life.> Her voice went quiet. <Short as it was.>

<So I gathered, watching the rest of you eat it,> Jeb said quickly. Anything to pull her from the memories. He studied the fruit, rubbing his thumb over the uneven bumps scattered across its thick red skin. <Here goes.>

He bit in, the outer flesh resisting slightly before surrendering to his teeth. The stringy white flesh within gave off a surprisingly fascinating tart yet tangy flavor. <That's... quite tasty, actually.> He popped the rest into his mouth, closing his eyes. <Not bitter at all. More of a tangy flavor? Think Janikk would let me eat another one?>

<Seriously? That's *not* what I tasted.> Urla's words were incredulous. <I don't know, Jeb. I'm starting to worry that

other fruit did something to you after all. I don't know how anyone could enjoy tasting *that*.>

<Hopefully nothing that'll stop me from helping.> Jeb rolled his shoulders, checking his Shielding as he made his way toward the portal. <You ready?>

<I'm ready.>

He inhaled, bracing himself for whatever challenge awaited him and Urla beyond. He rubbed his watch for reassurance as he checked his Shielding, running quickly through his old mission checklist. However far Lawrence and Razick had gone, hopefully he'd catch up to them quickly.

The portal hummed and snapped in front of him, beckoning him onward. With a deep breath, and a quick look back at the vine and its petrified tree, he stepped through into the unknown.

42

"Raz?" Jeb blinked in the harsh lighting, every muscle tense, his pistol gripped tightly in his fist. An assortment of Sparnelli military personnel, commissioned and enlisted alike, shuffled past him in the hallways, intent on their present tasks.

<Are you seeing this?>

<They don't seem to care that we're here,> Urla confirmed, confusion in her voice. <Why would Janikk send us through a portal to Sparnell? And how'd she get through the tyrellium shielding of SAF Headquarters? It's impenetrable to magic!>

<Maybe it's not Headquarters? Just something made to look like it?> Jeb ducked into one of the rooms along the corridor to gather his thoughts.

"You're not supposed to be here." An elderly katanoj bearing the badge of an instructor grabbed his shoulder, claws digging through the fabric of his brown and khaki working uniform as she glared. Jeb couldn't help but notice she felt mildly familiar, although he couldn't place from where.

"I'm so sorry, Ma'am. I was just looking for–"

"Down the hall to your right, third door on the left," she growled.

Jeb tugged at his hair. "Excuse me?"

"Turn right down the hall, third door on the left. You really *are* as stupid as they say, aren't you?" She eyed him disapprovingly. "You were looking for your class, right?"

"Oh. Uh, yes. Thank you," Jeb sputtered.

Rude.

"Good. Now get out. You're no longer welcome here." Only then did Jeb notice the room behind him was full of new recruits, watching him with their own mix of disdain and pity.

"Oh. Uh. Yes. Right."

Swallowing, Jeb stepped back into the hallway, turning to his right as directed. The hallway's occupants continued to ignore his presence. <What do you think *that* was all about? What *is* this place?>

Urla remained uncharacteristically silent.

Locating the described doorway, Jeb carefully entered to find another classroom, more sparsely attended, the students within watching his entrance with a mix of hope and dread. The Instructor stood at the front, slouching over a potted plant with his back to the class, his words muffled and mumbled.

Looking up at Jeb's approach, a shadow of sorrow passed over his eyes. "There you are. I was starting to hope you'd been removed from my roster."

"You don't want me here?" Jeb's brows furrowed as he tugged his hair again. He faintly wondered why he found the thought disappointing.

I *don't want to be here.*

He had to find Razick. And Lawrence.

"Was hoping, for your sake, they'd made a mistake. That maybe they'd reassigned you someone more prestigious and fitting of your Family name." He sighed. "But no matter. You're here now. Take a seat." He patted at the pockets on his apron, muttering absent-mindedly. "I have a letter here somewhere..."

Jeb remained standing. "Sir, do you know where I could find Kane Razick?"

"Kane?" The Instructor paused his search to eye Jeb quizzically. "They're a middling Family at best. Well-known, certainly, and with a level of prestige not often found in a Family of their ranking, but they dilute that by allowing too many underperformers to remain. No, prestigious Families such as yourself are best served limiting your contact with the lesser Families."

<This doesn't make any sense.> Jeb tugged at his hair, distraught. <I *am* a Kane.>

Shaking his head, he returned to his search, pulling a large, embossed envelope from one of his many oversized pockets with a grin of triumph. "Here we are! Why don't you see what your Family wants, and rejoin us when you can, yes?"

He glanced at the envelope, then stared, running his finger over the purple eye-shaped hurricane of the Valcore Family seal, and the name scripted on the front in painstakingly precise lettering. *Urla.*

<Oh.>

<Yeah.> The heartbreak in Urla's tone cut Jeb to the core. <This memory is mine.>

He bit his lip. <Why did the Valcore Family send *you* a letter?>

The Sparnell Confederation's Family-based politics had led to a system of elite ruling-class Families, well-known for their prestigious contributions to the Sparnelli war machine, and subsequently awarded a voice of their own in decisions regarding the governmental policies of the Confederation itself. The Javon, Margold, and Selkirk Families had practically defined the defensive, civil, and offensive policies of the faction, respectively, for the past several centuries.

The Valcores rose above even that, the other Families owing the entirety of their influence to their proximity to Fleet Admiral Valcore Sil's ear. Only the Rakethorne Family could be argued to rival Valcore Sil's stranglehold over Sparnell, and that was only if one chose not to believe the hushed rumors of Empress Rakethorne's possible demise at the hands of none other than the Fleet Admiral herself.

<I...> Even within their telepathic link, Jeb had to strain to hear Urla, the Hydroponics AI's voice achingly subdued. <Open it. You'll see.>

Jeb hesitated. <Are you sure?>

This wasn't his memory, and this didn't feel like it was *his* secret to learn. He'd been focused on his sister, as if she was the only one who mattered, as if his regrets in not being the protective brother he thought she needed were the biggest problems in the universe.

But the sorrow in Urla's voice had brought him crashing back to reality.

She was quiet for a long while, to the point Jeb was beginning to question his own Telepathy, when she sighed. <You deserve to know the truth. Yes. I'm sure.>

With unsteady hands, he unsealed the letter.

Urla,

The Family has reviewed your academic record. Despite your talent and magic aptitudes, your selection of studies has continuously failed to align with the Valcore Family Values. You have received several warnings to cease your misguided pursuits and realign your studies with the coursework we have already prepared for you. As you have failed to do so, you leave us no choice.

It is therefore with heavy heart the Valcore Family Council decrees you Disowned. You are to henceforth cease and desist your use of the Valcore Family name. The Family cannot afford the dishonor you seem intent to bring upon this Family.

Additionally, the Valcore Family Council has approved Admiral Kydell's request for your immediate and permanent reassignment to his fleet in the hope that, under his guidance, you may someday be permitted a re-evaluation of your revoked right to the Family name.

May your accomplishments bring glory to us all,

Fleet Admiral Valcore Sil

Valcore Family Council Chair

<Urla...> Jeb brushed at his eyes. <You were... I'm sorry... I didn't *know*...>

<Because I didn't *tell* you. Who wants to admit they were Disowned by their own Family? Who wants to admit to being a Disowned *Valcore*? The Fleet Admiral hasn't exactly avoided making enemies.> She laughed bitterly. <Do you know why I'm such a fan of your work?>

He'd wondered, but it had never seemed the sort of thing to talk about. <Why?>

<You had all these grand adventures, traveling away to distant planets to explore, discovering things the herbologists and alchemists will spend *decades* studying in detail. And you didn't stop there. Your work overturned everything people thought they knew about building an effective Nature Magic field inside a fleet. And even though the Confederation didn't value your achievements the way they should, your *Family* stood behind you, the whole way.>

Her voice turned wistful. <And here I was, shoved into a ship, reading about the discoveries of others. And even with all

the biologists around me, all with similar experiences, there was nothing to look forward to. Nothing to be proud of, for myself. So I decided I'd be proud of you, instead.>

Jeb bit his lip, exhaling. <Urla... If I hadn't known going in that you'd never been to the field before, I wouldn't have believed it. I *still* have trouble believing it. I've seen experts fail to handle challenges half as well as you have over the past several days. You've put my own talents to shame.>

<That's not true,> she protested.

<It *is*.> He rubbed at his chin, eyes closed to focus his full attention on the katanoj bound within his watch. <I've enjoyed learning more about your talents and skills during this mission. I'd love to do it again, too. The Confederation missed out, undervaluing your brilliant mind, and so did your Family.>

<What was your Family like, Jeb?> The sadness in her voice was underlined with a burning curiosity. <Are the Kanes really like the Instructor said?>

Rubbing the back of his neck, Jeb bounced on the balls of his feet. <Pretty much.>

He opened his eyes and surveyed his surroundings, the SAF classroom now gone and replaced with his childhood home. The dining room was meticulously set for dinner, the way Razick always preferred to keep it, while an oversized potted plant lurked in the corner near the doorframe to the kitchen. The heavenly smells of a lovingly prepared meal wafted from the kitchen, his mother humming happily to herself as she worked. His father sat at the dining table, calmly catching up on the news holos as he waited, laughing with Mama at the more ridiculous announcements.

<Kane is a large Family, because we don't Disown people. We stick together. Stick up for each other.> He inhaled slowly and exhaled even slower, willing his anger at Urla's Family to subside. <We hold our members as more important than the Family itself. The honor of the Sparnell Confederation, and the Family's honor within it, have never been able to compete. Even though a lot of the Confederation's prestigious achievements were built on the accomplishments of Kane battle mages.> He laughed. <As you can imagine, the Department of Prestige is less than pleased about this.>

<Because anyone who fails to put Sparnell before their own needs is a security risk. Right?>

<Something like that, I suppose. But it did mean that when I was reassigned as a botanist, the Kane Family supported me. Which helped. You remember how little recognition we biologists get.> Jeb frowned. <I mean... You're more than a biologist. But you know what I mean. I'm sorry I was wrapped up in myself. I didn't think to ask about your past. To help you carry some of the pain.>

<Hush.> There was an urgency to Urla's words now. <We shouldn't dwell on regret. If this is what I think it is, Janikk is only getting started. And whatever weakness we let her know, whatever high-emotion memory we dwell on, she's going to exploit it.>

Their surroundings shifted, dropping them on the bridge of some sort of spacecraft. Jeb was never good at identifying which class, but it reminded him of the *Inevitable*. <Is this memory one of yours, or one of mine?>

<Mine again. Sorry.> Urla's words were clipped, and Jeb could feel her anxiety digging into his skin. <You're about to learn how I died.>

43

Razick launched herself into the memory of her mother's dining room, a vision of fire and fury and deadly resolve. "You cannot have him!"

But it was Nya who greeted her, the fiery red-orange of her fiancée's thick, cracked skin spattered with blue and purple pie filling. "Raz, why?"

"Nya?" Razick dropped her spells, instead rushing forward to wrap the dracoling in a hug, ignoring the pie remains – and the tears now streaming freely down her face – as she wrapped Nya tightly in her arms.

"Why haven't you found me, Raz?" Nya's amber eyes drowned in a sea of accusation and pain. "Why haven't you *looked* for me?"

"Nya..." Razick faltered. She'd expected Kydell. Not... *this*.

"Why haven't you saved me, Raz? It's *your* fault he hurt me. Why won't you save me?"

Backing away from the disappointment in her lover's face, Razick struggled to come to terms with the new flood of emotions. What could she say? That she barely even remembered Nya? That she didn't even know where to *begin* her search? That for all she knew, Nya had moved on without her once she'd been manipulated into re-enlisting for Kydell?

"It didn't have to be this way." Admiral Kydell traced his fingers across Nya's shoulders from his position behind her fiancée's chair, golden eyes fixed on Razick. "I tried to help you. Tried to make you see."

"You get away from her!"

Razick lunged without a thought, only to find herself frozen, her eyes locked on Kydell's.

"I don't ask for much," the white-furred wolf continued. "Just your mind. Your complete and utter obedience." He shook his head. "There was no need for *Nya* to suffer for your foolish resistance to my will."

"Please, Raz," Nya whimpered, flinching as Kydell's claws dug into her shoulder. "Just... Give him what he wants. Please."

Helplessness overwhelmed her as she struggled against her renewed inability to attack her former admiral. He'd taken so much from her – her free will, her freedom, her future – and now it appeared he'd taken her fiancée as well.

But if *he'd* taken her...

But of *course* he'd taken her. She'd known that, from the beginning. Not once had she ever seriously considered any of the potential alternatives. She'd done the wolf's dirty work often enough to realize Kydell wouldn't blink at the thought of torturing others merely to send a message to someone else.

Especially if that someone was *Razick*.

"You let her go, wolf," Razick snarled, eyes locking on Kydell's. "She'll never be yours, and neither will I. Not anymore. I served my time."

"What are you going to do, Kane?" Kydell sneered back, teeth bared, lowering his head to rest his snout on Nya's shoulder. "I have your lover, and your mind."

"Don't let him hurt me," Nya begged.

"Which means I can find her," Razick spat back. "We have your files. We have your fleet. If you took her, *someone* will know *something*."

Janikk's hallucinations couldn't be trusted as fact, but they clearly drew from her own memories and insecurities. And Kydell's hunger for control and recognition meant the admiral kept meticulous records of most of his schemes. If he'd done anything to her, she'd find it in his records.

Clenching her fists, Razick fought off the sharp pang of guilt digging into her resolve.

"I *will* find you," she promised Nya. "I'm sorry your love of me led to him hurting you. I won't take the blame for his choices. I *can't*. But I understand if you blame me anyway."

"He wouldn't have hurt me if I didn't stand between him and you," Nya protested.

"I know," Razick agreed. "And while there's lots I still don't remember about you, if you're the sort of person I *think* I'd find attractive, you blame Kydell for that, too. Not me." She shook her head. "We've been victims too long, Nya. I'm still finding my way out. I won't let guilt drag me back. And I won't let him keep you, you have my word."

"What are you going to do? Please don't leave me!"

"I'm going to find my friend. And then he's going to help me find you."

And with that, she spun smartly on her heels and set off into the unknown at a stiff march, leaving her regrets to sob behind her.

"Put the claws away, Grim." Renkash's smile dripped with threat as he circled, dark fur with darker stripes blending into the shadows of the dreamscape. His tail beat an amused rhythm into the air. "I'm not here to fight. Not today."

"And why should I talk to you?" Shane spat with a snarl. "Why should I listen to *anything* you have to say?"

The cat's eyes flashed amusement, a pair of burning orange embers in the darkness. "Because my history is a part of yours, Dreamwalker. Don't you want to know what you think about yourself when you're not looking?"

"No. I want to *kill* you."

Renkash snorted. "You know you'll never kill me completely, even if you spend the rest of your lives trying. We're the same, you and I. You can dress it up however you like, but I'm seared into your soul." The imposing black katanoj sneered in triumph as he tapped Shane's chest, ears alert, whiskers splayed. "As long as you exist in the universe? So will I."

"We'll see about that." Shane lunged at Renkash's face, claws at the ready, hate in his heart.

The large cat phased away from the attack, emerging from the Afterlife to stand behind him. "We always did love violence, didn't we? Go ahead then. Let's get this over with."

Baring his fangs, the katanoj prepared for Shane's next attempt with the confidence of an apex predator.

He didn't have to wait long, Shane's next spell bending the mortal plane to bring him close enough to swipe at Renkash's neck, the large cat instead grasping Shane's wrist in an unyielding grip before spinning and immobilizing the human against his chest.

Shane winced at the contact, at the heat of Renkash's breath against his neck, his stiff collared epaulets the only barrier against the cat's fangs. Attempting to jump free, Shane struggled against Renkash's magic pinning him to the mortal plane until the resistance finally dissolved and he found himself in the higher dimensions of the Afterlife.

<<You still don't like being touched, right?>> Renkash taunted, seemingly content to remain on the mortal plane and await Shane's return.

Channeling his Necromancy, Shane elevated himself even higher, formulating a plan of attack. Concentrating his magic, he prepared the strongest Soul Shatter spell he could manage without drawing on the Void, wrapping it in a simplified version of his son's Shieldbreaker spell. "Should have killed me when you had the chance, cat."

<<Why?>> Renkash's voice held a feral excitement. <<We're having so much fun.>>

Launching himself from his perch, Shane cut through the ever-decreasing dimensions of the Afterlife until he landed once more on the mortal plane, face to face with the predatory cat. He released the Shatter with a roar, the spell dissipating in a disappointing shower of necromantic sparks against Renkash's Shielding.

The cat snorted, lips upturned. "Did you expect that to work?"

But it *should* have. Shane's nostrils flared as he stared down at his nemesis. Renkash had never learned Jake's Shieldbreaker spell. He shouldn't have been able to counter it.

"I know everything *you* know," Renkash purred, phasing to stand directly behind Shane. His voice was a low growl. "And everything *you* know, you owe to *me*."

The katanoj pounced but Shane was ready, phasing to add a healthy distance between them. The cat smiled, bloodlust in his eyes as he reversed Shane's efforts, instead pinning the human necromancer again. Renkash's claws lightly traced a bright red line below Shane's ear and along his cheek as he struggled to break free.

"No, Grim. If you want to fight, then *fight*. Don't waste my training." The cat's voice was patient, and tense with anticipation. "You'll never get anywhere if you keep holding back. *I* don't."

Shane paused his struggles to eye Renkash suspiciously. "Why are you helping me?"

"Don't tell me you forgot." Renkash met the question with a feral grin. "I *always* play with my food."

Steeling his resolve, Shane dug deep into his memories and deeper into his Imperium reserves, snapping Renkash's hold over him in the process.

<<Good,>> Renkash praised, wrapping himself in the Void. <<*Now* the fight begins.>>

The dreamscape erupted into a torrent of necromantic fury, the opposing predators countering and counter attacking in a perfectly balanced dance for dominance, a fight to the death of tooth and spell and sharpened claw across every plane of existence with a vitriol unmatched by all but themselves. The duel stretched onward in tense silence – hours, maybe days, Shane discovered he'd lost track in his single-minded focus on the demonic cat – Renkash perfectly shaking off Shane's efforts to win the upper hand with an infuriating smile and a feline grace.

Recognizing the stalemate, Shane dug to the very bottom of his reserves, summoning every last drop of his magic for one final effort to eliminate the memories of the dark shadowed cat from his mind. *All or nothing.*

Renkash grinned, pausing his own efforts to allow the full force of the blow to strike him squarely in the chest. His form dissolved, leaving Shane by himself once more.

I did it?

The victory felt hollow, the cat's final smug expression seared into Shane's mind, but there was no time to dwell on its meaning. Janikk's next test would start any moment.

Checking his remaining magic, Shane cursed under his breath. Renkash had cost everything he had. He couldn't afford another confrontation.

"Well, that was fun." Renkash casually paced back into his vision with a self-satisfied smirk. "I hope you feel better, now that you've gotten a little healthy aggression out of your system. I know *I* do."

"But... I just Shattered you."

"And now I'm back." Renkash purred, smoothing down black fur ruffled from their engagement, no trace remaining of his wounds from the fight. "I warned you. I'm *you*. As long as *you're* still here, so am I." He snorted. "How many times did you hit my soul with Shatter back on Loxira? What a mangled mess you make when you're angry and desperate. And yet you couldn't end my memory then, and you can't do it now."

Shane exhaled, shoulders slumping as the cat stalked closer. "So why haven't you killed *me*, then? You've had plenty of opportunities."

"That's not how this works, Grim," Renkash whispered in Shane's ear, his voice bearing promises of glory and violence.

"If you die, our conversation ends, and you wake up. But that's the easy way out, isn't it?" He ran a claw gently across Shane's throat, just deep enough to draw a trace of blood. "No, if you want me to leave you alone, you need to come to terms with our history. We can't move forward if you keep ignoring our past."

"I've put that past behind me," Shane scowled, immovable. "That's not who I am anymore."

"Oh, really?" Renkash erupted into laughter, jagged and cruel. "You keep telling yourself that. Violence is in our blood, in our bones, in our *soul*." He paused, his voice soft and drenched in threat. "Or have you forgotten already? Poor Razick. You think you could be friends, but she's not in our league. Even with all that training, she's little more than prey against a *true* predator."

Shane snarled, preparing to resume his attack, but stopped at Renkash's glare. "You leave her alone."

"Or what?" Renkash sneered.

Shane grappled with his words. "She deserves better than that."

"Of course she does," the oversized cat agreed. "They never deserve our cruelty. That's why it's such an effective lesson. Because if that's what we do when they *don't* deserve it..." He backed away, spreading his arms. "Well. Imagination is a powerful thing."

"I'm not like you." Shane turned away. "I don't *want* to be like you."

"You *are* me. We are the same. This is *your* dream, and as far as I can tell, I'm the embodiment of your most violent tendencies." Renkash shook his head, his black mane drifting across his shoulders at the motion. "You believed in our cause, once. We held the fate of the universe in our palms, all of existence, ours to subjugate. That could be us, again." The cat's face shone with malice. "And this time, *we'd* get to decide, not Admiral Kydell. You already have your own fleet. A planet to call home. A talented battle mage willing to give anything you want in exchange for your approval."

"They *trust* me," Shane snarled. "Kydell used me. Used *all* of us. I *won't* use them, too."

"They already gave you that authority. That's what power *is*. All that's left is to decide how to use it. Who will benefit." Renkash's eyes shone with a savage desire. "Why not us?"

Shane lamented his depleted magic, blinking in surprise as his veins filled with Imperium in response.

This is a dream, he reminded himself. *It isn't real.*

Here, he was only limited by his imagination.

Closing his eyes, he pictured his favorite twin blades, the weapons materializing in his hands with a welcome familiarity.

"More violence, then?" Renkash sounded *amused*. "Wanton destruction always *did* improve our mood. Help us think. Do you remember the time we–"

"I am *not* you," Shane snarled. Testing the grips of his swords, he launched himself at the cat once more. If he had to confront his past, he'd do it on *his* terms – rage in his heart, and blood in his teeth.

45

RENKASH WAS READY FOR Shane's assault, an identical pair of swords materializing in his grip to parry the attack before returning the favor. Once again the two dueled, the glint of sharpened steel lighting the dreamspace as both combatants bent reality and the Afterlife in their favor, twisting heaven and hell in a deadly dance of liquid fury and practiced muscle.

But this time, Shane was prepared for the stalemate, waiting until Renkash fell into a comfortable rhythm before twisting the Veil to obtain unobstructed access to the large katanoj's tail.

"Ow." Renkash paused, and Shane felt the unmistakable buzz of energy against the back of his neck as Renkash bolstered his Shielding before summoning the severed limb to his hand. "Well that's not fair."

"Never fight fair," Shane recited with a savage grin.

"But always fight honest," Renkash replied. "You *did* remember my lessons. Very good." Releasing his tail, Renkash allowed both swords to also fade into nothingness. "Of course, now that you've taken advantage of one of my weaknesses, I get to exploit one of yours."

With a twist of Renkash's hand, Jake stood before them, dressed in Confederation brown. His usual youthful expression had aged, replaced now with a hard determination, as he focused his attention on something or someone Shane couldn't see.

"And what's your name, Recruit?" a voice asked.

"Jacobus," Jake answered earnestly, his eyes still fixed on the unseen speaker. "Lawson Jacobus."

Shane clenched his fists, forcing himself to slowly exhale. This wasn't real. More mind games, from the dream.

"Lawson?" the voice asked with surprise. "You wouldn't happen to be Lawson Zane's son? Admiral Renkash's second? Never knew he had a kid."

Jake shrugged, and Shane's heart fell as he realized the boy showed no sign of duress at his present situation. "He didn't know about me."

The speaker laughed. "Yeah, that's always the risk, isn't it? Condolences about your father. He was a good, brave man. I'm sure you'll make his memory proud." There was a pause. "Saved me from Admiral Renkash a few times, only one I ever saw stand up to that damn cat. I owe him. If you ever need anything..."

The vision faded, leaving Shane clenching his fists in the ensuing silence.

No. Jake will never *become me.*

"Ouch," Renkash grinned, a toothy smile of pride. "No appreciation. No loyalty."

"Silence." Shane's voice was sullen with command, his mind a tangle of emotions.

No. This was a dream. Nothing more.

"That never happened. Why would you *show* me that?"

Renkash shrugged, the embodiment of smug muscle and gracefully contained lethality. "We only know what you know. Jake's already killed once. *Shattered* once. It's always easier the second time. And the third. And the fourth."

"Stop. Talking."

"Especially considering who he has for a father," Renkash continued pointedly, ignoring Shane's discomfort. "But a monster is only good at being a monster. Best to let that monster loose, let it do what it does best. Keeping it caged never ends well for anyone, once it breaks free. And it *always* breaks free."

Shane bit back his retort, instead staring at the dark-furred katanoj with wide eyes.

He's right. Violence and death were all Shane knew. All he was *good* at. But trying to keep that monster chained within wouldn't work forever. Every decision, every choice, he felt his old habits lingering beneath his thoughts. Fighting to resurface. *That monster is who I am.*

And what example was he setting for Jake, trying to deny a large part of who he was?

That didn't mean he'd let the monster loose. At least, not completely. But the universe *needed* the monster, he'd begun to realize after Baden. He'd helped save an entire planet that day, and countless lives. If he wanted to build a better life for Jake, he couldn't just hide and watch the universe tear itself apart. He needed to get his hands dirty.

And if most of that dirt was blood? Well, it was a small price to pay, for peace.

"You're right." Shane watched Renkash blink in surprise at the admission. "I have the power to change the universe, and I need to use it. Use the fleet." He scowled in warning. "But on *my* terms. *Not* yours."

"And what terms are those?" Renkash's whiskers splayed with curiosity, and Shane noted the cat's tail, now back to its original state, curling with satisfaction. "Are we rejoining the Confederation?"

"No." Shane crossed his arms, his attention fixed on the violent cat. "Currently, *I* hold the power. The fleet. The planet. The trust of Baden's citizens. Why would I give *any* of that to Sparnell?"

Renkash bared his teeth. "So what are we doing with this power?"

"We'll be the monster to keep the other monsters at bay. Protect the weak, against the strong who would devour them."

Protect Jake, so he never has to be what I've become.

"What's in it for us?" Renkash growled his displeasure deep within his throat. "You said we wouldn't surrender our power to others."

"More power, as more planets ask for our help. Prestige, as tales of our successes spread." Shane smirked. "And your favorite, blood and violence. But instead of trying to stop us, they'll beg for *more*."

"And the fleet?" Renkash licked his lips.

"My people are *mine*. You can't have them." Shane fixed the bloodthirsty cat with a pointed stare. "We will *not* hurt them again. And whatever they need, we'll make sure they get it, no matter the cost." He shook his head. "We won't hurt those who look to us for guidance or protection. Never again."

"It'll be more difficult to keep them in line," Renkash cautioned.

Shane stood firm, crossing his arms across his chest. "That's *my* concern. Not yours."

He'd always be the villain. He recognized that now. But that didn't mean he had to be one to his own people.

"And our enemies?"

It was Shane's turn to bare his teeth, darkness filling his eyes. "Hold nothing back."

46

JEB WATCHED AS THEN-VICE Admiral Kydell stalked across the bridge of the *Inevitable*, teeth bared in a snarl. "I don't understand the delay. I gave an order, I expect you to follow it. Yet no one has done as I've commanded."

Every instinct in Jeb's mind screamed to run, to escape the fate awaiting Urla.

But she'd asked him to stay. So he'd stay, for her.

Somehow.

"Captain Renkash already submitted his objection to your choice. And I concur with his assessment." The human commander crossed his arms, chin set in defiance of his superior's protests. His skin was a deep tan despite his posting aboard ship, although not as dark as the long, brown hair cascading down his back in a haphazard ponytail. "She's not just a botanist. Her skills in Zokinesis alone make her more valuable in the field."

<Is there any magic you *don't* know?> He'd already realized she was talented, but the more he learned the more he realized how little he knew of her credentials. <Do you think that's why you feel Janikk's network stronger than I do?>

<Maybe,> she answered, thoughtfully, before shaking off his question with a hushed urgency. <Listen. Please. We can talk about it after.>

"And where *is* your captain?" Kydell sneered, pausing his pacing to stare his subordinate in the eye.

The commander met the wolf's gaze, unflinching. "Something came up. An issue in Telemetry."

<Brave man.>

<Lawson looked out for us,> Urla agreed. <We all mourned for him, after Loxira.>

"Hiding, is he? He knows he can't disobey a direct order." Kydell stepped closer, his snout mere inches from Commander Lawson's nose. "And neither can you. As his executive officer, you're bound to carry out my orders in his absence."

"I'm bound to ensure the efficiency and effectiveness of his ship and its crew." Lawson leaned forward, his voice soft but firm as he addressed the wolf with a glare of his own. "I'll do whatever it takes to support this ship and her captain, just as you've conditioned me, sir. And this recent choice of yours? A waste of a talented resource."

There was sorrow in Urla's voice as she narrated her thoughts. <None of us deserved what Kydell put us through. What the Confederation *allowed* him to put us through.>

Kydell backed away, once more locking eyes with the insubordinate XO. "You know as well as I she's the only viable option we have to fill the position. The less talented candidates still have Families to protest my decision. Even that worthless Kane Jeb and his reckless drive to volunteer for everything has managed to gather a following back home. But the Valcores remanded First Petty Officer Urla to my command *and I will do with her as I wish.*"

<How could your Family *do* that to you?> Jeb couldn't contain his fury, clenching his fists at his sides. <Abandon you like that?>

<I was a liability to the Family honor.> Urla sighed. <It was for the best, really. I'd rather be the person I am than the person they wanted me to be.> Her voice grew quiet. <Not that I don't wish they'd have accepted me for who I am. You Kanes are lucky. That doesn't happen often, in the Confederation. I hope you know that. Value what you had.>

"I will *not* allow you to *kill* someone just to fill an *AI* position!"

"You don't have a choice." The wolf bared his teeth in triumph. "Your refusal to obey is a detriment to the effective operation of this ship. The *Inevitable* requires a Hydroponics AI, and I've already determined how you will fill that requirement. *Kill her*, or get the *hell* off the bridge."

Lawson spun sharply at the command, his ponytail swinging behind him as he marched from the bridge. He fixed them with an apologetic glance as he passed. "I did my best," he mouthed. "Run, if you can."

Jeb suppressed the urge to follow Lawson's advice. Urla had asked him to stay. This was important to her.

"Security," Kydell continued calmly. "Escort Urla to me. Then guard the door, to ensure your defiant Commander can't return." He smiled coldly. "And once we're done here, bring Captain Renkash to the bridge. It's become clear I've fallen behind on our sessions. Another failing I intend to correct today."

Jeb fought against Urla's memories then as security grabbed his shoulders, dragging him toward the admiral.

"It's no use, struggling." The wolf eyed them with amusement as he held out his hand, receiving in return a rather wicked-looking knife. "I've already decided your fate, and it *will* happen. All that's left now is to enjoy it." His lips turned upward in a menacing smile. "At least, *I* will enjoy it."

"No. Please..." Jeb protested, attempting to twist away.

Urla sighed. <It's a memory, Jeb, you can't change it. It already happened. Please. I need you to understand.>

"You think anyone'll risk their own necks for someone as *unimportant* as you?" The knife gleamed in the artificial lighting of the bridge as Kydell brought it into position. "It appears I'll have to kill you myself. Lieutenant Commander Yiven. As the only necromancer on the bridge, prepare the binding spell."

"I want *no* part in this," Alanis spat from the Navigations console. "If that damned lap cat of yours won't even do it, maybe that should tell you something."

<I was angry at Alanis for a long time. But she couldn't have changed anything. She was just as much a victim as I was, and always extra kind to me after. Guilt, at first, I suspect. But she became a good friend.>

"I'd hate for anything to happen to those brothers of yours. What were their names...? Oh yes. Elwyx and Osygg." Kydell's words dripped with bloody menace. "Such talented mages. Twins, even! I've put in a request to add them to my Collection. The other admirals want to split them up, but Family should always stick together. Isn't that right?"

"I'm sorry, Urla." Alanis' voice was strained. "They still have a chance. You understand, right?"

Kydell's knife hand plunged to Jeb's chest and pain followed, bringing with it a welcome darkness.

47

Razick felt free for the first time in her life.

And the last time.

She stared up at the Sparnell Armed Forces Headquarters, the imposing building of glass and angles reflecting the morning sun back at her and the capital city below them from its perch on the clifftop. Her fellow recruits jostled past along the giant walk up the Cliffside, its edges lined by statues of the long-dead that refused to be forgotten.

A pair of quick-footed katanoji almost knocked her backpack from her shoulder where it hung by a single strap, too absorbed in their own excitement at adulthood to pay any mind to the red-headed sixteen-year-old fighting down her own panic at the prospect of meeting the same fate as her father.

"What's the matter, Fireball? Are you *scared*?" A dark-furred canid paused his own progress, teeth bared in a threatening snarl. "Afraid of a *building*?"

Before Razick could react, a dark feminine voice sounded from behind her. "Who you calling Fireball?"

The canid backed up, swallowing hard. "Not you, *her!* I *swear!*"

"What if I don't believe you?"

"Well, then, I, uh..."

Razick burst into laughter as the canid turned tail and ran, pushing past several others in an effort to squeeze through the door first as one of the Instructors took off after him.

She'd always loved this memory. Her first meeting with Nya. She couldn't believe she'd forgotten it.

Turning, she greeted her future fiancée, a red-scaled dracoling with fierce amber eyes and a grin to match.

"They like to act tough, because it makes them feel big. But show you're not afraid of them and they'll be afraid of *you*, instead. Even some of the Instructors." She hefted her backpack higher on her shoulders. "Name's Nya. What's yours?"

"Raz." She grinned. "You been here awhile? Thought they wouldn't let us leave the building until our training finished."

"Had some big Family thing. Dad pulled some strings so I could go. Been here a month, otherwise." Nya rolled her eyes. "Feels like decades, though. Doesn't take long to figure out what they want from us. Hard part is figuring out how to make them think you're giving it to them, without losing yourself in the process." She winked. "Lucky for you, I've learned a few tricks, and I don't mind sharing."

She'd distrusted Nya then. She knew better now. "Thanks for the help."

"Saw the look in your eyes, staring at the building. Reminded me of my first time here." Nya shoved her hands in her pockets, turning to glare at Headquarters. "So. Let me guess. Battle mage in the family? Didn't do so well coming home?"

Razick nodded. "Father. Said I'd be better off if I died, rather than come home."

"He's wrong." Nya shook her head, brows furrowed. "My mother was the battle mage. She *did* die, ended up with one of those awful TAGs. Her admiral tried to keep her, after her conscription was up, but the Family threw a big stink. They'd already arranged her marriage to my father and everything, wasn't about to let the SAF ruin their political investment. So they had to let her go, but there wasn't much left of her by then. She's my own mother, and I barely know anything about her."

Razick shuddered. She hadn't known what a TAG was, then, but that was before she'd almost been assigned to Admiral Kydell's Selkirk. "I'm so sorry, Nya. I know what that's like." Razick squeezed Nya's shoulder, and felt the dracoling relax at her touch.

Nya grinned at her, a mischief in her eyes. "Race you to the door?"

"Actually," Razick interrupted, squeezing Nya's shoulder harder. "You don't remember me. I barely remember you. But we were close, and I trust you, and I'm hoping you can help me with something?"

The dracoling's brows furrowed. "What are you talking about?"

"This is a dream," Razick explained patiently. "A Dreamwalk, really. I've lost a friend inside. I promised I'd keep him safe but I lost track of him and he needs me. I'm hoping you'll agree to help me save him."

"What do you need me to do?"

Razick grinned. "Who's the scariest person you know?"

"My grandfather," Nya answered instantly. "Absolutely terrifying."

"This is a dream," Razick reminded her, "but do you think you could pretend to be him? Do I have enough memories of him?"

Nya's wicked smile shouted a definite yes. "*So* much better than class. You always did know how to have fun."

"Wait until I summon you," Razick told her. "I've a few more people to recruit first."

The scene shifted around her, and Razick wrapped her arms around herself instinctively before snorting. This was a dream. She didn't have to be cold unless she wanted to be.

Instead she surveyed her surroundings, recognizing one of the many planets she'd been sent to "soften up for annexation," as Fleet Command always called it.

She remembered getting in a fight with her Instructors over the phrase. Battle mage training included frequent reminders not to think, merely to follow orders "for the good of us all."

They hadn't liked it when she reminded them that "us all" never seemed to include the good of the planets themselves.

But there was no time to dwell on the past subjugation of planets, particularly pretend ones. She'd been unable to fight against Kydell's commands then, and she was a different person now.

And Lawrence needed her.

"Vernell! Cunningham!" she shouted into the silent, snow-covered trees. "Get out here!"

There was no answer, and she rolled her eyes. "That's an *order*, Petty Officers. Get your butts out here or I'm not the only one who'll be chewing out your asses. Move it!"

"This is a *stealth* mission," Vernell whined, dusting the snow off his Void-black fur as he emerged from beneath it. His tail jerked in agitation. "This isn't very stealthy, sir."

"Change of mission," she told him. "We're rescuing a friend of mine."

"You have *friends*?" Cunningham barked, emerging from the overgrown evergreen she'd adapted into her hiding spot. The pine needles sticking every which way from her thick, blonde braid combined with her red, scale-like skin gave her the appearance of a rather large red porcupine lizard, and Razick had to suppress a laugh.

"Don't talk to the Sub-Officer that way," Vernell growled at the dracoling before turning back to Razick with a perfect salute. "I hope you'll see fit to give me a glowing report for my performance today, sir."

"We'll see," Razick offered, only to watch the ever-obedient Vernell stretch taller, ears and whiskers perfectly arrayed in attention. Apparently dream-Vernell was from the days before she'd broken him from that habit.

She'd been hard on him, then. Annoyed at his constant efforts to please.

But that was before she'd learned his mother was a TAG. Razick would've been the perfect example of obedience, too, if she'd been running from *that*.

"We're stuck in a dream," she informed them instead, "and there's an important officer stuck here with us. We need to find him and save him."

"An admiral?" Vernell asked hopefully.

Cunningham merely scoffed. "Another escort mission. Great."

"A commodore," Razick told them. "Gather your teams. Find me on my signal."

Vernell saluted again. "Yes, sir!"

But the scene was already changing again as Razick moved to the next useful memory.

"I'm coming, Lawrence," she promised. "You don't have to fight your demons alone."

48

"You've finally won, Grim." Renkash bowed slightly with a predatory grace, eyes still locked to Shane's, tail twitching in anticipation of the battles to come. "We have a deal."

The cat dissolved as he spoke the words, and with him, the dream.

Groaning in emotional exhaustion, Shane blinked at his new surroundings, shaking himself free from the roots dangling through cracks in the ceiling to gently hold him in place. He noted the Kanes still sleeping in a similar arrangement on either side of him.

The room itself was small, hewn from the same rock and tyrellium Shielding as the cave, yet with a cozy and intimate feel rather than the impersonal indifference of the previous passageways. Small sparks of light warmly illuminated the space with surprising ease, inspection revealing their source as an assortment of bioluminescent fungi and the small winged insects feeding on them.

He jumped backward involuntarily, skin itching at the memory of the obnoxiously loud crickets that had swarmed his skin before they'd entered the cave, falling to his knees as the full weight of his claustrophobia hit him in the same moment. The light in the room dimmed slightly as he pulled heavily on Janikk's network of life to stave off his fears, the planet somehow stronger within his mind and even more alive.

"Dirkkataa Klaael nikkeer! Kajj Flesyk rekkorae Flesykoj niwok?"

Shane started at the sound, quickly turning to spot the satisfied spirit of a young woman in an ornate, oversized necklace and beautiful Runework-embroidered robes now standing at the center of the room, tilting her head as she watched him expectantly.

Janikk.

Shane bowed politely to the spirit, summoning all the deference he could muster into his voice. "Greetings, Janikk. You have my thanks for granting us an audience."

She blinked slowly, waiting, and he sighed. Of course she wouldn't know Galactic Common. By his estimates, she was ancient, and therefore her language likely predated anything spoken today. Still, he decided to run through the languages he *did* know, just in case. Courtesy of Feels' Phoenix Assembly and the language spell they provided upon his arrival to Baden, he had a larger than standard selection to choose from.

Sparnick? The Confederation had sent several landing parties, and while the reports didn't include any dialog with Janikk, perhaps she'd learned a few phrases. "Hello. It's a pleasure to finally meet you."

Janikk's words betrayed her frustration. "Flesyk nekksilae Flesykoj, nudarrekknae."

That would be a no. Legionese, perhaps? "Thank you for granting me the honor of speaking with you."

"Nudarrekknae."

Shane exhaled. The rest were even less likely, but... Loxiran? "Oh gracious planetary spirit, I'm hoping you can help us."

Janikk watched silently, her face blank.

Okay, then maybe... Yarvish? "Janikk? We'd like to request your help."

She burst into laughter, although she attempted to hide it behind her hands, and Shane couldn't help but crack a faint smile. Not exactly the language of diplomacy, Yarvish. He'd always known it was a backwater planet.

He scratched his chin, switching into his final known language, Badenese. "You probably can't understand this either, can you?"

Janikk tilted her head again, watching silently.

He exhaled, turning to observe Jeb, still wrapped in protective roots. He'd have to wait until the biologist was done, then hope he knew one of the telepathic translation spells.

But Janikk was clearly unwilling to admit defeat, instead motioning for Shane to join her near the small plant growth in the center of the room. He nodded, cautiously moving forward until he stood before her.

Immediately he felt the foliage attempt to encircle his wrists and ankles, causing him to jump backward with a snarl. "No."

"Tsekeht tenaa Flesykoj aja Ecknaab." Janikk's voice held a kindness as she motioned him to once again step forward, adopting a pose with her feet spread slightly apart, hands not quite relaxed at her sides, palms facing forward and up. "Turikkaa yukkan. Darrekknee."

Eying her suspiciously, Shane cautiously approached again, mimicking her pose and eliciting a grin of approval. The vines returned to wrap around him, slower than before, and this time he permitted it without protest, keeping his attention locked on Janikk.

As much as he disliked the thought of being restrained, this was her planet. If he wanted her to permit his people to settle here, he'd need to gain her favor. And right now, that required his cooperation.

If it was a trap, he should hopefully be able to phase out of it easily enough.

But the growth stopped soon after, the planet's structure gently supporting his entire body much the same way his exosuit supported his core, offering little resistance against his efforts to move.

Not a trap, then. A safety feature, perhaps?

He dialed up the settings on his body brace as an extra precaution. "Okay. What's next?"

The vines burst into bloom, light purple flowers filling the center of the small cave with a delicate and enticing fragrance. Shane felt his breathing slow and his eyelids begin to droop as Janikk drifted closer, a sorrowful smile gracing the delicate features of her face. "Darrekknee." She reached for his forehead, and Shane felt the telltale sensation of her ghostly touch.

His vision went dark, his consciousness not far behind.

He awoke wrapped in roots, much like he had upon completion of his negotiations with Renkash. Turning to the center of the room to confront Janikk about whatever she'd just done to him, Shane instead found a living woman with long, blonde hair and proud eyes, her attention on the young men and women before her.

Blinking, he surveyed the room to discover many more individuals still wrapped in roots, ranging in age from elderly to barely adult. The Kanes weren't among them.

He shook his head, scratching against his temple in an effort to puzzle out this new development, only to discover his hair much shorter than it had been mere moments ago.

Now in a panic, Shane pulled at his neck before rubbing his face, only then pausing to exhale in relief. This wasn't his face, it was *hers*.

"This is your memory, isn't it? That 'Tsekeht' you sent us through. You did it, too."

Observing the room itself, Shane nodded in understanding. The age-weathered walls that greeted him the first time were now covered with subtle but colorful figures of nature and cultural events, faintly visible beneath the bioluminescent life clinging to the stone.

His vision shifted, this time revealing a treetop village bound together with rope bridges, the houses twisted and formed from the branches of the tree itself. Young children ran happily underfoot despite the height, laughing and teasing as they navigated the tree with ease, their brightly colored clothing a stark contrast to the natural shades of the village. Here he watched Janikk learn, apply, and teach various Nature Magics, hunting skills, and combat techniques, defending her village against an assortment of the planet's ferocious wildlife even as she led parties to hunt them in return, all accompanied by a rising reverence from her peers until finally Janikk herself stood in the role of observer as others sought her attention and guidance.

"Were you their leader, Janikk?"

Her thoughts turned sorrowful, and suddenly they stood in a clearing with a collection of mourners, those closest wearing the bright clothing of Janikk's village, the other groups each donning what Shane assumed to be their own unique cultural variations. Shane counted idly as each sent a single mourner forward to lay a fruit upon the chest of the deceased elderly woman at the center, whispering a short mantra over her body before stepping away.

Fifteen. Just like the poles.

Janikk was last, gripping the woman's hand and bowing to press their foreheads together before carefully removing the large wood and metal necklace – a twin to the one worn by the ghostly visage of Janikk in their conversations – from the dead woman's chest. She placed her fruit and retreated to her former position, delivering the colorful piece of jewelry to the attendant to her left.

All eyes turned to Janikk as she nodded to the mage at the woman's feet. On her signal, the woman's body rose into the air, the funeral attendees turning to watch as the telekinetic mage reverently set her upon the ledge, an assortment of scavengers already gathering in the fading light to pick over her bones.

"Janikk esaukkaa Ecknaab," Janikk said solemnly.

"Janikk esaukee Ecknaab," the mourners replied, bowing briefly at Janikk before parting to allow her entrance to the cave within the cliff face.

The door slid shut behind her, and Shane's vision darkened. "You took the Tsekeht again? Why?"

But Janikk had her own agenda, shifting his vision once more to view the planet, now torn by an invading force. A stranger. *Redistael*. Outsider.

He watched as Janikk, now wearing the ornate necklace from the prior memory, gathered her entourage beneath the planet's surface, each individual attempting to shout louder than the others.

"Nekksilee!" Janikk scowled, silencing the argument. "Janikk esaukae Ecknaab."

"Janikk esaukkae Ecknaab," they repeated solemnly, bowing in respect and backing away to exit the room.

At their departure, a young man emerged from the back corner to slowly approach her with a small, gleaming knife in his hand. He closed his eyes, shifting his grip on the weapon as she backed against the wall, vines erupting from the stone to wrap around her wrists and ankles and hold her fast.

"Nubudokk."

At her word, he opened his eyes, stepping forward to begin the slow and careful task of carving Runework across her arms, legs, and chest.

Shane felt Janikk's pain as his own, studying the runes through her memories.

"I don't recognize most of this, but these runes…" He motioned toward the fresh Runes across her upper chest. "This is Necromancy. A binding spell. A strong one." He shuddered inwardly. "They bound you here, forever, to watch the planet. Didn't they?"

Janikk's voice held an infinite loneliness as she finally addressed him. "Darrekknee, Tergerael. Darrekknee."

Understand.

The vision faded, depositing Shane back in his present reality. Shaking himself free from the vines, he found himself collapsing onto his hands and knees, his strength spent.

"Carefully," Janikk cautioned kindly, her words foreign and yet somehow familiar. "The magic hasn't worn off yet."

"I can understand you now?" he gasped in surprise, blinking as he struggled to sit. Razick's masterwork of an exosuit admirably performed the bulk of the effort.

"I think it worked this time." Janikk sounded pleased at his reaction. "I've not had cause to use this spell for many generations. I made an error in my first attempt. But now, you know my history, and so you understand the intentions of my words. But I do not know yours." Her spirit settled to the ground before him, reaching her hands toward his as she adopted a sitting pose. "You have many questions. Share your Trials with me, so I may understand and answer."

Shane hesitated. With the exception of Jake and Feels, he hadn't shared his full history with anyone. So many secrets, so many regrets he'd tried to keep hidden.

But the fleet was counting on him.

He could certainly wait until Jeb completed his own tests. Rely upon the biologist's Telepathy to bridge the language barrier. But the woman before him had bared her soul to grant him this opportunity, and respect demanded he meet her on equal footing. If that meant he and Jake needed to go back into hiding afterward...

He waited, but his conditioning remained silent, seemingly considering the exchange a fair trade.

Nodding his head, he allowed her to take his hands in her own.

He opened his memories to her curiosity, guiding her through the key moments of his own life. His childhood on a Yarvan farm, the Legion attack that had claimed his parents' lives, the all-consuming rage for vengeance which had driven his military career. He showed her his reawakening with the discovery of Jake on Loxira, his subsequent efforts to provide for his son while hiding on Baden, his decision to murder and imprison Feels in a misguided effort to keep his secrets, and the attack by Kydell's fleet – now *his* fleet – which had completely altered his plans.

Exhaling, he cautiously met her eyes, finding not the condemnation he expected but rather a sorrowful compassion.

"I understand you, Tergerael."

Repentant One.

"Please… Don't tell anyone."

"I won't betray your trust. Just as you won't betray mine." Her words held both promise and threat. "I am bound to uphold the Ecknaab, the Balance of life upon this planet. So are you and your people, if you choose to remain."

Shane's brows furrowed. "You'll let us stay? Just like that?"

"You have passed the Tsekeht, the Leadership Trials. You have offered yourself to the Tenecknaab, and it has accepted. The Ecknaab has spoken, you are part of the Balance." She tilted her head, watching his confusion. "I am Janikk. Guardian. Teacher. I protect the Balance. I do not decide where it falls."

"But many others have tried to settle here, and you killed them all." Rubbing the back of his neck, Shane struggled to make sense of her words and her sudden acceptance of their presence. "Why us? Why have we been allowed to succeed when the others have failed?"

"I have not allowed anything." Her smile hinted at a patient amusement. "Those who came before sought to subjugate, and met the results of their failure. But you…" She motioned to the Kanes, still asleep within their vine cocoons. "The Leadership Trials confront each Pilgrim with the worst of themselves. Their deepest fears, their worst regrets. All our leaders must pass the Trials, no matter their method of leading. Our teachers, officers, and governmental and spiritual leaders each passed the Trials, when beginning their career and when achieving important milestones."

"Like requesting permission to settle your planet."

She nodded, slowly. "You brought your leaders, and the Trials will decide if the Balance recognizes their leadership. Already, you have passed, and so on behalf of the Balance, I bid you welcome. You and your people respect the Balance, and have earned its respect in return." Closing her eyes, she tilted her head as if listening. "Even now, they search for you. Reach into the Tenecknaab. You will see."

Following her lead, Shane reached his consciousness into the strange network encompassing the planet's diverse array of life. His mind filled with the local planetary wildlife, overwhelming his senses until he adjusted his focus, applying filters to narrow his search to Feels.

And suddenly there they were, his beloved empath, accompanied by several other lifeforms. Three were faint, not yet part of Janikk's network, but the others… He counted two fylox, plus…

"Haveid?"

Janikk laughed. "I like Munokkael. I hope they stay."

The Hunter.

"But then why–"

"So many questions, Tergerael!" she interrupted with a smile. "But the wrong ones. We will speak later, once your friends awaken."

Shane's attention drifted from Janikk to glance at where the Kanes remained sleeping within their vined cocoons, his thoughts still overflowing with questions. Turning back toward the planetary spirit, the necromancer instead discovered Janikk's departure, with no trace of her presence remaining on either side of the Veil.

49

Urla opened her awareness to find not Janikk, but the same household they'd visited prior. The same woman stood in the kitchen preparing vegetables, while the brown-haired man sat watching holovids.

<What the hell? This is a *Dreamwalk*. When we died, we were supposed to wake up. That's the *only* reason I showed you that.>

<You picked that memory on *purpose?* Why would you *do* that to me?> But the anger in Jeb's voice dissolved quickly into sorrow. <Urla... I'm sorry. I didn't understand. I wish you would have *told* me.> He paused, his voice calmer when he spoke next. <Still. I'm glad you showed me now, even if it's just because you thought it would end the memories.>

<The Grand Navarch suggested I be more honest with you.> She sighed in frustration. <He was right, so I'm trying, but it's *hard*. I don't want you to think less of me.>

<Think *less* of you?> Jeb's voice cracked. <Urla. You've been through so much, and gave up so much, just to remain true to yourself and your beliefs. I don't think less of you! I'm in awe of your strength.>

That... wasn't the reaction she'd expected.

She hadn't felt appreciated in a long time, but ever since the Grand Navarch's boarding of the *Inevitable*, and her chance opportunity meeting Jeb...

<Thanks. That means a lot.>

"Think fast!" A freckled teenager with unruly red curls and shining green eyes bounced into the room, tossing some sort of metallic object at Jeb.

He deftly caught it, lobbing it back at her before she darted out of the room.

It missed, and she stuck out her tongue at him before disappearing from sight. "Can't catch me!"

"Would you stop that ruckus?" the man shouted from the dining room table. "I'm trying to watch the news vids here. I don't want to miss anything!"

"Enjoy it while you can, Sweetheart," the woman sang from the kitchen, her voice shifting to a sudden sadness. "You've missed so much already, and she'll be sixteen soon enough."

<Is this your Family?> Urla watched with envy.

<Yeah.> Jeb tugged his hair. <Before Razick was conscripted. I remember this one.>

"Does she have to go?" Jeb's voice questioned.

<And I guess you get to see it, too, now,> Jeb added quietly.

"Darling, you know the law," Jeb's mother answered, resuming her work. "We all have to do our part. Keep our planets safe."

"But I don't want her to leave," Jeb pouted. "I want her to stay. With me. Howard told me not everyone comes back from conscription!"

"They're the lucky ones," Jeb's father growled from the dining room. "If Razick's lucky, she'll never come back, either."

"Carl!" Jeb's mother dropped her knife with a clatter, turning to glare at her husband, hands on her hips. "We do *not* say things like that in this house. *Especially* not about your own *daughter*! I've worked hard for this family and I will *not* have you tear it apart again."

<Only time I ever saw them fight.> Jeb had a sadness to his voice. <Mama was never the same, after Razick left.>

"Sorry, ma'am." Jeb's father bobbed his head, switching off the holographic projector as he rose slowly from his seat. "I'm trying. I'll go get some fresh air. Be back in an hour to help with dinner?" He wrapped Jeb's mother in his arms, planting a kiss lightly on her cheek as she resumed her cooking.

"Thanks, Dear." She leaned into the embrace. "I know how hard this is for you."

"Damn the Confederation and their damn wars," his father agreed, granting Jeb his own kiss on the top of his head on the way out the door. "You be good for your Mama, alright?"

"Yes, Papa." Jeb nodded.

<I didn't understand it at the time,> Jeb explained as the scene dissolved. <But I think I'm starting to.>

<Your father was a battle mage, too, wasn't he?>

<Yeah...> Jeb's voice faded. They stood in silence in the empty darkness for several moments before he spoke again. <What were you studying, anyway? That would make your Family Disown you like that?>

<That was the anthropology.> Urla laughed bitterly. <Behavioral archaeology. Ethology, about animal behaviors and how they adapt.> It felt good to open up to Jeb. <I like knowing why we act the way we do. Wanted to learn Psychometry and become a therapist, but the Valcores managed to block that, so I found the next best thing. Always wished I was born a Margold. Heard they encouraged study like that.>

Jeb tugged his hair. <That's why you were so fascinated with those large birds trying to eat us earlier.>

<Grand Navarch called them gromdornox. Fascinating pack tactics. Would love to study then, see how they adapted to hunt despite Janikk's warning network... From a safe distance, of course.> She was at risk of rambling now, but decided she didn't care. She was safe, with Jeb. <And the drawings in that temple back where we ate the fruit were *superb*. I want to go back. There's so much to study here!>

<The Grand Navarch...> Jeb couldn't hide the excitement in his voice. <You served on the *Inevitable*! You can help me figure out who he *is*! When we boarded, Lawrence mentioned he'd been in Renkash's landing party to Loxira—>

<Jeb. Stop.> She cut him off. <I already know who he was.>

She'd assumed he was dead. Shattered. That's what the reports had said. But there was no mistaking Grim. If she'd held any doubts before, Jeb's confirmation he'd been to Loxira confirmed it.

Jeb's voice was giddy with excitement. <Who was he?>

<No.> This clearly wasn't the answer Jeb expected, but Urla pressed on before he could interrupt. <He wants a fresh start. And he's *trying*. I won't be the one to keep that from him. >

<Urla...>

<Don't misunderstand. When he says he's not a good person? He means it. He's caused more harm and pain that most could accomplish with several lifetimes.> She grew quiet at the memories. <But he's always done right by me. We didn't interact often, but he never forgot I was more than just some unimportant Hydroponics AI. That meant the universe to me then, and it still matters now. I won't betray his secret. Not even to you.

<You're staying, aren't you?> Jeb sighed, running his fingers through his hair. <You're not coming back to Baden with me, are you? You're staying with him. With the fleet.>

<Yes.> She felt his breath catch. <Jeb... You have a Family. A *real* family. I want to know what that's like, and the fleet... The fleet's the closest I've got.>

<We could be a family. I'm right here.>

<I want to *live*, Jeb. A real life, with accomplishments of my own, and a living, breathing body. I have so many dreams, and

he's my best hope at a chance to accomplish *any* of them. It's not that I don't appreciate *us*, it's just...>

<I understand.> He didn't hide the sadness, but she could tell he *meant* it. <I *love* you Urla. You deserve all of that. And he can get it for you. I can't.> His voice cracked, but he pressed on. <But I put that life behind me. Built a new one, on Baden. And I can't... I'm not ready to give that up.>

<Jeb... You're more than I ever dared dream you could be.> This was *hard*, and his understanding made it *harder*, but she finally had the opportunity to live her own life and she couldn't afford to give that up.

Not even to bask in the shadow of Kane Jeb.

<But you've missed out on so much,> Jeb finished. <And you have the opportunity to make up for lost time. You need to take that chance, and I'd only hold you back. Just... Remember me, okay? I'll always be here for you. And who knows, maybe someday things will work out and we'll be able to try this again?>

She didn't even try to hide her relief at his understanding. <I'd like that.>

And with that resolution, the Dreamwalk dissolved, Janikk's cave materializing around them once more.

50

Jeb attempted to rub the last bits of induced sleep from his eyes, stiffening at an unexpected resistance against his hands and arms. He blinked against the dim bioluminescent lighting surrounding him, recognition dawning as he recognized the now-familiar underground walls of Janikk's manufactured cave system, this time surrounded with a tangled mass of vines along the periphery, Lawrence standing proudly at the center.

"Good. You're awake," the necromancer greeted him, slowly sinking to the floor.

Exhaling, Jeb focused his Agrokinesis, directing the vines encasing him to slowly loosen their hold and release him to the ground. He eyed Lawrence with confusion as the necromancer reached into one of the many pockets of his jacket to pull out a thick roll of fabric. "What are you doing?"

Lawrence raised an eyebrow as he calmly began unlacing his boots. "I'm changing into dry socks."

"You're..." Jeb threw up his hands, motioning toward Razick, still asleep in her own tangle of vines. "My sister's still stuck in that dream thing, and you're here worrying about your socks?"

"I'm not *worrying*. I said I'd bring extras, and I mean what I say." He pulled out a second pair, as tightly rolled as the first. "I brought more, if you want a pair."

"If I..." Jeb began to protest, then stopped himself. Razick had always teased him that for someone with the patience to deal with plants, he often forgot how to use it on people.

And with everything else on his mind right now, dry socks sounded like a good idea.

"Thanks," he said instead, plucking the socks from Lawrence's hands before plopping down beside him on the moss scattered throughout the cave.

"Anytime," Lawrence said automatically, before pausing to tilt his head. "Provided I have more than *I* need," he amended.

For some reason, the way he said it reminded Jeb of the whole absurdity of everything since that first conversation with Lawrence in the bathroom of the Baden City Academy not even a month ago. The foolish yet somehow successful attempt to defend a planet with two Instructors, a janitor, and a student, and how Razick hadn't even hesitated to assume they'd succeed. The strange adventure across Janikk as she enlisted deadly predators to lure them into a dream-cave thing. His falling in love with the most brilliant woman he'd ever met, bonding over their research of a foreign planet, only to lose her on that same planet to that same brilliance.

He filled the cave with his laughter. He couldn't *help* it, although he tried. Voids, he tried. The love, the pain, the uncertainty, the joy, all merged into some sort of unhinged chorus of emotion.

Lawrence, to his credit, ignored it, the necromancer's attention focused wholly on his socks, which only made Jeb laugh all the more. All-powerful necromancer. Brought to his knees by tight spaces and wet socks.

The story of Jeb's life these days.

Urla's concern hovered on the other end of their telepathic link. <Jeb. I'm sorry. I hope you're not upset with me.>

He had to pull himself together. For her sake, and Razick's.

<Of course not,> he reassured, after a few moments. <I'm proud of you. It's just... I'm also sad for me. I've never met anyone like you, Urla.>

<Maybe you will again.> Her words were hesitant. As if she wasn't sure whether to say them. Or believe them.

He didn't believe them, either. But she needed the ruse, so he'd play it. <Maybe.>

<I'm sorry I can't be who you need me to be.>

<I need you to be you,> he told her, fiercely. Despite everything he felt right now, that part was true. <Just... Let me know, okay? If you want to try this again.>

<I will,> she promised.

"How are you?" This time it was Lawrence checking in, his voice light, his hand even lighter as it rested, briefly, on Jeb's shoulder.

"That was more thinking than I'm used to." Jeb wrinkled his nose at the realization of how that sounded. "I mean… I think *a lot*, I just don't often think about *people*, you know?" No, that wasn't right either. "I think about *people*, I just don't…"

He shrugged helplessly. He was in no state to explain it. Better if he stopped trying.

"I understand," Lawrence said, simply. And it was enough.

"Is she okay?" Jeb asked, waving one hand at Razick. Anything to change the subject.

Plus he was worried.

"She's safe."

"But is she *okay*? She's been in there a long time." Jeb pressed. He'd already lost Urla, although at least she'd kept the door open for later. He couldn't imagine what he'd do if he lost Razick, too. "I mean, if you made it through, with all your regrets of the past… What's keeping her in there?"

"I don't know," the necromancer answered honestly. "But I want to help her. And I need your help to do it."

Jeb didn't hesitate. "What do you need?"

The faint request of an apotheturgic link settled into the back of Jeb's mind. "I need your mother's help. I need you to Call her."

Jeb accepted the link, blinking as the raw power of the Void behind the Veil settled into his mind. "Wow. This is what your magic's like? All the time?"

"No." The necromancer scowled. "We're still isolated here, so I need Janikk's help, too."

Jeb felt the Void shift within his mind as the necromancer began to cast. <If this is only a fraction of his power, I'm glad he's on *our* side.>

<Me, too!> Urla laughed. <You have *no idea* what he's capable of.>

Jeb tugged at his hair as a thought occurred to him. <I wonder what memories *he* saw?>

"Okay. Hopefully she can help with what I need." Lawrence motioned to Jeb as a young woman in ornate robes materialized in the middle of the room, watching them expectantly. "I want to help my friend. She's still stuck in the Trials and I'm worried about her."

Janikk frowned. "Flesyk nulinae eckitnae."

"I'm not asking you to." Lawrence shook his head. "But the same construction holding your magic in these caves is keeping my magic out, and we need it. Was hoping you could help me access the Afterlife from here."

"Budokkae ivoj eckitni zegee."

"She's my friend and I'm helping her. Tell me how," Lawrence snarled.

Janikk let loose with an excited babble of information, none of it understandable despite Jeb's best efforts. <When did he

learn how to speak to Janikk? We weren't in that dream thing *that* long, were we?>

"Jeb. Up." Lawrence's voice was rich with command as he pointed to the loose roots next to Razick. "Wrap yourself in those again. They've dug through the tyrellium shielding and will help us bypass it to reach the Void. Let me know when you're ready, and I'll walk you through the Soul Call spell."

Inhaling deeply, Jeb followed the necromancer's instructions, entangling himself in a thick root cocoon before turning to the necromancer for further instruction. "Done. What's next?"

"I'll need you to reach out over the Tenecknaab – er, the planetary network thing – until I can bridge across it to reach the Void. Does Urla want to help?"

<Of course I do!>

Jeb nodded. Moments later he felt Urla's magic join with his in the apotheturgic link, her familiarity with Zokinesis further strengthening his own efforts to map Janikk's planetary life network. Closing his eyes, Jeb allowed the overwhelming life of the planet to flood his mind and was rewarded with a rush of necromantic power in return, strands of the Void mingling and twisting themselves throughout the planetary network and Jeb's thoughts.

<Amazing. Obviously I've been to the Afterlife, being dead and all, but it's never felt this... *alive*.>

"*This* is what my magic's like," Lawrence purred triumphantly, eyes closed as he greeted the Void. The necromancer pulled at the Veil, wrapping himself in the higher planes of the Afterlife like a comfort blanket. "I feel whole again. But this isn't the goal of this exercise."

Lawrence turned to fix Jeb with a pointed stare. "Focus on your mother. Everything you can remember. What she looked like. What she smelled like. Any quirks or habits that really stood out to you. Whatever you can remember about her, hold it in your mind."

Jeb filled his thoughts with the comforting chops of freshly diced vegetables, the soothing alto of his mother's voice, the subtle tones of her flowery perfume, and her laugh of parental pride when he shared his accomplishments with her, no matter how insignificant they felt now. "What's next?"

"Gift those memories to the Void." Lawrence snorted at Jeb's alarmed expression. "You'll still remember them! You're letting your mother know you remember *her*, and sending out a beacon for her to find you, if she wishes."

Focusing his thoughts, Jeb released them to the Afterlife, Lawrence's magic mingling with the memories to amplify their signal. They held the spell for what felt like an eternity until finally a familiar presence twisted around Jeb, settling next to his heart with an anxious urgency.

<<Sweetheart? What's wrong? Is everything alright?>>

"I'm fine, Mama." He choked back a sob. He hadn't realized how much he'd missed her. "But Raz might be in trouble. My friend says he can help her, but only with your help."

Mama was instantly all business, just as always when someone in the Family was in trouble. <<What does she need from me?>>

Lawrence, in comparison, was the perfect model of awkward politeness. "Ma'am, I'd like to pull you to the mortal plane for this, if that's alright with you."

<<Whatever you need to help my Raz, you just let me know.>>

With a twist of his finger, Lawrence bent the Afterlife, depositing Mama on the cavern floor between them in a bundle of freckles and short white and red curls. Jeb resisted the urge to run up for a hug. He'd have time for that later. Right now, Razick needed her more.

"Thank you, Ma'am." Lawrence offered a faint bow, rubbing the back of his neck as he addressed her. "I'm worried she's stuck in a Dreamwalk, reliving old memories."

Mama bit her lip, sorrowful eyes turning to inspect Razick, asleep in the tangle of roots. Jeb had to strain to hear his mother's next words. "What memories?"

Lawrence eyed Jeb before returning his attention to Mama. "The way it works... She's reliving her greatest traumas. She told me about her relationship with her father. I'm hoping you'll help us."

Jeb scowled. <Papa wasn't *that* bad!>

Mama blinked slowly at Lawrence. "My Raz is reluctant to trust these days. She told you about that? She must trust you."

<She's your older sister, right?> Urla said softly. <There's probably more going on than you remember.>

"She's my friend." Shane shifted his weight, rubbing the back of his neck. "I'm not used to having any."

Mama tilted her head, watching Lawrence closely. "What are you willing to do to help her?"

"*Anything.*"

She grinned. "Then tell me what you need."

"I want her to know she's not alone," Lawrence explained slowly. "She missed you, so having the opportunity to talk to you – the *real* you, not a dream version – will help."

"And you?"

Running his fingers through his hair, Lawrence shifted his weight. "She told me how much she wanted her father's approval. I want to try to give it to her."

"Papa loves her," Jeb protested, preparing to argue until Mama placed her hand on his shoulder.

"Sweetheart, your father's a lot different now than he was when you were little." She smiled sadly. "Razick's been through a lot... But it started at home, and I wasn't the person she needed me to be to Shield her from it."

"But she seemed fine to *me*..." Jeb looked quickly between Mama and Lawrence, seeking answers. "We were *happy*."

Mama sighed. "We all have our scars, Jeb. Some are deeper than others, and not all are visible from the outside."

<And sometimes we hide them from those we love because we don't want to worry them,> Urla added. <We want to be

the strong one, and don't always recognize that reaching out for help when we need it is also a strength.>

<Like you not telling me about your past.>

<Exactly that,> Urla agreed. <I'm sorry.>

Jeb shook his head. "I wish I'd realized. I would have helped! But I can help now. What do you need?"

"I've still got that Divination magic in my bloodstream, so I should be able to get us inside her Dreamwalk, but your mother and I will need a telepathic link to make sure we stick together." The necromancer bit his lip. "I hate betraying Razick's trust by sharing all this with you, but I don't see a better option."

"I do. You stay here, Sweetheart. Razick wouldn't want you to see her like this. I'll do the link."

Mama wrapped Jeb in a hug, and he let her, closing his eyes and sinking into her embrace.

Lawrence failed to keep the surprise from his voice. "You know Telepathy?"

"Where do you think I learned it from?" Jeb quipped. "Certainly not the SAF."

"In that case then, I think we're all set." Lawrence moved to stand beside Razick's root-cocooned form, wrapping his arms around her to provide additional support. "Jeb, Urla, let her down gently."

Channeling his Agrokinesis, Jeb did as directed, watching as the necromancer carefully cradled Razick in his arms before lowering her to the floor. Making himself comfortable beside her, Lawrence gently leaned her head on his shoulder, against his neck, and wrapped himself around her much as she'd done with him the night prior.

"She's going to expect this kind of treatment all the time, now," Jeb teased.

Lawrence scowled at him before turning to Mama. "We ready? Send me the link, and I'll take us in."

"Tergerael arrnae ekki fylox." Janikk crossed her arms from her observation point, shaking her head as she smiled.

"What did she say?" Jeb demanded.

"She says I think like a fylox." Apparently noting Jeb's furrowed brows, he elaborated. "Those red furry things that tried to eat us."

Jeb tugged at his hair. "That doesn't sound like a compliment."

"It is, from Janikk." Shane smirked, offering his hand to help Mama settle to the dirt next to them.

<What did we get ourselves into?> Jeb lamented, untangling himself from the roots, but Urla only laughed.

"Here goes." Closing his eyes, Lawrence settled back against the wall, and promptly fell asleep.

<I hope this works,> Urla admitted, her voice edged with concern.

"Me, too," Jeb whispered to himself, watching his sister's still form on the floor. "Me, too."

51

"Where's Lawrence?" Razick growled again, bringing her face mere inches from Admiral Kydell's. "I know you know. Tell me, and this will all be over."

"I told you, I don't know," Kydell snarled back, fighting against the twisted metal restraints holding him to the chair. "But if you come back to me, set me free, we can find him together." He looked wildly around the hidden room Lawrence had hidden him in after Baden, the small space now overflowing with the allies she'd gathered from her memories. "It's me. You know me. You didn't need all these other people."

"Cunningham? Shock him," Razick ordered.

"With pleasure."

"He's an *admiral*," Vernell protested weakly. "Shouldn't we... You know... Be taking orders from *him* instead?"

"And miss out on the fun?" Cunningham laughed, Electromancy coursing through her fingers and the chair holding Kydell as the wolf snarled and grit his teeth. "Don't tell me you've never wanted to do this." She grinned at Razick. "Can I punch him next?"

Razick felt a pang of guilt at the sheer glee in Cunningham's face, but pushed it down. She wasn't a violent person anymore, but this was *Kydell*, and it wasn't even the real version. She'd fantasized about killing him for *years* after she'd escaped. The Dreamwalk was no different than that.

Right?

A deep purple dracoling with piercing ice blue eyes moved to stand beside Vernell, his uniform bearing the single thick stripe and twin double stripes of a vice admiral. "You can take my commands, if you'd rather."

"No, no, I'm fine, Admiral Vox, sir!" Vernell announced with a salute to Nya's impersonation of her grandfather. "Uh, I mean, I'll follow your orders, of course I will, sir!"

This wasn't working. She'd thought that maybe gathering all her allies would have made the whole task easier, but she was used to working with already-formed units, trained to pursue a common goal. This time, she'd amassed the numbers but it was taking all her energy to corral everyone, leaving her none to search herself.

She didn't know how Lawrence did it.

She briefly wondered at her father's career, and whether any of the ribbons he'd buried in the box in his closet had involved similar chaos, and if so, how he'd handled it – but pushed the thought aside quickly. The Father she remembered would be no help to Lawrence. She couldn't afford the distraction.

"Razick?" And there he was, summoned by her thoughts and looking around the crowded room with a sense of bewilderment. "What... What *is* this?"

"Not now, Father," she growled back at him, her attention still focused on Kydell. "I'm *busy*. So let's get this over with. I'm not a coward like you are. You spend all your time hiding from yourself and your past, always looking for something that'll change you into someone else you like better.

"But the truth of it is, you can't live with yourself, or the things you did. You say you did what you needed to survive... But this *isn't* surviving, and I won't pretend it is. I *refuse* to set myself up for a future like yours. I'm *not* you. And I *never* want to be."

She turned to glare at him where he stood beside her silent mother. "I used to think I needed your approval, but I *don't*. I already have my own. Now you can either help me find Lawrence, or get out of my way, because he's my friend and he needs me. You already had your chance, and you didn't want it."

Her father blinked at her, and then suddenly the room shifted around her and it wasn't her father standing there beside Mama, but the necromancer.

Launching herself at him with her Telekinesis, she wrapped him in a hug. "Lawrence! You're safe! I've been tearing this place apart trying to rescue you."

He shuddered in her arms, but didn't move.

"We came to rescue you," Mama told her. "But I guess you didn't need it."

"Mama?" Releasing Lawrence, she rushed to Mama instead, burying her face in her mother's neck and sobbing. "I missed you so much. Are you...? Is this really you? Did Lawrence...?" She glanced at the necromancer, who hadn't moved since their hug, before returning to search Mama's face with her eyes. "Did he bring you back for me?"

"Just for a little while." Mama ran her fingers reassuringly through Razick's hair. "I'm here. But I wasn't always there for you when you needed me. I knew I could rely on you, and so I relied on you too much. Pushed you to grow up too fast, to be stronger than I had any right to ask of you. Because I couldn't rely on your father, and I wasn't strong enough to do something about it. It was unfair to you, and I'm so, so sorry."

"Mama..."

"Hush, Raz. It's alright. An apology, long overdue."

"But if you're here, then that means..." Her eyes widened, and she pushed away from Mama. "Lawrence! I thought I was talking to Father, not... Not..."

"I'm okay." His words were cautious as he turned toward her, blinking slowly. "Everything you said is true."

"That's not how I feel about *you*." She poked him squarely in the chest, waving her other hand across the now-empty room. "You saw what I tried to do to save you."

"I've reached my own arrangement with my past," he told her, finally meeting her eyes. "You didn't need to save me."

"Now we're *all* in trouble." Razick grinned up at him, before sobering. "You told me earlier there was no shame in worrying about those I felt responsible for." She poked him again. "Even if they're big scary necromancers. You're my *friend*, Lawrence."

"Shane," he corrected again, frowning.

"Shane," she agreed, and this time, it felt *right*. Wrinkling her nose, she reached up and pat him teasingly on the cheek. "Have you figured out how to get out of here? I'm *starving*. You better not have lost *my* backpack."

But the room was dissolving around her as she spoke, and she was on the alert again, surveying their new surroundings and its occupants. Jeb, Shane, Mama...

And a strange woman in the center of the room.

She stiffened. "Who are you?"

"Janikk," Shane offered, and the woman smiled warmly. "It's okay. We're safe here. The biggest threat in the room is me."

"For now." Razick snorted. "Why am I in your lap?" She sat taller. "You *missed* me! You told me you weren't my body pillow, and yet here you are again when I wasn't looking!"

Shane rubbed at the back of his neck. "It made sense at the time?"

She stood, resisting the sudden urge to tousle his hair before moving to her mother. "Mama. Is that *really* you?"

Her mother nodded, tears streaking down her cheeks in slow, uneven paths as she wrapped her arms around Razick. "Your friend Called me back. Said you needed me."

"I didn't," Razick said honestly, her tears mingling with her mother's as she leaned into the hug. "But I'm glad you're here, all the same."

"I wasn't here for you like I should have been. I wasn't going to fail you again."

"Oh, Mama..." Pulling away, Razick rubbed her knuckles against her eyes to dry them. "We have so much catching up to do, but I have some things I need to talk to Shane about first, if that's okay?"

"Of course, Sweetheart." Razick felt her mother's hand settle against her shoulder blade, a warm and comforting presence, even as Mama turned to offer a knowing smile to the necromancer. "You two take all the time you need."

"Do you need me?" Jeb shifted his weight, smiling happily at Mama. "Because if not... I'd like to spend the time with Mama."

"Go, Jeb. I'll be fine."

His face lit up, and Razick couldn't help but remember his younger self and their exploits together, causing trouble for each other and pretty much everyone else who had the misfortune to cross their path.

And then she was alone with Shane, the necromancer looking down at her with an even more unreadable expression than usual. Raising her chin with a confident defiance, she met his subdued gaze with her own fire. "You wanted to be friends, right? So now you're stuck with me. Too late to change your mind."

"Okay."

"Which means I'm going to be a pain in your ass, because I know I can get away with it," she continued firmly. "If I'm going to keep going on these missions with you, I need some answers, and you're going to give them. So let's start with the basics. *Who were you?*"

52

Shane growled. "I can't tell you that."

She was his friend. He wouldn't risk her safety with that knowledge. Already he felt the conditioning coiled deep within his mind, planning its attack should she press the issue.

Although the instinct was quieter than usual. Less sure of itself, as if his conversation with Renkash had shifted something. Unbalanced its usual certainty.

Razick sighed, shaking her head. "Was worth a try. But if I'm going to keep you safe, I need to know what to expect from you. I'll work best when I can shore up your own weaknesses, rather than duplicating your strengths."

"You already know my weaknesses." He shrugged, happy for the change of subject. "My greatest fears are enclosed spaces, myself, and wet socks." He snorted. "Although that second one, not as much as before tonight."

"What did you see? In the dream? Did you get to talk to your parents?"

"No." He'd hoped to see them, once he'd realized what was happening, but the Trial apparently had other plans.

"How are they these days?"

"Dead."

Razick's brows furrowed. "Yes... But you're a necromancer. You brought my mother back to talk today. Jake Calls his all the time. Don't you speak with yours?"

"I've tried, but... They've never answered. Either they've already passed too far beyond the Veil, or..." He scowled, clenching his fists. "I just assumed they were too ashamed of me. I should've never allowed the Confederation to twist me into who I became. My parents taught me better than that."

"Hey." He felt Razick's hand land tentatively on his upper arm. "They'd be proud of you, now. And all the good you're doing."

"I just hope it's enough."

Razick pointed up. "You saved a whole fleet so far, and it hasn't been a month yet."

He found he couldn't argue with her.

"And that's ignoring Jake. Which, honestly, is rather difficult to do."

Shane laughed at that. "How do you think I ended up on Baden?"

"I know it's a tough topic, but I want to better understand you." Razick looked away to run her feet along the moss of the cave floor before once again meeting Shane's eyes. "What happened that day? At Yarva?"

Shane stiffened in surprise. "Yarva? Not Loxira?"

Everyone always wanted to know about the assault that had ended his bloodlust for the Confederation, but nobody had ever asked about the attack that had started it in the first place.

"Figure I already know as much as you're willing to share about Loxira." Razick crossed her arms, turning her head to watch him as she leaned against the wall. "But Yarva's a big part of why you are who you are, isn't it? Both your choices, and Kydell's manipulation. If I want to understand you, I need to understand Yarva, don't I?"

Running a hand through his hair, Shane nodded. "Yarva was a civilian farming planet. Should have never been a military target, but I guess when you're the largest food producer in the sector, and ruled by the bloodthirsty Confederation... Well, that changes things, doesn't it?" He sighed. "Space Defense Legion is smarter than the SAF gives them credit for. Confederation likes to focus on how they don't have the advanced magic capabilities we have, but that also means they don't have the same weaknesses. And they're *damn good* at exploiting our weaknesses."

Razick nodded agreement. "They can't match us in mage power, but they don't *have* to. My superiors always underestimated that technology of theirs. Every time one of my missions went sideways? SDL. Every last one."

"Confederation doesn't like to talk about their failures, either, so instead of teaching about them, instead of *learning* from them, they bury the losses and keep repeating the same mistakes."

He looked away to compose himself, nodding gratefully as Razick squeezed his shoulder. "Yarva was no different. Legion attacked a nearby military target, one of those armored moons the Confederation used to play around with, so of course the SAF responded with a fleet of their own. Big one. Most of our available ships. Legion jumped to a different target, and the fleet followed."

"I've heard about their guerilla tactics. Our Void necromancers just can't keep up. They rely too much on being able to get anywhere in a jump." She frowned. "Er, no offense."

Shane snorted. "None taken. It's true! Takes a lot of magic to Hyperjump a ship, but Telekinesis loses directionality in a portal, and the Confederation hadn't been able to effectively replicate the Legion's engine tech on anything bigger than a small corvette. And even then you're in for a wait to get the whole thing through the portal. Not ideal in a combat situation."

The Legion was vulnerable enough when hopping portals. Confederation ships, with their weaker engines, were practically sitting ducks.

He's always found military tactics a fascinating subject, but the next part of this discussion hit closer to home. "As you can guess, once they were sure they'd worn out the fleets chasing them, Yarva was their next target. And the Confederation had left us wide open, damn the Legion and their damn portal drive. Jumped in what ships they could, of course, but there's only so much unescorted small craft can do against a capital fleet, even if death is merely an inconvenience." He let out a hollow laugh. "A lot of Sparnelli military careers died for that mistake... As did my parents, and my entire village. Same story across much of the planet."

Razick reached to pull Shane into a hug, but he shook his head.

"You can guess at the rest. I carried my anger around with me for a long time, until Loxira opened my eyes. War is hell. On everyone."

"It is," Razick agreed. "And I appreciate you telling me all this... But that's a history lesson. I want to know about *you*. What happened to *you* that day?"

Shane swallowed. He'd never told *anyone* that story. Not even Feels. The pain ran too deep.

"Take your time, Shane. But I need to know."

Razick's voice carried a deep compassion, as did her use of his name. She was his friend. She *wanted* to be his friend.

Closing his eyes, Shane pictured his old family farm, his father finishing up the day's labor while Shane helped his mother with meal preparations. She'd been on edge for much of the afternoon, but she'd met his father's concerns with a warm smile and a complaint about having one of her headaches again. To all appearances, it was a day like any other.

Until suddenly, it wasn't.

"Dad ran inside with a strange look on his face. Told Mom she needed to go outside. I wanted to go, too, but he told me to finish up dinner for her in the kitchen, then grab some for myself without them." He felt his breath catch, but pushed onward. "I'd barely started eating when they rushed inside. Told me to climb in the fireplace."

"The fireplace?" Razick's brows furrowed. "Mama always wanted a fireplace. Father wouldn't allow it. But I thought Yarva was a tropical planet?"

"Most of it is." Shane smiled sadly. "Including where we lived. We'd never used it, but Mom wanted one, and Dad never said no to her, so we had one." He let out another laugh, of beloved memories and simpler times. "He always talked about how lucky he was that she chose him. Called her his orchid in the wheat, and wondered why a woman like her would ever be content to stay on Yarva. She'd just smile, and remind him she was tougher than she looked."

Razick smiled wistfully. "I wish my parents had a relationship more like that. Jeb seems to think Father was like that, but I never saw it. What was your father like?"

"He was a good man... unlike me. Loving. Hardworking family man, with simple needs. The kind I try to be, for Jake." Shoving his hands in his pockets, Shane began to pace. "He adored my mother. Anything she wanted, he'd figure out how to make it happen. She meant the world to him. And so did I."

He shook his head, trying to forget the heartbreak in his mother's eyes, and the fear in his father's, the last time he saw them alive. "Dad shoved me into the fireplace, made me promise not to leave no matter what, and started barricading me in. Mom made sure I brought my dinner with me, and then..." He paused, screwing his eyes shut as he reached beneath his shirt to grasp his mother's necklace. "She gave me her locket. That's when I really knew we were in trouble. It had been in her Family for generations and she never took it off. Not for *anything*."

His breath turned jagged at the memory, his footsteps staggering as he resumed his pacing to clear his head, whispering an inaudible thanks to Razick for pausing her questioning to allow him to recover. He'd been grateful to have the locket, an intricate mechanical antique of Legion manufacture, the holographic recordings of his grandparents replaced instead with those of his own parents sometime before the attack... But the memory of the desperate hope in his mother's eyes as she'd slipped it around his neck and tucked it beneath his shirt always brought him to tears.

He gripped it tighter, focusing on his breathing as he sent another futile Call into the Void. "I never forgot you, Mom. Or Dad. I'm sorry I didn't grow up into the son you wanted. Even at my worst, even knowing your disappointment in me, I never stopped loving you."

Razick said nothing, merely keeping pace with him as she waited for him to continue.

Emotions quelled, at least for the moment, he paused again with his back to her. "They sat outside the barricade, sharing their favorite memories as the SDL rained destruction down on the planet. I tried to be strong, for them. I couldn't see what was happening, but I *felt* it. Several times it felt like the house took a direct hit – the whole *building* would shudder – but my parents would laugh nervously about the close call and resume their stories. If I didn't know any better I'd have assumed someone was Shielding us, but we didn't know any spells like that, so we must have just been lucky." He exhaled, slowly. "And then we weren't. Everything shook, and suddenly my parents just... weren't there anymore."

Razick reached for him again, but he brushed her away.

"Shane, you don't have to–"

"Yes! I do!"

His words came out harder than he'd wanted, and she flinched as he turned to face her. But she reached for him anyway, tracing her finger through the air to follow the tear making its way down his cheek.

"Sorry, Raz. It's just... I haven't told anyone. And maybe I need to."

Her hand settled on his arm, and he allowed it this time, savoring the comfort of her presence.

"Like me, about Father. Some things just need to be spoken. To know we're not alone."

"I *was* alone." Shane's voice cracked, but he pressed on. "Three days in that chimney before the rescue crews found me.

They wouldn't tell me what happened to my parents, but it wasn't hard to figure out. The fireplace was the only thing still standing of our house." He reached to press his hand against Razick's, and squeezed. "Confederation put me on a ship back to Sparnell, and that's when I found out I was a Void mage."

"I remember you told me about that. I'm so sorry. That should have been good news."

"Except for Kydell, it might have been." He shook his head. "You can guess the rest. Wasn't old enough for conscription yet, and the rest of the Family wasn't willing to take me in, so they sent me to one of the war orphanages on Sparnell. Then Admiral Kydell himself came to Claim me on my sixteenth birthday." Shane snorted. "Said he'd asked for me personally, that he'd read what happened in my file, and hoped to be like a father to me. I thought I was special. Claimed by Kydell himself! What a fool."

Razick's hands were on his cheeks as she directed his face toward hers. "Look at me."

Resisting the urge to pull away, he obeyed.

"What Kydell did to you is not your fault. Not anyone's fault but his, and Fleet Command's for letting him get away with it. You were vulnerable, and he took advantage of that. Of you. Just as he did to me, and all the rest of us."

"But–"

"No." She cut him off. "It wasn't your fault that you believed what we were taught to believe. Do you understand?"

He stared at her, silently, then nodded. "I... Thank you."

"Nya had orange eyes, too, you know. More of an amber, really. Deep and rich, with a smoldering fire to them. I could have stared into those eyes for hours. How did I forget that?"

"Kydell really did a number on us, didn't he?"

Razick sighed, biting her lip. "Growing up with Father, I learned not to trust. Not to open myself up, not to get close to people, because it would always end up with me getting hurt. But Nya... There's still so much I don't remember, but... She just had this way about her. From the very first time we met, I just *knew* I could trust her. With *anything*. We started as old friends, but we were two flames from the same spell. We needed *more*..." Her voice broke, her fists clenching and unclenching at her side. "And Kydell may have had her killed for it. May have made *me* kill her for it."

"We'll find her," Shane promised.

"I want to go through Kydell's encrypted files," she told him. "See what I can find."

"We have so many in the fleet who deserved better," Shane added softly. "My next task, I want to work with Feels to reclaim their old Underground network on Baden. They did resurrections..."

"Shane. What if she's *dead*? *What if I killed her?*"

"Then it's a good thing you're friends with a necromancer," he told her firmly, grasping both of her shoulders. "Whatever happened to her, whatever Kydell did, we'll find her. Okay?"

"But what if she hates me now? What if–"

"No." Summoning decades of command into his voice, he felt Razick calm at the confidence of his words. "Didn't you just tell me it's not my fault? And I *encouraged* Kydell, at least in the beginning. So if it's not *my* fault, it sure as *hell* isn't yours."

Razick backed away, wiping her eyes on her sleeve. "Thanks. For always being there for me."

"I wouldn't go that far," he laughed softly. "You should talk to your mother."

"I have so many things I want to say to her," Razick agreed, turning to watch Jeb and her mother engaged in a lively conversation. "Are you going to be okay? I asked you all those emotional questions, and now I'm running away."

"Go," he reassured. "Please. I'll be fine."

The bounce in Razick's steps to join her family brought a wistful smile to Shane's face as he longed for a family reunion of his own.

But he had a new family now. Jake and Feels both brought so much light and love into his life, and he'd been slowly growing to consider the Turncoat Armada and his other allies from Baden as an extension of that family. His conversation with Renkash had further cemented that thought.

But first he had to find a way out of this room, and back to them.

Absent-mindedly caressing the locket as he worked, Shane began running his fingers along the wall in search of an exit when suddenly a section of wall recessed of its own accord, the full weight of the Void once more flooding into Shane's mind and washing away his previous thoughts. Gasping within the unexpected deluge, Shane re-centered his emotions on his love for his family, and felt a familiar exuberant affection wrap around his mind in return.

Feels.

53

They'd followed the furred creatures for what felt like hours, wrapping around the cliff face and wandering through the trees, grasslands, and even a small creek before locating the remains of an ancient weathered staircase carved into the rock. Feels watched Haveid eye the steps with concern, tentatively poking at the crumbling structure with their bad ankle as their four-legged friends yipped encouragement from above.

"I don't think I can go any further, even with my Telekinesis," they admitted at last with a sigh, disappointment radiating from their thoughts. "I'd rather not face Javon's wrath for risking my fur twice in the same day."

Feels smiled inwardly, thoughts on their necromancer and his slow but steady realization of their own concerns for his safety. "As I'm the only one with wings," they volunteered, "I'll fly on ahead and let you know what I find."

"Not by yourself," Lieutenant Tashford protested. "I'm not eager to explain to the Grand Navarch why we left you unprotected, should something go wrong. Petty Officer Yaevin?"

Their young, gray katanoj escort stepped forward to salute Tashford, tail twitching a staccato cadence as he grinned. "Yes, sir?"

"Escort our friend. If there's any trouble waiting for them, make sure you find it first."

Green eyes glittered in the starlit night, accompanied by an eager anticipation. "With pleasure, sir."

And I still need to get used to the concerns for my safety.

Feels smiled. "Very well. Lead on."

Progress was slow despite the petty officer's clear talents in mountain climbing. The rock face was crumbling and chossy, while the former steps added more hazard than help from their centuries of neglect.

Feels marveled at their escort's ability to navigate the challenges in the dark. At several points the muscular cat began to slide toward the cliff edge, Feels preparing an emergency healing spell in case of the worst despite Yaevin's constant emotions of confidence, but the katanoj always managed to snag a pinch in the stone just in time. Haveid's red-furred friends continued ahead, their own progress slowed to accommodate their companions, their delicate footpads barely disturbing the fractured stone beneath.

And then the stairway shifted, the pathway now turning to cut deep within the rock, and Yaevin grinned, their emotions shining with relief.

"*This* is more like it."

Bracing his back against one wall, his boots and hands the other, the young climber easily shimmied up the remainder of the ancient passageway, accompanied by the delighted yips of their four legged escorts.

"Wait," Feels cautioned, eying the crumbling archway before them, the darkness within hinting at some sort of cave system. "We can't see what's inside."

The katanoj's smile grew bigger. "*I* can."

With a snap of his fingers the cave lit up in a myriad of colors and information, Feels' vision now covering an assortment of spectrums in addition to augmenting the faint dawning light able to penetrate their pathway into the rocks.

"Oramathea," Feels whispered in admiration. "Always wondered how you vision mages saw the world. It's beautiful."

"Helped a lot with that climb, too," Yaevin laughed with a subtle pride, following the furred creatures' eager leaps into the cave. "You're clear to enter. Just us in here, and the cave's holding. Hope this was worth the trip!"

Tuning out any possible distractions, Feels studied the interior of the cave, their enhanced vision revealing an array of decorative crystals embedded in the roof of the cavern and a collection of intricate artistry only partially obscured by the damages of time. Scenes from everyday life adorned each mural displaying treetop villages, processes for the nurturing of plant and animal life, scenes of family and community and education… A whole ancient extinct society on display.

But none of this helped find Grim. "I suppose I should fly back to the others, let them know what we found."

"No need," the katanoj purred. "Telepathy. I'm an advanced scout, not a battle mage. Want me to link you to the fleet captain? Or someone else?"

"In that case… Sub-Lieutenant Xalis." As much as they should notify Haveid, their first concern was Grim's safety, and Feels knew from experience that necromancers were adept at finding each other.

<Yes, sir?> Xalis' polite greeting did little to hide her eagerness to assist.

<The petty officer and I found another cave, and I think it's related to the one you believe the Grand Navarch entered. Could you come take a look?>

She hesitated. <I'm with the fleet captain right now. Should I bring the rest of your team?>

Perfect. <Yes, that will do nicely.>

<On our way.>

She dropped the sending, and moments later Fleet Captain Haveid materialized in the center of the room, accompanied by Xalis, the remainder of their battle mages, and a very grumpy Tarvick.

"Hyperjumping is bad enough when I'm dead," the biologist grumbled. "This is too much for one day."

"You know you're happy leaving Hydroponics for once," Haveid teased, and Feels caught a flash of joy from Tarvick at the reminder.

Xalis ignored them both, instead turning to Feels, eyes sparkling in the dark. "Same exercise as before?"

"If you'd be so kind." The empathic fae sent thoughts of gratitude her way, both for her assistance and her discretion.

Grim needed them, but that didn't mean everyone needed to know the full extent of their relationship.

She nodded, and Feels recognized the concentration in her eyes as she cast her spellwork, carefully tracing the Oath tether to an unadorned section of the wall. "Here." Her fingers dipped slightly into the stone, and through their still-augmented vision Feels saw the heat of her fingers brush against the Tyrellium Shielding beneath. "By the shape of the missing portion of the Afterlife, it slopes down here to a large chamber at the bottom."

Feels perched lightly on her shoulder. "So how do we get inside?"

The room suddenly came alive as if the cavern itself decided to answer, the morning sun lining up with a previously hidden gap in the cave's ceiling to illuminate the crystalline structure embedded within the room and reflect its light throughout to dance along the walls. The door before them opened, sliding inward to reveal an intact set of steps. The emotions of love and startled relief flooded Feels' thoughts from their Insight to Grim.

"Send me back to the Afterlife," they breathed, thoughts focused on a calming affection. "Let me go to him."

And suddenly they were on the higher planes again, following their Oath to take up residence within the necromancer's locket once more.

Don't scare me like that. Are you okay? Is everyone else okay? I missed you so much. Don't you ever disappear like that again.

"We're all fine," he told them, emotions shifting to a sheepish apology at their admonishments. "Janikk had a test she wanted us to take, but we passed. We can stay here. The planet's ours, as long as we take care of it."

You're hurt! Casting a quick spell to heal the deep cut against his shoulder, recognizing the telltale signs of basic field treatment on the wound, Feels quickly ran a healing diagnostic to hunt for any other injuries. *You're never leaving my sight again*, they ordered, bracing for the argument in return.

"I'm sorry I kept sending you away, Feels," Grim apologized. "From now on, it's your choice, not mine, where you want to be." They felt his grip tighten against the locket, his voice soft with longing. "Please stay."

I thought you'd never ask.

He was theirs, finally, completely, and they'd never leave him without a fight. Not unless he asked.

"Thank you." Grim's gratitude was overwhelming now, underlined with a deep-set worry. "I... wanted to talk to you about something else. About the test."

Listening as their necromancer described his vision of Jake as a Confederation conscript, Feels felt his concerns for the boy blossom into fears and doubts, confronted with a possibility of the very future he'd fought hard to avoid.

Lawson. Not Lawrence? they asked when he'd finished.

"Lawson." Grim's voice sank. "The more I pick apart the pieces, the more it doesn't make sense. Or the more I don't *want* it to make sense. Why would the Tsekeht show me this? What is it trying to tell me?"

Maybe it's nothing?

"There's strong Divination magic in the Tsekeht, Feels. It means *something*. I just can't puzzle out *what*."

Jake's a smart kid. He knows the power of Family names in Sparnell. Grim had kept his word to always remain truthful with the boy, and there'd been a lot of questions about Sparnell in the early months after the events at Loxira. *Everyone expects you to follow the legacy of your ancestors. Lawrence will come to mean the Sparnelli defeat at Baden. But Lawson is a small family, a respectable family, and you've instilled in Jake a lot of the Lawson family values.*

"That makes sense..."

But by the doubt filling his thoughts, Grim wasn't convinced.

"In the dream, Razick said I was conditioning him. Just like Kydell did to me."

There's a difference between teaching your son, and forcing him into becoming who you want him to be. Visions are never what they appear on the surface. Even the Valcore Oracle could never predict things perfectly. Feels felt Grim snap to attention at their mention of the fleet admiral's mother. Even those who scoffed at prophecy had to admit the Oracle's gifts had exceeded the standard limitations of the art. And they'd *still* launched a three-way civil war over disagreements in interpretation. *If it was a true vision, I think it means Jake will be okay. He'll remain true to the values he's learned from you and his mother, and adapt to the situation, no matter where he finds himself in the future.*

The necromancer's thoughts calmed slightly. "I like that interpretation. That's what I've been trying to teach him."

He'll be fine. It's not like he picked the name Renkash.

Grim's short snarl carried the memory of violence past. "I'd worry about *all* of us, if that were the case. Not just him."

You don't give yourself enough credit, Grim. You're a great father, and a kind leader. Wrapping the necromancer's thoughts in their own confidence in him, Feels felt Grim relax further, a calming love slowly taking the place of his self-doubt. *We're all lucky to have you.*

"Someday I hope to be the man you think I am, Feels."

You already are. You just won't admit it to yourself.

"Yeah, yeah..." His voice faded, his thoughts taking on a mischievous eagerness. "Been thinking about what we need next. I took so much from you, and it's time I give some of it back. What do you think about visiting some old friends?"

Feels had to admit he'd piqued their curiosity. *What are you planning...?*

"As I recall, one of us was a criminal mastermind back on Baden before I came and mucked up your whole enterprise." Rather than his usual guilt at this turn of conversation, Grim's thoughts tightened into the steadfast craftiness that always accompanied one of his more reckless endeavors. "How would you like to help me take back the Phoenix Assembly? Could start planning it out over breakfast. Over more of that tsijturikk fruit, perhaps?"

And you claim you're not romantic.

54

Jeb excused himself from the conversation with Mama at Razick's approach, earning a quick smile from his sister and a hand squeeze from his mother in the process. She'd been through so much, first from the SAF and then from whatever Mama had meant about her and Papa. She needed this. More than he did.

He surveyed the small cavern, noting Lawrence doing the same, when a section of wall by the necromancer disappeared to reveal a rough stone staircase, seemingly of its own accord.

A rush of plant life filled his mind, Urla's thoughts transmitting over their telepathic link at the same moment. <The barrier's down, I can feel more of the network again. Company incoming. Four belong to Janikk.>

Jeb caught Lawrence moving away from the door, the necromancer's attention now claimed by the locket beneath his shirt. <Guessing they're friendly. Search party from the *Relentless*?>

<I don't sense any danger,> Urla conceded. <They must have noticed when we got cut off in the cave.>

But there was little time for speculation. Jeb braced himself as a pair of fylox bounded into the room, attempting and failing to position himself between Razick and the new threat as their excited yips and barks filled the cavern. He saw Razick stiffen at the intrusion, no doubt preparing her spellwork in case the creatures attempted to continue their attack from before, but they seemed content to chase each other around the indoor room, periodically pausing to sniff at random plants and objects, or cast quick glances at the door. Despite their apparent disinterest in the other occupants of the cave, Jeb only relaxed when several uniformed officers from the *Relentless* materialized by the doorway. The fylox shared the sentiment, halting their investigations to prance around the limping Fleet Captain Haveid like small children seeking praise.

"Glad to see you're all in one piece." The katanoj grinned, surveying the room as they scratched both fylox behind the ears. "We sent a search party as soon as we realized you'd disappeared, but it looks like you didn't need us after all."

"We're fine," Jeb reassured, glancing at Razick animatedly talking with Mama. It was good to have his sister back. Get her the closure she'd needed, whatever that had been. "Janikk wanted to ensure we'd respect her and her planet, so she set up a test, but we seem to have passed."

The fleet captain's lips pulled upward into a feral grin, their excitement clearly matched by the others in their party. "So we can stay, then?"

"Yeah." Jeb tugged at his hair. "At least, she *seems* to like us. Lawrence can tell you more. Void knows I have no idea what she's saying, but they understand each other somehow."

Urla's voice interrupted his thoughts. <Since the barriers are down and you have this well in hand, I'm going back to the *Relentless*. We've got a lot to do before we can settle the planet and I'd like to pull some thoughts together for the Grand Navarch on ways to speed things up. Will you be okay?>

<You do what you need to do.> He smiled, rubbing his watch. <I love you.>

<Thank you.> Her words carried warmth as she severed the link.

"...because I like this planet." Haveid continued, and Jeb realized he'd missed a large chunk of conversation. "Janikk took a liking to you, then?"

Jeb ran his fingers through his hair, remembering the planet-wide efforts to herd them into the cave by any means necessary, the Dreamwalk they'd each undergone, Lawrence's strange newfound understanding of her unfamiliar words, and Janikk's willingness to work with the necromancer to help Razick. Returning his attention to his sister, Jeb studied her movement as she spoke with their mother, no sign of the cautious and reserved battle mage who'd returned from the war.

When he met Haveid's gaze, his words were quiet. "Yeah. Somehow our ragtag band of Sparnelli outcasts won her over. Even after she'd seen all of us, especially Lawrence, at our worst."

Jeb winced as the words came out, harsher than he'd intended. Despite his openness about the darkness in his past, Lawrence had always done his best for them.

Haveid's own smile faded, their face growing serious in the flickering lights of the cave. "Cass told me he was former Sparnelli. We all carry our regrets of what we've done. I've personally killed a lot of undeserving people. Not as many as your sister, but we've all done what we must to survive."

Jeb's eyes widened at the reminder of what Razick had likely done, the things she'd never talk about, but Haveid was already smiling again, their hand resting heavily on his shoulder.

An unfamiliar human took his place beside the fleet captain.

"But we've got a chance at a new life now, don't we?" Only then did Jeb recognize the voice of his fellow botanist, Tarvick. "Grand Navarch Lawrence will see to it."

"I appreciate the vote of confidence."

Jeb jumped as Lawrence's voice emerged from behind, his psychomorphic fae perched lightly on his shoulder as the pair rejoined the group. "I'll assume Jeb has informed you we've been granted permission to colonize the planet. What he hasn't shared, because he doesn't know yet, is the agreement I've made with Janikk to earn that right."

The young gray katanoj in the party nodded knowingly. "Always a catch."

"Not that kind of agreement." Lawrence shook his head. "We'll be part of Janikk, and the Balance of life that lives on her. We won't own her, and never will. In a way, she'll own us."

"With that network thing your fae was telling us about?" Haveid scratched their chin, whiskers twitching.

"Exactly like that." Lawrence nodded, his eyes locked on Haveid's, and only then did Jeb notice his faint connection with the large cat.

"You're already in the network, aren't you?"

Haveid nodded at Jeb's question, one of the fylox at their feet leaping upward to place its front paws on the fleet captain in a bid for more attention. Haveid seemed more than happy to oblige, rubbing the creature's chin, much to its apparent delight. "These little rascals brought me something to eat. Would have been rude to refuse."

Jeb poked Lawrence gently on the shoulder, the necromancer turning to him with curiosity. "I'm going to check in with my sister, if you no longer need me."

Lawrence brushed him away with a nod, his attention quickly reclaimed by the search party.

"I'll need to talk to you before we leave." Feels left the necromancer's shoulder to hover lightly in Jeb's field of vision. "I'd like to borrow your Telepathy, so we can learn Janikk's language. But it can wait."

Nodding, Jeb acknowledged the request before slipping away. His mother and sister greeted him with warm smiles and warmer hugs.

"I've missed you both, so much," Mama admitted, her fingers cold against Jeb's neck before she pushed him away to hold him at arm's length, her eyes dancing with pride. "What's this Razick says about a girlfriend?"

His shoulders slumped. This wasn't the conversation he'd intended to have, but he may as well tell them. "We're not together anymore."

"Oh, Sweetheart..." Mama wrapped him in a hug. "I'm so sorry."

"Was it because of the Tsekeht?" Razick frowned in concern.

"No..." Jeb shook his head, summoning a halfhearted smile. "She's had so much of her life taken from her, by the SAF and Kydell. She has the opportunity now to reclaim it, to live her own life and make her own name for herself." He ran his fingers through his hair, tugging at a knot where the vines from the cave had entangled. "I encouraged her not to waste it."

"You're a good man, Jeb." Mama squeezed him tighter, lightly kissing the top of his head, and he felt himself relax into her arms. "How are you feeling?"

"I'm sad for myself," Jeb admitted, before meeting Mama's eyes. "But happy for her. And proud. Finding out who she is, now that she can decide."

He shook his head, freeing himself from Mama's embrace before shoving his hands in his pockets, his attention on his feet. "A flower can't bloom in the shade if all she longs for is the sun. If she stayed, she'd be trying to grow in *my* shadow." He straightened his shoulders, meeting his mother's gaze once more. "But she was born to do great things on her own. She knows I'm here for her, if she wants me. And that will have to be enough."

Razick's voice was soft as she placed her hand on Jeb's shoulder. "Sometimes we meet the right people, at the wrong time–"

"No." Jeb shook his head. "I'd like to think we met at just the right time. She's been told most of her life that she wasn't good enough, and now she's finally pursuing her dreams." He smiled. "And I got to be a part of it."

Mama's face shone with tears as she wrapped her arms around him once more, tugging on Razick to join them. "I'm so proud of you, Jeb. I'm so proud of you both."

Jeb closed his eyes, relaxing into the hug as Razick wrapped her arms around them both. The future was far from uncertain, but today? They were together, and happy, and wasn't that all that really mattered?

55

SHANE RUBBED THE BACK of his neck, surveying the excitement on the bridge of the *Relentless*. It had been several hours since they'd concluded their business with Janikk, Jeb and Feels working together with the ancient planetary guardian to extract her memories of the language of her people and craft them into an easily-shared telepathic language module, much to Janikk's fascination. Shane squeezed the locket in his fist, his thoughts focused on gratitude and appreciation for his empath's clever suggestion to tie the language to the Tenecknaab, as well, limiting its use to those already joined into the planetary network.

A caress of love filled his mind.

We make a good team, Grim. Feels' emotions shifted into a pleading sadness, concern overtaking their words. *Please don't make me leave.*

"Never again," Shane promised softly, his grip tightening on the locket. "It's time I admit it. I love you, I need you, and I don't feel whole unless you're here with me."

His emotions shifted, unbidden, into a serene calm, Feels' Psychomorphation dancing through his mind. *I can help with that...*

And suddenly his emotions shifted, Shane's knuckles white around the locket as he gasped, his every thought now locked into a possessive longing for his beloved spouse.

But this is more fun.

Closing his eyes, Shane savored the moment, his own enjoyment mixing with the manufactured emotions until Feels let go with a satisfied sigh.

You have work to do, they reminded him. *But perhaps we can finish this later.*

"I'll hold you to that," Shane whispered, his thoughts focused on mischief as he caressed the locket once more before allowing it to settle beneath his shirt, his focus now entirely captivated by the task at hand. He squared his shoulders, directing his next words to the entire bridge. "I need to jump to the rest of the fleet. Tell them we have a home. Think I'll pick up Jake first, too. He deserves to hear this. Jeb, Razick, are you staying here or would you like me to bring you back?"

Razick shook her head, motioning to Haveid and the holographic display between them. "I'd like to stay here, work with Fleet Captain Haveid on our plan for getting everyone prepared for the planet."

Haveid nodded. "We want to ensure they understand what they're getting into, since Janikk confirmed that joining the network can't be undone. Everyone deserves to make that choice for themselves."

"Have to be careful how we say it, though," Razick added, her brows furrowing as she glanced at Haveid. "We still have Kydell loyalists. Don't want to hand them anything they'll hurt us with later." She wrinkled her nose at him, grinning. "You'll have to stay alive without me."

"A challenge."

"I trust you."

"A mistake," he told her.

"Perhaps. We'll see if I survive it," she answered back, smiling warmly.

It was *nice* to have friends.

He turned to Jeb. "And you?"

"*Someone* has to keep an eye on you." The biologist crossed his arms in front of his chest, voice stern, but he was smiling. "Urla's been working with Janikk to learn how her people built housing. We think we can use Agrokinesis to grow it out of living plants, but neither of us know much architectural engineering. She's asked me to liaise with your neighbor, see if Tom and Gabbie are willing to help us out."

Shane swelled at pride in his team, and felt Feels' own pride in him race through his mind in turn. *This* is what he'd been hoping for, to encourage his newfound family to work together, using their own skills and experiences to forge their own paths rather than waiting for him to dictate their every decision. It would take time, especially among those more accustomed to Admiral Kydell's micromanagement of their every thought, but the more Shane himself approved of those who took initiative, the more courage the rest would find to try it for themselves.

"A solid plan. Let me know if you need my help to push through any barriers." Several eyes on the bridge widened at his words, the phrasing carefully sidestepping any implications his approval was required. *Good*. They could chew on that for a while.

"So... Am I preparing to Hyperjump, or...?" the Navigations AI questioned.

"No, the *Relentless* will stay at Janikk. Jeb and I will jump back solo." Shane grinned at the disappointment in the AI's voice. "You'd only leave me behind, anyway."

"I would *never*," Navigations protested, but Shane caught the amusement beneath his indignation even before Feels' confirmation.

"We've all left officers behind to flex the power we hold on the ship." Shane crossed his arms, growling, before relaxing with a shake of his head. "Even me. Didn't like my performance review. Although, in hindsight, it *was* accurate."

"Bastard." And suddenly a grizzled canid stood on the bridge, his black fur graying with age around his hands and muzzle, green eyes watching Shane with a calculated intelligence.

The canid saluted and Shane followed before relaxing, motioning for the wolf to do the same.

"Just wanted to say, I'm behind you, Sir." The wolf hung his head. "Sorry I've been such a pain in the ass. I've been bound in the *Relentless* for most of my Oath. Wanted to make sure I could trust you, before I committed to remain. Poke at you until you showed us all who you really were, since my role gives me more leeway than most." He shook his head with a snort. "And yet with all my best efforts, I couldn't even make you angry."

"Trust isn't a right, Navigations. It's a privilege." Shane placed his hand on the officer's shoulder and squeezed. "Thank you for gifting me with yours."

The Navigations AI raised his head, meeting Shane's eyes. "What's next for us, Sir?"

Every eye on the room was upon Shane now, the full weight of the question hanging heavily in the air.

"That's up to you," he answered, choosing his words carefully. "I can help get the tools and resources you need, but you each have a real opportunity to decide what your life will look like from this point forward, and I *won't* choose that for you. Some of you will choose to remain with the fleet, to defend each other and eventually, I hope, to defend those who look to us for help and inspiration. And some will choose to find ways to make Janikk more of a home for yourselves, and for all of us. We're all in this together. Each and every one of you is important to our success."

"What about those of us who no longer wish to be dead?"

Shane recognized the voice as Tarvick, the *Relentless'* surly Hydroponics AI, and lowered his voice to carry the necessary gravity befitting the question. "What the Confederation has done to so many of you is reprehensible. I intend to do everything within my power to undo the worst of it." He concentrated his magic, pulling Feels to the mortal plane beside him. "Some have already labeled us as space pirates. So, let's prove them right. I've decided we need to branch into the criminal underground, too. My partner," he nodded at Feels, "once ran the Phoenix Assembly on Baden, before I so rudely murdered them."

"The Grand Navarch has agreed to help me rebuild it," Feels cut in, correctly interpreting Shane's pause, their love coursing through his thoughts. "The Phoenix Assembly was my answer to Sparnell's disregard to our well-being, to allow deserters and dissidents an opportunity at a new identity, a new face, and a new life away from the Confederation. We intend for it to do so again."

A murmur of excitement rippled through the bridge as Shane motioned for Jeb to stand closer for the Hyperjump to Baden. The Phoenix Assembly had been well known in certain Confederation circles, and the knowledge that Shane was responsible for its destruction and soon its resurrection was certain to travel quickly through the fleet.

Good. Best they knew more of his failings, but also his resolve to set them right.

There was the small matter of not angering Baden further, of course. Although considering the depths the Assembly had fallen to after Feels' disappearance, Shane hoped the planetary government would take it as one more sign of him helping keep them safe.

Assuming they even found out *he* was behind it.

He motioned Jeb closer, grabbing the biologist's arm as he addressed the *Relentless'* bridge one last time. "I'm grateful for your trust in my intentions, and, with your help, I intend to reward that trust with a better life for all of us."

Dropping the spellwork holding Feels to the mortal plane, heart resting lighter as the fae settled contentedly into the locket against his chest, his thoughts filled with the empath's affection, and *home*.

56

RABERT PASTED A SMILE over his misgivings, earning an encouraging smile from his wife and son in return. The fleet had sent a young human with broken Galactic Common to serve as his therapist, Veris identifying the woman as the same medical professional who had delivered him back to Baden in the first place.

Unlike those provided by the Baden Defense Force, he'd found himself unable to send her away, despite his attempts to form the words. Thrilled at his perceived acceptance, his family had requested she begin their sessions immediately, and she'd seemed suspiciously eager to oblige.

He had to admit it was nice to be able to interact with his family again, his desires to isolate from them receding with each session, although he couldn't help but wonder if he was putting them in danger in the process. The constant anxiety in the back of his mind continued to churn and twist within his gut at every interaction.

And yet Veris and Fiara showed no signs of sharing his concerns, their infectious exuberance as he abandoned each of his newly constructed defenses almost heartbreaking to watch. Even the typically wary Fangela openly cheered his every moment of weakness, to the point he wondered if maybe his fears were all in his mind.

But something was wrong.

There it was again, those foreign thoughts attempting to dictate his actions. The power of its suggestions curled deep within his emotions in an attempt to strangle his free will, the sensation gone again as soon as he acknowledged it, leaving him wondering yet again what was real and what was imagined.

And whether or not his choices were his own.

"Is everything okay, Mr. Asik?"

Veris' new friend – Jake, he reminded himself – sat across from him at the table, eyes lined with concern as he gently poked the remains of cake on his plate.

Rabert remembered faint mumblings from his captors prior to his release, a hurried effort to fulfill orders from 'the Kid' and the even more harried discussion about updating some sort of important plan. The boy across from him now carried none of the optimism of the others, and Rabert wondered just how much this kid had to do with those plans. Veris had sworn Jake had been instrumental in his release, but the fact a young preteen wielded that much power only served to heighten Rabert's distrust.

"I'm fine," he lied, tugging at the fabric of his trousers beneath the table. "It's just a lot to get used to, after…"

His voice trailed off, his dearest Fiara rushing to his rescue with a flurry of words meant to soothe, sending their son to fetch him a second slice of cake as Fangela darted away in search of another of those awful scented candles she'd taken to lighting around the house. And yet Jake still sat there, brows furrowed in concentration as he studied Rabert, as if he, too, had concerns that lurked just at the edge of his thoughts.

Rabert had a sudden urge to ensure the boy remained unable to voice those concerns. It was bad enough this influential stranger was encouraging Veris to keep secrets, the two of them often smiling conspiratorially in the sudden silence whenever Rabert entered the room, but now the young man had clearly identified himself as a threat to Rabert's secrets, too.

Not that Rabert himself knew what those secrets *were*, but there was no way this young human child would learn them before Rabert. The importance of this task rose within his mind to consume all other thoughts.

But before he could formulate a plan, Fangela was rushing to him, a large candle held triumphantly in each hand as she grinned, positioning them on the table with a nod to Jake. "Your father's outside waiting. Whatever he was doing, looks like he succeeded." She turned to Rabert with a good-natured scowl.

"Maybe now you can finally thank the man who saved your life."

Rabert felt the knot in his stomach tighten, his breath suddenly shallow as he gripped his trousers in his fists, focusing on his breathing in the hope they wouldn't notice the terror in his heart. He didn't understand why, but he couldn't afford to be in the same room as their new visitor. He needed to leave. *Now*.

"Father?" Veris dropped the cake slice in front of him, reaching to steady his chair as Rabert pushed away from the table. "Is everything okay?"

"Yes... I...." Rabert cleared his throat, clenching his fists as he stood seeking his words.

They didn't come.

"Let him go," Rabert heard Jake admonish his family, but he was already stumbling up the stairs to his bedroom as if his life depended on it. "My Dad will understand."

A flurry of protests followed but Jake prevailed, the murmuring voices instead shifting to greet the boy's father and make apologies for Rabert's continued absence.

He should feel guilty, his continued avoidance of the man who'd apparently saved his life doing much to undermine the gratitude of his family for that rescue. But he couldn't find the emotion – couldn't afford to *feel* the emotion, his mind corrected – and so instead Rabert stumbled into the bedroom he and Fiara shared.

The once comforting space was now filled with an assortment of items meant to cleanse the worries from his mind or some such nonsense. An activated carbon fan scrubbed the air, its dull whine grating on Rabert's thoughts – although at least the air purification had been helpful for his allergies. Less helpful were the collections of dried herbs scattered about the room, intended to ward off restless spirits or some similar superstition but only serving to aggravate those very same allergies.

But worst of all was the pair of cleansing candles perched upon the dresser, the twin flames flickering ominously like the cruel yellow eyes of the white-furred wolf haunting his dreams.

57

SHANE EMERGED ON THE bridge of the *Inevitable*, releasing his hold on Jeb and Jake as he turned to greet Navarch Javon with a triumphant smirk.

His son eyed him for a moment before wrapping him in a quick hug, burying his face in Shane's chest. "I want to go home."

"Soon," Shane promised, ruffling the boy's hair affectionately.

"Let's let your father work," Jeb said quietly, motioning for Jake to follow him.

Jake had missed him. An unsurprising outcome, given this was the longest they'd been apart since they'd first met. He squeezed his son's shoulder, the unspoken promise passing between them as Jake followed Jeb to the observer seats at the edge of the bridge.

He'd make up for lost time later. Right now, the fleet needed him first. And Shane needed Jake here, listening. To understand what it was for, and why it mattered, and just how far Shane would go for those who looked to him for help.

Especially Jake.

"You've done it then?" There was no question in Javon's eyes, or the feline grin spreading rapidly across her face.

Shane's eyes danced in return as he instead addressed the AI systems of the flagship. "Communications? Connect me to the fleet. I have an announcement."

<Done, Sir,> the AI confirmed moments later. <You're live with the fleet.>

Inhaling slowly, Shane closed his eyes to gather his thoughts as he stood at attention on the *Inevitable*'s bridge. When he opened them again, he was the epitome of the commanding yet caring leader he aspired to become.

<I know you have a lot of questions,> he began, the Telepaths from each ship within the Turncoat Armada dutifully transmitting his message to their crews. <We stand at a threshold, and this isn't where you thought you'd be standing at this point in your lives. You want to know, what comes next? And where do you fit in?>

Shane paused to allow his questions to sink in, noting the *Inevitable*'s bridge crew nodding before he continued. <Allow me to answer that first question now. So much has been taken from us by the Sparnell Confederation, and Admiral Kydell.

Our hopes and dreams, our futures, our families, our lives, even our very minds. Starting today? We're taking it back.>

He allowed a brief, faint smile as the murmur of excitement reached his ears, his face hardening as he continued. <Janikk has graciously agreed to adopt us as her own people. To allow us to build our lives upon her surface and defend us from outsiders, provided we agree to do the same for her. We have a home, somewhere we are welcome just as we are, and it's up to us to decide what that means.> He exhaled slowly. <Which brings us to the second question. Where do you fit? What's your role in this new life?>

The bridge crew leaned forward as they awaited his answer, Feels reporting an overwhelming anticipation radiating from the entire fleet. These were people accustomed to orders, in many cases orders which controlled every aspect of their lives.

That would end today.

Shane allowed the tension to build before speaking again. <That's *not* my question to answer. It's yours. Our future rests in your hands. What do you want to build? Who do you wish us to become? This is as much your question to answer as it is mine, and I look forward to experiencing and encouraging each of your endeavors as we make our own journeys and determine our own fates. Together.>

He shook his head, his voice projecting resolve and determination. <We're no longer outcasts or disappointments, turncoats or traitors. We don't owe our loyalty to a leadership who could care less about our welfare unless it furthers their

glory. We are *not* Sparnelli. We reject their values. That's not what we stand for. We deserve *better*.>

Shane's voice hardened further, his experiences from decades of command converging to power the emotions of this one pivotal moment. <From this day forward, we owe our allegiance to no one but each other. We'll build our own Family with those we've worked beside. With those who value the blood, sweat, and tears of our efforts. Today we claim our own path, and choose our own goals, for we are *Mordena*.>

He'd labored over that name, knowing they needed one. Something his people could rally behind, more than just the Turncoat Armada moniker they'd given themselves. Before they'd left he'd poured through Jake's dictionaries, looking for just the perfect word.

And then he'd remembered that night on Baden, when Razick had dragged him to dinner at one of the still-intact restaurants to celebrate the planet's survival. They'd toasted to their loved ones, hurt by Kydell. Mom and Dad. Osygg and Elwyx. Nya. Raz. Alenahs.

Mordena. A promise to those past, to build a better future.

He turned to watch Jake, the boy's eyes locked onto his from across the bridge as he kicked his feet under the guest chair, ignoring the buzz of excitement surrounding them.

He'd build a better future for Jake. Whatever it took.

You did it, Grim. Feels' excitement echoed the fleet's, the bridge of the *Inevitable* visibly charged with a fierce anticipation at the promise of a future where their personal choices mattered. *They'll follow you anywhere.*

Want to know more about Urla's work on Janikk after the events of *Spirits of the Relentless*?

Join the Vazdimet mailing list to read a free bonus chapter: https://link.vazdimet.com/rmmd2

Note from the author: I was relentless with edits for this novel, cutting a great many scenes short or removing them entirely to tighten up the plot into the book you now hold in your hands. I'm proud of those results, and don't miss any of those deleted chapters... Except this one.

I'd have loved to include Chapter 58, but the book could only end properly with Shane's speech, and so with heavy heart, I cut the chapter.

I share it here instead, for those who wish a sneak peek into the efforts to build a new home on Janikk, and what that means to the people involved.

Morjakk Glossary

The story in this novel is intended to be understood without understanding the constructed language sprinkled throughout its pages. With the recognition that some people like to know anyway, I've provided the following glossary.

If you'd like to explore this constructed language further, you can find more at its worldbuilding page:

https://link.vazdimet.com/morjakk

Vocabulary

darrekknee - understand

Ecknaab - The Way of the Balance, a belief that death and life are equally importance, and that each gives power and importance to the other

fylox - a cunning, predatory quadraped known for pack behavior and exceptional problem solving

gromdornis - A large, multicolored bird with a draconic appearance, also called a "dragonbird." They grow to exceed three times the size of an average person. Highly intelligent and organized, they generally live and hunt in a family group. (plural: gromdornox)

Janikk – Teacher; Guardian; Master; Ruler

Klaael - pilgrim; Soul Seeker

klaaetael - journey tree, a vining plant infused with the distripate spell. Consuming its fruit, the klaaeturikk, begins the Tsekeht Trials. The vine will only flower and fruit when subjected to Agrokinesis, typically by the Rekkael administering the Trials.

klaaeturikk - journey fruit, eaten by Klaael in preparation for the Tsekeht

Munokkael - The Hunter

munokkae - to hunt; to be hunted

Nekksilee - Listen (to me)

nikkeer – welcome; a formal greeting of respect

nubudokk – I'm ready

nudarrekknae - I don't understand.

Redistael - Outsider

Tenecknaab - The Link to the Balance, the neural net that links all creatures on the planet

tekkirkk – danger cricket, a loud, winged insect with a shrill, droning screeching call for attracting mates and warning off predators

Tergerael - Repentant One; one who laments their past actions; one who agonizes over their decisions

Tsekeht – test or trial; metamorphosing challenge; The Leadership Trials

tsijturikk - A round, fleshy pitted fruit with a gold-flecked purple skin and a highly nutritious juicy nectar, known as "burst fruit."

yinit - white furred omnivorous pack animal with long snouts, sharp teeth, and thick claws built for burrowing in the snow and ice

yukkan – sanctuary; a strong sense of belonging

Janikk's Phrases

Chapter 19

"Darrekknee ivox Tenecknaab." - Understand our link to the Balance of existence.

"Nurekkee Tsekeht." - Follow the Trials.

Chapter 22

"Zegae ivojox yukkan. Munokkee. Yukkanee." – You seek a sanctuary of your own. Eat. Belong.

Chapter 33

"Turikkael ij Tergerael. Nikkeer." – The Generous One of the Repentant One. Welcome.

"Klaaelox dirkkatae aja Tsekeht." – The pilgrims are seeking the essence of themselves through the Leadership Trials.

"Tsekeht esaukkee yukkan." – The Trials will provide/prove them worthy of sanctuary.

Chapter 48

"Dirkkataa Klaael nikkeer! Kajj Flesyk rekkorae Flesykoj niwok?" – Welcome, Soul Seeker! May I grant you knowledge?

"Flesyk nekksilae Flesykoj, nudarrekknae." - I'm listening to you, but I don't understand.

"Tsekeht tenaa Flesykoj aja Ecknaab." - The Leadership Trials know you're with the Balance.

"Turikkaa yukkan. Darrekknee." - You've been offered sanctuary. Understand.

"Janikk esaukkaa Ecknaab." - The Teacher served the Balance

"Janikk esaukkae Ecknaab." - The Teacher serves the balance

"Janikk esaukee Ecknaab." – The Teacher will serve the Balance.

"Darrekknee, Tergerael. Darrekknee." - Understand me, Repentant One, Understand Me

Chapter 50

"Flesyk nulinae eckitnae." – I am not permitted to interfere.

"Budokkae ivoj eckitni zegee." – I'm not convinced your distraction will help.

"Tergerael arrnae ekki fylox." – The Repentant One thinks like a fylox.

ACKNOWLEDGEMENTS

To you, Reader. Your love and support keeps Vazdimet alive, and me writing. I have so many more adventures in my head, eager to make their way to the page, and I can't wait to share them with you.

To TJ Trewin. Your excitement about my books, and their covers, is infectious and has carried me through many a self-conscious day.

To my sister, Janine. I know fantasy books aren't your thing, so you might never see this, but you've always supported my dreams regardless of your own personal interests, and that means the world to me.

To my beta readers, Amy Winters-Voss, Laura, Julian, and notahumanhand, and my editors, A. Dani and Emily Vair-Turnbull. Your thoughts have been invaluable in helping *Relentless* reach and exceed the vision in my head when I first began, and I offer you my gratitude.

To my Discord friends. Your boundless support, enthusiasm, and motivation help keep me going.

Without you, this novel, this *universe*, would not exist. From the bottom of my soul: Thank you.

About the Author

MORGAN BISCUP IS THE founder of Vazdimet Studios, and the creator and lead author of the Vazdimet universe. An electromechanical engineer by education, she enjoys exploring the impacts of technology and magic on people, cultures, and personal interactions. When she is not hiding in the bedroom to write, Morgan enjoys spending time with her husband, her two amazing daughters, and a highly opinionated cat.

Find Morgan Online

Website: https://www.vazdimet.com
Discord: https://link.vazdimet.com/discord
Newsletter: https://link.vazdimet.com/newsletter

Other Vazdimet Books

For a detailed list of books by Morgan Biscup and others set within the Vazdimet Universe, including recommended reading orders: https://link.vazdimet.com/books

Ambitions of Atonement

SPIRITS OF THE RELENTLESS is the second installment in the Mordena Dawn space opera fantasy series, detailing the founding of the costly Mordena mercenaries and their rise from piratical deserters to ferocious and effective defenders of the independent Freehold planets. When powerful galactic empires seek to devour innocents whole, there's no hired force better prepared to stand against them.

https://link.vazdimet.com/mordena-dawn

The exploits of Shane Lawrence and his allies continue in
Mordena Dawn, Book 3:
Ambitions of Atonement, by Morgan Biscup
https://link.vazdimet.com/atonement

Sometimes the biggest threats are the closest allies.

Void necromancer Shane Lawrence needs resources for his new fleet to help his people secure the futures once stolen from them. The resurrection network formerly led by his deceased partner, Feels, could provide that aid. But in the fae's absence, the Phoenix Assembly is under new, enigmatic management, and the organization has morphed into an ominous force that casts shadows over every illicit corner of Baden.

But while Shane tries to build a new future by atoning for his past, Feels is restless and longs for parts of that past. When a chance discovery threatens the very foundation of everything they've built together, Shane and his allies are left once more grappling with the aftermath of betrayal. Can Shane rebuild what was lost, or will his efforts for atonement lead only to deeper despair?

www.ingramcontent.com/pod-product-compliance
Lightning Source LLC
Chambersburg PA
CBHW061855310726
48972CB00004B/1033